CATCH THE GIRL

A Mercy Harbor Thriller: Book Three

Melinda Woodhall

Cover designed by Michael Rehder

This book is a work of fiction. Names, characters, places, and incidents either are products of the author's imagination or are used fictitiously. Any resemblance to actual persons, living or dead, events, or locales is entirely coincidental.

Melinda Woodhall
Visit my website at www.melindawoodhall.com

Printed in the United States of America

First Printing: July 2019
Creative Magnolia

ISBN: 9781081604745

For Michael

CHAPTER ONE

The high-pitched creak of rusty metal pierced the stillness ahead, sending a shiver of alarm down Ruth Culvert's back. She crouched at the edge of the forest, her eyes darting around the empty parking lot before settling on a battered sign swaying in the cold breeze. Pale moonlight lit up the faded outline of a coiled snake.

"It's the old Cottonmouth filling station," Ruth hissed into the darkness behind her. "We must've veered off track."

Her heart sank as she noted the shuttered windows and the boards nailed over the door. There was no one to help them, no one to offer them a ride. She reached back to take Candace's hand, half expecting her friend to have disappeared. But cold, trembling fingers clutched at her, pulling on her sleeve, stretching the thin homemade material of her dress.

"I don't feel very good," Candace whimpered.

She moved closer to Ruth, seeking warmth in the frigid air, unused to the icy wind that was so rarely felt in Florida. The first few weeks of December had proven unusually cold, and Ruth suspected that the falling temperature may drop below freezing before the sun came up.

"We need to get to the main highway," she said, not sure why she was still whispering.

1

No one had followed them as they'd left the compound. No one had accosted them as they'd made their way through the boggy forest and along Little Gator Creek. No one seemed to be chasing after them.

As far as Ruth could tell, she and Candace were alone in the night, and free to talk as loudly as they wanted. Maybe they would be allowed to leave after all. A soft rustle in the thick cluster of trees behind her started her pulse racing again.

On second thought, probably best not disturb the snakes and gators.

Ruth looked toward the narrow road that wound past the parking lot, hoping to see a passing car or approaching headlights.

Someone's got to come along eventually, right?

Ruth rubbed her arms, wishing she'd worn something warmer than the thin sweater she'd knitted herself the previous winter. The air cut right through it, and she shivered at the thought of the long night ahead. They would need to find shelter before it got too cold.

She reached in her pocket and felt around until her fingers closed on a thin piece of paper. She hadn't lost the address. She knew where they were going; now she just needed to find a ride, or maybe a telephone to use. Her eyes flicked to the building.

Don't places like this usually have a pay phone?

She tried to remember driving by the old gas station before. Had there been a pay phone hanging on the wall outside the restrooms? She thought so. But would it still be there after all this time?

"Wait here, Candy. I'm gonna see if they have a phone."

When Candace didn't reply, Ruth hesitated. She turned to stare into the girl's frightened blue eyes. Beautiful, vivacious Candace had always seemed fearless to her before, but now she stood frozen in terror. Ruth felt a surge of fury.

"It's gonna be okay. We'll get you out of here, and he'll never be able to lay a hand on you again. You hear me?"

Candace nodded, wiping at her nose with a small, trembling hand. She tried to say something, and Ruth noticed that her teeth were chattering, and her lips had taken on a bluish tint.

"I'm sorry, Ruthie. I'm real sorry I got you mixed up in all this."

Candace's words stoked Ruth's fury even higher.

"Don't you apologize, Candy. Once you're all safe and sound I'm going back there and giving that man a piece of my mind. He can't treat people like this."

Giving Candace's hand a firm squeeze, Ruth stepped out of the muddy forest onto the cracked asphalt of the parking lot. Gravel and rocks crunched under Ruth's rubber-soled shoes as she made her way toward the convenience store.

The old building seemed to sag under the weight of the cold night air, its roof littered with branches and debris that had blown in from the surrounding wetlands.

When Ruth reached the island of concrete and metal that had once held a trio of gas pumps, something hard and scaly moved against her bare legs. She held back a scream as an armadillo trundled past, heading toward the deserted road. She watched the gray form disappear into the night before she continued up to the building and around back toward the restrooms.

A black metal payphone hung on the wall. It was positioned between the men's and women's restrooms, right where she remembered.

Ruth hurried toward the phone and lifted the receiver with a heavy hand, already knowing what she would hear, but still devastated when she detected only dead air.

She banged the handset back into the cradle and sighed, dropping her head into her hands.

What now? Do we start walking, or do we hunker down for the night?

A faint buzzing made her lift her head. She picked up the receiver, hoping the sound was coming from the phone. The phone was still dead. The buzzing grew louder; it seemed to be closing in.

Is that a boat? Is someone on the water in the middle of the night?

Most of the land and waterways in the area were part of the protected Cottonmouth Wetland Preserve, but local poachers found ways around the restrictions, and night hunting wasn't uncommon. As the buzzing abruptly stopped, dread began to settle in Ruth's stomach. She felt sure that someone was out there in the dark. She had to warn Candace.

Spinning on her heels she ran back toward the forest, her heart pounding as a faint light appeared, bobbing up and down as it made its way through the thick branches of the palm and cypress trees that flourished in the soggy marsh. They were no longer alone.

"Candy?"

Ruth rushed toward the spot where she'd left Candace, her voice a hoarse whisper in the night. The trampled ground where they'd stood was now empty.

She called out again and again, her voice low and frantic with fear, her mind swirling with regret. Why had she left Candace on her own in the woods? Why had she ever agreed to her plan in the first place?

The snap of a stick directly behind her made Ruth jump and scream. She ran toward the cover of the trees without looking back, driven by blind instinct to get away from whatever or whoever was behind her.

Dodging thick tree branches and jumping over roots and puddles, Ruth made her way further into the forest, stopping only when she felt her feet begin to sink deeper and deeper into the soft, wet ground beneath her.

She'd reached the edge of the swamp that lay at the heart of the preserve. To go any farther she'd need a boat and a good deal of courage. Navigating the swamp at night wasn't for the faint hearted;

four-foot long cottonmouths and alligators twice that length glided through the dark water, their glowing eyes watching from the murky shadows.

Although Ruth had grown up in the area, she wasn't foolish enough to think she knew how to navigate the swamp on her own. Standing still, Ruth closed her eyes and listened to the night.

At first she heard only her own ragged breathing, but then, in the distance, she thought she heard voices.

A woman was talking. Ruth strained to listen. The voice sounded familiar. Was that Candace, or someone else? Just then a terrible shriek filled the night, turning Ruth's blood to ice.

"No, please, no..."

The pleading voice belonged to Candace. There was no doubt in Ruth's mind as she stood transfixed, listening to the now-rustling bushes, cawing birds and the heavy, ominous splash of water nearby. The creatures of the night had heard the scream, too.

"Sister Ruth? Where are you, girl?" The stern voice carried clearly in the frosty air. "You come on out now before you get hurt."

There was a cold edge to the voice that made Ruth instinctively crouch lower in an attempt to hide behind the long tufts of cordgrass that edged the water. Despite the urge to turn and run, she began to creep toward the voice on shaky legs.

I have to check on Candy. I have to make sure she's all right.

Another voice muttered beyond the trees, but the words were too low for Ruth to hear. As she drew closer a whispered conversation ended in an angry rebuke.

"You've caused enough harm," the cold voice snapped in frustration. "Now, go get the boat ready while I finish this."

Heavy footsteps pounded into the underbrush; branches snapped and cracked as someone forced their way into the wall of trees and barreled past Ruth, who had ducked behind a thick sabal palm.

She waited until the footsteps had died away before stepping forward and raising a hand to push a tattered frond out of the way. She peered into the inky darkness beyond, seeing the outline of someone kneeling on the ground. Ruth was only a few yards away, but the person's back was to her, and she couldn't see clearly from the cover of the trees.

Forcing herself to step out into the open, she looked up into the sky, where a thin sliver of moon hung within a spray of pinpoint stars. Dawn was only an hour away. If she could find Candace they might still have a chance to make it to the highway by daylight. They could flag down a truck.

She stepped toward the hooded figure and cleared her throat.

"Wh...where's Sister Candace? We're leaving the congregation. You...you can't stop us."

The figure stood and moved aside, revealing Candace's crumpled body. A sticky mass of blonde hair surrounded the girl's pale, lifeless face. As Ruth stared in horror, the figure raised a hand.

Moonlight glinted off the metal blade of a knife. The hand swung down in a violent arc and the knife sunk into soft flesh with a sickening thud.

"Now, see what you made me do," the voice said with disdain. "If only you and Sister Candace had followed the rules, none of this would have had to happen."

Ruth opened her mouth to scream, but her throat was too dry. The only sound that escaped was a guttural sob. Before she knew what she was doing, she sprang forward, grabbing for the knife in mindless fury.

She clawed at the hand holding the knife, trying to wrestle it free, her feet slipping in the long grass, now wet with the first official frost of the year. Ruth braced herself as she fell backward, but before she could hit the ground, a strong arm wrapped around her throat and pulled her back against a rock-hard chest.

"I've got you, Sister Ruth...I've got you now."

A bird cawed overhead, and a deep growl sounded from the shadows of the forest. The wetlands were alive with creatures just as dangerous as the one holding Ruth by the neck; they would smell the fresh blood pooling on the sodden ground.

"We can't stay out here. It'll be daylight soon."

The man's words were thick and slurred. Ruth recognized his voice; her eyes widened in shock and disbelief.

"Take her into the station," the cold voice commanded. "Hurry."

The arm tightened around Ruth's neck as the man began to drag her roughly toward the dilapidated building. She clawed at his hands as her head began to spin. She couldn't breathe and she couldn't loosen his grip.

This is it. Candy is dead, and now I'm gonna die, too.

Ruth's fading mind tried to make sense of what was happening. She couldn't understand why they'd killed Candace. She didn't know why they wanted her dead. She struggled to keep her eyes open, looking back at Candace's prone body, fearing she would never see her friend again.

The man's arm suddenly fell away, and Ruth collapsed in a heap on the cracked floor of the grimy restroom. She gasped for air, looking around the tiny room in confusion. Only a few rusty pipes and the cracked boards of the old stall remained.

"You shoulda' kept your nose outta this, Ruth."

His grim words reached her through a fog of fear. Was she going to die in the filthy room? Would her body ever be found?

"Tie her up and leave her to me."

A shadow had appeared at the door, blocking the last streaks of moonlight. Ruth saw the man's hands clench above her.

"But...what are you gonna—"

"Don't worry about that. You just get the boat ready."

7

The man pulled out a big folding knife and opened the blade. Ruth braced herself for a blow, but he only pulled off her sweater and used the knife to cut it into strips. He tied a strip around her wrists and another around her ankles. He tightened both the knots, then hesitated, looking down at her with wide, glassy eyes. She thought he was going to say something, but then he turned and disappeared through the door.

A soft rattling in the shadows made Ruth snap her head around. A thick snake was coiled in the corner, its head raised, its eyes trained on Ruth. Through the shadows she made out the pattern on its back; black diamonds decorated the scaly skin. Ruth stifled a scream, slowly raised her bound wrists to her mouth, and began to tear at the strip of material with her teeth.

Just as her hands broke free, another warning rattle sounded from the corner. The big triangular head rose higher, revealing a thick bulge just below the snake's mouth: his midnight snack. Ruth inched toward the door, untying the material around her ankles as she slid across the grimy floor. She peered around the door frame and saw that Candace still lay on the ground. No one else was in sight.

Maybe she's still alive. Maybe it's not too late.

Ruth stood on trembling legs, took a deep breath, then darted across the uneven ground to kneel beside Candace. She gently shook one shoulder and bent to look into her friend's face. Large, bloody letters had been carved into the smooth, pale flesh of her forehead. Ruth read the word in shocked silence.

JEZEBEL

Her mind buckled, refusing to accept the horror of what she was seeing. Voices sounded behind her and she jumped to her feet and ran across the parking lot and into the thick forest of trees on the other side of the lot. She scrambled through the scrub and foliage, ducking under branches and jumping over the roots of trees as she ran.

The sun had appeared over the east end of the forest by the time Ruth stopped and leaned against a tree to catch her breath. A sudden noise behind her caused her to jump. She turned to run again, not seeing the jutting root of the massive cypress tree until she was tumbling forward. Her head slammed against the massive tree trunk, and the world went dark.

CHAPTER TWO

Eden Winthrop crossed to the coat rack and took down the thick white sweater she rarely got an opportunity to wear. The sudden cold snap was a pleasant surprise in the lead up to Christmas, even if the chilly air in Mercy Harbor's administration office was better suited for the heat of a summer day. Eden slipped her arms into warm sleeves and wrapped the soft cotton sweater around her with a happy sigh.

It's finally beginning to feel like Christmas.

Moving back toward her desk, Eden paused to consider the crystal blue sky outside her window and the sunlight sparkling down on the Willow River below. It was a picture-perfect day in Willow Bay, and for the first time in months she felt relaxed and almost optimistic.

"What can go wrong on a day like this, Duke?"

The golden retriever was curled up on the long sofa nestled under the window. He gave Eden a sleepy blink, then closed his eyes. Apparently the cold weather during their early-morning walk had gotten him in the mood for a mid-morning nap.

Eden was pleased to see Duke so content. He seemed to have fully recuperated from his recent injuries, both mentally and physically. She wondered if she too could be considered fully healed after her own awful ordeal.

Pushing back the disturbing images of the night she'd survived both a category four hurricane and a prolific serial killer, she told herself yet again that it was best not to dwell on her narrow escape. Better to be grateful both she and Duke had made it through alive. Better to just get on with things. After all, she had Hope and Devon to keep her busy, as well as a new relationship that needed her attention.

Eden let her eyes linger on the framed photo she'd recently added to the collection on her credenza. Leo Steele's handsome face stared back at her, his dark eyes and strong jaw softened by a teasing smile. Her pulse quickened as she recalled their cozy dinner at his place the weekend before.

Yes, things are definitely starting to look up around here.

Eden was still gazing at Leo's picture when the phone on her desk lit up, dragging her out of her daydream. She pressed the intercom button.

"This is Eden Winthrop."

"Ms. Winthrop, this is Edgar down in security."

Edgar coughed, then cleared his throat.

"I'm sorry to disturb you, but I've got someone here who's...well, she's asking to see you."

Eden stared at the phone, noting that Edgar's usual bantering tone had been replaced with a nervous hesitation.

"Does this person have a name...or an appointment?"

Edgar paused, clearly uncomfortable.

"Well, ma'am, I asked if she had an appointment, but she says she's not sure. When I asked her name, she refused to say."

Eden raised her eyebrows, still staring at the phone, imagining the security guard's disapproving face on the other end.

"She doesn't want to give her name?"

"No, ma'am. From what I can tell, she's had a...well, a rough time. Seems to be looking for help; she's asking for you specifically."

"Well, bring her up, then," Eden said, intrigued, and confident that Edgar wouldn't allow anyone that posed a threat past the security station.

Clearing away a pile of folders and papers on her desk, Eden stood and walked out to the glassed-in reception area to wait. She smoothed back a lock of blonde hair, adjusted the collar of her silk blouse and fidgeted with one of the pearl buttons on her sweater.

Finally, the elevator doors slid open and Edgar stepped out. He turned back and motioned to someone within.

A young woman emerged from the elevator. She was rail-thin, with a pinched, narrow face and anxious eyes. Disheveled red hair hung to her shoulders in limp strands. She took several timid steps into the corridor then stopped and jerked her head around, as if sensing someone behind her.

Eden opened the glass door separating the administration suite from the corridor and beckoned for them to come inside. She tried to smile, but her smile faltered when she saw the girl's muddy shoes and threadbare dress. The girl twisted her hands nervously in front of her, and Eden saw they were crisscrossed with cuts and scratches.

"Hello, I'm Eden Winthrop."

She stepped back to fully open the door.

"Please, come inside."

As the girl shuffled in, Eden turned to Edgar, her green eyes full of questions. He shrugged and raised his eyebrows.

"The mailman dropped her off. Said he picked her up walking along Highway 42 out past I-75. Basically, the middle of nowhere."

Eden glanced back, noting the sprinkling of freckles on the girl's otherwise alabaster skin. Bluish circles ringed her eyes, and her lips were chapped and dry.

"Okay, but why did he bring her *here?*"

A soft voice sounded behind Eden.

"Because of...this..."

The girl's eyes flicked toward the corridor, then down to the floor; her voice faltered. She reached into the pocket of her dress and pulled out a folded sheet of paper. Eden reached for the offered paper, taking the opportunity to study the girl's appearance.

There were no visible track marks on her arms, and her pupils weren't dilated. She was nervous but didn't appear jumpy. Eden decided she didn't look like an addict.

Studying the thin circle of bruises around the girl's slender neck, Eden scanned for additional injuries. She noticed an angry, discolored lump under a sticky strand of hair that had wilted over the girl's forehead. She'd been beaten, may still be in shock.

"You're hurt," Eden stated, keeping her voice neutral, unthreatening. "You need to see a doctor. We can get you to a hospital."

Edgar nodded and stepped forward, his hand settling on the handheld radio affixed to his security belt.

"I can put in a call now if you like."

The girl shook her head. Her eyes returned nervously to the corridor again and again.

"I don't like hospitals. I just need a place to...to stay."

Eden hesitated, worried by the dazed look in the girl's eyes. She might have sustained a concussion. She might even have some sort of brain injury. But Eden knew that, for the time being, it wouldn't be a good idea to press the issue.

Working at Mercy Harbor's network of domestic abuse shelters had taught her that pressure only served to scare away most women. Victims of abuse often resisted going to the hospital at first. They wanted to avoid the questions and suspicions of doctors and nurses that might feel obligated to notify authorities.

Many of the battered women that ended up at Mercy Harbor had initially tried to handle a violent situation on their own, too ashamed or scared to seek help. Some even went so far as to ignore broken bones or internal injuries.

Eden turned to Edgar, realizing she wasn't likely to get much information out of the scared woman with the older man hovering nearby.

"Thank you for your help, Edgar." Eden held open the door. "I'll let you know if we need anything else."

Surprised by his sudden dismissal, Edgar paused, cleared his throat loudly and hitched up his pants.

"Well, if you're sure, Ms. Winthrop…"

Eden gave a firm nod and a reassuring smile.

"Yes, I'm sure. And thanks, again, Edgar."

Once the security guard had disappeared into the elevator, Eden turned back to face the girl.

"We're alone now, and I promise not to tell anyone you're here unless you give me your permission. Okay?"

The girl nodded and swallowed, her eyes fighting to meet Eden's sympathetic gaze.

"So, will you tell me your name? It'll be easier for us to get to know each other that way."

Eden kept her voice casual, wanting to lighten the atmosphere.

"I'm Ruth."

The words were barely a whisper, but it was a start. Eden nodded and stuck out a hand.

"I'm happy to meet you, Ruth, and welcome to Mercy Harbor. Let's go into my office. It's a bit warmer in there."

She led Ruth inside and waved toward the sofa where Duke was still sleeping. The dog lifted his head as Ruth approached. He sniffed in her direction, and she returned his gaze, producing a shy smile.

"Hi there, doggy. Can I sit here with you?"

Ruth's sweet, high-pitched voice reminded Eden of her niece, Hope, although it was clear that Ruth was no longer a teenager.

She looks young, but I'd say she's at least twenty, maybe older.

Questions swirled in her mind as she watched Ruth place a small hand on Duke's soft coat. The room was chilly, and Eden imagined the dog's warm body was comforting to the girl, who had been out in the cold wearing only the thin dress.

With a guilty start, Eden looked down at her own warm sweater and tugged it off. She crossed to Ruth.

"Here, put this on. You must be freezing."

Ruth stared at her in confusion, then slowly stuck her arms into the sleeves and allowed Eden to wrap the sweater around her thin body. Eden sat next to Duke and joined the girl in scratching the golden retriever's back.

"Ruth, what happened to you, and why does that paper have my name and address on it?"

Ruth's hands grew still, and her back stiffened.

"I...I can't remember. I woke up and...it...it was in my pocket."

A pained look passed over her narrow face, as if she were trying to remember something. A disturbing thought popped into Eden's mind.

Or maybe she's trying to forget.

"Take your time, Ruth. You've hit your head. You may have a concussion. Maybe you're a little confused?"

Ruth nodded, her chest starting to hitch in and out as if holding back a sob.

"I woke up in the woods," she said, her voice thick with unshed tears. "I was scared...so scared...and my head hurt. I knew I had to get away before..."

Ruth gazed down at her injured hands then closed her watery eyes, letting her voice trail away as she rocked back and forth.

"Before what, Ruth? What happened? Who hurt you?"

But even as she asked the question, Eden suspected that whatever had happened to Ruth in the woods had been too traumatic for the girl to talk about. She needed time to rest and heal.

Eden knew that survival instinct could force a shattered psyche to block out disturbing memories. She'd been in a similar state of mental distress herself after her sister, Mercy, had been murdered five years earlier. Eden had been the one to find her sister's body, and she'd locked away memories of the tragic day for years.

It had taken therapy, patience and plenty of time for her to overcome the resulting anxiety and allow herself to remember what had happened. Eventually she'd been able to make peace with what she'd seen and done that long-ago day.

But she could see that Ruth's journey was just beginning. First the frightened girl would need a place to rest. A quiet place where she could begin to feel safe again. Once she'd gotten Ruth settled into a shelter, Eden would bring Reggie in to help.

With counselling and therapy from the kind-hearted director of the foundation, Eden was confident Ruth would find the courage to face the truth and seek help. Maybe she'd even be willing to tell the police what had happened and who had beaten her.

With luck we'll get the abuser off the streets and behind bars before he can hurt anyone else.

CHAPTER THREE

The congregation's extensive vegetable garden was flourishing under the bright rays of the winter sun; neat rows of lettuce, arugula, collards, kale and spinach decorated the dark, rich soil in varying shades of green.

"Sister Marie, you comin' in soon? It's getting cold out here."

The man's voice pulled Marie out of her troubled thoughts and back into the brilliant blue Florida morning.

"Yes, I'm coming. Just need to pull another head of lettuce."

Marie felt Eli's intense gaze on her as she knelt by the lush bed of greens and set her basket on the ground. When he didn't turn to leave, a ripple of irritation fluttered down her spine.

He's just worried about Ruth and Candy. I'm sure everyone is.

Marie had woken up that morning to discover the main house of the CSL compound in an uproar. Two young women, Ruth Culvert and Candace Newbury, were gone. It appeared they'd left in the middle of the night with only the clothes on their backs. No one knew what to make of it. Marie suspected she was the only one who'd known they were planning to leave, although she hadn't known they would go so soon.

"I can wait for you and help carry your basket up to the house...if you want."

Marie heard the eager plea behind Eli's suggestion, and another wave of irritation caused her back to stiffen.

17

Why won't he just go away and leave me alone?

A twinge of guilt stirred at her unkind thought. Perhaps it was unfair of her, but she resented the young man's obvious infatuation all the same. She'd joined the Congregation of Supreme Love hoping to find peace, willingly leaving all her worldly cares and problems behind.

But after two years living within the cloistered world of the commune, she was still restless, still racked with resentment and regret. Forming any kind of romantic relationship was out of the question, at least for now. And, in any case, the quiet, awkward Elijah Dunkel was not her type.

"You go on ahead, Brother Eli. I'll be in soon."

Ignoring his look of disappointment, Marie trained her eyes on the ground, pretending to look for the perfect head of lettuce. She waited until Eli had walked back toward the big house before raising her head and looking out at the river. Her thoughts returned to the previous evening and her last conversation with the girls that were now missing.

"I've gotta get out of here."

Marie offered up an exasperated smile at Candace Newbury's whispered confession. They were clearing off the dinner table and sweeping the floors of the big dining hall.

"Yes, I know, Candy. You've been telling me that for ages."

Marie rolled her eyes and continued sweeping.

"No, this is different. I mean it, Marie."

Candace put an impatient hand on her arm.

"This is serious. Like, life and death serious. I'm leaving...soon."

The tremor in Candace's voice caused Marie to look up in alarm. The girl's pretty face was tense, her blue eyes wide.

"Why? What's going on? Has something happened?"

Candace cast a guarded look around the room, as if someone might be watching them, or listening in on their conversation.

"We can't talk here," Candace hissed. "Let's go to Ruthie's room."

They hurried to the long, low building that was home to the commune's single women. Candace paused when she saw several women talking in the hall. They all exchanged nods as Candace knocked quietly on Ruth's door.

"Sister Ruth?" Candace called out in a calm voice, smiling over at the other women, trying to act casual as she rattled the doorknob, anxious to get in.

Ruth peeked out the door, then stepped back to let them enter the tiny room. Marie saw immediately that Ruth was even more agitated than Candace. Her concern deepened at the girl's words.

"You can't tell anyone that we're going. No one can know."

Marie nodded, but Ruth insisted.

"You have to promise you won't tell."

"Okay, I promise. Now what is going on?"

"I've done something stupid," Candace whispered, looking over her shoulder as she spoke as if scared the women in the hall might be listening outside the door. "I'm in trouble, and I've gotta get away..."

Ruth interrupted; her thin, plain face twisted in anger.

"It takes two people to get into her kind of trouble...although men rarely see it that way and-"

Candace turned to Ruth with a panicked expression.

"We don't have time for all that. What's done is done, but I gotta get away before..."

"Before what?" Marie asked, her patience wearing thin at the hushed voices and half sentences.

Ruth reached over and pushed up the sleeve of Candace's dress.

"Before he does something more serious that this!"

Marie gasped at the angry stripes of purple and blue around Candace's upper arm. Her eyes narrowed in outrage as she realized someone's fingers must have left the ugly marks.

"*Who?*"

Marie's voice was quiet, her eyes wide.

"It doesn't matter who," Candace said, her eyes watering. "It was all a big mistake. I never should have come here in the first place."

Ruth flinched as if she'd been struck, and a guilty look flitted across her face. When she saw Marie watching her, she turned to face Candace.

"Candy's gonna leave, and I'm gonna help her," Ruth said, straightening her back and raising her chin. "But I'm not sure where she should go. Willow Bay's the closest town and...well, I thought you might know someone there."

Marie shook her head, denial kicking in automatically.

"I don't know anyone there." She met Candace's eyes, then looked away. "Well, not anymore."

But as Marie stared at the bruises on Candace's arm, an idea began to form. She closed her eyes, trying to decide if she should get involved. If she did, the information she provided could lead back to her; the refuge she'd found at CSL would be in jeopardy. Finally, she looked at Ruth.

"You have a pen and paper?"

Ruth pulled out a small notepad and a ballpoint pen. Marie scribbled down a name and address on the top sheet of paper and handed it to Ruth. She thought for a minute, then wrote the same name and address on the next sheet and gave it to Candace.

"This place helps women that have been...hurt," Marie said.

She'd seen the name in one of the bundles of newspapers the commune collected to recycle. The headline on the front page had made her heart stop, and she'd impulsively torn out the article, hiding it under the nightgowns in her drawer. Each night since she would stare at the words, knowing they only served to remind her of the past, but too weak to resist.

"They might be able to help you there, and-"

A sharp rap on the door interrupted her words.

"Sister Ruth? I'm brewing a fresh pot of tea."

The door opened. A tall woman with a mass of curly black hair stuck her head into the room and looked around with a smile.

"I'm brewing up some of Ma Verity's special tea. She thought you girls might like a cup before lights out. Said it'll help you sleep."

Ruth swallowed hard and nodded.

"Thank you, Sister Judith. That would be nice."

Judith beckoned the girls to follow her, but Marie excused herself, wanting to be alone, needing to think about what she'd heard and seen.

Back in her room Marie changed into a modest cotton nightgown and got into bed, pulling the hand-made quilt around her, unused to the chilly night air. She lay awake for a long time before she sat up and switched on the bedside lamp.

She pulled out the newspaper article and read it several times. Her eyes returned to the same name, over and over, until finally she forced herself to tuck the article away and close her eyes. When she opened them again, someone was knocking on her door. Ruth and Candace where gone.

The sound of voices and doors slamming brought Marie's mind back to the garden. She looked around to see if anyone had caught her daydreaming. The wide expanse of lawn and garden was empty, but a CSL produce truck had pulled up to the barn, ready to be loaded for the day's deliveries.

Marie's eyes fell on Jacob Albright's tall, muscular frame. As if sensing her stare, he turned and looked at her, his face grim and his eyes hard. He heaved the heavy crate of radishes he was carrying onto the truck, then turned in her direction and began to stride across the lawn with impatient steps.

"You seen Ruth or Candace today?"

The words were out of Jacob's mouth before he'd reached her, and Marie's mouth went dry. She stared at him for a long beat, unable to reply as she registered his barely concealed anger, noting the way he'd declined to use the commune's long-standing tradition of calling each member Brother or Sister.

Guess he doesn't consider runaways to be part of the family anymore.

Swallowing a thick lump in her throat, Marie shook her head and attempted to look innocent.

"No, I haven't seen them since last night."

Jacob's eyes narrowed, then strayed to her hands, which were nervously shredding the crisp head of lettuce she'd just placed into her basket.

"You sure about that, Sister Marie?"

Jacob's voice grew softer as he said her name, and he cocked his head, letting his eyes wander up from her hands to the neckline of her simple dress. The heat of his gaze was impossible to miss, and Marie felt a blush spread across her face.

"Yes, I'm sure I haven't seen them, Brother Jacob."

Marie looked past him to the men and women loading the big truck. She noticed a petite figure watching them from the shadows of the big back porch.

"Perhaps your wife has seen them? Sister Naomi's right over there if you want to ask her."

Jacob didn't turn his head. He just studied Marie with pale blue eyes that had suddenly turned colder than the icy wind blowing in from the river. Pulling her sweater tighter around her, Marie stood, then bent to lift the basket. She could feel Jacob watching her as she adjusted the basket against one hip and walked past him. His words stopped her halfway to the barn.

"I'm the leader here now, whether everyone likes it or not. I made a promise to my father to watch after this place, and I intend to keep it. So, if members of my congregation go missing, it's my duty to find them."

Marie nodded without looking back, her eyes wet with sudden tears at the mention of Jacob's father.

"Of course, Brother Jacob. I understand."

She moved briskly toward the barn, not wanting anyone to see her before she had a chance to wipe away the tears. The time was past to mourn Father Jed. He'd been gone for over a year, and she and the rest of the congregation had to move on and accept Jacob in his new role. It was what Father Jed had wanted; his dying wish was to see his son at the helm of the commune he had so lovingly created during the last twenty years.

Marie hung her basket on a hook in the barn then blotted her wet eyes on the sleeve of her sweater. Scolding herself for her weakness, she turned to a wooden bin and scooped out an armful of carrots to add to the basket.

If only you were still here, Father Jed. You'd know what to do.

Marie smiled at the remembered face of the dear old preacher. He'd saved her during the lowest moment of her life, and then suddenly he'd been gone. Her smile faded.

But you were wrong about Jacob. He's not the man you wanted him to be, Father Jacob. He's not...you.

A sick feeling settled into Marie's stomach. In the end Father Jed had been like everyone else who'd left her or let her down. He was no different than her father or her mother after all.

Straining under the weight of the overloaded basket, Marie emerged from the barn just as Eli pushed one last crate of broccoli into the truck and pulled down the sliding door, ready to leave for the day's deliveries. He called out to a thin man with fuzzy red hair and worried eyes who had been helping to load the truck.

"Zac...come on...time to go."

The young man jogged over to the truck and climbed into the passenger's seat without a reply. Before Eli could hoist himself into the driver's seat, Jacob appeared by his side, a bulky carryall slung over one muscular shoulder. He whispered into Eli's ear then handed him the bag.

23

Something about the furtive exchange between the two men caused Marie's already heightened sense of unease to grow. She kept her eyes on the truck as it rolled out of the gates and headed toward Highway 42.

For the first time since she'd arrived at the commune, Marie wished she was the one leaving. The big fence and solid walls that had always made her feel safe and protected were beginning to feel more like a prison than a refuge.

CHAPTER FOUR

Jacob Albright watched the truck disappear around the bend, unsure if Eli Dunkel could be trusted with the assignment he'd been given. The young man had proven to be a loyal member of the commune so far, but he could be hot-headed, and lately he'd been unpredictable.

Jacob cocked his head and narrowed his eyes, suddenly wondering if Eli had started dipping into the supply of pills and powder they stored and transported along with the crates of organically grown vegetables.

It's the oldest story in the book isn't it? Some idiot gets hooked on his own stash and screws everything up?

But Jacob hadn't gotten any complaints that the deliveries had been tampered with, and he wasn't even sure Eli knew what was in the big carryalls they used. They'd never talked specifics, and Eli wasn't the type to ask many questions. He'd been told to make the deliveries and not let anyone else know. So far, he'd done as he'd been told.

Jacob wasn't sure what it was about Eli that had been bugging him. Something just seemed off. He finally turned away, deciding it didn't matter one way or the other.

What other choice do I have? He could be a fucking psychopath for all I know. Doesn't matter to me so long as he makes the deliveries and keeps his mouth shut.

Jacob sat down on the steps leading up to the main house, wanting a minute alone to relax, his nerves still on edge after the nasty shock he'd gotten that morning.

Shrill voices had sounded in the yard below his window just after sunrise, and he'd jumped up with a start, sure that the compound was being raided. He'd peeked through the curtains, expecting a swarm of black-vested DEA agents, but saw that the front gate was still securely locked and that the long driveway was empty. His new business operation hadn't been uncovered, at least not yet.

Another excited voice from below had penetrated the still room.

"...and Sister Candace is gone, too. Her bed hasn't been slept in."

Naomi had stirred then, sitting up in their big, four-poster bed, her dark curls forming a halo around her angelic face. The green eyes that had sparkled with happiness on their wedding day now shone with an emotion that was harder for him to read.

"Sister Candace is gone." Her voice was flat. "I guess that must spoil your plans for the day."

She'd turned away, as if to go back to sleep, and Jacob had quickly dressed and pounded down the stairs two at a time, his anger growing with every step.

That little bitch had better not be playing some silly game.

But he soon confirmed for himself that Candace Newbury was not hiding in any of the buildings, gardens or sheds that made up the sprawling compound. She was in fact missing, along with her friend, Ruth Culvert.

Both girls had been seen in their rooms before lights out the previous evening, but their rooms were empty by the time they were summoned for breakfast duty that morning.

Jacob was sure they hadn't gone out during the night, at least not through the front gate; he fastened the big bolt each evening himself.

The girls had simply vanished.

The front door opened. Slow, dragging footsteps sounded on the porch behind him, but Jacob didn't look around.

"You find those girls, yet?"

"No, Ma, I didn't. I guess they've run off."

He heard his mother settle herself into the big rocker she'd taken to sitting in most days, and he finally turned to look at her. What he saw worsened his already sour mood.

Verity Albright had been a healthy, vibrant woman when Jacob returned to the CSL commune two years before, but the glow had faded from her face in the year since her husband's death, and she now looked considerably older than her sixty-five years. And worse than her worn appearance, was the vacant look in her eyes.

The bright blue eyes that had been quick to notice his misbehavior as a child, and just as quick to forgive him any transgression, now seemed washed-out and empty. How had it gotten to this point?

"Ma, you feelin' all right?"

He watched her, noting the way her hands clutched at the arms of the wooden rocker, her knitting needles forgotten in her lap as she rocked quickly back and forth.

"I'm fine, Jed. Quit fussing."

Jacob's stomach dropped, and he shook his head again.

"Ma, it's me, Jacob. Daddy's gone. You know that."

Verity looked up and smiled uncertainly, her eyes confused. The rocker started moving faster, and the boards underneath squeaked in protest.

"Yes...yes, of course. I know that. Your daddy's gone." After a few more frantic rocks, she murmured, "He's coming back soon though, you know."

Jacob froze, staring as his mother closed her eyes and balled both hands into fists.

"He's coming back to me, son. He told me so. He told me..."

27

The door behind Verity swung open and Judith Dunkel stepped out, her worried eyes immediately taking in the older woman's distress.

"Oh, dear, what's the matter, Ma Verity?"

Jacob watched, feeling helpless, as Judith knelt beside the rocker and wrapped her hands around his mother's clenched fists.

"Ma Verity?" Judith's voice was soft but firm. "Everything's okay, but we need you to calm down. You're going to be fine."

Verity squeezed her eyes shut and shook her head.

"No!" she cried out, making Judith jump back in surprise. "Jed's coming home. He told me so."

The door opened again, and this time Naomi stuck out her head. Her face hardened when she saw Jacob sitting on the steps, and she turned to the women.

"Sister Judith? What's wrong with Ma Verity?"

"She's just tired, I think. Sometimes grief is just too much to handle. It can make a soul tired."

Naomi nodded, her eyes filling with tears, but she didn't say anything. Jacob dropped his eyes, guilt stirring at the thought of what his wife had been through lately, then giving way to anger.

They'd all been through a lot. Hadn't he suffered, too? He'd found his way back to his father after five years away, only to lose him. And his mother was now slipping away as well.

Naomi wasn't the only one suffering. She'd tried to trap him, and it hadn't worked out the way she'd planned.

Karma's a bitch sometimes, isn't it?

Jacob stood up and stretched his long legs, wishing he was anywhere but at the little commune, surrounded by grieving, whining women.

"Sister Judith, I've got some urgent work to take care of. Can you watch after Ma?"

Judith stood and turned to face Jacob. She was a tall woman, almost as tall as he was, and her body was strong and solid-looking. Her thick black hair settled around a smooth, practical face and alert eyes that appeared amber in the morning light.

"Of course, Brother Jacob, you go right ahead and do what you have to do. I'll get your mother some herbal tea and settle her in upstairs for a nice nap. She'll be good as new before you know it."

Jacob heard sympathy in Judith's voice, and a stab of resentment knifed through him as he realized the woman was having to care for his mother because his own wife wouldn't. He turned to glare at Naomi, his resentment building as he saw tears had spilled onto her porcelain skin.

"Thank you, Sister Judith. You're a real big help."

He ignored Naomi's tears, pushing past her into the hall, needing to get away from the prying eyes that seemed to always surround him. He hurried into his office, locked the door behind him, and collapsed into the desk chair. When he raised his eyes, he was staring at the framed photo of his father that hung on the opposite wall.

I did it again, Dad. I've screwed everything up all over again.

Jacob wasn't sure how he'd gotten himself into his current situation. He'd come back to the commune after five years away. He rarely told anyone where he'd been during those long years, and his parents had never rubbed it in. They'd welcomed him back with open arms, the beloved prodigal son returning to the fold.

At first it had all seemed so right. He'd gotten his life in order; he'd stopped partying and started working. He'd tried to stay on the straight and narrow.

But then boredom set in, and pretty little Naomi got under his skin. She distracted him; manipulated him. Before he knew it, she was pregnant and he was standing in front of his father promising to love, honor and cherish a girl that had already started to get on his nerves.

I tried to do the right thing for once, Dad. I wanted to please you.

Unfortunately, his father hadn't stayed around to witness his sacrifice and selflessness for long. His father, a robust man who'd still had a thick head of white hair, and who had turned seventy only the month before, had dropped down dead without warning. Everything Jacob had given up in order to please his father had been for nothing.

Jacob opened the desk drawer and pulled out the thin laptop he kept hidden away. The congregation would be shocked to know he'd been using the computer and a smartphone, both of which were against the commune's long-standing rules.

Jedidiah Albright had founded the Congregation of Supreme Love just before the turn of the millennium, driven by a growing aversion to the worldly vices and temptations he felt had ruined society. The ominous talk about computer viruses that would throw the world into chaos on the first day of the new millennium scared him. He had decided to completely outlaw computers and any other electronic gadget that would allow the outside world to corrupt their refuge.

As Father Jed had told his adoring flock over and over, he wanted the CSL compound to be an oasis in a sea of sin. He believed the little community could offer peace and light in a world otherwise covered in conflict and darkness.

Turns out that some of us like a little sin, Dad.

Jacob opened the computer and clicked on a camera icon. As the application loaded, he crossed to the big framed photo of his father, lifted it off the wall, and slid it into the closet. He felt better without his father's eyes on him as he returned to the computer and surveyed the screen, reading down the list of active options. Clicking on a link would activate a live stream view from one of the cameras hidden throughout the commune.

Jacob felt a warm rush of blood throughout his body as he clicked on the camera labeled MFR. After a slight pause, the application opened a new window, revealing a small room with a neatly made twin bed and a small dresser.

A slim woman sat on the bed reading a book. She wore a pale pink shift dress, and her long dark hair hung over one graceful shoulder. Jacob swallowed hard at the memory of what lay underneath the delicate material.

"Night can't come too soon, sweet Marie," he whispered to the unsuspecting woman displayed on the screen.

He watched as Marie stood and dropped the book on the bedside table. She paused, then opened a drawer and reached under the folded clothes inside to pull out a torn piece of newspaper.

"What the hell is that?" Jacob murmured, curious about the quiet girl that seemed content to pick vegetables and do chores.

For the first time he wondered what Marie Ferguson hoped to find at CSL. With her looks she could likely have any man she wanted.

So, why's she wasting time around here?

The girl touched the paper with one finger, tracing the words. After a few seconds she tucked the newspaper back in her drawer and closed it. Jacob watched until Marie left the room.

Looks like somebody besides me has a little secret.

CHAPTER FIVE

The bright blue Neon Prius sped along Highway 42, cutting in and out of the long-haul semis, dusty pickups and loaded-up RVs that used the county road as a shortcut over to Florida's west coast. A long, loud blast sounded from an eighteen-wheeler that had suddenly materialized behind the Prius. Pete Barker was tempted to give the old trucker a middle-finger salute.

Stay focused, Barker. Pissing off some trucker isn't going to help you find Taylor any faster.

Ignoring the truck now glued to his bumper, Barker kept the car humming along at seventy until he saw the sign for his exit. He steered toward the offramp and headed west. Two uneven lanes of cracked asphalt made up the rural road, and a faded billboard on his right announced that he was two miles away from the Cottonmouth Wetlands Preserve.

Barker slowed down and began looking for his turn-off. Minutes later he was pulling into the surprisingly busy parking lot of the Little Gator Creek Diner. A neon sign blinked off and on, illuminating a grinning alligator that had seen better days.

Barker's pulse started to race at the thought of walking inside. What would he say if Taylor was in there?

And how the hell am I going to cope if she isn't?

The need to find his daughter, to make sure she was safe and well, had intensified in the aftermath of his investigation into two cold case murders. He'd uncovered a serial killer's lair, along with a heartbreaking photo collection of young, female victims. For one terrifying moment Barker had thought Taylor was one of the girls in the photos.

The pain he'd felt then had been worse than the heart attack he'd suffered the previous year, and once he'd realized that the girl in the photo was not Taylor, and that his only child was still alive, still out there somewhere, he'd been on a mission to find her.

Whatever disagreements they'd had, and whatever painful things they'd said, no longer mattered. His baby girl was alone in the kind of world that produced killers like Douglas Kramer and Adrian Bellows: monsters that disguised themselves as men and blended into society. Innocent young girls like Taylor, girls on their own, would be seen as easy targets.

A black Dodge pickup truck pulled into the space next to Barker. Three men in baseball caps, jeans and work boots stepped out, slamming the doors behind them as they hurried toward the diner. The driver paused and studied the little blue car suspiciously, pushing up the brim of his bright orange Florida Gators baseball cap to get a better look at Barker.

Barker raised a hand in greeting and pasted on a broad smile. The man frowned, then nodded and turned to walk toward the diner.

Not used to strangers around here I guess.

He picked up the folder on the passenger seat, tucked it under his arm, and stepped out of the car, his foot sinking into a pile of moss and broken branches, his eyes automatically scanning the surrounding area.

A thick forest spread as far as the eye could see, an army of unruly weeds and rough scrub threatening to encroach on the concrete parking lot and the narrow highway that cut through the thick foliage. He moved toward the diner, surprised to feel a shiver run up his back as the cold air filtered through his thin shirt and crept beneath the unbuttoned collar.

The diner's atmosphere was warm and welcoming compared with the chill outside. Barker sat at the counter and looked around with anxious eyes.

"Afternoon. You need to see a menu?"

A woman had appeared at Barker's shoulder, her voice friendly but hurried. She wore a white apron over jeans and a t-shirt, and her graying hair was slicked back into a bun at the nape of her neck.

"Sure, that'd be great."

Barker accepted the thin, paper menu but didn't bother to open it. His eyes flicked around the room, searching for Taylor. A dozen tables and booths were arranged around the room, and the stools at the counter looked into a small kitchen. A tiny alcove on one side had been fashioned into a makeshift convenience store stocked with a limited selection of groceries and sundries.

"Chester, you enjoyin' this weather?"

Barker looked over his shoulder. The man in the orange Gators cap was now sitting at a table in the corner with his buddies, grinning up at an older man holding a tray of drinks.

"Hell no, I hate the cold. And if you had any sense you would, too."

The old man passed out the drinks: a coke for the man in the orange cap and cans of Bud Light for his two passengers.

"Oh, yeah, why's that?"

Chester raised an eyebrow and cocked his head.

"Anyone'd think you didn't grow up in citrus country, Buck. You should know a freeze means hard times all around."

The middle-aged couple at the next table looked over with grim expressions, nodding their heads at Chester's words as the old man shuffled away. Barker noted the man's uneven gait, and the faded tattoo on his forearm, then pretended to look down at the menu as the man passed by.

"You ready to order?"

Chester stood behind the counter looking at Barker. He didn't smile but his voice was friendly.

"I'll just have a cup of black coffee, please."

As the old man turned to the coffee pot, Barker cleared his throat.

"And I was wondering...is Taylor working today?"

The coffee cup clattered as Chester arranged it on a saucer and set it clumsily in front of Barker. Thin brown liquid sloshed over the rim of the cup and dripped down the side.

"Taylor?"

Frown marks appeared between the man's eyes, and he left the name hanging in the warm, slightly greasy, air. Barker nodded, careful to keep his features neutral and relaxed. No need to let the man know he was desperate to find his daughter. Desperation scared people away and kept them quiet.

"Yeah, Taylor Barker. She a waitress here, right?"

Chester shook his head, and for one heart stopping minute Barker thought he had gotten it all wrong, that the one lead he'd managed to find after months of searching had been a dead-end.

"Well, she *used* to work here, but that was a few years back. She's moved on. Too smart and too damn pretty for this old place I guess."

Barker swallowed hard, his disappointment at not finding his daughter made bearable by the knowledge that he'd uncovered a clue. It was a start.

"So, where she'd go once she quit here?"

Barker wasn't surprised when the old man raised an eyebrow, put both hands on his bony hips, and puffed out his chest.

"Aren't you a little old to be chasing after a girl her age?"

Barker didn't react. The decades he'd spent as a detective had taught him how to read people, taught him how to determine the best way to get the information he needed. He could see the man in front of him wasn't the type to suffer fools.

"I'm her father."

Barker let the words sink in as he sipped at his coffee.

Chester stiffened, then sighed. He opened his mouth to speak, then closed it and turned to the waitress who had given Barker the menu.

"Minnie? I'm goin' out back. You watch the front for me."

The woman nodded and Chester motioned for Barker to follow him through the little kitchen and out the back door. His limp became more pronounced as he stepped out onto hard-packed dirt. The area behind the diner held a dumpster, a rusty propane tank and a baby blue El Camino that, from what Barker could see, had been carefully maintained over the years.

Barker stuck out a hand.

"I'm Peter Barker. I live over in Willow Bay."

Chester ignored the hand.

"And I'm Chester Gosbey. I own this diner. Have for near about forty years. Took it on after I got back from Vietnam."

Barker nodded, his eyes moving to the tattoo on the man's arm. His uncle had come back from the war with something similar.

Chester cleared his throat and put a hand up to shield his eyes from the glare of the sun. It was noon, and the sun was high and bright, even though the air didn't seem any warmer.

"So, you're Taylor's father? The one she was runnin' from?"

Chester's words hit Barker in the gut. His jaw clenched along with his fists, and he couldn't stop himself from snapping back at the old man's quietly spoken accusation.

"Yeah, I guess that's me."

Barker ran a hand through his thick thatch of dark hair, which, in the last few years, had become increasingly sprinkled with gray.

"According to my daughter I did everything wrong. I'm a selfish father...responsible for her mother's death. But I'm here now, and no matter how angry she is, I need to find her."

Chester didn't speak, he just looked at Barker, who stared defiantly into the old man's pale blue eyes. Barker thought only old folks seemed to have eyes that particular shade of blue; it was the color of weariness and faded memories.

"Look, I just need to know she's okay."

The words came out as a plea, and Barker dropped his gaze, his anger draining away into the cold air.

"I wish I could help you, Mr. Barker, but when Taylor left here, she didn't leave a forwarding address."

Barker's fists unclenched and his hands fell limply to his side.

"Did she say anything about where she was heading?"

"She said she wanted a quiet place to *find herself*, or some such thing. She was a troubled girl. Downright depressed, I'd say."

A sick ache started in Barker's stomach at the thought of Taylor sad and alone. He looked out into the dense spray of trees and scrub that surrounded the old place and wondered where she could be now.

"You think she might have done something stupid? Maybe even hurt herself?"

Chester shook his head.

"Your daughter seemed like a smart girl to me. I'm sure she wouldn't have done anything stupid."

Barker thought he saw a flash of pity in the man's face, but it was quickly replaced by a curious frown.

"How'd you hear she was workin' here anyway?"

Barker shrugged, feeling inept as he thought of how little he'd been able to uncover about his daughter's whereabouts.

"Somebody saw one of my posts on Facebook asking about her. Said they'd seen her waiting tables at a diner out by the preserve."

Barker didn't mention the derogatory comments the person had made about the diner and its clientele. No need to insult this old man who appeared to care about Taylor, and, as far as Barker knew, was the last person to have seen her before she disappeared without a trace.

Minnie stuck her head out the back door and rolled her eyes.

"Buck Henry's tryin' to pay with a hundred-dollar bill. I need change."

Chester nodded and waved her away.

"Be right there."

Once the door had shut behind her, Chester turned to Barker.

"I suggest you go on back to Willow Bay, Mr. Barker. When Taylor's ready to come home, she will. Kids usually do in the end."

* * *

Barker headed back to the highway with a heavy heart, picking over everything Chester Gosbey had said.

Does the old man know more than he's saying?

Barker knew he should be planning out his next steps, but he couldn't concentrate. The thought of Taylor waiting tables in the backwoods diner made his mind churn with questions.

How'd she end up there? And why'd she leave? Is she still running from me, or is something else going on?

Squinting into the distance, Barker pulled down the sun visor to cut back the glare, seeing the two men at the last possible minute. He wrenched the wheel just in time to avoid hitting a truck that had pulled off on the narrow shoulder, partially blocking the road. The men had been standing by the truck, staring down into the engine, oblivious of any cars going by.

The Prius screeched to a halt and Barker stepped out, his pulse still jumping at the near miss.

"You guys nearly got run over."

The two young men stared over at Barker in surprise, apparently unaware they'd almost been killed. When they didn't speak, Barker sighed and walked toward them.

"You need some help?"

The men were both young and slim. One had a blonde crewcut while the other was a redhead, his hair a frizzy halo around freckled cheeks. The blonde man finally nodded.

"Truck broke down. Not sure why. Neither of us know much about engines."

Barker smiled, realizing the men were only kids really. Neither looked to be more than twenty-years-old. Younger even than Taylor.

"I don't know much about engines myself, but you can use my cell phone if you want to call for a service truck or a tow."

The redhead shook his head and took a step back.

"We don't have anyone to call, mister."

The blonde nodded, his eyes scanning the road behind Barker and finding the blue Prius. He looked back at Barker, then down at the ground.

"Okay," Barker said, nodding toward the car. "I can give you two a lift if there's somewhere you can go for help."

"That'd be nice, thanks," the redhead agreed, already walking toward the Prius.

"Brother Zac, we can't just leave the truck here like this," the blonde man said. "Someone could drive past and steal everything."

Barker raised his eyebrows at the comment.

"*Brother* Zac? What...are you two monks or something?"

Barker's tone was amused, but the men didn't smile.

"No, we belong to the CSL," Zac explained, his eyes wide and earnest. "Our community is like a family; everyone's a brother or sister. I'm Brother Zac, and this is Brother Eli."

"CSL?" Barker asked. "What does that stand for?"

39

"It's the Congregation of Supreme Love," Eli muttered, his small eyes flashing and his chin jutting out.

Barker put up a placating hand.

"I didn't mean any offense."

He sighed and waved over toward the Prius.

"So, you all want a ride?"

"Nah, one of us can hike back through the woods for help while the other one waits with the truck. It'll be safer that way."

Barker saw Zac's face fall at Eli's stiff words. He looked at the big white box truck. The words *CSL Organic Produce* had been painted on the side in green letters.

"Okay, suit yourselves, but you might want to push your truck further onto the shoulder. Otherwise the next car that drives past might not miss you like I did."

Zac nodded, his face still downcast.

"I can steer if you two want to push," Barker offered.

Eli stepped in front of the driver's side door protectively.

"No. It's like I said...we don't need any help."

Barker nodded, his detective radar giving off a warning.

Brother Eli doesn't want me near his truck. I wonder what he's hiding.

Looking past the men into the thick woods, Barker's curiosity rose even higher.

"Your, uh... *community*...it's in the woods?"

Zac nodded, his arm automatically swinging up toward the trees.

"Yeah, the CSL compound's over that way. It's–"

But his words were cut off by Eli's impatient rebuke.

"No need to waste this man's time, Brother Zac. I'm sure he needs to get going."

Barker decided to give up. He didn't need to spend his time trying to help someone who just wanted to be left alone.

Giving Zac an apologetic shrug, he headed back toward the Prius. He hadn't gone far when his thoughts returned to Taylor. He reached for the photo in his pocket, checking to make sure it was still there. Clutching the photo, he swung around.

"Hey...can I ask you guys for just one favor before I go?"

He hurried back toward the truck, holding out the picture of Taylor he'd started to carry with him wherever he went.

Zac was already heading into the trees. Apparently he'd drawn the short straw and would have to traverse the thick woods to the commune to get help.

"Have either of you seen this girl around here?"

Eli stared at the picture with angry eyes, then shouted over to Zac, who had begun to trudge back toward the truck.

"You go on, Zac. I can handle this."

When Zac hesitated, Eli's face reddened.

"I said go on. We don't have all day."

He turned back to Barker and shoved the picture away, his hands balled into tight fists, his eyes angry slits in his narrow face.

"I never seen that girl. We don't meet many folks outside the compound. We like to be left *on our own*."

Sweat dripped from Eli's face in spite of the cold air, and Barker began to wonder if the young man was on something.

It's either drugs or serious anger issues. Maybe both.

Whatever it was, Barker suspected the man had recognized Taylor's photo, and that he'd wanted to stop Zac from seeing it.

Barker put his hands up in surrender and backed toward his car.

"Whatever you say, *Brother*."

But when Eli turned away, he slipped out his phone and snapped a picture of the truck's license plate. As soon as he got back on the highway he would call Detective Nessa Ainsley. His old partner still worked in the Willow Bay Police Department. She'd run the plates for him.

With help from Nessa maybe I can find out exactly who Brother Eli really is, and what it is he's hiding.

CHAPTER SIX

T he victim's statement in the police report made Leo Steele's stomach turn. He wanted to close the folder and never open it again, but he knew that wasn't an option. Criminal defense attorneys didn't have the luxury of being squeamish. The man charged with the nauseating crime was his client, and Leo was determined to get the flimsy case against him thrown out before the WBPD railroaded another innocent man into jail for a crime he hadn't committed.

Oscar Hernandez had been arrested following a brutal attack on a local woman the week before. The crime had taken place in an upscale gated community that was home to many of Willow Bay's most prominent citizens, including Mayor Hadley, and had caused outrage throughout the town.

In the flurry of news reports and press statements that followed, the WBPD had rushed to find a suspect. The battered department was desperate to take attention off of the public relations nightmare they'd been going through since the previous chief of police, Douglas Kramer, had been arrested for a series of kidnappings and murders that had gone back more than a decade.

Leo knew the department couldn't afford any more bad press. He figured they'd jumped on Oscar in an attempt to calm the public. All they had to hear was that he'd once dated the victim and had a prior arrest for assault. This had given the police a convenient excuse to question the young man, who had agreed to speak with them without a lawyer present. By the end of the interview Oscar was in handcuffs and the lead investigator on the case, Detective Marc Ingram, had made up his mind that Oscar was the perp.

By the time Leo had been assigned as Oscar's public defender, the arrest, along with Oscar's mugshot, had been the lead story on Channel Ten's nightly news, diminishing any hope of finding an impartial jury in Willow Bay.

Leo ran a tired hand through his dark hair, mentally sorting through the information he'd reviewed so far, still disturbed by the violence of the crime. The details in the report didn't match up with the quiet, scared man Leo had visited in the jail that morning.

A soft tinkling announced the arrival of someone at the outer door to the law office, and Leo used it as a welcome excuse to push the folder away.

"Still fighting the good fight, Leo?"

Pete Barker strode into the office before Leo had a chance to stand up. He crossed the room and dropped into the chair in front of Leo's desk without waiting for an invitation to sit down.

"I'm still trying. Your old pal, Detective Ingram, isn't making it any easier though."

Barker nodded, rolling his eyes at the mention of his ex-partner.

"He always was a pain in my ass. Glad he's moved on to someone else's ass now."

"Very funny, Barker," Leo said, noting the bags under the retired detective's eyes and the way Barker's hands were clenched into fists on his lap.

I'm guessing it's not a good time to complain about my own problems.

Leo sat up straight in his chair and folded his hands in front of him on the desk. Barker wouldn't have come by just to chat. Something was up and Leo needed to be ready to listen.

"Okay, so what's going on? New info on Taylor?"

Barker nodded and pulled out a sheet of paper that he'd shoved into the pocket of his black bomber jacket.

"Yeah, I got a lead that Taylor had been spotted waiting tables at some diner near the Cottonmouth Preserve. When I went out there the old guy that owns the place said she had worked there."

Leo felt a bolt of adrenaline; this was the first real lead Barker had shared with him in months. If Taylor had been spotted, there was now a physical trail to follow.

"Hold on, don't get too excited," Barker said, reading the hope on Leo's face. "The old timer said Taylor took off almost two years ago. He's not sure where she went. Said I should just go home and wait for her."

Leo could see from the stubborn set of Barker's jaw that he had no intention of following the old man's advice, but there was something else bothering his friend. He could see the tension in Barker's shoulders and hands, and he sat back and waited for Barker to tell him the rest

"Then, when I was leaving, I almost ran into these two young guys on the side of the road. They were from some sort of commune or cult or something. Called each other Brother Eli and Brother Zac, like they were in some kind of religious order."

Leo frowned, confused.

"And you think these guys know something about Taylor?"

Barker blew out a frustrated breath and sat back in the chair.

"Maybe. I mean, it's a pretty isolated place. I don't imagine there are many restaurants around there, and not many girls who look like Taylor. If she was working at the diner, these young guys were bound to have seen her."

Leo nodded, wanting to support Barker but wondering if the ex-detective was grasping at any random connection in his desperation to find his daughter.

"Anyway, one of the guys acted like he had something to hide. His truck broke down, but he didn't want any help. Then when I showed him Taylor's picture, he got all angry."

Barker pulled out his phone and tapped on the screen.

"I got their tag number. Thought Nessa could run it for me and find out who these guys really are. Unfortunately, she didn't respond to my call. Some big case going on, I guess."

The sick feeling settled in Leo's stomach again. He wondered if Nessa was working the assault case against Oscar Hernandez. Forcing his mind to turn back to Barker, he opened his laptop and rested his long fingers on the keyboard.

"So, what's the name of this commune? Maybe we can find some information online."

"Yeah, I already looked it up. They don't have a web page or anything, but I found the Congregation of Supreme Love registered as a non-profit in Florida. Got their address and the name of the guy that runs the place."

Leo nodded, glad that Barker was thinking logically, feeling a little guilty for assuming the worst.

"All right, so I assume you've already googled the address and have the directions?"

It was Barker's turn to nod.

"Yeah, but I didn't want to go out there on my own. You hear crazy things about some of these communes. They have names like Congregation of Supreme Love, but then they'll stockpile a warehouse full of firearms and put up a barb-wire fence around the place."

Leo cocked his head and raised one eyebrow.

"I doubt this little group is dangerous."

"Oh yeah? That's probably what the cops in Waco thought before they had the shoot-out with that cult out there," Barker said, his voice grim. "That guy was a real nut job."

Before Leo could respond, a loud voice boomed out from the doorway.

"Hey, Barker, you talkin' about me behind my back again?"

Leo watched Frankie Dawson swagger into the room, his lanky frame hidden beneath an over-sized windbreaker. He had the jacket's hood pulled up over a black knit beanie.

Barker shook his head and then stood up to face Frankie.

"How'd you guess? You're getting good at this investigation work, Frankie. Maybe you should open your own PI firm."

The two men glared at each other, then their faces relaxed into grins, and Barker laughed.

"You preparing for a snowstorm? It's not that cold out there."

Frankie rubbed his bony hands together and shivered, then pushed back his hood. He left the beanie on and pulled the jacket tighter around him.

"This is like the artic for a Florida boy," Frankie said, turning to Leo. "And where's Pat today? She finally get smart and quit on you?"

"She had to take Tinkerbell to the vet, but I'm sure she'll be upset to find out she missed this unexpected visit."

Frankie crossed to the coffee pot and poured himself a cup, inhaling the steam that floated up from the freshly brewed liquid.

"Unexpected? I'm offended. I got a personal invitation from Detective Barker."

He noticed Leo's raised eyebrows.

"Yeah, man, I was surprised, too. Figured Barker must be pretty hard up to call on me."

"You got that right," Barker said, sitting down and growing serious. "You both told me you'd help me find Taylor once we'd taken down Kramer. So now I'm here, asking for your help."

Guilt burned Leo's cheeks as he looked into Barker's haggard face.

I've let him down. After everything he did to find my mother's killer, and after he helped save Eden, I've done nothing.

Coffee sloshed over the rim of Frankie's cup as he set it on Leo's desk and plopped into the chair next to Barker.

"I'm sorry, man. I shoulda' checked in with you sooner." Frankie put a hand on Barker's arm. "I guess I suck at being a friend."

"Me, too," Leo added, wondering why he'd allowed himself to get pulled back into work instead of following up on his promise to Barker.

"Thanks, but it's not your fault, either of you. I tried to play lone wolf, but it's not really working out. I need some help if I'm going to find Taylor, and something's telling me I don't have much time."

Frankie frowned and stuck his hand into his pocket, searching for a cigarette.

"What do you mean? What have you found out?"

Leo was glad to see the hand come back out empty. Apparently Frankie was sticking to his vow to quit.

Barker began to explain what he'd learned at the Little Gator Diner, and how he'd met the two men on the road.

"I just have a bad feeling that they all know more than what they're saying. Besides, I can't find a trace of Taylor after she quit the diner. It's like she just disappeared."

Leo's fingers flew across the keyboard, searching the city records while Barker spoke. He searched the property deed database as well, beginning to make connections.

"It looks like a man named Jedidiah Albright registered the Congregation of Supreme Love as a non-profit back in 1999. He and someone named Verity Albright were listed as directors."

Both Barker and Frankie listened intently as Leo talked and continued to tap on the keyboard.

"The latest filing was just this past year, only now someone named Jacob Albright is the registered agent. He and Verity Albright are listed as directors. The address is the same...a rural road off Highway 42. No phone listed."

Barker nodded, adding, "Yeah, it's out there near the Cottonmouth Wetlands Preserve..."

"I see in the county death notices that Jedidiah Albright died last year, but no additional personal information was provided. Doesn't look like the family put an obituary in the newspaper-"

The buzzing of Barker's phone interrupted Leo.

"Hey, Nessa. Thanks for calling me back."

Leo watched Barker's face as he spoke to the woman who had been his last partner before retirement. The softening around the older man's eyes revealed just how close the two detectives had gotten. They still watched out for each other even though they were no longer partners.

"You get a chance to run the plates off that truck?"

After a few more questions and pauses to listen, Barker grunted his thanks and disconnected the call. He stared over at Leo and Frankie, a stricken look on his face.

"Nessa ran the plates. The truck belongs to Jacob Albright, so no surprise there. But-"

Leo could see Barkers hands tremble as he fidgeted with his phone and cleared his throat.

"-but she ran his name through the system and got a hit. He's got a criminal record. Apparently he served time in Pensacola for felony assault before being paroled back in 2017."

A thick silence hovered in the room as each man thought what none of them wanted to say: Jacob Albright had been paroled around the same time Taylor Barker disappeared.

"I know a dude that lives out that way," Frankie said at last, breaking the silence. "You remember my friend Little Ray? Well, his cousin owns one of them airboats that takes people out into the preserve to see gators and shit."

Barker stared at Frankie.

"And what the hell does that have to do with finding Taylor?"

"Well, his cousin must know all the people around there. He could take me to ask around. Maybe I can find out if anyone knows this Jacob dude, and if anyone's seen Taylor."

Barker gave a grudging nod.

"I guess it's worth a try."

Trying not to look at the Oscar Hernandez file or think about all the work that needed to be done on the case, Leo smiled at Barker.

"And I'll drive out to the commune with you tomorrow. We'll find out if anyone there has seen Taylor, and we'll talk to Jacob Albright."

Barker stood and stuck his phone back into his pocket.

"Okay, and I'll ask Nessa to send me all the details she can get on Albright's record."

Barker was quiet as he followed Frankie to the door, agreeing to meet Leo early the next morning. Leo returned to his office and surveyed his desk. Instead of picking up the case file, he took out his phone and dialed Eden.

"Leo, I was hoping you'd call."

Eden's soft voice acted like a balm on his frazzled nerves.

"And I was hoping you'd answer," Leo replied, wishing he didn't have to cancel their plans for the evening.

"I need to stay with an unexpected arrival at one of the shelters tonight, so I won't be able to meet you for dinner."

Leo stared at the phone, surprised to hear the words he was about to say coming from Eden.

"Oh, well, okay."

"You aren't mad, are you?" she asked.

Leo pictured the delicate frown line that appeared between Eden's green eyes when she was worried, and he rushed to reassure her.

"No problem. I promised Barker I'd help him look for Taylor tomorrow, so I need an early night. And I have a case file to keep me busy until then."

49

There was a pause, and when Eden spoke her voice had stiffened, the warmth gone.

"So, you've accepted the Oscar Hernandez case?"

Leo blinked, looked down at the phone in surprise, and pushed back a flash of irritation.

"Yes, I have accepted the case. Is that a problem?"

He regretted the coldness of his words as soon as they'd left his mouth, but he couldn't deny that her judgmental tone irked him.

"Well, I'm here trying to save a woman that has been battered and abused, and you're there defending a man that's accused of a horrific assault. I guess it's hard for me to accept."

Closing his eyes against visions of the injuries depicted in the case file, Leo drew in a deep breath and then exhaled slowly.

"If I thought Oscar Hernandez had committed the assault I would have a hard time accepting it, too," Leo said, keeping his voice low and calm. "But I'm convinced he didn't do it. And it's up to me to prove it before another innocent man's life is ruined."

After another pause, Eden's voice had lost its edge.

"I'm sorry. Leo. It's not my place to judge. I should know you'd never defend a man you believed could do those things. I'll leave you to your work. I hope you and Barker have luck tomorrow."

She'd said all the right words, but after they'd hung up, Leo wasn't convinced her heart was in them. And he was starting to think she may never be able to fully understand or accept his responsibilities as a defense attorney.

He picked up the case file and opened it again.

First I've got to find a way to get Oscar out on bail. He's got a job, a wife, and a son to take care of. He's counting on me.

But Leo's mind refused to concentrate on the information in front of him. He had to find a way to manage the Hernandez case and help Barker without letting anyone down, and without losing Eden in the process.

CHAPTER SEVEN

The streetlights flickered on just as Eden Winthrop looked out the shelter's front window onto Waterside Drive. Streams of office workers had already made their way past the nondescript building, disappearing into bars offering two-for-one happy hour specials or trudging toward parking garages that quickly emptied out once the clock struck five.

A few stragglers hurried past the Mercy Harbor shelter with their jacket collars up and their heads down, unused to the frigid wind that was blowing in off the water. Eden watched as two women waited to cross the street, their mingled breath a delicate mist in the cold air around them.

"I'm glad we're inside, Duke. It's getting colder by the minute."

Duke stood beside her, his big brown eyes trained on the sidewalk outside, his tail wagging hopefully.

"Don't tell me you want to go out again?"

An amused laugh sounded behind Eden and she turned to see Reggie Horn, the director of the Mercy Harbor Foundation.

"The cold air must agree with Duke. He's got that lovely fur coat to keep him warm."

"Well I'm not quite as lucky," Eden replied, rubbing her arms over the thin silk of her blouse. "I gave Ruth my sweater and don't have a backup."

Reggie knelt next to Duke to rub his soft golden fur.

"Maybe you just need someone to keep you warm," Reggie teased. "You could call on Leo. I'm sure he'd be happy to oblige, although I haven't seen him hanging around in a while. Everything okay between you two?"

"He's been busy with a case, and he's helping a friend look for his missing daughter. It's been hard to find time."

A gleam came into Reggie's eyes. She looked up at Eden with sudden intensity.

"A friend? Is it that detective? You know, the big one. What was his name?"

Eden raised both eyebrows and grinned.

"You mean Peter Barker? Are you trying to act like you don't remember his name?"

"And why should I remember his name?"

They both laughed and Reggie sighed.

"Okay, I have to admit he seemed...interesting. And I haven't been interested in anyone since Wayne died."

The frank admission took Eden by surprise. She stared at Reggie with wide, green eyes, before recovering her composure enough to respond.

"That's...great. I guess. I mean, you should ask him out."

As soon as the words slipped out, worrying thoughts began to circle inside Eden's mind.

Didn't Leo ask Reggie to counsel Barker? Isn't he still in mourning for his late wife? Would a date constitute some type of ethics violation?

Reggie gave Duke a hug, then stood up.

"Well, your boyfriend asked me to meet with Peter. He thinks he needs grief counselling." Reggie cleared her throat. "But I'm sure you can understand that my personal interest in the man disqualifies me to provide him with any type of counselling."

Eden nodded, relieved that Reggie was one step ahead of her as usual.

"But I'm not sure how I can explain the situation to Leo without making myself look like a fool. I mean, Peter Barker probably doesn't know I'm alive. He'll think I'm deranged if I say I can't counsel him because I have the hots for him."

A nervous giggle escaped before Eden could hold it in. She'd never talked about Reggie's love life before, and the thought of the older woman having the hots for anyone had never crossed her mind.

"Don't worry, Reggie. I'll tell Leo. He'll understand."

Reggie rolled her eyes and sighed.

"I'm not sure why he would understand, since I don't, but thanks. I'd appreciate avoiding that particular conversation."

A man jogged past the window, a chocolate Labrador trotting lightly by his side, and Duke's tail began to wag furiously as he stared after them.

"Why don't I take Duke over to the Riverwalk? Let him stretch his legs and enjoy this fresh air. It'll give you a chance to check in on our new resident."

"That would be great, Reggie. Hopefully Ruth's feeling better. And maybe she'll be ready to talk about what happened to her."

Reggie's small hand reached out to grasp Eden's arm.

"Don't rush her, dear. You know as well as anyone that it takes time. Be patient."

Eden nodded, then waited as Reggie retrieved a cherry-red trench coat and matching knit cap. She watched through the window as Duke dragged the petite director down the sidewalk and around the corner toward the river.

Walking past the muffled conversation and clattering of coffee cups that drifted out of the main dining room, Eden made her way to the north wing of the building, stopping in front of the last door on the left. She knocked softly before waving her card key in front of the automated lock.

The door clicked open and Eden stepped into the room.

A light had been left on in the tiny kitchenette, and the television in the sitting area was on and tuned to Channel Ten News at Six, giving off a cozy glow.

Eden regarded the room with satisfaction; it seemed to have been designed specifically to accommodate the women and children that turned to the foundation, desperate to find a safe haven.

The building had originally been a boutique hotel catering to cost-conscious business travelers. Unfortunately, Willow Bay's modest business community hadn't attracted enough visitors to keep the little hotel running, and the newly vacated space went on the market just as Reggie and Eden had started looking for a new location for their main shelter. The proximity of the building to the Mercy Harbor administration offices had sealed the deal.

Eden saw that the door to the bedroom was ajar.

"Ruth? Are you awake?"

As she entered the bedroom a chill surrounded Eden; the room was freezing. She stared across to the window. The blinds had been raised, and the window was open. A bitter wind swirled into the room, carrying the scent of the river with it.

Eden ran to the open window, staring out into the receding light. The evening was still and silent. Across an expanse of manicured lawn lay the Riverwalk Promenade, which bordered the dark water beyond.

"No.... please.... no."

The soft moan of distress made Eden jump. She stepped back from the window, her eyes moving to the bed positioned against the far wall. Ruth huddled under a thin white sheet. The thick comforter had fallen to the floor, pushed off the bed by the girl's restless movements.

Eden turned back to the window and pulled it shut with a loud thud, before securing the latch and lowering the blinds. She then hurried to the closet and pulled down another blanket.

Looking down at Ruth's sleeping form, now motionless, her thin figure seemed almost childlike. Eden bent to tuck the extra blanket around the girl, her eyes coming to rest on the pale, freckled face and the fragile, bruised neck.

A hot burst of anger erupted in her chest at the thought that someone had purposefully inflicted those bruises, and that yet another violent abuser roamed Willow Bay.

Eden forced herself to turn away, waiting for the rage to morph into the fierce determination that allowed her to keep fighting.

Ruth's going to get past this. And I'm going to help her. The monsters don't get to win this time.

She froze at a soft sound from the outer room, then looked toward the doorway. A shadow flickered past. Eden's heart started to pound. Her mouth was suddenly dry as her mind raced.

Why was the window open? Did someone get inside?

Relief flooded through her as she heard the patter of paws and familiar snuffling sounds Duke made when he was exploring new territory. She stuck her head into the sitting room.

"Duke! You nearly scared me to death."

The golden retriever looked at Eden with curious eyes, then continued sniffing around the room. Reggie appeared in the doorway behind him and smiled.

"How's she doing? Any better?"

Eden put a finger to her lips and waved Reggie out into the hall. She guided Duke out as well and closed the door behind them.

"She's still sleeping. Obviously restless, but I think she'll be out most of the night. We'd better wait until tomorrow to try to talk to her."

Reggie nodded, rubbing her hands together, trying to warm them.

"It's colder out there than I thought. Even Duke wanted to come back in once we felt the wind coming in off the river. He couldn't get back inside fast enough."

A smile touched Eden's lips as she looked down at Duke. He'd been her support animal for years now, and she felt like she knew him better than anyone. It didn't surprise her that he'd wanted to come in from the cold.

"Duke's a smart dog," Eden laughed. "And he likes his comforts. Besides, he grew up in Florida, which means he has thin blood."

Eden's smile faded as they began walking back toward the front of the building. They'd have to find a way to get Ruth to talk soon. They needed to make sure she was safe, and that her abuser wasn't out there hurting anyone else.

"Reggie, will you talk to Ruth tomorrow? See if you can get her to open up? I'm worried...whoever hurt her is still out there."

"Of course. I'll do whatever I can."

But Reggie didn't sound optimistic.

"If we can find out more about Ruth, it could lead us to the man who abused her," Eden urged. "Even if she can't remember everything, or won't give us his name, any information could help."

Reggie stopped outside the dining room and turned to Eden.

"Have you called the police? Asked if anyone matching Ruth's description has been reported missing?"

Eden bit her lip and shook her head.

"No, not yet. I was hoping to have more to go on before I involved anyone else, but maybe you're right. Maybe someone has reported her missing. It can't hurt to ask."

* * *

Eden left Reggie and Duke in the main dining room. The lively conversation of residents and staff faded away as she moved down the hall to the lobby. Sinking into a comfortable armchair by the window, Eden inhaled deeply, then took out her phone.

Let's hope Nessa will still take my call.

The last time Eden had called Nessa Ainsley for help, she'd gotten the detective involved in a frantic search for a serial killer that had ended in the arrest of the town's chief of police.

The WBPD was still struggling to redeem itself in the eyes of the Willow Bay citizens, and Mayor Hadley was still looking for a new police chief capable of rebuilding the demoralized department.

But as Eden scrolled through her contacts for Nessa's number, her phone rang. A familiar name appeared on the display, then Nathan Rush's voice boomed into Eden's ear.

"Eden, why haven't you returned my call? Is everything okay?"

The concern in Nathan's voice had become a habit. Ever since Eden had left her role at Giant Leap Data to open the Mercy Harbor Foundation, her ex-partner had worried about her safety, sure that one day she would go too far in her quest to save the world.

"I'm fine, Nathan. Just busy. How are things out there? San Francisco still surviving without me?"

"Nothing's the same without you, Eden," Nathan said, his voice relaxing as they fell into their usual banter. "Which is why I want you and the kids to come out here for Christmas. I need to see you. I have some important news."

Eden laughed, sure that this was just one of Nathan's ploys to make her feel guilty for neglecting him. Although they were no longer a couple, they were still friends, and she knew he often felt left out of her life.

"Sure," she teased. "Why don't I just bring the whole gang and stay through the new year."

"That would be great. It'll give us plenty of time to talk. You all can stay with me. I have plenty of room in my new place."

Eden had seen pictures of the elegant house Nathan had purchased with his profits from the technology start-up they'd founded together. She knew the price for such a house in San

Francisco must be eyewatering, but it was well within his means after their company had gone public with a record-breaking IPO.

Eden had used much of her profits from Giant Leap to open Mercy Harbor. She was grateful that the continued success of the company ensured she would be able to fund the foundation for years to come. It was her way of honoring Mercy's memory. The only way she knew to make amends for failing to save her sister.

"You can't be serious, Nathan. I can't just leave the foundation for weeks to go galivanting off to the west coast."

"So, who says you have to galivant? Maybe you and the kids could just hang out. Spend some time away from the drama."

The words came out as a reprimand, and Eden felt her back stiffen. She didn't like Nathan's implication that the kids were under undue stress. Hope and Devon were her number one priority. And besides, she was looking forward to spending Christmas with Leo. It would be their first Christmas together.

"I can't, Nathan. The kids and I have plans and-"

"Plans are meant to be changed. Besides, I need to talk to you. And you keep telling me you'll come out to tie up the loose ends here. What better time than when the kids are out of school?"

Eden knew Nathan was probably right. She owed him a visit, if only to settle the matter of her remaining shares. He deserved that much after everything they'd been through together. They'd worked so hard to make Giant Leap a reality, and in the end the business had allowed her to fulfil her promise to Mercy.

"I'll think about it, Nathan, but I can't promise anything."

As she disconnected the call, she pictured the hurt she would see in Leo Steele's dark eyes if she told him she would be going to visit her ex for Christmas.

Although Leo had never complained about her friendly relationship with Nathan, she sometimes imagined she could feel him tense up when her ex-partner's name was mentioned. And she doubted he'd be pleased to have her leave town just before the holidays.

Eden lifted her phone again, scrolling to find Nessa's number.

I can't think about that now. I need to find out what happened to Ruth first. Everything else can wait for tomorrow.

CHAPTER EIGHT

Ingram's desk was meticulously organized, its surface polished to a gleaming shine underneath a tidy stack of neatly labeled files. Detective Nessa Ainsley looked over her shoulder, listening for any tell-tale footsteps in the hall, half-expecting Ingram or Ortiz to burst into the office demanding to know why she was rifling through their files.

And what'll I say then? I don't even know what I'm looking for.

All Nessa knew was that Detective Marc Ingram had been assigned as lead detective on a high-profile assault, and that his overly aggressive efforts to quickly solve the case had raised her suspicions.

Ingram was up to something. Just what that was, Nessa still wasn't sure. But she intended to find out before the high-strung detective could do something to further disgrace the WBPD.

The fallout from Chief Kramer's recent arrest had left the entire Willow Bay Police Department reeling; the detectives that worked with Nessa in the Violent Crimes unit had been hit especially hard. Marc Ingram, his partner Ruben Ortiz, and Nessa's partner, Simon Jankowski, had all worked under Kramer for most of their careers. They were understandably shaken to find out that for the last decade their chief of police had been kidnapping and murdering young women.

Nessa worried the shock might have been too much for Ingram to deal with. He'd started working late most nights, and some mornings when she came into the office she noticed he was wearing the same suit and tie he'd worn the day before, as if he'd never gone home. And now, looking at his pristine desk, Nessa was concerned.

What detective in their right mind has a desk this neat?

Gingerly opening the top file in the stack, Nessa froze, her eyes scanning the document within several times before she registered that she was reading a letter of recommendation from one of the city council members. Apparently the council member was convinced that Detective Marc Ingram should be Willow Bay's next chief of police.

A sudden buzzing from her cell phone startled her. She jerked her hand back, knocking the folder off the desk and spilling the stack of letters onto the floor. She scurried to collect the papers, her heart plummeting as she saw that Ingram had gotten a letter from almost every councilman in Willow Bay.

Shoving the papers back into the folder, Nessa backed out of Ingram's office and closed the door behind her. She took out her still-buzzing cell phone. Dazed by the terrible possibility that the weasel-like Detective Ingram may soon be her boss, she didn't look at the display as she connected the call.

"Nessa, it's Eden Winthrop. Do you have a minute?"

The soft voice on the other end of the connection was a surprise, prompting Nessa's reply to slip out before she could censor herself.

"Sure, just please don't tell me another girl is missing."

Nessa bit her lip and sighed. She hadn't meant to sound so ungrateful. Eden's efforts to help abused and vulnerable women had resulted in the take down of several violent criminals in the last year, getting them off the streets of Willow Bay and saving innocent lives in the process.

"I'm sorry, Eden. That didn't come out right. How can I help?"

"No problem. After everything that happened the last time I called asking you for a favor, I imagine my voice is the last thing you wanted to hear."

Eden's understanding tone made Nessa feel even worse.

"When I think about what could have happened if you hadn't called...well, I should be thanking you, not avoiding your call. In fact, this whole darn town should be thanking you."

As the truth of her own words sank in, Nessa shivered. Chief Kramer had killed so many innocent people. If Eden hadn't started the search for Kara Stanislaus he would likely still be out there hunting for more victims.

"I appreciate the thought, Nessa, but I don't need any thanks. What I do need is your help."

Nessa stepped into the office she shared with her partner, sat at her desk, and pulled out a thick pad of paper and a pen.

"Okay, you got it. What can I do for you?"

"You can check to see if anyone's reported a missing person. Someone that matches the description of a girl that arrived at Mercy Harbor earlier today. She's clearly been abused, but says she can't remember what happened, or who hurt her."

Nessa raised her pen over the notepad, then paused.

"So, you're telling me that this time you're not reporting a girl missing. You're reporting, uh...a girl you *found*?"

"Yes, I guess you could say that. Although it's more like the girl found me. She walked into the Mercy Harbor administration building carrying a piece of paper with my name, along with Mercy Harbor's address."

A frown settled between Nessa's eyes as she listened.

"Does this girl have a name?"

"She says her name is Ruth, and she looks to be about twenty years old. She's got red hair and brown eyes. Average height, but very slim."

"And you think someone may have reported her missing?"

Nessa's hands were already moving on the keyboard, navigating to the search screen for the department's database.

"It's possible," Eden said. "She's obviously been hurt, and from the looks of her shoes and clothes, I'd say she's been outside at least overnight."

As Nessa had expected, there weren't any active missing person cases in the area. She widened her search to include the state and national databases.

"We haven't had any reports of missing women in the area," Nessa said, her eyes on the search results. "And I don't see anything that matches the description you gave in the state or national databases."

Eden sighed on the other end of the connection, but Nessa wasn't ready to give up yet.

"I'll run a deeper search using the information we have on the woman...on Ruth...through the FBI database as well. They have cases going back decades. Maybe we'll get a hit."

"Thanks, Nessa. I'd feel a lot better if you did that. And I've already asked our therapist, Reggie Horn, to meet with Ruth tomorrow. Hopefully, once Ruth has had a chance to rest, she can clear up some of these questions."

Loud voices sounded in the hall, and the door to the office swung open. Detective Simon Jankowski pushed his way in, followed by Detective Ruben Ortiz. The men quieted down when they caught sight of Nessa's disapproving look and the phone in her hand.

"I'll plan on stopping by in the morning as well," Nessa said, keeping her narrowed eyes on Jankowski's face. "Just to make sure everything is okay and see if Ruth wants to make a statement."

After she'd disconnected the call, Nessa turned her full attention on Jankowski and Ortiz.

"You boys seem to be all riled up. You got news to share?"

They exchanged glances and Ortiz produced an embarrassed grin.

"Ortiz was just sharing some gossip," Jankowski said. "Nothing you'd be interested in I'm sure."

A sneaking suspicion grew in Nessa's mind.

"Actually, maybe I would be interested."

She stood next to her desk and crossed her arms in front of her.

"Maybe you two have heard that Ingram fancies himself the next chief of police around here."

Both Jankowski and Ortiz gaped at Nessa.

"What?" Jankowski's voice reverberated around the little office. "That uptight little..."

Ortiz began backing toward the door. From the flush that had reddened his handsome face, Nessa figured he knew about Ingram's file full of recommendation letters.

"Now, now, Jankowski, let's not say anything about our future boss that we're going to regret."

Nessa knew her sarcastic comment, delivered in her strongest southern accent, was bound to irritate Jankowski, but she couldn't help herself.

"Did you know about this, Ortiz?"

Jankowski turned around just as Ingram's partner slipped out into the hall. He stared at the empty doorway, then looked back at Nessa.

"We can't let that happen, Nessa. Ingram is the worst person I can think of to take on the role. He's not a leader. And..."

"And what?"

Nessa stared up at her partner. His hazel eyes were blazing, and his jaw was clenched under an impressive five o'clock shadow.

"I don't trust him."

Jankowski's words surprised Nessa. She knew he didn't like Ingram, few people did, but she hadn't thought he distrusted the man that had already been a detective back when Jankowski was still riding patrol.

"Okay, so how do you plan on stopping him? I hate to tell you, but he's got the backing of almost everyone on the city council."

Jankowski ran a distracted hand through his hair, shaking his head in disgust. He collapsed into his desk chair and stared over at Nessa with brooding eyes.

"We've got to find another candidate for Mayor Hadley and the council to consider. Someone with a little more sense and a lot more personality than Ingram."

Nessa's heart quickened as she remembered Jerry's words from the night before. He'd been standing in the bathroom door watching her brush her teeth, his tall frame reflected in the mirror.

"You'd make a mighty fine chief of police, Nessa."

His casual statement had taken her by surprise, but the idea, once planted, had quickly germinated and sprouted overnight, filling her mind.

Yes, I would be a damn good chief, but Hadley would never hire a woman. Would he?

She felt her phone buzz in her hand.

"It's Barker."

Jankowski grunted, still watching her, his eyes thoughtful.

"I think I've got an idea about who could be a good alternative to Ingram," Jankowski whispered as Nessa lifted the phone to her ear.

Waving him away, she spoke into the phone.

"Hey, Barker, what's up?"

Barker sounded depressed.

"I just wondered if you could run a full background on Jacob Albright. Leo and I are going to go out to his commune tomorrow, and it'd be nice to know what we're dealing with."

"From what I remember, it looks like you'll be dealing with a sexual predator."

She tried to think of something to add that would make her old partner feel better.

"But I'm sure he's got nothing to do with Taylor."

Barker ignored her last comment.

"So, he was doing time for a sexual assault?"

"Yeah, Jacob Albright went down for five years. Assaulted a minor. He's a registered predator."

"Well, that may explain why he's living out in the woods. He's hiding away from society."

"Lucky society," Nessa murmured, refusing to let her mind drift back to Ingram.

"Yeah, he sounds like a real charmer. Can't wait to meet him."

Barker's voice had taken on a belligerent tone that worried Nessa.

"You best be careful out there in the woods. Make sure you and Leo watch out for Albright. He sounds like a real-life big, bad wolf."

CHAPTER NINE

The dusky evening was fading into night as Frankie sat in the passenger's seat of the pickup, staring out the grimy window. The slightly battered Chevy had one headlight out, and the single beam bounced along the uneven road, illuminating gnarled tree branches, clumps of hanging moss and patches of the swampy terrain that now surrounded them.

"Are you sure you know where you're goin', dude?"

The big man sitting next to Frankie grunted, his eyes sticking to the road ahead. Raymond Miles, better known as Little Ray to his many friends, had driven the road enough times to be cautious. Fallen tree branches, frisky raccoons, and even the occasional deer could appear suddenly; one instinctive turn of the steering wheel would send the little truck careening into the swamp.

"Hell yeah, I know where I'm going. I grew up around here."

Frankie watched Ray's meaty hands clutch the steering wheel, wondering for the first time about the background of the man he'd befriended in prison. He hadn't known the bulky, bearded man was from the backwoods, and he hadn't met many people that had grown up in rural Florida. At least none that admitted to it.

"I thought all you Florida crackers kept to yourselves," Frankie said, his eyes searching the night ahead for any sign of life.

"You think we spend all our time hunting snakes and gators?"

Ray risked a look over, a grin lifting his plump cheeks.

"Yeah, I guess," Frankie admitted, wondering belatedly if the term Florida cracker could be considered an insult.

"Well, you're not too far off, at least not when it comes to Hank and Dooley. They're out in the swamp hunting most nights."

A sign up ahead caught Frankie's eye, and he watched as the white words and sun-faded wood grew closer.

Viper Airboat Rides operated swamp tours out of a modest wooden building perched on the edge of the massive Cottonmouth Wetland Preserve. Two airboats were tied to a dock that jutted out into a wide tributary; the dark water beyond fed into the preserve's interconnecting chain of lakes, rivers and swamps.

A man wearing a hoody, dirty jeans and flip-flops stood on the dock. His lank, white-blond hair fell over his sunburned face as he surveyed Ray's pickup.

"What's up, Little Ray?"

A pudgy man with a sweat-stained cap had materialized at the driver's side window. He leaned into the cab to stare at Frankie.

"Who's this?"

The man's eyes were close-set, and his nose was slightly upturned; the overall effect was vaguely porcine. Ray pushed the man out of the window and threw open the truck's door.

"Back up, Dooley, you idiot. Give me some fucking room."

Ray stepped out, towering over Dooley by at least a foot. He turned to the man on the dock and waved.

"Hey, Hank. You boys takin' the boat out tonight?"

Both men regarded Ray with slack faces, their eyes moving to Frankie, then back to Ray, who sighed and motioned for Frankie to get out of the truck.

Frankie stepped out into the cold air, zipping his windbreaker and pulling up the hood.

"That idiot's my cousin, Dooley." Ray gestured toward the chubby man in the stained cap. "And that's his business partner, Hank."

Hank and Dooley nodded in unison, and Ray moved toward the dock with a confident swagger.

"And this here's a buddy of mine. His name's Frankie."

Frankie returned the nod and followed behind Ray, keeping a nervous eye on the water's edge.

"So, you boys catch any gators lately?"

Hank shook his head, his eyes flicking to Dooley before he spoke.

"Season's over, Little Ray. No more gator huntin' til next year."

Ray's laughter boomed across the water as he threw back his head and closed his eyes.

"Since when...since when has that...stopped you two poachers?" Ray gasped out between bursts of laughter.

"You boys found Jesus or somethin'?"

Dooley's indignant, piggish eyes glared over at Ray before settling on Frankie.

"Don't you go talking bad about Jesus now. Me and Hank go to church as often as the rest of the folks around here."

This comment only served to make Ray laugh harder, and Frankie started inching back toward the truck. He'd come out to the middle of nowhere to find out if these men knew anything about the CSL commune, or anything about Barker's daughter. From what he could see they weren't likely to be much help.

"Don't worry, Frankie, they're harmless," Ray said, his laughter dying away although a grin still plastered his face. "They're scared you're an undercover game warden or some shit like that."

Frankie raised his hands and kept backing away. He felt his foot sink into a soggy patch of ground and grimaced.

"I'm no undercover nothin."

Frankie absently reached into his pocket hoping to find a cigarette.

"I'm just trying to find out what's the deal with that CSL commune. You know the guy that runs the place?"

Hank jumped down off the dock onto the muddy bank, his flip-flops making sucking sounds as he walked closer. Frankie saw what looked like a jailhouse tattoo on his forearm and a faint scar across his throat.

"Yeah, we know Jake. What do you want with him?"

Frankie blinked at Hank's familiar use of Jacob Albright's name and the edge of hostility in his voice.

"Hey, Ray, I thought you said these guys were cool." Frankie kept his eyes glued to Hank's approaching figure. "I'm not getting cool vibes right now."

Ray hooked a thick arm around Dooley's neck and gave a playful squeeze.

"You guys are cool, aren't you?"

Ray's voice turned serious as he stared at Hank.

"My friend here wants to know about this Jacob guy and the little commune he runs. What's your problem?"

Hank raised his hands and shrugged.

"I don't got no problem, Ray. I just don't like strangers snooping around askin' questions. The Albrights are from around here, and they're good people. Although I don't see Jake much, not after he-"

Dooley held up a grubby hand to silence Hank, then shrugged off Ray's arm.

"Listen, Ray. We don't want to piss off Jacob Albright or the folks over at CSL. This is a small community. We don't want any trouble."

Frankie cocked his head and frowned.

"So, you're saying this Jake guy is trouble? What...is he some kind of badass? You guys scared of him?"

Ray chuckled and rubbed his hands together, watching Hank and Dooley with raised eyebrows.

"Hell, no, we're not scared. But he's done serious time, and lately he's been-"

"Shut up, Dooley."

Hank shuffled closer to Frankie and lowered his voice.

"Let's just say that Jake Albright's been expanding his business ever since his daddy passed last year. Sending out lots more deliveries. Seems like there's some new folks over there, too."

Dooley nodded, then produced a leering grin, revealing an uneven set of yellow teeth.

"Yeah, some of them new girls are real pretty."

Frankie looked away, his eyes falling on Hank's forearm. He studied the crude tattoo. He'd seen plenty like it when he'd spent time in prison for an armed robbery he hadn't committed. Luckily Leo had managed to prove he couldn't have been at the scene of the crime. If it wasn't for Leo, Frankie imagined he'd still be behind bars. Maybe he'd even be sporting one of those jailhouse tats.

"Where'd you get your ink?"

Hank shrugged, then looked down at his arm and pushed up the sleeve of his hoodie to give Frankie a better view.

"I did some time down in Brevard county. Got homesick so I got this here viper put on to keep me company."

Nodding as if impressed, Frankie looked over at Dooley.

"Sounds like we all spent some time in the joint."

Dooley shook his head and rolled his little eyes.

"Oh, no, not me. No sir. I'm not going to jail. I'm a law-abiding citizen. I work here and...and..."

"And go poaching in the swamp every night," Ray finished for him, the grin reappearing.

A blush spread up Dooley's neck.

"That's a damned lie."

A disapproving scowl spread across the little man's broad face as he turned back to Frankie.

"But Jacob Albright, now he did real time. Five years in the state pen. Not sure what all he did. Some sort of sex thing."

"And then he just came back home after that?" Frankie asked, widening his eyes for effect. "Just like nothin' ever happened?"

Dooley shrugged his plump shoulders.

"He did his time. That's all there is to it."

"You guys seen anything suspicious going on over at the commune? You said you saw some pretty girls? Did they seem okay?"

As Hank stepped forward, Frankie looked down at the man's muddy flip-flops, shivering at the thought of the cold air on bare, wet feet.

"Them folks at the commune are fine. They're real religious. Keep mainly to themselves except when they sell produce from their farm."

A furtive look passed between the two men, and Frankie wondered what it was they weren't saying. A stiff wind blew back his hood, ruffling through his tangle of hair, and his teeth began to chatter.

"You wanna come out with us on the boat?" Dooley asked, his suspicions about Frankie forgotten. "You'll love the swamp at night. Could even bring back a gator if we're lucky."

"Won't you guys get in trouble?" Frankie asked, looking out at the black water, half-expecting to see two glowing eyes staring back at him.

"Well, gator season is over," Dooley admitted, "but there are more than a million of 'em in Florida. They're a damn nuisance. Me and Hank just want to help."

Hank nodded and folded his arms over his thin chest.

"Yeah, if we *did* go out poaching we'd be performing a public service. Folks should be thanking us for saving lives."

Ray slapped Dooley on his back, sending him stumbling forward. He glared over his shoulder, then turned to face Frankie.

"You look scared. You scared of gators?"

"Hell yes," Frankie said, walking back to the Chevy. "And I'm sure as hell not going in the swamp at night."

Hank's eyes took on a malicious gleam.

"We could drive you past the back of that commune you're so interested in. You could see for yourself what they're gettin' up to."

Frankie hesitated, his hand already on the door handle.

I promised to help Barker, and now I'm being a chicken-shit.

But before Frankie could change his mind, Ray marched over to the truck and wrenched open the door.

"I don't have time for joy-ridin' around the swamp tonight. I gotta work the night shift. Some of us have real jobs, you know."

Weak with relief, Frankie climbed into the passenger seat and buckled his seat belt.

I'll call Barker and tell him what I found out. I can always come back another time and go out in the boat. Like in about a hundred years.

He waved to Hank and Dooley as Ray did a three-point turn in the muddy lot and nosed the Chevy back out onto the road. He didn't relax until they had crossed the Willow Bridge and were headed back into town.

CHAPTER TEN

Barker slowed the Prius as they passed the entrance to the CSL compound, his eyes scanning the automated security gate and the thick concrete walls that shielded the compound from curious eyes. A large *No Trespassing* sign was prominently displayed. Barker noted that the bright white sign looked conspicuously new next to the chipped and faded paint on the walls.

"Looks like they aren't expecting any visitors today."

Barker glanced over at Leo, who was riding shotgun. The lawyer's long legs pressed against the little car's dashboard as he tapped impatiently on his cell phone.

"The map's saying there's a crossroad up ahead." Leo motioned for Barker to keep driving. "We can turn around there, head back this way, then find a place to park along the road. Try to see who's coming or going."

A flash in the rearview mirror caught Barker's eye. He eased his foot on the brake, slowing to a crawl. The box truck he'd seen the day before had appeared on the road behind them; it stopped next to the gate. Someone jumped out and tapped a code into the security panel. Barker recognized Brother Zac's bright red hair.

"I think I've got a better idea. Hang on."

As Barker steered the car into a wild U-turn, Leo braced his legs against the floorboard and reached for the grab bar. The right tires of the Prius skidded off the asphalt briefly, then the car bumped back onto the road, pulling up behind the CSL truck just in time to follow it through the open gates.

A tall, leanly muscled man with dark, wavy hair walked toward the truck, waving the driver toward a barn on the left side of the courtyard. His eyes widened as the truck trundled away, revealing the electric blue car.

"That's Jacob Albright," Barker murmured to Leo. "Nessa sent me a mugshot. It's definitely him."

A frown creased Jacob's forehead as he watched Barker and Leo climb out of the car.

"You gentlemen lost?"

Barker produced his most innocent smile, taking his time zipping up his bomber jacket, allowing Jacob a glimpse of the gun he had holstered on his belt. The smile on Jacob's face tightened.

"Looks that way," Barker said, his eyes scanning the compound. "What is this place anyway?"

"This place is private property, actually."

Leo stepped forward, throwing Barker an impatient look that told him the defense attorney wasn't in the mood for games.

"According to my records this is the listed address for a non-profit religious organization called the Congregation of Supreme Love. Am I right?"

Jacob hesitated; confusion clouded his face.

"Yeah, that's right. Who are you?"

"I'm a lawyer. I'm looking into the disappearance of a young woman. I have reason to believe she might be in this vicinity."

A group of women began to stream out of the two-story house that sat across from the barn. The soft murmur of their voices fell silent as they spotted the men in the courtyard.

"Ya'll go on back to the garden," Jacob called out. "There's work to do."

Barker's eyes searched every face as the women dispersed around the corner of the house, his pulse racing at the thought that Taylor might be in the group of modestly clothed women. None of the faces looked familiar.

"What's the woman's name?"

The sullen words snapped their attention back to Jacob. Leo spoke before Barker could find his voice.

"Her name's Taylor Barker. She's twenty years old–"

"Twenty-one. She had a birthday in November," Barker interrupted, his voice wavering on the words.

Swallowing hard, Barker pulled Taylor's picture out of his pocket and held it toward Jacob, but the man ignored it.

"We don't have anyone called Taylor in the congregation." Jacob kept his eyes on Barker's as he shook his head and shrugged. "Now, I'm gonna need to ask you to leave. As I said, we have work to do."

Leo plucked the photo out of Barker's grasp and held it in front of Jacob's face. His voice was hard as he stepped closer, invading the younger man's space.

"I suggest you look at the photo, Mr. Albright."

Jacob glared at Leo, then let his angry gaze flicker to the photo. His blue eyes darkened; Barker imagined he could see the man's pupils dilate even in the bright morning light.

"You know her?" Barker asked, holding his body rigid as he waited for the reply. "She's here?"

Slowly Jacob shook his head, but his eyes remained on the photo. The sound of approaching voices startled him into action.

"No, I've never seen her before. Now you two best get going."

Barker could feel Leo's eyes on him, could feel the question behind the gaze.

Leo's not buying Jacob's story either.

The door to the main house opened. A frail looking woman with a long white braid stepped out onto the porch. She was leaning on a cane, and her arms shook with the effort to steady herself as she shuffled toward a big, white rocker. A tall, robust woman followed behind, keeping an eye on the older woman's progress until she'd settled herself safely in the chair.

"Everything okay, son?"

The older woman's brittle voice cracked in the air, and Barker was sure he saw Jacob's features tighten.

"Nothing for you to worry about, Ma. These men are just leaving."

But his mother's voice rang out again.

"You forgot your manners, boy?" Her words were slow, almost slurred. "Invite your guests to sit a spell. Offer 'em some...some tea."

Jacob turned back to Barker, his fists clenching at his sides."

"No, Ma. These men can't stay."

Barker opened his mouth to protest, when he noticed that the tall woman on the porch was calling to someone inside the house. He held his breath, expecting Taylor's face to appear in the door frame.

Instead he saw a man's face; it was the man he'd met the previous day. The sun reflected off Brother Eli's white-blonde hair as he joined the women on the porch.

"Hey, Brother Eli," Barker called out, looking over Jacob's broad shoulder. "You get that truck fixed yet?"

Leo placed a firm hand on Barker's arm and squeezed.

"He's got a gun," Leo muttered under his breath. "Stay calm."

Eli held the rifle casually in his right hand, the barrel pointing down, almost touching the wooden floor. When he noticed Barker and Leo staring at it, he lifted the rifle and cradled it in the crook of his arm. He ignored Barker's greeting.

"This is private property, and you're not welcome here."

Eli began to descend the steps, the rifle still held loosely in his grip. The tall woman on the porch watched the scene with wide eyes. As Eli reached the bottom step she called out.

"Eli, you be careful, now."

Eli didn't look around.

"Don't worry, Mama. I know what I'm doing. We can't let these men bring their worldly problems into our congregation."

The woman in the rocking chair nodded in apparent agreement.

"Leave him be, Judith. Your son's a man now, like my Jacob. They have to keep the evil out, you know. They...they..."

The weak voice trailed off, and the older woman's head slumped toward her chest, falling against the long white braid that snaked across her shoulder and ended in her lap.

"Ma Verity?" Judith knelt beside the rocker. "You okay, Ma?"

She put a solid hand on the older woman's thin shoulder and gave a slight shake. Verity moaned and nestled deeper into the chair.

"I think she needs a little nap."

Judith looked up with a rueful smile; it faded when she saw that Eli stood only a few feet behind Jacob, the gun held firmly in both hands.

Jacob studied his mother's slumped form, impatience seeming to override any concern he was feeling. He turned to Judith.

"Go to the back garden, Sister Judith. Make sure everyone stays there until I give the all clear. I don't want anyone getting hurt."

He watched Judith scurry down the steps and around the building, then swung his gaze to Barker.

"I'm going to ask you politely for the last time. Please *leave.*"

Eli raised the rifle, the barrel pointing straight ahead, his face impassive. Barker wondered what lay behind Eli's stony exterior.

What's happened to cause this supposedly religious young man to feel comfortable holding a gun on two strangers?

Leo pulled on the sleeve of Barker's jacket.

"Let's go, Barker. We don't want any trouble."

But Barker wasn't so sure. Maybe trouble was the only thing that would lead him to Taylor. Sitting around and playing it safe certainly hadn't worked. He laid a big hand on the butt of his own gun.

"Something's way off around here," Barker said, his eyes boring into Jacob's. "You profess to be a congregation of love, and here you are threatening us with a gun? And your mother's up there almost comatose and you don't seem to give a damn? What's going on here? What are you hiding?"

Jacob narrowed his eyes and clenched his jaw.

"The only thing wrong around here is *you*. We're doing just fine on our own. We don't need you causing problems."

Out of the corner of his eye Barker saw Eli begin to shake. The rifle trembled in the young man's hands, and he couldn't seem to keep it steady. If Eli pulled the trigger, even accidentally, someone could get hurt. Leo might be shot. Barker was willing to risk his own life, but he couldn't risk anything happening to Leo.

"I'll be back," Barker said, his voice hard, "and next time, I'll bring the police with me."

Jacob's handsome face twisted into an exaggerated smirk, but Barker saw fear behind the scorn.

"You just be sure any cops you bring have a warrant with 'em. If not, they won't be allowed in either. This is a private community and it's gonna stay that way as long as I'm in charge."

Leo pulled Barker toward the Prius.

"Come on, this isn't getting us anywhere. Let's go for now."

Barker allowed himself to be propelled toward the car. As he opened the driver's side door a thin voice drifted through the air.

"You fellows want to have some tea? It'll warm you up."

Ma Verity was once again awake, squinting at them with a vague smile. Barker didn't bother to respond. He sank into the driver's seat, pushing back the feeling that he was missing something important. As he backed out of the compound, he saw the chair on the porch begin to rock back and forth.

CHAPTER ELEVEN

The gates closed behind the Prius with an unsettling clang that echoed inside Jacob's head. He shut his eyes and breathed in deeply, trying not to panic, forcing the photo of the girl out of his mind. He needed time to think.

"Brother Jacob?" Eli's voice broke the silence. "You think they'll really bring the cops out here?"

Shaking his head, Jacob glanced at Eli, then looked away.

"Nah, they're just bluffing. They don't have justification for a warrant. And we sure as hell won't let 'em in without one."

He stomped toward the barn, his boots crunching over gravel and dirt, fear burning through him at the thought of the cops raiding the place. He replayed the conversation, wondering how the two men had found their way to the compound. He straightened, then turned to glare at Eli.

"That man recognized you. He asked about the truck..."

"Yeah, he's the one I told you about. The one that stopped and offered to help. I sent him on his way though."

Understanding washed over Jacob.

"You and Zac are the ones that led him here. Ya'll must've told him something that made him suspicious. What was it?"

Eli frowned and shook his head.

"We didn't tell him nothin'. He was asking questions. Showed me that picture-"

Without thinking Jacob reached out and grabbed Eli's arm in a tight grip.

"You saw the picture?"

"Yeah. I saw it."

"What'd you tell him? You admit you knew her?"

Wrenching his arm away, Eli regarded Jacob with hot, angry eyes. A flush turned his pale skin red.

"I didn't tell him nothin'," Eli snapped. "The old man smelled like a cop to me. And besides, I wouldn't go tellin' a stranger our business."

Jacob sighed; he believed Eli was telling the truth. He'd kept his mouth shut about knowing the girl in the photo. The young man was strange, but he'd proven himself trustworthy time and time again.

And he hates cops just as much as I do. Maybe more.

Regarding Eli with solemn eyes, Jacob wondered how far he could push the young man. He had no choice but to find out.

"We can't let anyone from the outside ruin our congregation," Jacob said, his voice dropping. "That's why I need your help."

A wary look entered Eli's eyes, but he remained quiet, as if sensing he wasn't going to like Jacob's request.

"I need you to go find Sister Candace and Sister Ruth. I need you to bring them back here."

"Why the hell do you want me to do that?" Eli's voice shook with outrage as he frowned up at Jacob. "Them girls took off and abandoned the congregation. They don't wanna be here, and they don't *deserve* to be here."

Jacob nodded his agreement, knowing he had to placate Eli if he was going to manipulate him into finding the two runaways before they could cause more trouble.

"I know," Jacob said, adopting the stern, disapproving expression he'd seen his father wear countless times. "I'm pretty disappointed in their behavior as well. They've already caused a lot of people distress, which is why I need you to bring them back before they cause any more harm."

"I told you from the beginning that Sister Candace was nothing but trouble," Eli insisted. "I thought you'd be happy to see the back of her."

Eli crossed both arms over his thin chest and cocked his head before continuing.

"And I bet Sister Naomi wouldn't be pleased to see that...that *Jezebel* back here."

Jacob blinked, then let out an involuntary bray of laughter. He hadn't been prepared for the old-fashioned word to come out of the little man's mouth.

"What the hell are you talking about, Eli?"

But an unpleasant thought began to form in the back of his mind. Once again he gripped the smaller man's arm.

"What do you know about Sister Candace anyway?"

Eli tried to throw off Jacob's hand, but the bigger man tightened his grip and pulled Eli closer, lowering his head so that he was staring into Eli's wide, scared eyes.

"You know something about Sister Candace that I should know about? You know where she went?"

"No...I just know...she was trying to..."

Jacob pushed Eli away, watching with narrow eyes as Eli lost his balance and sat down hard on the dirt floor of the big barn. Looming over Eli with both hands balled into fists, Jacob stared down at him with contempt.

"I didn't bring you here to sit in judgment of me. I brought you here to be my...my right hand. I brought you here because I thought you'd have my back, no matter what."

"I do Jake...it's just-"

"Don't call me that here, you idiot," Jacob spit out, raising a big boot, tempted to kick the man cowering before him. "I'm *Brother Jacob* now."

He stepped back, frustration building at the thought that he might have misjudged Eli's abilities. When he'd met Eli in prison, Jacob had discovered that the simple man was easy to manipulate, and that he was unafraid to do almost anything if he thought Jacob would be pleased.

Then, once Jacob had been paroled, he'd decided to ask Eli to join the commune. Even back then, when Jacob had been determined to rebuild his life in a way that would please his father, he'd suspected he would eventually need someone on his side that wouldn't ask too many questions. Someone desperate enough to do whatever was asked.

"After everything I've done for you, you're gonna try to tell me what to do? You think you should be running this place?"

Eli shook his head, but his eyes still held a defiant gleam that worried Jacob.

"Just what is it about Sister Candace that you think you know?"

Standing up and dusting off the back of his faded jeans, Eli dropped his eyes and cleared his throat.

"She...she was trying to...to steal you away from Sister Naomi. And she was trying to cause trouble around here. Talking about you to the others..."

His voice trailed off and he raised his eyes to Jacob's.

"I don't think Sister Naomi will like it if you bring Sister Candace back here."

Keeping his face carefully neutral, Jacob shrugged.

"Sister Naomi is my wife, and a member of this congregation. She will submit to the decisions of her husband and her spiritual leader."

Jacob watched Eli's reaction, choosing his next words carefully.

"In fact, all members of this congregation must abide by the decisions I make. I'm the leader now. My father's gone, and it was his wish that I lead his flock. It's the sacred duty of the congregation to follow."

The words flowed from Jacob's mouth in a rough imitation of his father. He enjoyed using the authoritative tone that had come so naturally to Jedidiah Albright, feeling as if he was a child playing dress up.

Only instead of wearing my old man's clothes, I'm wearing his holier-than-thou attitude.

A twinge of shame passed through Jacob as he remembered his father's kind face and worried eyes, but he pushed the image away, fixing his face into a grim mask as he waited for Eli's response.

"Okay," Eli agreed, his voice resigned. "I'll go out and look for them tonight."

❋ ❋ ❋

Dinner in the big dining hall was normally a cheerful affair, the airy room resounding with the conversation and laughter of men and women pleased to be relaxing after a long day in the gardens and workshops. But the atmosphere in the commune had grown increasingly tense after the disappearance of Candace and Ruth, and the unexpected arrival of the two strangers in the courtyard earlier in the day had prompted a flurry of rumors to spread through the congregation.

Jacob noted the whispered conversations and anxious faces around him with concern and realized with dismay that Sister Marie wasn't at any of the tables. He wondered what she was doing.

Maybe she's in her room. Maybe she's undressing right now.

His eyes glazed over as he pictured the long, graceful legs and shapely figure Sister Marie hid under her modest dress.

"Brother Jacob?"

A soft voice behind Jacob made him pause with a bite of boiled potato halfway to his mouth. He put down his fork and turned to see Judith Dunkel hovering behind his chair.

"Yes, Sister Judith?"

Jacob tried to keep the irritation out of his voice. He was anxious for dinner to end so that Eli could begin the search. If the girls were still hiding out in the woods or the swamp, they needed to be found soon, if they had any hope of being found at all.

Unless the gators have already got to them.

The thought fluttered through his mind as he waited for Judith to say whatever it was she had to say and let him get back to his dinner.

"Eli says he's got an errand to do tonight, and I was just wondering if that is such a good idea. It's cold outside and I think-"

Jacob winced as a high-pitch laugh pierced the air next to him, obscuring the rest of Judith's words. Naomi was seated at the table to his right. He'd almost forgotten she was there.

"Stop being such a nag, Sister Judith." Naomi's teasing tone didn't match the hostile gleam in her eyes. "Your son's a grown man now. He doesn't need his momma speaking for him I'm sure."

Jacob resisted the urge to slap the spiteful smile off Naomi's pretty face. Instead he turned back to Judith.

"Sorry about that, Sister Judith. You'll have to excuse my dear wife. She doesn't understand what it means to be a devoted mother."

He couldn't suppress a smile when he felt Naomi stiffen at his words. He motioned for Judith to continue.

"Well, I don't mean any disrespect, of course. I'm just worried about Eli's health. He hasn't seemed well lately."

Glancing over at Naomi, Judith bit her lip and twisted her hands in front of her. Her eyes widened as she took in the pale, stricken expression Naomi now wore.

"But then maybe Sister Naomi is right. Perhaps it isn't my place to interfere. I'm sure you know what's best."

Jacob watched Judith's tall, solid back retreat into the kitchen, then turned to Naomi. She stared down at her salad, her eyes wet with tears.

"You know better that to insult a member of the congregation. She's just trying to look out for her son. Something you wouldn't know anything about."

Not waiting for a reaction, Jacob stood and left the room, striding toward the sanctuary of his office with long, impatient steps. Locking the door behind him, he sat at his desk and once again pulled out the laptop. He clicked on a folder and waited for the files to display.

A collection of thumbnail images appeared, each one showcasing Candace Newbury's supple young body in a different pose. Candace was smiling in some of the photos, and in others she was looking directly at the camera with a seductive pout.

It was fun while it lasted. But then nothing lasts forever.

Jacob clicked on the *Select All* option, then, with only a slight pause, he tapped the *Delete* key.

"Bye-bye, Candy," he muttered, moving the cursor to the live-stream app. "Hello, my sweet Marie."

The whispered words had just left his mouth when he heard an angry rap on the office door, and the familiar whine of his mother-in-law's voice filled the room. In a panic he slammed the lid closed.

"Brother Jacob? I need to speak to you. It's about Naomi."

Jacob banged his fist on the desk, then forced himself to stand and shove the laptop back into the drawer. He took a deep breath and tried to smooth out his features. He opened the door wearing a stiff smile.

"Sister Priscilla, what a lovely surprise."

Priscilla Putnam looked remarkably like her daughter. Her hair was just as dark, and her eyes just as green. In the soft, intimate light of Jacob's study he wondered if he should have chosen the mother over the daughter.

She'd know how to treat a man properly. And she wouldn't be obsessed with having a baby.

But his mother-in-law had other things on her mind. She was worried about Naomi. The girl hadn't been acting like herself lately. Had he noticed anything wrong?

Quickly growing bored with Priscilla's barrage of questions, Jacob let his mind drift. With Candace gone, and his wife growing increasingly hostile, there was no reason he couldn't begin his seduction of Marie right away. As he ushered Priscilla out the door, he'd already determined his next move. It was just a matter of time.

CHAPTER TWELVE

A ngel bent to scoop up another egg, her basket already heavy with the morning's collection, her back and legs still aching from her recent mission into the swamp. The air in the chicken coop was icy, and she pulled her shawl tighter around her shoulders, shivering as she walked back into the early morning sunshine.

Just a quick stop in the potting shed and I'll be ready to go.

It was her turn to get the eggs to Chester Gosbey's diner before the morning rush began, but she wanted to check on the devil's weed first. She had feared they would succumb to the cold weather, knowing the toxic plants were sensitive to frost, so she'd been careful to cover all the pots the previous evening.

The little wooden shed was nestled behind a cluster of ancient, moss-covered oak trees. Angel ducked inside, pulling back a makeshift cover to reveal a long tray of delicate purple blossoms. She surveyed the elegant, trumpet-shaped flowers and the deadly pods resting below them, gathering a few leaves and one plump, walnut-sized pod. Hiding her stash in a shoulder bag under her shawl, she hurried back into the sunny morning.

The two-mile walk through the woods to the Little Gator Diner usually provided Angel with a welcome break from the bustle of the compound's never-ending chores. It was her time to think and plan.

A chance to drop the act she was forced to maintain when at the commune, where it was getting harder to keep up the pretense.

I should just burn the whole place down and be done with it.

But she knew that wasn't an option. Not while Jacob was there. She had other plans for him. And besides, CSL was the only home she had now. It had become both a prison and a sanctuary.

But that is about to change. I'll do what needs to be done, and then I'll be the one calling the shots around that place. Things will be very different.

Her legs ached as she walked through the boggy woods toward the diner, and she breathed a sigh of relief when she saw the sign up ahead. Chester hadn't turned on the lights yet. Although he was still smiling, the alligator on the sign seemed sad without the neon to liven him up.

Chester appeared at the door, squinting into the morning light, his pale eyes translucent. He waved and limped forward, leaning on his cane for support.

"Thought you weren't comin' today."

Angel ran a hand through her dark hair and forced herself to take a calming breath. It was time to fall back into character.

No use letting the old cripple get under my skin.

"I'm here now." She held up the heavy basket. "And I have plenty of eggs for you."

Chester led her inside. He watched as she lifted the heavy basket, noting the grimace of pain that crossed her face.

"Sorry, I'd offer to help, but my damn leg's actin' up again, and that new doctor at the clinic doesn't know why."

He started counting the eggs as Angel stretched her arms and rolled her shoulders, not bothering to respond to the old man's usual complaints about his prosthetic leg.

"Everything okay? You look a little under the weather."

She bristled at his words, offended by his prying, but attempted a neutral smile.

"Everything's just fine, Mr. Gosbey."

The old man studied her with his curious, baggy eyes, then turned to the cash register. He inserted a key and the drawer popped open. Taking out a small stack of bills, he licked his thumb and began to count.

"You know," he said, his thumb pausing over a ten-dollar bill, "CSL hasn't been the same without Jed."

Angel stiffened with resentment, but didn't respond, her eyes resting on the cash in Chester's hands.

"No offense, or nothin'," the old man continued, "but Jacob isn't the man his father was. There's no denying that."

Sticking out a hand for the payment, Angel allowed a sharp edge to enter her voice.

"Things are good at CSL. No need for you to worry."

He handed her the stack of bills and sat back on the stool behind the counter, watching as she stuck the money into her shoulder bag.

"I was surprised that Jed wanted Jacob to take over," Chester rattled on. "Although maybe it's not appropriate for me to say. But I always thought Tobias would be the natural choice. Him or one of the older men with more experience."

Rage transformed Angel's face into a distorted grimace. She leaned over the counter, staring into Chester's shocked face, her eyes blazing with contempt.

"You'll stay out of our business if you know what's good for you."

Chester's hand instinctively tightened around the head of his cane, and Angel followed his gaze to the heavy stick. Her mouth widened into an ugly smirk as their eyes met.

You don't have the guts to use that, old man, and we both know it.

She walked to the door, then stopped and turned around.

"What do you know about Sister Marie?"

Her voice matched the ice-cold look in her eyes as she waited for his response.

"Who? Sister...Marie?"

Angel paused, studying his confused reaction.

"The girl that worked here as a waitress," she said, her voice calmer now. "The young one that went to school with Candace."

The confusion on his face was replaced by a look of concern.

"Ok, yeah...Marie. She's a good girl. Why do you ask? She okay?"

She ignored his question.

"What do you know about her? Other than she went to school with your granddaughter? She have any family around here?"

Chester dropped his eyes, revealing his impending lie.

"I don't know nothing, why? She in some sort of trouble?"

Without another word, Angel pushed through the door and walked back toward the woods. She knew she should never have revealed her true face to the old man. After this he would no longer trust her. He might even tell Jacob what she'd said.

Maybe I'll have to pay the nosy bastard another visit. Make sure he doesn't cause any trouble. But I have other things to take care of first.

First she needed to find out where Ruth had gone, and then she needed to uncover Sister Marie's true identity. She could tell from Chester's reaction that Marie was not the girl's real name, and Angel wasn't surprised.

She knew firsthand how convenient it was to use someone else's name. She'd done it herself most of her life, and now using her real name was no longer an option anyway. But she always thought of herself as Angel. And after her first kill, she began to pretend she was a real angel. Of course, she was an angel to some, the angel of death to others. It depended if they were useful, or if they were in her way.

And Sister Marie and Sister Ruth are definitely in my way.

CHAPTER THIRTEEN

The door to the office opened, revealing Ruth Culvert's thin frame. Reggie jumped up and crossed the room, noting with relief that a crisp cotton blouse and black jeans had replaced the thin, homemade dress Ruth had arrived in the day before, and that her red hair had been brushed back into a loose ponytail.

Reggie's relief vanished when she saw the fading bruises around the girl's pale neck and the angry welt on her forehead.

It'll take more than a good night's sleep and new clothes to help this one.

"Come in, dear," Reggie said, motioning for Ruth to take a seat in one of the comfortable armchairs near the window.

Ruth hesitated, hovering in the doorway as Eden Winthrop's familiar voice sounded behind her.

"It's okay, Ruth, go on in," Eden coaxed from the hallway. "Reggie's the director here, and a really good therapist, too. She just wants to talk to you. She wants to help."

Hurrying toward the chair farthest from the door, Ruth lowered herself onto the seat, keeping her back straight and her hands clasped in her lap. She searched the room with nervous eyes as Eden followed her in and stopped beside Reggie.

The anxious expression on Eden's face was mixed with hope, and Reggie wished she could reassure her that the girl would be fine. Truth was, healing took time and patience; there was no guarantee that Ruth would ever recover her peace of mind or her memory.

"Don't you worry, now," Reggie said, reaching out to give Eden's hand a reassuring squeeze. "I'll take good care of her. We're just going to talk for now."

"I can't remember anything, you know." Ruth's voice was soft, almost a whisper. "I've tried to remember, but everything's...foggy."

Fear clouded Ruth's wide, gray eyes, confirming Reggie's worry that it wasn't going to be easy to get her to open up.

The poor girl doesn't want to remember, and I don't blame her.

Reggie wasn't sure if Ruth's physical head injury was causing her memory loss, or if she was subconsciously blocking the memory of the abuse she'd suffered. Some things were too painful to remember.

"Eden, why don't you go and get some work done? Ruth and I will be fine here. We'll get to know each other and talk a little."

"But...I was hoping..."

Eden bit her lip, searching for the right words.

"It's just, shouldn't we try to get a description of the person who did this to her? So that we can tell the police?"

From the corner of her eye Reggie could see Ruth's legs begin to jitter up and down. She understood Eden's desire to catch the perpetrator who had hurt Ruth, but it wasn't the right time to put pressure on the girl. Forcing her to relive the details of the abuse before she was ready would only cause further distress.

"It's possible Ruth won't be ready to remember anything today," Reggie said, hating the crestfallen look that appeared on Eden's face at her words. "But we'll see what we can do."

She turned and moved toward Ruth, realizing only after she'd sat down in the chair across from the girl that Eden hadn't left the room. Reggie raised her eyebrows.

"Yes, Eden, is there something else?"

"Well, I know I'm not the expert here-"

"That's right, you're not," Reggie said in a patient voice, glancing over at Ruth, then back at Eden. "So, please, leave it to me."

93

Clearing her throat, Eden gave Reggie an apologetic smile, then held up a single finger.

"I just want to ask one more thing. You see I was wondering if maybe you could try hypnosis. I mean, if Ruth can't remember after you guys talk, maybe that would help."

Reggie sighed, exasperation mingling with a grudging admiration at Eden's persistence. Eden didn't give up if she thought there was the slightest chance to stop another woman from getting hurt; she'd do whatever was necessary to get another abuser off the streets.

"I'll evaluate that possibility," Reggie agreed, gesturing for Eden to leave. "Now, good-bye."

Once Eden had slipped out the door, Reggie turned to Ruth.

"Okay, then. I imagine you want to know who I am before we start talking. It's never easy to share painful experiences with anyone, so it's important you feel comfortable with me before we begin."

Reggie paused, waiting to see if Ruth would react. When she didn't, Reggie continued.

"Well, my name is Dr. Regina Horn. I'm a psychiatrist and the director of the Mercy Harbor Foundation. Most of my patients start out calling me Dr. Horn but end up calling me Reggie, so let's skip the formality in this case."

Reggie watched Ruth's hands ball into fists in her lap.

"I don't need a psychiatrist," Ruth blurted, her voice shaky. "I'm not crazy."

"Of course, you aren't," Reggie agreed matter-of-factly. "Psychiatrists provide therapy to help people stay mentally and emotionally healthy, especially if they've experienced trauma."

Ruth swallowed hard, then shook her head from side to side, a soft whimper escaping.

"I just keep seeing these...terrible...things."

Reggie hastened to bring Ruth's focus back to their conversation.

"No need to think of that right now. Tell me a bit about yourself first. All I know is your name is Ruth. What's your last name?"

"It's...Culvert. Ruth Culvert."

"How old are you, Ruth?"

Reggie waited, keeping her face placid and relaxed.

"I'm twenty-two."

Reggie nodded and smiled.

"Do you live in Willow Bay?"

Ruth shook her head, her eyes widening in panic. Reggie moved on to the next question, letting Ruth know she wouldn't be pressured into answering any questions she didn't want to answer.

"Is there anyone you want us to contact for you? Anyone that might be worried about where you are right now?"

Again, Ruth shook her head. A single tear dripped down her cheek as she closed her eyes and let out an anguished sob.

"I'm...I'm scared," Ruth whispered, keeping her eyes tightly shut. "I don't know what happened. I was...I was in my bed one minute, and then the next...I was in the...the woods..."

Reggie leaned over and tucked a tissue into Ruth's small hand.

"Was this yesterday morning when you woke up in the woods? Is that when the mailman found you?"

Ruth nodded, blotting her eyes with the tissue.

"When I woke up my head was hurting, and I had...blood on me. I looked around. I didn't know where I was, but I could see the road past the trees. Somehow I made it through...the trees...to the road..."

She stared into space, watching the events play out in her mind.

"And a man in a truck stopped to help you?"

"Yes. He asked if...if I needed help...where I was going. I opened my hand and showed him the paper with a...a name and address."

Reggie leaned back in her chair, trying to rein in her curiosity.

"And you don't remember how you got the paper?"

Frustration passed over Ruth's face for the first time, and a frown creased the pale skin of her forehead.

"I'm not sure. Every time I try to remember, I get so scared."

Reggie hesitated. Maybe Eden was right. Someone had assaulted Ruth, and that someone was likely still out there free to hurt other women. She had an obligation to try to get details from the girl.

Maybe then we can file a report in time to save someone else.

Making her decision, she turned to Ruth.

"I'd like us to try a relaxation technique. It'll help you feel safe while allowing you to remember what happened."

"You mean, you want to hypnotize me like Ms. Winthrop said?"

Reggie nodded, although she didn't like to use the word hypnotize; the idea often scared patients and set unrealistic expectations about the process. But if she could get Ruth in a relaxed, receptive state, the girl might allow herself to remember how she'd ended up in the woods, and how she'd gotten Mercy Harbor's address.

"I don't know," Ruth said, her eyes wide. "I'm scared."

"No need to be scared, Ruth." Reggie's voice was gentle. "We'll just focus on breathing. That should induce a state of deep relaxation where you'll feel safe. Once you feel ready, we'll talk about the events that led you to Mercy Harbor. If you start feeling too uncomfortable at any time we'll stop right away."

"Okay," Ruth agreed, much to Reggie's surprise. "Let's try."

But the raw fear on Ruth's face made Reggie hesitate.

"Are you sure you feel ready?"

Ruth nodded, her eyes wide.

"Yes. I *have* to remember. I have a...a bad feeling that if I don't remember, something...terrible will happen."

The tortured words sent a shiver down Reggie's spine, but she managed to keep her expression calm. The girl was determined, and she wanted to remember. Reggie pushed the remaining doubts from her mind.

Not the right time to chicken out now, Reggie.

As she walked Ruth through the initial stages of hypnosis, Reggie was surprised at how quickly Ruth sank into a deep, trance-like state.

"Now Ruth, I want you to think back to the night before you arrived at Mercy Harbor. You said you remember getting into bed. Tell me about that."

Ruth spoke in a soft, melodic voice, her face passive.

"I remember getting into bed, but I wasn't comfortable. I had my nightgown over my dress, and it felt strange. I laid there for a while waiting for Candy to come..."

The words faded, and Ruth's fingers began twisting in her lap

"You're safe here, Ruth. Nothing here can hurt you. It's okay for you to remember what happened next."

When Ruth didn't speak, Reggie gently prodded.

"So, you're waiting for Candy? Who's Candy?

"She's my friend. But...she's in...in trouble."

Ruth's forehead furrowed and her voice deepened.

"He...hurt her and I'm going to help her. We've got to leave tonight." Ruth's eyes remained closed, but Reggie saw movement underneath her lids, as if she were watching someone. "Candy's here for me and we're sneaking out. We can't let them see us but it's dark..."

"Where are you and Candy going?"

"We're cutting through the woods by the swamp. We have to find the road so we can get to Willow Bay. Marie wrote down the name of a lady that can help Candy."

"Who's Marie?"

Ruth didn't seem to hear Reggie. She wrapped her thin arms around herself and whimpered again.

"I hate the swamp at night. It's so cold. So scary. We can't find the road." Panic entered Ruth's voice. "I see the snake."

"What snake, Ruth? What do you see?"

"The snake on the sign. We're at the old gas station by the preserve, but it's...it's closed down. I think...I think we're lost."

"What do you see, Ruth? Is anyone else with you?"

"Someone's here." Ruth whispered. "We've got to hide."

Reggie waited, noting Ruth's quick, shallow breaths, unsure if she should allow Ruth to continue. The girl stiffened, then spoke in a hoarse whisper.

"Candy? Are you okay? Candy?"

Ruth's sudden shriek pierced the air, causing the hair on the back of Reggie's neck to stand on end. She swallowed hard, then spoke quickly, careful to keep her voice calm.

"Ruth, listen to my voice. I don't want you think about the swamp right now. Take yourself back to your room. You're safe and warm in your bed."

But it was too late. Ruth's eyes opened, glassy with terror as she relived the events in the swamp.

"No, Candy, run. Please, run...no, please don't hurt her!"

Reggie stood and crossed to Ruth, kneeling in front of the chair, her face positioned in front of Ruth. She took Ruth's hands in hers.

"Ruth, listen to me. You're here with me at Mercy Harbor, and everything is okay. We're fine. Look at me, Ruth."

Ruth's frightened eyes fell on Reggie's calm face. She blinked, as if surprised to see her, then looked around the room.

"That's it. Now slow your breathing. Inhale slowly, now exhale."

Keeping eye contact with Ruth, Reggie breathed in deeply, then let out a slow breath of air, urging Ruth to do the same.

"That's it. Just relax and breathe. Everything's going to be okay."

"No, it's not okay," Ruth gasped, shaking her head from side to side, trying to catch her breath. "*Candy's* not okay."

Bolting up and out of her chair, Ruth stared past Reggie, seeing only the horror of the dark swamp, crying out in anguish.

"She's *dead.* They...they *killed her.*"

* * *

Reggie stood over Ruth's sleeping figure, her forehead furrowed with worry, her heart still pumping hard from the effort to get Ruth sedated and back to her room after her startling revelation and the panic attack that had followed.

A frantic knock announced Eden's arrival. Reggie closed the bedroom door behind her and crossed through the sitting room to open the door.

"What happened? Is Ruth all right?"

Eden hurried inside, looking around at the empty room. Her eyes moved to the closed bedroom door.

"She's sleeping now, Eden," Reggie said, dreading what she was going to have to say next. "But she did remember what had happened. At least some of it."

Eden turned and stared at Reggie in silent expectation. The therapist lowered her small frame into a chair, her legs still shaking.

"I need to sit down."

Reggie looked up at Eden, not bothering to wipe away the sheen of perspiration that lit up her ebony skin. She didn't have time to waste. She had to tell Eden the truth quickly. The police would need to be called. An investigation would have to be started.

"And I think, when you hear what Ruth told me, you're gonna want to sit down, too."

CHAPTER FOURTEEN

The stress in Eden Winthrop's voice was palpable even over the phone. Nessa motioned for Jankowski to close the door to their shared office, trying to concentrate on Eden's frantic words. Jankowski rolled his eyes and sighed, then stood and pushed the door shut. He turned back to Nessa, crossing his arms over his wide chest, eyebrows raised.

"Eden, hold on a minute," Nessa interrupted. "Detective Jankowski's here with me and I'm gonna put you on speaker phone."

Nessa watched Jankowski stiffen, noting the wary look that appeared in his eyes at Eden's name.

Folks around here think a call from Eden Winthrop means trouble's on the way. That and more bad press.

"Now, slow down, Eden, and tell us what's happened."

Nessa laid the phone on her desk. Both she and Jankowski stared at it as Eden's anxious voice erupted from the speaker.

"Ruth's the girl I told you about yesterday, the one who couldn't remember how she'd gotten injured, or how she found Mercy Harbor's address. Well, she met with Reggie today and was able to remember some of what happened."

Nessa met Jankowski's eyes over the phone, seeing that he too was braced for the worst. Eden cleared her throat, her voice turning hoarse as she continued.

"Ruth said she and a friend, a girl she called Candy, were being chased in the swamp. She said whoever was after them caught Candy and they...they killed her."

Jankowski leaned on the desk with both hands, his voice hard.

"You're telling us this woman witnessed a homicide?"

Nessa heard Eden's sharp intake of breath at Jankowski's blunt question. She threw her partner a disapproving glare, then bent over the desk to grab a pad of paper and a pen.

"Eden, we need to know exactly what Ruth told you. We're gonna have to investigate, of course. But please remember, the girl could be mistaken. You said yourself she couldn't remember, that she was upset. Let's hope this is some sort of misunderstanding."

"I don't think so, Nessa." Eden's voice was firm. "Reggie has had lots of experience treating traumatized patients. She thinks Ruth is telling the truth. She thinks seeing her friend get killed is likely what caused Ruth to block out the memory and–"

Jankowski interrupted, sounding irritated.

"We won't know anything for sure until we investigate. Can Ruth...what's her last name?"

"Culvert," Eden offered. "It's Ruth Culvert."

Nessa scribbled down the name.

"Well, can Ms. Culvert come down and give us a statement?"

"She was hysterical," Eden snapped back, her tone heating up at the impatience in his voice. "Reggie had to sedate her. She'll likely be out most of the night."

Nessa winced. If Ruth's friend had been hurt, or even killed, every minute would count. And she knew firsthand that if there really was a body out there in the swamp, the wildlife would quickly destroy any evidence.

"Eden, what can you or Reggie tell us?" Nessa asked, gesturing for Jankowski to stay quiet. "What information did Ruth provide that you can pass on? I don't think we can afford to wait until tomorrow to look into this."

"Well, the mailman who brought Ruth to Mercy Harbor said he found her off of Highway 42 past I-75."

Nessa nodded, taking notes on the pad.

"And Ruth said she and Candy had gotten lost in the swamp and ended up at a closed gas station near the preserve."

"Did she give any other details about the gas station?"

"Well, Ruth said there was a snake." Eden sounded unsure. "She told Reggie she'd seen a snake on a sign over the gas station."

Jankowski leaned over the phone again.

"She saw a snake hanging on a sign? Did he give her directions?"

The sarcasm in his voice earned another glare from Nessa, and this time she scooped up her phone, turned off the speaker, and turned her back on Jankowski.

"Sorry about that, Eden. I think that's enough for me and Jankowski to go on for now. We'll take a drive out that way and see what we can find."

"Thank you, Nessa. Please let me know...whatever you find."

The gratitude in Eden's voice produced a guilty flush on Nessa's face. While she and Jankowski could drive out to the area and look around, it was unlikely the two of them would be able to find anything in the thousands of acres of wetlands that made up the Cottonmouth Preserve.

"I will, Eden. And I'll also come by to check on Ruth later. We'll need a statement from her as soon as possible. Without a reliable eyewitness account, it'll be hard to get more resources assigned to the case. It's a big swamp out there, you know. It'll be hard to find anything without an organized search party."

"I understand," Eden said, her voice somber. "But, Ruth seems to believe she's still in danger, so please, do whatever you can."

* * *

Nessa turned on the heater in her Charger, holding a numb hand in front of the vent as she sped down I-75.

"It wasn't this cold last December," she muttered toward Jankowski, who was studying a map on his laptop as they hurtled along. "I took the boys to the beach on Christmas Day. They still had sunburns on New Year's Eve."

When Jankowski just grunted instead of replying, she looked over.

"You find anything interesting yet?'

More silence. Finally, Jankowski raised his head and pointed to a sign on the side of the road.

"Follow those signs to the Cottonmouth Preserve. They'll take you to Highway 42 which runs parallel to the preserve."

He looked down at the computer again, clicking on a message in his inbox. He drummed his fingers on the dashboard as he read the message.

"Shit." He snapped the laptop closed. "There's no record of a Ruth Culvert in any of the databases. According to the State of Florida, she doesn't exist."

Nessa shrugged, keeping her eyes on the road ahead. A trio of semi-trucks had formed a convoy, slowing traffic.

"I'm not surprised. Lots of folks in the backwoods keep to themselves. It was like that in Georgia, too."

"I thought that accent of yours was fake. I didn't know you really are a...a..."

Nessa smiled, glad to finally see a flush spread over Jankowski's handsome face. Maybe there was a trace of shame left in his brawny body after all.

"I think the word you're looking for is red-neck."

Jankowski shook his head, a wicked gleam lighting up his eyes.

"No, I was thinking more along the line of hillbilly."

Nessa scowled at her partner, but she was glad to see him smiling again. He'd had a hard year. First his wife had cheated on him, leading to a bitter divorce, and then Chief Kramer's crimes had been exposed, causing Jankowski to question everything he'd been taught during his dozen years on the force.

The ping of an incoming text message erased Jankowski's grin.

"Gabby," he muttered. "Again."

Nessa stared straight ahead. She knew better than to get involved in Jankowski's love life. The slightest comment could set him off. They both needed to stay focused on the task at hand.

"Take the exit," Jankowski growled, pointing to a sign overhead.

"Yes, *boss*," Nessa said, rolling her eyes as she steered the big car off the interstate and onto Highway 42.

The rural road was in visible need of repair, and Nessa felt the Charger's right tire bounce over a sizable pothole. An oncoming car swished past them, retreating quickly in the rearview mirror, leaving the road empty as far as the eye could see.

"It's creepy out here," Nessa said, more to herself than Jankowski, who was staring sullenly at the passing scenery.

Dense clusters of trees lined the road, making it impossible to see past the towering tree line. The sun reflected off the water around the thick, gray roots of the cypress trees, hinting at the wetlands just beyond. They'd driven for another fifteen minutes before Nessa spotted a faded road sign: *Cottonmouth Gas and Snacks – Next Exit.*

"You see that sign?"

Jankowski nodded, turning to Nessa.

"Yeah, I saw it, but I don't see an exit yet."

Nessa squinted at the road ahead, waiting for the exit sign to appear. Jankowski thumbed his phone, accessing a map app and searching for nearby gas stations.

"Nothing's showing for Cottonmouth Gas on the map. In fact, it looks like there's nothing else on this road until we pass the welcome center, which is another five miles."

Craning her neck to see Jankowski's phone, Nessa let the Charger drift to the left, earning a blaring honk from a big, black pickup truck hurtling past them in the opposite lane. She glared back at the driver in her side mirror.

I wasn't even over the line and there he is making a fuss.

As the truck sped out of sight, something glinted in the mirror. They'd passed a sign nearly hidden by an overgrowth of vegetation. Nessa lowered her foot on the brake and pulled to the side of the road.

"What the hell are you stopping for?"

Jankowski looked up from his phone just as Nessa maneuvered the car into a wide U-turn and drove back toward the sign. He followed her eyes to the now-obvious dirt road that led off the highway.

Guiding the car slowly onto the overgrown road, Nessa could see glimpses of a building beyond the army of sable palms lining the shoulder. Within seconds the Charger stopped in front of a boarded-up gas station which stood abandoned about fifty yards off the highway.

Jankowski pointed to the lopsided sign hanging from one rusty chain. The faded outline of a coiled snake was still visible, although the lettering on the sign was hard to make out.

"I think it says Cottonmouth Filling Station," Nessa murmured, uneasily peering into the woods around them. "I guess we'd better look around."

A loud rustling from the bushes startled Nessa as soon as she'd stepped out of the car. Her hand instinctively reached for the gun in her holster, then fell to her side as an enormous racoon trundled into the clearing, passing Nessa without a sideways glance.

"You aren't scared of 'coons are you, Ellie May?" Jankowski teased. "I thought you'd feel right at home out here."

"Shut up, Jankowski." Nessa walked toward the front of the station, her eyes scanning the boarded-up windows and doors. "We're looking for a possible victim, remember?"

She saw him freeze beside her, turning to see him hold a finger up to his lips.

"Shh!" he whispered, gesturing ahead toward a dirty expanse of ground. "Footprints."

Nessa looked down. Several sets of footprints in the mud led around the old building. Once again she reached for her gun, but this time she pulled it out and held it in front of her with both hands, following Jankowski as he crept toward the back of the station.

Catching sight of a thick pool of dried blood on the grass several yards away, Nessa's eyes followed a trail of blood drops leading toward the rear of the building.

"Over there," Nessa whispered, pointing her gun toward the restrooms. "I think someone's in there."

Jankowski was already advancing on the doorway to the men's room. He pointed his gun through the door, arms extended, then took a quick glance inside. Looking back at Nessa, he shook his head, before stepping fully inside and taking a good look around. When he emerged he nodded, giving a silent thumbs-up.

Inhaling deeply, Nessa turned to the women's room. She held her weapon in front of her with steady hands despite the pounding of her heart. Standing beside the doorway, she peeked in quickly, noting at once that no one was in the room.

As she entered the little room, she noticed a pile of material had been thrown in the corner, along with a long coil of something else. It took Nessa a minute to realize she was staring at a snake. Or at least what was left of one. She hurried outside.

"All clear," she said, her voice quiet but shaking. "At least, all clear of humans, but there's something reptilian in there."

Jankowski brushed past her, his big shoulders blocking the entrance as he surveyed the room.

"Snakeskin," he said, crossing to the corner and bending to pick it up. "It's a diamondback rattler. Big one, too. Gotta be six foot."

He held the skin up to show Nessa it was almost as long as he was, but her eyes were glued to a narrow door in the back wall. A smudge of red on the doorframe had caught her eye. Jankowski followed her gaze, then stepped closer to examine the mark.

"Looks like a bloody handprint, or at least a partial print."

Jankowski's voice was a grim whisper. He met Nessa's eyes, then held up his hand, silently counting down with his fingers.

Five, four, three, two, one.

Wrenching the door open, Jankowski pointed his gun into the utility closet, every muscle in his body tense and ready to fight.

A foul stench emanated from within, sending Jankowski stumbling backward. Nessa gagged, then lifted her hand to cover her mouth and nose. She approached the open door cautiously, already knowing from the horribly familiar smell what she was going to find.

The girl's body hung from a hook mounted on the closet wall. Her simple dress was covered in an apron of blood. Nessa raised her eyes to the poor girl's face. She gasped, turning away in horror as she saw the word that had been carved into the dead girl's forehead.

She felt Jankowski beside her, heard his sharp intake of breath.

"What's it say?" he asked.

Nessa's voice caught in her throat as she choked out the name.

"Jezebel."

CHAPTER FIFTEEN

The fireplace danced with flames, warming Eden's living room against the cold snap that had deepened overnight. The floor was strewn with rolls of brightly colored giftwrap, silky bows, and tags adorned with snowmen, reindeer, and Christmas trees. A stack of presents for Hope and Devon teetered on the sofa, waiting to be wrapped.

"You don't think I'm spoiling the kids, do you, Duke?"

Duke stared at her from his position in front of the fireplace, the light from the flames reflecting in his big brown eye and warming his golden fur. Eden sighed, then turned to eye the gifts she'd ordered online the previous weekend, too anxious to enjoy the cozy scene she'd set in an effort to get her mind off Ruth.

Even the Christmas classics on the radio hadn't managed to lift her sprits. She grimaced as a Channel Ten weather bulletin interrupted Bing Crosby singing *White Christmas*.

"Temperatures are expected to drop below freezing tonight while local farmers scramble to save the citrus–"

The buzzing of Eden's phone drowned out weathergirl Veronica Lee's grim forecast. Switching off the radio, Eden's pulse quickened as she noted the caller's number on the display.

"Nessa? What did you find?"

A momentary silence was followed by Nessa's ragged voice.

"We found a girl's body. She'd been...killed. We're still waiting for the crime scene techs and the medical examiner, but there's no doubt that this is a homicide."

The words confirmed Eden's fear with a sickening finality. She'd known deep down that Ruth had been telling the truth but had held on to a fragile hope that the young woman had been mistaken.

No more hope now. Just more death...and another monster out there killing innocent women.

Eden gripped the phone to her ear and cleared her throat.

"So, what do I tell Ruth?"

"Actually, I'm more interested in what Ruth can tell us right now," Nessa said. "We need to talk to her as soon as possible...get a formal statement. At this stage she's the only one who knows what happened, and until we find out more, she'll be considered a person of interest."

Eden gasped.

"A person of interest? You mean, like, a *suspect*?"

"I mean a person of interest. And a possible witness, of course."

The implications of Nessa's words stunned Eden into silence. Her mind spun with the possibilities.

Is Ruth a reliable witness? Could she have something to do with the murder? Could she have blocked the memory because she knew the killer, or...she killed the girl herself?

Shaking her head against the thoughts, Eden spoke more forcefully than she intended.

"No, that's not possible. Ruth is a *victim*. She needs protection, not an interrogation."

"Calm down, Eden." Nessa's voice was weary. "I'm not accusing Ruth of anything, but a girl is dead, and we need to keep an open mind as we begin the investigation."

The soft nudge of Duke's nose against her hand made Eden look down. She smiled into the golden retriever's worried eyes, glad to have his stabilizing presence next to her. They'd been through so much together already. They'd get through this as well.

"Does Ruth need a lawyer?" Eden asked, her thoughts quickly turning to Leo Steele. "If she's a suspect, she should have legal counsel and–"

"Whoa there, Eden," Nessa interrupted, "you're getting way ahead of yourself here. First we need to talk to Ruth, and we need time to investigate the crime scene. Only then can we determine who's a suspect."

Eden thought of Ruth sleeping fitfully at the shelter. The girl was so broken, so fragile. How would she respond to an interrogation by Nessa and Jankowski? Jankowski's hard face filled her mind.

"Nessa?"

"Yes, Eden?"

Eden swallowed hard, tears springing to her eyes.

"Promise me you'll be there with Ruth when she's questioned? Promise you and Detective Jankowski won't be too hard on her."

Nessa's sigh was long and heavy, and Eden could picture the detective's kind blue eyes on the other end of the connection.

"For now, Ruth's a witness and a possible victim. Of course, we'll treat her accordingly," Nessa agreed. "But we need to talk to her right away."

"She's sleeping now. She's sedated. She'll likely be asleep for hours, if not all day."

Eden's protective instinct sharpened her voice, and she had to remind herself that Nessa was only doing her job, only trying to help catch the person who'd killed Ruth's friend.

Nessa's a good detective, and she's on our side...isn't she?

But Ruth was asleep, and even when she woke up, there was no guarantee she'd remember what she'd said while under hypnosis. No guarantee she'd remember what had happened to her friend. An aggressive interrogation would only damage Ruth further.

"I'll let you know as soon as Ruth wakes up and is ready to talk."

Eden knew she had no choice. If she wanted the WBPD to find the killer quickly, they'd need all the information they could get, and Ruth was the only one who had seen what had happened.

Once she'd disconnected the call, Eden tapped on Leo's name in her favorites list. No answer. She hung up before the call rolled to voicemail, then tapped in the number for his law office.

"You've reached Leo Steele's office. Pat Monahan speaking."

Eden was relieved to hear Leo's long-time paralegal. The motherly woman kept close tabs on Leo's schedule.

"Hi Pat, it's Eden. I'm looking for Leo. He in the office today?"

"No, dear, he's in court this morning."

Resisting the urge to ask what he was working on, and when he would be back, she thanked Pat and ended the call.

I bet he's working on getting Oscar Hernandez out of jail and won't have time to help Ruth convince the WBPD she's a victim, not a suspect.

Without warning Eden's heart began to pound in her chest and her throat constricted. She'd suffered for years from anxiety after her sister had been killed, but with Reggie's help she'd gotten control, or at least she thought she had. Now, standing in the cozy room, staring into the fire, she wasn't so sure.

A familiar feeling of dread descended over her, making it hard for her to breathe, convincing her that she was heading toward a full-blown panic attack.

An incessant buzzing in her hand brought her attention back to her phone. Nathan Rush was calling.

She hesitated, not wanting her ex-partner to hear the anxiety in her voice. She'd assured him her anxiety disorder was no longer a problem. Had she been lying to him as well as herself?

"Nathan, this isn't a good time."

She struggled to keep her voice calm, sinking onto the sofa and pulling Duke in for a hug.

"What's wrong?" he asked, hearing the stress in her voice. "What's happened? Is something wrong with the kids?"

"No, Hope and Devon are fine. Great in fact. But..."

She felt a lump rise in her throat, and for a horrible minute she thought she was going to burst into tears. Pulling herself back from the edge, she straightened her back, squared her shoulders and took a deep breath.

"We're all okay, but there's something going on...a woman at the shelter's been involved in a...a homicide. I need–"

"Not again, Eden," Nathan said, his worry growing into frustration. "You can't keep putting yourself in danger. Come out here for Christmas. Let the police handle things there."

Eden held the phone away from her ear, not wanting to deal with Nathan's disapproval, not wanting to disappoint him yet again.

"I'm sorry, Nathan, but I can't come for Christmas. I need to stay here and take care of this...situation. And the kids want to stay here. This is our home, and they need stability right now."

When he didn't respond Eden looked at her display. Had they gotten disconnected?

"Fine, then I'll come there," Nathan finally said, his voice firm. "I need to talk to you, and I want to make sure you're okay."

"No, Nathan, please just let me handle this. I–"

A beep on the line alerted Eden that she had an incoming call.

"I'll call you later Nathan. I've got to go."

Eden disconnected the call and took a deep breath.

No time for panicking now. Reggie's on the other line.

She'd have to tell Reggie about the body the police had found. Then they'd need to talk to Ruth and tell her the police wanted to question her, and that there was no way to avoid it.

After all, Ruth's the only one who's seen the face of the killer.

CHAPTER SIXTEEN

A single white cloud hung in the otherwise brilliant blue sky as Iris Nguyen stepped out of the crime scene van, pulled up the zip on her protective coveralls, and surveyed the gas station. Yellow crime scene tape cordoned off the area to the right of the station, and she could see Alma Garcia standing in an expanse of dirty ground, camera in hand. The senior crime scene technician was fully covered in protective wear from head to toe; Iris could see only her eyes as she looked up and waved.

"Should I unload the gurney now, or do you want to inspect the body first?"

Wesley Knox stood at the back of the van, his white coveralls straining to cover his tall, thick body.

"Let's see what we've got first," Iris replied, looking around for Nessa. "This one sounds like it might be...difficult."

Willow Bay's chief medical examiner wasn't sure what to expect. Nessa had phoned with the news that they'd found a body hanging on a wall, and Iris hadn't wasted time asking questions. She'd simply requested that they leave the body in situ until she arrived.

"Iris, over here!"

Iris recognized Nessa's southern drawl and turned to see the detective coming around the corner of the building, a baggy protective suit covering her clothes and shoes.

Grabbing her camera from the car, Iris took a few steps toward the crime scene tape, then looked back.

"Come on, Wesley, and bring my bag, please."

The forensic technician nodded, grabbed the heavy bag that Iris took to every scene, and fell in step behind his diminutive boss. They ducked under the yellow tape and crossed to Nessa, who pulled down her face mask and offered a tired smile.

"This is a bad one, Iris. Real bad."

Iris nodded, scanning the surrounding woods and taking in the dilapidated building.

"Let me guess...the animals got to the body?"

Nessa blinked, then shook her head.

"No. Well, at least not the kind of animal you're talking about."

Nessa pointed toward the spot where Alma stood with her camera.

"It looks like the girl was killed over there, then someone moved her. Probably trying to hide the body, but who knows? Maybe they wanted to keep the wildlife away."

Gesturing for Iris and Wesley to follow, Nessa turned and walked to the women's restroom, stepping aside to let Iris pass.

The smell of death greeted Iris as she approached the room. She had time for a fleeting thought about the stench not being as strong due to the cold weather, then stopped abruptly at the sight of the bloody body suspended in the closet.

An irrational urge to hurry forward and release the girl from her tortured position flooded through Iris, but she pushed it away.

It's too late to save her now. All I can do is determine how she died. Maybe then the police will find whoever left her mounted on this filthy wall.

Needing a few minutes to prepare herself for the examination that lay ahead, Iris stepped back outside. She looked past Wesley's questioning gaze to stare at Nessa.

"Okay. So, how'd you guys even find her in there?"

"Eden Winthrop called in a report of a possible homicide. A girl at one of her shelters claimed to have seen her friend get murdered."

Iris nodded to Wesley, hoping the young technician was prepared to see the macabre sight. He'd proven to have a strong stomach in the past, but you never knew.

"Okay, Wesley, let's do this."

She stepped back into the room and paused to raise her camera, knowing she'd want to have pictures from every angle when she went to write up the report. She felt Wesley jerk to a stop beside her.

"Jesus, what the...no, it can't be her..."

Wesley's garbled yell reverberated in the little space, causing Iris to jump and spin around. She watched as Wesley tore off his face mask and crossed to the closet. He raised a big hand to push back a stiff tangle of blonde hair, using the other hand to lift the girl's chin, revealing a bloated, discolored face with a series of bloody cuts across the forehead.

"Candy? Oh, dear God, it...it is her. It's Candy."

Wesley backed away, bumping into Iris before turning and rushing through the door. Iris followed after him, watching as he sank to his knees by the payphone, vomiting up the lunch he'd eaten just before they'd received Nessa's call.

"What is it, Wesley? Do you know the...the deceased?"

Iris glanced up to see Nessa hovering over her shoulder, waiting for Wesley's response. Putting a gentle hand on his back, Iris asked the question again.

"You called the...the girl Candy. Why? Do you know her?"

Wesley nodded, a lock of brown hair falling over his forehead as he again leaned over and retched onto the dirty ground. When it appeared he had nothing left in his stomach, Wesley looked up at Iris, his eyes bloodshot and swollen.

"That's Candy Newbury. She...she used to go to Willow Bay High."

Nessa crouched beside Wesley.

"You went to school with her?"

Wesley nodded again, a self-conscious expression appearing as he saw Iris, Nessa and Alma gathered around him.

"How well did you know her?"

Nessa's question seemed to confuse Wesley. He frowned and shrugged.

"We dated a few times, but that was a while back. I haven't seen her in years. I thought...I thought she'd gone away to college or something."

Before Nessa could respond, Detective Simon Jankowski appeared over her shoulder. He looked down at Wesley, then over at Iris.

"Your tech knows the victim?"

Iris nodded, her throat suddenly too dry to speak.

"Then he can't be at the scene." Jankowski's voice was firm. "But before he leaves we'll need to take a statement from him."

Nessa and Jankowski exchanged a glance that sent a ripple of unease down Iris' spine. She tuned to Wesley, her concern growing at the glassy look in his eyes.

"I'll take his statement," Nessa said. "We can sit in my car."

Wesley stood up, his legs shaky, his eyes returning to the restroom door. He stared in horror, face pale, before allowing Nessa to lead him toward her Charger.

Feeling Jankowski's eyes on her, Iris forced herself to clear her mind and focus on the scene. A girl had been viciously killed and it was her job to find out how. It wasn't the right time to think about anything else. She squared her shoulders, walked back into the room, and lifted her camera.

* * *

It was almost an hour before Iris was ready to load the body into the crime scene van. She'd taken photos, thoroughly examined the body and surrounding area, then called Alma to help her take the girl down from the wall. She soon realized that the body had been held upright by a hook that had gotten caught on the back of her dress. A few snips with her scissors and the girl was free.

As Alma left to continue her investigation of the scene outside, Iris recorded the body temperature as well as the air temperature in the restroom, eager to give the detectives a tentative time of death. Colder than usual weather would mean slower decomposition, and the additional protection provided by the closet meant less bug activity to analyze.

A shadow in the doorway blocked the sunlight. Nessa turned to see Detective Jankowski leaning against the doorjamb.

"You need any help, Iris?"

His voice was deep and his words soft. He sounded weary, and she looked up at the big detective with curious eyes. One minute he was hard as nails, the next he was playing Mr. Helpful.

"I need to lift her onto the gurney. May need some help with that since Wesley is...unavailable."

"You mean, you want me to *touch her?*"

She cocked an eyebrow at his squeamishness.

"You're not telling me that you're afraid to touch a dead body, are you?" She felt a flash of satisfaction at his embarrassed shrug. "I thought you were some kind of tough guy."

It was Jankowski's turn to raise an eyebrow.

"Me? A tough guy? Maybe when I'm chasing live perps, but not in this situation. I'm definitely not tough when it comes to...*this.*"

Iris shook her head and sighed.

"Well, you don't have a choice. This is your scene, and I need some help. Come with me."

Jankowski followed her back to the van, watching as she took out the gurney and lowered the wheels.

"You take the rear," she said, not really needing his help to push the lightweight gurney but liking the idea that she was making him uncomfortable.

The smell assaulted them again as they stepped through the doorway and Iris could see Jankowski hesitate.

"It's okay, I've already got the sheet underneath her, so all we need to do is lift the sheet up and slide her onto the gurney. Ready?"

Jankowski nodded, but his hands shook as he lifted the sheet. As soon as the girl's body was on the gurney, Iris covered her with a clean sheet and secured the straps. She watched the detective step back and release a deep breath.

"We done here?"

"Help me push her back to the van and load her in," Iris said, her tone dry. "Then you're done."

Once they'd closed the van door behind the gurney, Iris pulled down her mask and pushed back her hood. Her thick dark hair was gathered in a low bun, and she felt the cold air on the bare skin of her neck as it slipped under her coveralls, sending a chill up her spine.

"So, what's the cause of death?" Jankowski asked, his voice all business again.

Opening her mouth to give her usual disclaimer about needing time in the lab to determine the cause of death, Iris found herself instead telling Jankowski her real opinion.

"She was stabbed multiple times. I count over forty wounds from my superficial examination. I wouldn't be surprised to find more when I get her back to the lab."

Iris nodded toward the pool of blood on the ground.

"And she lost a considerable amount of blood. I'd say it's a homicide by stabbing. Case of death exsanguination."

"And the murder weapon?"

Iris bit her lip, picturing the deep stab wounds and angry slashes.

"A fixed blade knife, probably about four inches long. Not the kind you'd find in most homes. Maybe something used for hunting or farming. Once I have exact measurements I can try to find a match."

Jankowski swallowed hard, and Iris suddenly felt guilty for mocking him. She'd heard he was a good cop. She also heard he'd gone through a bitter divorce with the city's high-profile media relations officer.

From what I've seen of Gabriella Jankowski, he has his hands full.

Iris tried not to stare as Jankowski folded muscular arms over his broad chest. She'd never noticed before how strong he was. The lack of eligible men in Willow Bay must be getting to her.

"What about time of death?"

Bringing her thoughts back to the subject at hand, Iris paused, hesitant to be too specific based on the recent change in temperature.

"I'd say it's been at least twenty-four hours, but no more than forty-eight."

Jankowski's grunted, clearly unimpressed.

"Great, so we have a twenty-four-hour window to work with?"

"It's the best I can do for now," Iris replied, opening the door to the van. "If you want to sit in on the autopsy I may be able to narrow it down."

Jankowski produced a tired grin.

"Oh, I'll be there all right, whether I want to be or not."

As Iris backed down the dirt road and pulled onto the highway, her thoughts returned to Wesley. Although she'd examined hundreds of bodies and performed countless autopsies, she'd never had the bad luck to find the body of someone she knew at a death scene.

Poor Wesley must be devastated, but he may be able to shed some light on the victim. And now her family will know what happened to her.

Thoughts of the girl in the back of the van, and the family that would never see her alive again, prompted Iris to push her foot down harder on the gas pedal.

She needed to get the police her results as quickly as possible. They'd all need to work quickly if they hoped to find the person capable of such a vicious attack.

CHAPTER SEVENTEEN

The sky outside her window was dark; the day having faded away while she'd slept. Ruth lay in bed staring out at the night, wondering where she was and how long she'd been asleep. The last thing she could remember was Reggie Horn's worried eyes and soft words.

Sleep now, Ruth. Everything will seem better once you get some sleep.

But everything wasn't better. Ruth knew that now. When she'd arrived at Mercy Harbor she couldn't remember what had happened the night she and Candy ran away. But the terrible truth had come crashing back during her session with Reggie, and now, no matter how hard she tried, she couldn't get the image of Candy's ruined face out of her mind.

Voices in the hall startled Ruth. She wasn't ready to face anyone yet. She didn't want to answer all their questions. Closing her eyes, she forced herself to take in a long, slow breath, then release it.

"Ruth?" Reggie's voice sounded outside the door along with a quiet knock. "Ruth, are you awake?"

The door opened, but Ruth kept her eyes closed, her body limp.

"Let her sleep, Reggie."

Eden's soft words sounded sad, and Ruth was tempted to sit up and reassure her that she was okay. She been so nice to her, but Ruth just wanted to be left alone.

"The police want to talk to her," Reggie said, "and they won't be happy about waiting until tomorrow when they have a dead body on their hands."

Ruth's heart stopped.

So, the police have found Candy. It really wasn't just a bad dream.

Tears pooled in Ruth's eyes as she thought of her friend. Poor Candy had been so scared at the end. She'd just wanted to get away from the trouble she'd gotten herself into at the compound, but it had all gone so terribly wrong. A surge of fear passed through Ruth at the thought of the man who'd caused the trouble, and the man who'd chased her through the swamp.

If I tell on them, will they come looking for me? Will I be next?

Her thoughts turned to the dark figure in the swamp: the person who had killed Candy. Ruth could picture the hood, and the terrible motion of the arm raising up and down, stabbing over and over again.

Was it him? Was he the one who killed Candy? Or was it someone else?

She shook her head, frustrated. She couldn't be sure. It had been dark, and she'd been so upset.

"Come on," Eden whispered. "We'll check on her first thing in the morning. Nessa will just have to understand."

Ruth waited until the door had closed behind the two women before sitting up. Pulling the blanket around her shoulders, she slipped out of bed and crossed to the window. The moon shone bright in the clear sky, adding an eerie glow to the lawn and the riverbank beyond.

It'll be a full moon tomorrow night.

She leaned her forehead against the windowpane, liking the cold feel of the glass against her warm skin. A sudden rap on the window made her jump. She'd fallen asleep.

Looking around in confusion, Ruth saw a figure standing outside her window. She opened her mouth to scream, then recognized the familiar face that stared back at her. Her hands shook as she released the latch and pushed open the window.

"What are you doing here?" Ruth whispered, looking over her shoulder, sure that Eden or Reggie would be standing behind her along with the police. "You won't believe what happened. Someone killed Sister Candace."

"I know," the woman said, smiling sadly. "That's why I came to help you. You need to be with your family now, not with these strangers."

Ruth hesitated, confused.

"But how did you know I was here?"

The woman shook her head and laughed.

"Always so many questions, Sister Ruth. You must have faith. We don't have time to talk now. We have to go."

"Go where?" Ruth asked. "I don't want to go back to the compound. Not with–"

The woman put a finger to her lips.

"Shh, no need to talk now. I've taken care of everything, but we have to leave. You aren't safe here."

When Ruth hesitated the woman shrugged, stepping back.

"I can't force you to come with me," she said, looking around nervously. "But they know you're here. They'll come for you, too."

Ruth watched as the woman turned toward the river, her breath a cloud of white in the dark night.

"Wait," she called. "Let me get my shoes on."

The woman paused, then turned and hurried back to the window. She offered a hand to steady Ruth as the slim girl slid outside and jumped to the ground.

"I see the strangers have already given you new clothes," the woman said, eyeing Ruth's jeans with disapproval. "What else have they given you?"

"They've been really nice," Ruth insisted, already regretting the worry she'd cause Eden and Reggie when they discovered her gone.

The woman grabbed Ruth's hand and pulled her toward the river.

"What have you told them?"

The words were accusing, and Ruth drew her hand away, suddenly unsure about what she was doing.

"I didn't tell them anything." Ruth's voice was defiant. "But maybe I should have."

The woman turned and raised her arm, and Ruth cringed, holding up a hand defensively, reminded of the figure in the swamp and the arm that had been raised again and again over Candy's body.

But when Ruth looked up she saw that the woman was signaling to a figure standing behind a cluster of trees. Ruth's eyes widened as the man approached.

"No...no...it can't be..."

She turned to run but the woman was right behind her. She grabbed Ruth's arm and pulled her close.

"You betrayed the congregation, Sister Ruth. You turned your back on everyone who trusted you. I can't allow that."

"You can't allow that?" Ruth asked, her voice incredulous. "Who are you to tell me what I'm allowed to do?"

A malicious smile spread across the woman's face, and Ruth saw a flash of silver. She looked down to see a knife gripped in the woman's hand.

"I'm the angel of death, Sister Ruth. And I'm here for you."

CHAPTER EIGHTEEN

The sounds and smells of the commune's early morning activity penetrated the small room off the kitchen where Eli Dunkel lay sleeping. He lifted his head, felt a wave of dizziness wash over him, then dropped back onto the pillow. The smell of frying eggs and burnt toast made his stomach clench, and he struggled not to retch.

What's the matter with me? Feels like I've been hit by a bus.

He sat up slowly, his head pounding. squinting against the sliver of morning sun shining through the little window over his bed. The window had been left open, letting in a draft of cold air.

Looking down at his bare chest in confusion, he saw four long, red scratches that started at his shoulder and ended just above the waist band of his jeans. He lifted a finger to trace the marks and saw cuts on his hands. Pain shot up his arm as he tightened his hand into a fist.

So, it wasn't a nightmare. It really happened. Again.

A pile of clothes had been thrown over the straight-backed chair in the corner, and Eli hefted himself off the bed and shuffled toward it, wincing at the shock of the icy tiles on his bare feet. He looked down, expecting his feet to be coated with the muddy remains of his nighttime trek through the swamp. His jeans were filthy, but his feet were clean.

Angel must have washed me up before she left me here.

Details of the previous night's events were slowly coming back to him, although everything after dinner seemed more like a bad dream than a memory.

He shook his head as he buttoned up his shirt, trying to chase the image of the girl from his mind. Angel had warned him not to think about Ruth anymore. She had betrayed them all and didn't deserve to come back to the commune.

Angel's stern voice played in his head over and over again.

God's will must be done, Eli. It isn't our place to question Him.

Of course, that was what she always said when she wanted him to do something he didn't want to do, and he never could resist her.

She's an angel after all, isn't she?

He thought of her stony face, grim and determined, but eerily calm as they'd walked home through the woods after the bloody night. The memory of the blood made him feel sick again, and this time he couldn't stop his stomach from heaving up its contents.

He spat bitter mouthfuls of bile into a trash can by the door, then looked around for a tissue. He dug his hand into the pocket of his jeans, coming up empty.

He wiped his mouth with the back of his hand, then froze.

Where's the piece of paper?

He stuck his hand back into his pocket, digging around even though he could feel that it wasn't there.

After checking his other pockets, he searched through the sheets on the bed and examined the floor, even dropping to his knees and looking under the bed.

The blood-stained piece of paper he'd taken out of Sister Candace's lifeless fingers two nights before was gone. He'd had it with him last night. Had gone to the address listed for Mercy Harbor. From there he'd only had to wait for Eden Winthrop to come out and lead him to the shelter, and to Ruth.

It had all gone more smoothly than he could have hoped. But now the paper was gone, perhaps dropped at the scene.

He looked down at his battered hands.

And my fingerprints and blood are probably all over it.

Dread settled over him at the thought of what Angel would say if she found out he'd left evidence behind. It may be God's will that they were carrying out, but he doubted the police would care.

As Angel had told him before, the police and everyone else outside the commune were against them. All it would take was one stupid mistake and they'd rush in and shut the place down.

CSL will be closed, and I'll be back in the pen for good this time.

Eli thought about the promise he'd made to himself when he'd gotten out of prison. The promise that he'd go straight, and that he'd never go back. And he'd arrived at CSL determined to live a good life.

But that was before Father Jed had died, and before Jacob had been led astray. Wickedness had seeped into the commune, and then Angel had come to him, saying she'd had a vision: Eli had been chosen to be the instrument of God, and it was up to them to save the congregation from ruin.

Exchanging his stained jeans for a new pair from the cupboard, Eli stuffed his feet into his work boots, and glanced out the window, tempted to run back to the river and search for the paper. But no, it was too late, the sun had risen, and the compound was already bustling with activity. He'd have to have faith that Angel was right: they were on the side of the righteous and good fortune would follow.

A graceful figure crossing the courtyard caught Eli's eye. He watched as Sister Marie stopped in front of the barn to talk to Tobias Putnam. She looked up at the older man with a shy smile, and Eli felt a pang of fear.

"Whatever happens, I can't let the police find out what I've done, cause if they do, I'll never see Sister Marie again."

CHAPTER NINETEEN

The line of cars leading onto the East Willow Bridge were at a standstill. Nessa strained her neck, trying to see around the minivan in front of her. A few drivers honked. After several minutes of idling a pregnant woman in the Chevy pickup next to Nessa climbed into the bed of her truck and stared out over the traffic toward the bridge.

She looked over at Nessa and called out, "Looks like there may be an accident, although I don't see any cars banged up. But there's a police car...lights flashing."

Nessa hadn't heard anything that morning about an accident on her police radio, but then she'd been preoccupied, wondering how she was ever going to find time to go Christmas shopping for Cole and Cooper when she was lead detective on a murder investigation.

I guess getting up at the crack of dawn didn't make a bit of difference.

She'd hoped getting on the road early would give her a head start on the day. She hadn't counted on the traffic jam ahead.

Unwilling to wait any longer, Nessa activated the bar of emergency lights on the Charger's dashboard, pulled onto the shoulder of the road, and began bouncing past the row of cars. She followed the flashing lights to a WBPD cruiser parked on the grassy slope next to the bridge. Someone called out to her as she climbed out of the car.

"Over here, Detective!"

Nessa pulled on a police-issued windbreaker as she turned to see Officer Dave Eddings emerging from the shadows of the bridge's bulky concrete abutment. His face was pale as he strode toward her, his eyes wide beneath a dark WBPD cap. Despite the near-freezing temperature beads of sweat trickled down the young officer's face.

"What's going on, Dave?"

Eddings opened his mouth to speak, then closed it again, swallowing hard. Nessa thought his expression would have been comical if it wasn't so disturbingly similar to the one she'd worn the day before when she'd found Candace Newbury's body.

"It's okay, Dave. Take a deep breath and tell me what's happened."

Pointing down the grassy slope toward the water, his chest heaving in and out, he fought for a breath of air.

"You found something...someone...in the river?"

Nessa felt her pulse quicken at the thought of finding another body in the water.

It couldn't happen again, could it? Not so soon after the last time?

She often thought about the dead girls they'd found in the Willow River the previous summer; they made regular appearances in her nightmares.

When Eddings shook his head vigorously back and forth, Nessa sighed, relieved and suddenly impatient to find out what was going on. She needed to get to the Mercy Harbor shelter downtown, had hoped to beat Jankowski there.

I promised Eden I'd be there when we question Ruth Culvert.

And after they talked to Ruth, she and Jankowski would have to rush to the medical examiner's office. Iris had agreed to wait for them before she began Candace Newbury's autopsy. It was going to be a busy day and this unexpected interruption threatened Nessa's carefully planned schedule.

"So, then, what is it, Dave?" Nessa asked, her voice brisk. "Your cruiser's blocking traffic. There's about a mile back-up into town."

"Not in the river..." Eddings choked out. "She's under the bridge."

Nessa froze at his words. Her mind suddenly thick and heavy.

"She?" Nessa asked, grabbing the arm of his bomber jacket. "What do you mean *she's under the bridge*?"

Eddings turned and pointed to the water again. Nessa's eyes followed his arm toward the shadows that hid the bank of the river and the pier beyond.

Forcing her feet to move, she walked down the slope, the air growing colder as she approached the river's edge. The bright morning sunlight faded into the gloom under the bridge and she blinked, waiting for her eyes to adjust.

The gurgling of the river accompanied a faint *creak, creak, creak,* producing a disturbing melody that raised the hair on Nessa's arms. She stumbled forward and lifted her face to stare toward the sound.

The frail body of a young woman hung suspended over the water.

Nessa took a step back, stumbling on the uneven ground, fighting her instinct to turn away from the terrible sight. She put her hand on her holster and drew out her Glock, keeping a tight grip on the cold steel of the gun as her eyes searched the dark crevices for possible hiding places.

Someone had killed the girl, that much was obvious. Her hands were tied behind her back with the same thick rope that formed a noose around her neck. That alone made Nessa decide suicide was unlikely, but the bloody letters carved into the girl's pale forehead left no room for doubt.

JUDAS

Nessa could hear shouts from the top of the bridge. The crowds would be gathering up there; the news would spread quickly. They'd managed to keep the discovery of Candace's body under the radar for the time being, but there would be no hiding this from the public while they figured out what happened. A woman had been found hanging from a busy bridge. Someone had committed murder, someone that may still be nearby.

A heavy hand on Nessa's shoulder startled her. She twisted around, Glock still in her hand, a scream hovering in her throat.

"Holy shit."

Jankowski stared past Nessa, not seeing the look of terror on her face or the big gun in her hand. His eyes were on the broken girl, his face stricken.

"It can't be her.... can it?"

Nessa shook her head, confused.

"What do you mean? Her who?"

She looked back, noting for the first time the way the girl's red hair contrasted with her snow-white skin. Eden Winthrop's words echoed in her head.

...she looks to be about twenty years old. She's got red hair and brown eyes. Average height, but very slim...

Jankowski put his hand back on her shoulder.

"I just came from Mercy Harbor," he said, his eyes holding hers. "They went to get Ruth Culvert and found her room empty, her window open. I thought she'd run off, but..."

Nessa closed her eyes, let her head fall forward.

"We were too late, again," she said, her voice thick. "We didn't get to her in time to...save her."

"We did what we could," Jankowski protested, although his words sounded hollow. "The psycho who did this is to blame, not us."

Nessa knew he was right, but it didn't make her feel any better. She pulled up the hood of her windbreaker and began to walk back to her Charger.

"We need to let Iris know what's happened. She'll need to be on scene here before she can perform Candace Newbury's autopsy."

Jankowski pulled out his phone.

"I'll let her know. She can perform postmortems on both victims once she's done here."

Nessa nodded, both mind and body numb, wondering if she should go ahead and call Jerry to let him know she would be working late. Maybe even hint that he should do the Christmas shopping for the boys this year without her.

Afterall, it's going to be a very busy day.

CHAPTER TWENTY

The alarm clock emitted a shrill beep that would've woken the dead, but it was wasted on Barker; he was already awake. He'd been up half the night searching the internet for more information on the Congregation of Supreme Love and Jacob Albright. He'd finally fallen into bed sometime after two in the morning, dozing fitfully until just after six when a mockingbird outside his window began to warble, ruining any chance he had of going back to sleep.

He brought his fist down on the snooze button, silencing the alarm. He studied the old clock radio, its black plastic case scratched and faded with time. It had occupied a place beside the bed for so many years, it seemed like a permanent fixture now. Caroline had set the alarm every night, always producing a sleepy smile when Barker awoke cursing at its incessant beeping in the morning. The thought of that smile sliced through him.

Barker stood and stretched, wondering if it was too early to call Nessa. He wanted to run his suspicions by her. She was one of the few people whose opinion he trusted, and one of the few people who would care enough to listen.

After hours of brooding over the situation, Barker had convinced himself that Taylor's waitressing job at the Little Gator Diner must have brought her into contact with someone at the CSL commune. From what he saw the day before, there were dozens of people working and living in the compound. One of them must have seen Taylor.

Jacob Albright's handsome face flashed into Barker's mind, and he grimaced as he remembered what both Nessa and Frankie had told him. The man was a sexual predator. He'd spent five years in state prison. And Jacob had been released from prison about the same time Taylor left her waitressing job. It seemed like a strange coincidence to Barker.

Or maybe I'm just grasping at straws because I don't have a fucking clue where Taylor is and if she's all right.

Picking up his cell phone, Barker tapped on Nessa's number. She answered on the fifth ring.

"Hi Barker. Hold on a minute..."

Loud voices sounded in the background as Nessa spoke.

"Sorry about that, but I'm at a crime scene and I can't really talk now but...well, I just want to tell you...not to...not to worry. I mean, when you see the news."

Barker frowned, confused.

"Why would I worry?"

A siren sounded behind Nessa and Barker could hear someone yelling for everyone to back up.

"A young woman's body's been found, and well, it's a long story, but, um, it isn't Taylor. I just...didn't want you to worry."

The air left Barker's lungs in one big rush, and it took a minute for him to catch his breath again.

"Barker? Listen, I've gotta go. It's bad here. I'll...call you when I get a chance."

Before Barker could respond, the call had been disconnected. Nessa was gone.

Barker threw his phone on the bed and walked into the living room wearing only his pajama bottoms. He picked up the remote and flipped on the television, navigating to Channel Ten news. If anyone had coverage of Willow Bay's latest crime scene, it would be Channel Ten. The special news bulletin across the top of the broadcast made his heart sink: Body Found Hanging from East Willow Bridge.

A reporter in a fluffy white parka and knee-high black boots stood in front of the old bridge. Crime scene tape and a few uniformed offers were keeping the reporters and the gathering crowd away from the scene, but Barker could see Nessa's red curls peeking out from the hood of a WBPD jacket.

"Detective Ainsley?"

Nessa turned to the reporter calling her name and raised an eyebrow.

"My sources tell me this is the second woman's body found in two days. Can you confirm this information? Should the women of Willow Bay be worried?"

The guarded look in Nessa's eyes told Barker the reporter's sources had indeed been correct. Two young women were dead.

And don't forget Taylor is still missing while I sit around in my pajamas waiting for someone else to figure out what's going on.

Jamming his thumb down hard on the *OFF* button, Barker hurried into his bedroom to get dressed.

* * *

When Barker arrived, Nessa stood just behind the crime scene tape talking to a slim woman with a shiny bob and a well-fitted trench coat. Gabriella Jankowski had wasted no time getting in front of the news cameras. Her position as Willow Bay's media relations officer suited her, Barker thought, watching Jankowski's ex-wife pose for a passing reporter.

"Hey, Gabby, when are you going to have a statement for us?"

A barrel-chested reporter with thick glasses and bad skin hovered just beyond the tape, his microphone gripped in his hand like a hammer. Gabby produced a brilliant smile, although Barker noticed the sparkle didn't quite reach her eyes.

"We'll schedule a press conference as soon as we have something to share, Boyd," she said, glancing at Nessa. "Won't we, detective?"

Nessa glared at the reporter then turned away, ignoring Gabby's question. Barker scooted under the crime scene tape and grabbed Nessa's arm.

"I need to talk to you, Nessa." Barker's face was tense, his usual sardonic grin missing. "Please, just give me a minute."

He saw Nessa's eyes searching the scene. He imagined she was looking for Jankowski. Her bulldog of a partner wouldn't want Barker horning in on the scene or distracting Nessa from her duties.

"I saw Jankowski heading back to his car," Barker said, dropping his hand. "I just want to know what's going on. If women are being killed, I need to know the details. I need to know if Taylor could have been-"

"I told you, Taylor's not one of the victims we've found."

Barker nodded. Nessa wouldn't lie about something so important.

"I know. I believe you. It's just...maybe the perp who did it...maybe he's done this before."

A look of pity crossed Nessa's face before she could conceal it, and Barker realized she must think him pathetic. Here she was trying to solve a real-life murder, and he was conjuring up farfetched theories to explain why his daughter had moved out, and why she wouldn't speak to him anymore.

"You know what...forget it," Barker said, running a hand through his graying hair. "I shouldn't be bothering you."

"Barker, come on, you know I'm not supposed to release details until the vic's next of kin has been notified."

She looked around, making sure no one else was within earshot, then lowered her voice.

"We're still tracking down the first victim's family. We found her out at an old gas station off Highway 42, but apparently she went to Willow Bay High a few years back."

Barker leaned forward, his eyes bright.

"So did my Taylor," he said, trying to keep his voice even. "What's the girl's name?"

"Candace Newbury," Nessa said, her voice weary. "She was a friend of the other girl...the one Eden Winthrop was trying to help...the one we found this morning under the bridge."

A wave of dizziness passed over Barker as he absorbed the girl's name. He closed his eyes to steady himself.

"You okay, Barker?' He opened his eyes to see Nessa's worried face. "You aren't having another one of those cardiac infarction things are you?"

"No, I just...didn't stop to eat breakfast. My blood sugar must be playing up."

Nessa looked doubtful, but she spotted Jankowski walking toward them and waved Barker away.

"You can't mention that I told you anything, Barker. I'll never hear the end of it if Jankowski finds out I've compromised the investigation before I've even left the scene."

Slipping under the tape, Barker made his way back to the Prius, which he'd parked on the side of the crowded street, one wheel up on the curb. When he was back in the car he dialed Leo's number.

He wanted to tell Leo that a girl's body had been found only a few miles away from the CSL commune, and that the victim had gone to school with Taylor. In fact, Candace Newbury and his daughter had been pretty good friends. They'd always seemed so happy hanging out together. But that had been years ago.

And now one of them is dead, and the other is missing.

CHAPTER TWENTY-ONE

Marie pulled the blanket up to her chin, snuggling under its soft warmth, her sleepy brain registering the unusual chill in the room. A sharp click pierced the stillness, followed by the faint squeak of a rusty hinge. Sitting up and pulling the blanket around her, Marie looked toward the door, expecting Sister Judith to begin scolding her for sleeping in.

Instead, Brother Eli stuck his head into the dimly lit room, his white blonde hair slightly damp, as if he'd just stepped out of the shower.

"Sister Marie? Sorry to wake you up, but it's gettin' kinda late. Brother Jacob wants us all to meet in the main house."

Keeping his eyes on hers, he stepped further into the room, prompting an irrational flutter of panic to sharpen her tone.

"Haven't you ever heard of knocking?"

She wrapped the blanket firmly around her body, her face arranged in an indignant scowl while her heart hammered a frightened beat.

What if he won't leave? Will anyone come if I scream?

Eli raised a hand to push back a lock of wet hair. Marie noticed scratches and cuts on his hand.

"Sorry 'bout that," he said, not moving. "I should've knocked."

The door swung open behind Eli, revealing Judith Dunkel's tall figure. Her eyes widened when she saw her son.

"What are you doing in here, Eli?"

Judith looked past him, a frown creasing her forehead when she saw Marie wrapped in the blanket.

"It's getting late, Sister Marie. We're all expected in the meeting hall by ten o'clock. Shouldn't you be up and dressed by now?"

Marie nodded, smiling at Judith, relieved by her timely arrival.

"Yes, I really should get going. Sister Ruth used to wake me up and I guess...well, I guess I'll need to get myself up from now on."

Judith returned the smile, but a shadow crossed her face at the mention of Ruth. Her eyes flicked back to Eli and her jaw tightened.

"Come on now, son. Let Sister Marie get dressed in peace."

Marie and Judith watched Eli leave, his pale face flushed pink under their scrutiny. Once he'd disappeared down the hall Judith turned to Marie, concern deepening the fine lines in her broad face.

"Hope my boy didn't bother you, dear. He means well, he does, but sometimes he just...gets carried away."

She sighed and bit her lip, as if trying to think of the right words.

"I try to keep an eye on him but...he's a grown man now, so maybe I should just do what he asks and...let him be."

As the tall woman turned to go, Marie reached out a hand, wanting to offer reassurance, feeling somehow guilty for adding weight to the woman's burden.

"It'll be okay, Sister Judith," Marie said awkwardly, drawing her hand back to clutch the blanket. "Sometimes people just want a little space from their parents, but that doesn't mean they don't need them anymore or that they don't love them."

Judith smiled back at Marie, her amber eyes lighting up.

"You must be a wonderful daughter to your own parents."

Marie flinched as if she'd been struck, quickly turning her face away, hiding the sudden tears that threatened.

Would Sister Judith still call me a wonderful daughter if she knew that my mother's dead and I haven't visited her grave or seen my father in years?

As Judith left the room, Marie glanced up, catching her own sad reflection in the mirror, the impulsive words she'd used about kids needing space from their parents replaying over and over in her head.

Maybe all I needed was some space. Maybe now it's time to go home.

* * *

The meeting room in the main house was packed full when Marie arrived. Every seat, bench, stool and spot to stand in was taken up by a member of the congregation. She couldn't remember seeing everyone come together like this since Father Jed's funeral the year before.

It seemed to Marie that the congregation's core mission had moved away from the loving fellowship and peaceful living that had drawn her in. Once Father Jed was gone, Jacob had begun pushing the congregation to work harder and harvest more, rarely gathering his flock for the kind of meeting which might negatively impact productivity.

"Quiet everyone, please!"

Jacob's voice filled the room, his stern tone silencing the crowd.

"I'm sure you're all wondering why you're in here when you have chores to do out there."

Standing at the front of the room, Jacob was tall enough to look out over the crowd. He searched each face before finding Marie near the back of the room. His eyes rested on her as he spoke.

"As you've all heard, two of our members have chosen to leave us. They left without even saying goodbye, and we have no reason to believe they'll be back."

Marie's stomach ached at the thought of her friends.

Where are you Candy and Ruth? Are you safe? Did you find help?

She stared back at Jacob defiantly, turning away only after she saw Naomi standing behind her husband, watching Marie with hostile, narrowed eyes.

"And you may have seen the outsiders yesterday," Jacob continued. "Strangers that came to us, uninvited, trying to cause trouble, and trying to bring their worldly problems into our commune...into *our home*."

A murmur of discontent stirred through the crowd. A brittle voice shouted out from beside Jacob. People strained to see.

"Father Jed didn't like strangers tryin' to tell us what to do."

It was Ma Verity. Her voice was slurred, and for an instant Marie wondered if the older woman had been drinking. The crowd pushed back, giving Ma Verity room to move closer to Jacob, who was nodding at her, an approving smile on his face.

"Father Jed loved each and every one of you," she hollered. "He built this compound to protect you. Now that he's gone we can't let evil get in. We can't let them ruin everything he built!"

"Amen!" Jacob called out, looking around at the people nearest to him, pulling Ma Verity and Naomi closer. "I made a promise to my father to protect my mother and my wife, and all of you. So, no matter what happens, I won't let him down."

Several men cheered. Tobias Putnam beamed at his son-in-law.

"Your father would be proud."

The crowd began to clap and several people around Marie surged forward, dragging her along. She tried to hold her ground but felt a wall of bodies behind her, pushing her forward.

Suddenly a strong arm circled her waist and guided her toward the side of the room, forcing the people around them to make way. Once they'd reached the edge of the crowd, Marie looked down to see that the arm belonged to Eli. She gaped at him, not knowing if she should be thankful or furious.

"Brother Jacob told us to protect our women," Eli said with a proud grin. "So, I thought I'd start with you."

She decided on furious.

"I don't need protecting, Brother Eli."

Marie tried to step back, but she was already standing against the solid wall of the meeting room. There was nowhere else to go. Eli moved closer, his chest only inches from hers.

"You may be surprised what you need, Sister Marie."

She swallowed hard, tempted to jerk her knee up between his legs the way her father had taught her. But something in his voice made her pause. He sounded sad, almost remorseful.

"I don't want to hurt you, you know." Eli's voice was almost a whisper. "I didn't want to hurt-"

A big hand fell on Eli's shoulder before he finished his sentence.

"You two stop whispering and come join in the celebration."

Jacob stood behind Eli, his cold blue eyes not matching the smile on his face. He pulled Eli toward the center of the room. Marie watched them go, curious about Eli's comment.

"I think Brother Eli likes you."

Naomi stood beside Marie, watching the men disappear into the crowd. She raised her eyebrows, her green eyes eager for Marie's reaction.

"But I guess you have your heart set on someone else?"

Small white teeth flashed behind Naomi's full lips as they twisted into a mocking smile.

"No, I don't actually," Marie replied stiffly. "I came to CSL to find peace. The last thing I want is...well, a relationship."

Naomi rolled her eyes, choking out an angry laugh.

"Oh, spare me the little virgin routine. You've had your sights set on my husband since you got here, just like your slutty little friend. He's told me all about it."

Marie gasped at the hateful words, stunned by the sudden attack.

"You must be pleased that Sister Candace is gone. Now you can have him all to yourself. At least until the next one of your kind comes along."

The crowd parted around them and Tobias Putnam made his way to Naomi's side. He stared down at his daughter with concern.

"You all right, honey?"

Naomi jerked away, pushing past Priscilla Putnam who had appeared behind Tobias.

"Naomi?" Priscilla looked after her daughter with worried eyes, then turned to scowl at Marie. "What did you say to upset her?"

"I didn't say anything." Marie took a deep breath, willing herself to stay calm. "I just stood here while she...talked about Jacob."

Tobias laid a hand on his wife's back and guided her away. He looked back with an apologetic smile.

"Don't take any notice of Naomi, dear," he said over his shoulder. "She hasn't been herself lately."

Ignoring the big man's words, Marie crossed to a table where drinks and snacks had been laid out. She picked up an oatmeal raisin cookie and poured herself a cup of tea. Adding a splash of milk and two tablespoons of sugar, she sank into an empty chair, trying to block out the conversations around her, her thoughts returning to Ruth and Candace.

"The devil lurks everywhere you know. Even here.... right here among us..."

Ma Verity's shrill words interrupted Marie's thoughts as everyone in the meeting hall turned to stare.

"Calm down, Ma," Jacob said, taking his mother's arm. "We're safe here and I won't let anyone hurt you. You go get some rest."

Judith hurried over in response to Jacob's words, her strong arms supporting Ma Verity's stooped frame as they slowly left the room. The momentary silence that followed was soon shattered.

143

"You say we should guard against strangers, Brother Jacob?" Priscilla Putnam stepped forward. "Then why'd you bring that Sister Candace here in the first place?"

A hush settled over the crowd as Jacob pulled himself to his full height and glared at his mother-in-law.

"Sister Candace didn't come here at my invitation, and she's gone now. Nothing more needs to be said."

He stared around the room, his face hard.

"Anyone who has a problem with that can talk to me *privately*. Now, please, get back to work, and remember, no strangers get past the gates without my okay."

As the crowd dispersed, Marie watched Jacob pull Eli to the side. They exchanged a flurry of hushed whispers, then Jacob hurried from the room. She assumed he'd head for his office as he did each day. She wondered what he did behind the closed door. What was he hiding?

The image of Jacob shoving the big carryall into the truck stuck in Marie's mind as she moved toward the exit. Something was going on, but what?

An icy wind cut through Marie's sweater as she stepped outside. She looked up at the sky, hoping to feel the warmth of the sun on her face, trying to make sense of everything that had happened in the last few days.

Would Jacob try to stop me if I just opened the gate and walked out?

She looked toward the fence and the narrow road beyond.

And what if I told him who I am, and who my father is?

Somehow Marie knew that whatever secret Jacob was hiding, the last person he'd want nosing around would be a Willow Bay police detective.

CHAPTER TWENTY-TWO

Pete Barker was standing in the driveway when Leo Steele pulled up in his BMW. Frankie Dawson slouched beside him in the passenger seat. As he lowered his window, Leo noted the drawn look on Barker's face and the bags under his eyes. The stress of searching for Taylor was leaving its mark on the retired detective.

"You in a hurry, Barker?" Frankie called, leaning over Leo to look at Barker. "Aren't you gonna invite us in for a cup of tea?"

Leo opened his door to step out, but Barker put up a hand to block him, foregoing his usual sarcastic comeback at Frankie's remark.

"We don't have time to mess around," Barker said, opening the door to the BMW's backseat and sliding inside. "There's another psycho hunting girls in Willow Bay, and I need to find Taylor."

Leo regarded Barker in his rearview mirror, wondering if the older man was making a bad joke, or if he'd been drinking. It was pretty early in the morning for alcohol, but he had been depressed lately.

Frankie turned in his seat and stared back at Barker.

"Are you on crack again, Barker?"

"I wish I was," Barker said, strapping on his seatbelt. "Then maybe I wouldn't have to accept that this is really happening. But I saw it on the news. And I confirmed it with one of my sources in the department."

Leo turned off the car. He twisted around to look back at Leo with raised eyebrows.

"I haven't seen the news yet," Leo said, his mind whirring. "I've been up to my eyeballs preparing for the Hernandez bail hearing later today."

Frankie threw Leo an impatient glare, then turned back to Barker.

"So, spill the beans, man. Who died?"

"The bodies of two young women have been found in the last twenty-four hours," Barker said bluntly. "They managed to keep a lid on the girl they found yesterday since it was discovered outside of town, but the one this morning was hanging off the East Willow Bridge. Reporters have already got hold of that one."

Leo's neck was beginning to ache. He turned around and once again consulted the rearview mirror.

"There's something else to all this, Barker. What is it? What's got you so worked up?"

"The girl they found yesterday was a friend of Taylor's from high-school." Barker met Leo's eyes in the mirror. "Her body was found out by Highway 42."

The words stunned Leo, and even Frankie seemed speechless for a minute while the implication sunk in.

"So, a girl's body was found out by the CSL commune?" Leo asked slowly. "A girl your Taylor knew?"

Barker nodded, his face grim.

"Yeah, her name was Candy Newbury. She was a good kid."

Leo's brain was already making disturbing connections. If Taylor knew the victim, and if the victim had been found in proximity to the last place Taylor had been seen...

"What about the other girl?" he asked, refusing to jump to conclusions. "Is there a known connection between the victims?"

Barker nodded, scratching the stubble on his unshaven chin.

"I don't know her name, but apparently she was friends with Candy. She'd gone to Eden asking for help, but..."

Barker paused, as if he just realized who he was talking to. He put a hand on Leo's shoulder and squeezed.

"Maybe you can call Eden and get more information? Find out who the other victim was?"

Leo's heart sank at Barker's words. If Eden knew the victim, she would be heartbroken.

Could the girl under the bridge be the unexpected arrival Eden had mentioned? The one she'd been trying to help?

A terrible question came to him.

"Does Eden even know the girl has been killed?"

Barker dropped his eyes.

"The police haven't released the girl's name pending official ID and notification to next of kin," he admitted. "So, Eden probably hasn't been informed yet."

Gripping the steering wheel with both hands, Leo forced himself not to take his frustration out on Barker. The man was suffering enough. It wasn't his fault Eden once again faced the devastating news that one of the women she'd tried to help had been senselessly killed.

"I've got to go tell her," Leo said between gritted teeth. "I can't let her find out from someone else."

"But I told Hank and Dooley that we were comin' for an airboat ride," Frankie protested. "They said they'd take us 'round back of the commune like Barker wanted."

Leo shook his head, pushing the button to unlock the doors.

"Get out, Frankie. You and Barker can go there now, and I'll catch up with you after I've had a chance to talk to Eden."

Huffing indignantly, Frankie got out of the car. Leo waited for Barker to climb out of the backseat and join Frankie on the driveway before he pulled out into the road and headed toward Eden's house.

* * *

Eden opened the door before Leo had a chance to knock. Her newly installed security system alerted her anytime movement was detected on the driveway or around the yard. She could then access an app on her cellphone to view a live video stream of the exterior. Leo had helped her select the system in the aftermath of her niece's kidnapping, so he wasn't surprised to see her already waiting for him.

"I thought you were going with Barker to look for his daughter," Eden said, foregoing a greeting, her voice wary. "What's happened to change your plans?"

Knowing it was pointless to delay, Leo reached out and took her hand, wanting to comfort her, wishing he could soften the blow.

"Let's step inside. Barker just told me something that I think you need to hear."

Eden nodded and stepped back to let Leo into the foyer. She turned to him with worried eyes, gripping his hand in hers.

"What's is it, Leo? Has something happened at the school? Has something happened to Hope or Devon?"

"No...nothing has happened to the kids,' Leo assured her. "But a body's been found, and Barker seems to think it was a...a girl you were helping."

Eden stared at Leo, then produced a sad sigh.

"I know about Candace Newbury already. Her friend, Ruth Culvert, came to Mercy Harbor. She's the one that told us about Candace. She's staying at the downtown shelter."

Leo shook his head, his face grim.

"No, Eden. Two girls have been found in the last twenty-four hours. Candace Newbury was found out by the Cottonmouth Preserve yesterday, but the other girl was discovered just this morning. She...her body...was found underneath the East Willow Bridge."

"Another girl? But, who...?"

Leo could see the alarms going off in Eden's head. She spun and ran to the kitchen, grabbing her cellphone off the table and tapping hard on the display. Holding the phone to her ear, her wide, scared eyes met Leo's.

"Reggie's not answering. She must be in with a patient. She has office hours this morning."

Quickly tapping in another number, Eden activated the phone's speaker and laid it on the counter. The call connected; they heard traffic and people shouting in the background.

"Nessa? It's Eden. Is it true? Did you find Ruth? Is she...dead?"

Leo held his breath, hoping that Barker had gotten his information wrong. Maybe it had been a mix up. Maybe the girl on the bridge was some other poor woman.

"We found a girl, but we haven't made an official ID yet. And as you know, I personally never met Ruth Culvert, so I can't be sure it's her, but...hold on a minute, Eden."

Leo drew Eden against him as they both stared at the phone. Eden tensed as Nessa's voice came back on the line.

"Sorry, but the ME needs my help. I've got to go."

"Please, just tell me if it's her," Eden begged. "Is it Ruth?"

Nessa lowered her voice.

"The woman we found is of average height, very slim, with shoulder-length red hair. She's wearing black jeans and a white blouse. Her shoes look...homemade."

Eden closed her eyes and sagged against Leo.

"We've confirmed that Ruth Culvert is not in her room at the shelter, and...well, the condition of the body leads us to believe that the perpetrator is the same person responsible for Candace Newbury's death."

Eden reached for the phone, her hand shaking.

"Then it really is her. Ruth is...gone."

"I'm sorry, Eden. I hate for you to find out like this. I shouldn't have said anything." Nessa's voice was resigned. "Are you going to be okay? Are you alone?"

Leo cleared his throat.

"I'm here with her, Nessa. I'll stay with her as long as she needs me. And, thanks for being straight with us. I know you could get in trouble."

"Don't worry about it, Leo. I'm already in so much hot water a little more won't make any difference."

After ending the call, Leo looked down at Eden, not sure what to say. Once again she was heartbroken, and once again he felt helpless to do anything about it.

Pulling away, Eden straightened her back and wiped her eyes, before crossing to the counter where she kept her purse and keys.

"Eden, where are you going?"

The angry, determined set of her jaw worried him.

"There's nothing you can do for Ruth now," he said, realizing too late how insensitive the words sounded. "What I mean is-"

"Actually, there is one thing I can do." Eden wrenched the door to the garage open, turning to glare back at Leo. "I can find the bastard who did this."

Leo followed behind Eden, standing in the cold garage as she opened the garage door and climbed into her white Expedition. Duke appeared beside him, his eyes sleepy, as if all the commotion had disturbed his nap. Eden lowered her window and leaned out.

"Watch Duke for me, Leo," she said, her voice hoarse. "I don't want anything to happen to him."

"At least let us come with you, Eden," Leo called out.

But she was already backing down the driveway.

"Don't worry, boy." Leo patted the dog's head. "She'll be back."

After the Expedition had raced away, Leo pushed back thoughts of Oscar Hernandez's bail hearing and followed Duke inside.

CHAPTER TWENTY-THREE

By the time Eden reached downtown, a cold drizzle had started to fall, and she realized, too late, that she'd left home without a jacket or an umbrella. The parking space reserved for her in the garage under Mercy Harbor's administration building was only two blocks away from the shelter, but it would seem much further in the icy rain.

Deciding to park in a metered space on the street just outside the shelter, Eden sat in the car's cozy interior, watching the raindrops trickle down the windshield, trying to gain control over her emotions. She already regretted her reaction to Leo's news; she shouldn't have taken her grief out on him or driven off in a huff. She couldn't risk acting badly in front of Reggie or the women in the shelter.

A sharp rap on the passenger side window made Eden jump. She released a high-pitched scream at the sight of a small figure standing beside the Expedition.

Reggie's dark eyes stared through the rain-spattered glass, and she motioned for Eden to unlock the door and let her inside the warm car.

"What are you doing out here?"

Reggie frowned, revealing a delicate pattern of fine lines around her eyes. She took in Eden's thin blouse and raised an eyebrow.

"And where's your coat?"

"I left in a bit of a rush," Eden said, her mouth suddenly dry. "Leo came by and told me some...upsetting news."

Reggie cocked her head and sighed.

"I'm afraid I've got some bad news as well, and there's no way to put this gently. Ruth snuck out of her window last night. She's not come back yet."

Eden ignored the heavy lump in her throat.

"I know," she said, reaching for Reggie's small hand. "The bad news Leo told me involved Ruth."

Reggie's frown deepened.

"What do you mean? How would Leo know that Ruth's gone?"

Rain trickled like tears down the window behind Reggie as Eden struggled to find the right words. It was harder than she'd expected.

Now I know how Leo must have felt when he told me.

She hoped Reggie would be able to handle the news about Ruth better than she had.

"The police found a body this morning, hanging from the East Willow Bridge," Eden choked out. "A very thin young woman with red hair. Based on the description I'd already given Nessa, they think it's...Ruth."

Reggie froze, then clamped both hands over her mouth, muffling a gasping sob as she shook her head from side to side.

"Why...who...?"

Reggie's voice broke, and she dropped her hands, staring into her lap with a tortured expression.

"I shouldn't have forced her to remember what happened and then just left her alone. I should have stayed with her."

"It isn't your fault, Reggie. If you want to blame someone for Ruth's death, then blame the monster that killed her."

Reggie stared over at Eden with wide, red-rimmed eyes.

"Killed her? Are you saying she...didn't...it wasn't...suicide?"

"No, the police are convinced Ruth didn't kill herself. They're calling it a homicide. They believe the same person who killed Candace Newbury somehow got to Ruth as well."

The remorse in Reggie's eyes blazed into anger as Eden's words sunk in. Wrenching open the car door, she stepped out into the cold air, the rain now just a light sprinkle, and looked back at Eden.

"I'm going to Ruth's room to see if I can find out what happened."

Having come to the shelter for just that reason, Eden now wondered if they should wait for the police. She looked out at the gray sky. Rain could erase trace evidence left behind. Even a civilian like her had seen enough detective shows on television to know that. It would be too risky to wait. The one clue to finding Ruth's killer may be washing away even as they stayed there talking.

"Okay," she said, turning off the engine. "Let's go catch a killer."

* * *

The window across from Ruth's unmade bed was still open, letting in a mist of cold, wet air that clung to Eden's bones as she surveyed the room.

"Her shoes are gone," Reggie said, opening the closet. "But the dress she came in is still in here."

Eden crossed to the window and stared out over the lawn toward the river. The rain had stopped, but an army of sullen, gray clouds blocked the sun. She raised her hand to the window latch, then hesitated. Best not to touch anything. There could be fingerprints or other evidence that would help the police.

"No sign of damage. I'd say it was opened from the inside."

Eden bit her lip, trying to picture the room as it had been when she'd left the evening before. She knew the window had been closed against the falling temperature, but had it been locked?

"And there's nothing inside the room that would suggest a struggle," Reggie added. "In fact, there's nothing here at all except Ruth's dress. It's like she just vanished."

Leaning out of the window, Eden saw a faint imprint in the mud below. It looked like a footprint, but she couldn't be sure.

"I see something outside," she said, turning to Reggie. "I think it might be Ruth's footprint. Or someone else's."

Reggie didn't waste time asking questions. She spun around, rushing down the hall and out the back door onto the lawn. Eden followed her out, stopping abruptly several yards from Ruth's window.

"Be careful not to step on anything," Eden warned, looking around at the soggy ground. "Nessa won't like us coming out here tripping over potential evidence."

Eden didn't want to think about Detective Jankowski's reaction to their invasion of a possible crime scene. He seemed to be high-strung at the best of times. She tip-toed across the lawn, carefully studying the ground ahead before each step.

"Look," Reggie called out, pointing beneath the open window. "It really is a footprint."

Eden could see the imprint of a shoe in the dirt directly under the window. Her eyes moved away from the window and she could see another print, and then another. It took her a few minutes to understand what she was seeing.

"Reggie, there's more than one set of prints here."

Following the trail of footprints with her eyes, she felt Reggie beside her, heard the intake of air as Reggie began to see the pattern that now seemed so clear.

"There was more than one person here last night," Reggie said, her voice hushed. "Ruth wasn't alone when she left."

Eden nodded, then began moving parallel to the prints along the lawn. They led out toward the grassy bank of the river, eventually disappearing into the deeper foliage at the edge of the water.

A flash of white caught Eden's eye. She bent to retrieve a crumpled piece of paper that had been discarded in the long grass. The paper was wet, and the words written on it were faded, some letters smeared with streaks of blood, but Eden didn't need to see all the letters to know what was written on it. She'd seen the paper before.

"Your fingerprints will be on that now."

Reggie's voice sounded far away as Eden looked at her own name written across the bloody paper.

"This is just like the note that Ruth had when she arrived," Eden said, dread settling like lead in her stomach. "Ruth showed me the note when she arrived at Mercy Harbor. She came to *me*, seeking *my* help, and now she's dead."

Reggie stared down at the paper, eyes widening as she made out the words. She put a thin arm around Eden's trembling shoulders, but Eden shrugged her off, raising a hand to stop the protest that was sure to follow.

"There's nothing you can say to change this, Reggie," Eden said, looking with haunted eyes toward the water. "I failed Ruth, and now her blood is on my hands."

CHAPTER TWENTY-FOUR

Jacob pushed open the door to Eli's room and slipped inside. He didn't know what he was looking for, but he was sure that Eli had lied to him earlier when he'd asked for an update on the search for Ruth and Candace. The flush on Eli's face, and the shifty look in the younger man's eyes, had made it clear he was hiding something, and Jacob needed to know what that was.

The small cot that Eli slept on had been hastily made, the sheets still vaguely rumpled and the pillows thrown carelessly against the headboard. Dirty footprints marked the tiled floor, and a filthy pair of jeans had been wadded into a ball and shoved into the trash can by the door.

Leaning over to pick up the discarded pants, Jacob recoiled from the stench. He pinched his nose closed with two fingers as he held up the jeans. Red streaks stiffened the material and patches of caked-on dirt ringed the bottom of each leg.

What the hell...it smells like a slaughterhouse in here.

A terrible suspicion sprang to mind as he shoved the jeans back into the trash can and left the room. Eli was an oddball and a petty criminal. He'd known that all along, but Jacob hadn't thought him capable of anything worse than burglary.

That's what Eli had served time for, after all. Wasn't it?

Jacob suddenly wondered if Eli had lied about that as well. He'd never bothered checking Eli's record before inviting him to come live at the commune. But then, why would someone make up a story about being a burglar?

Unless he's something even worse. Like a psychotic killer.

Jacob shook his head and chuckled.

The most that little weirdo would be capable of is armed robbery. Maybe a carjacking, at a stretch.

But the stench of Eli's room stayed with him as he went into his office and closed the door. The strange young man had become an essential part of Jacob's operation. Without Eli's loyal service, Jacob's plan would never work. He needed someone willing to do the dirty work. Someone who didn't ask questions and wasn't smart enough to realize what was going on.

Jacob's plan to escape had come to him slowly over the past year. Each excruciating day spent in the midst of the stifling commune and the ignorant congregation had worn away his resolve to make his father proud. And after Naomi had lost the baby, becoming increasingly bitter and suspicious, he'd known it was just a matter of time before he'd have to make a run for it.

Buck Henry and his boys had arrived on the scene just in time. The opportunity to traffic drugs and weapons for the local dealer would double the money the commune's produce business brought in. That meant Jacob would be able to start a new life somewhere far away twice as fast.

The only drawback of his plan was Ma Verity. Once he ran off, the commune's money and resources would disappear with him, and his mother would be left to fend for herself. The one thing he couldn't allow himself to do was to abandon his mother without providing for her care. He could live with anything on his conscience but that. A solution would have to found quickly.

Pushing aside thoughts of his mother and her deteriorating mental health, he opened the safe under his desk and picked up a stack of hundred-dollar bills. The safe was almost full. Just a few more months of raking in the cash, and he would be a free man.

Unless something, or someone, fucks it up first.

Doubt surfaced at the memory of the men that had come sniffing around yesterday. They'd be quick to call in the cops if they suspected two girls had gone missing. The picture they'd shown him brought another pang of worry.

If they get to Eli, will he admit to knowing the girl they're looking for?

Jacob couldn't let that happen. If the men were able to convince the cops to raid the compound looking for the girl, they'd surely find the barrels of drugs and guns in the storeroom. Shoving the stack of bills back into the safe, Jacob decided he needed to take extra precautions to ensure the police didn't show up and ruin his plan.

Once the cops show up, a life sentence is the only new life I'll be starting.

* * *

"From now on I want the gate guarded at night," Jacob said, scowling at Tobias Putnam and Zachariah Culvert. "You can set up a rotation of the men."

"Surely there's no need for that." Tobias shook his head, making his plump cheeks quiver. "The gate is securely locked each night."

Zac kept his eyes on his feet, his bright red hair falling over his forehead to hide the resentment in his eyes.

"I'll decide what is needed, Brother Tobias," Jacob snapped.

Looking at Zac's downcast eyes, Jacob realized the young man was sulking again. He'd been moping ever since his sister had gone missing, and his sour expression was starting to get on Jacob's nerves.

"Have you got something to say, Brother Zac? Something about your Sister Ruth, maybe?"

Zac raised his head and glared at Jacob.

"Why haven't you gone lookin' for 'em?" Zac demanded, his frizzy hair matching the bright hue of his cheeks.

"Because this isn't a prison," Jacob said, his voice taking on a self-righteous tone. "Folks are free to leave if and when they want to. Your sister's an adult, and she chose to go. There's nothing any of us can do about that."

Zac cleared his throat, obviously wanting to say more. Jacob figured the boy had heard the rumors about him and Candace. He'd have to figure out a way to prevent gossiping in the future. It was bad for morale.

"Now, it's best if we let bygones be bygones."

Jacob wasn't sure what the saying meant, exactly, but his father had used it often, and it usually convinced people to move on to another topic.

"So, back to what I was saying. I don't want anyone to enter or leave the commune without me knowing about it first."

Zac snorted and stared up at Jacob.

"I thought you said everyone was free to go when they wanted. Now you want to give your okay 'fore any of us leave?"

Jacob resisted the urge to lash out. Zac was just upset about his sister leaving without saying good-bye. It was a natural reaction. Besides, Jacob needed all hands on deck. He couldn't afford a mutiny now. Not when he was so close to sailing off into the sunset.

"Listen, Brother Zac. I understand your concern about Sister Ruth. How about I go into town tomorrow and ask around, maybe even file a police report and see if we can find her?"

The words had a visible effect: Zac's face softened as he nodded in relief, letting his shoulders relax. Jacob dropped a hand on the boy's thin shoulder and patted him in what he hoped was a fatherly way. Jacob reckoned the boy's false hope would buy him enough time to decide what to do about the missing girls.

"Excuse me, Brother Jacob. May I have a word?"

Jacob turned to see Priscilla Putnam at the door. He was becoming impatient with his mother-in-law's constant interference but knew it would do no good to protest.

"Certainly, Sister Priscilla. What's wrong now?"

Jacob's mocking words caused Priscilla to narrow her clear, green eyes. Tobias quickly stepped next to his wife and put an arm around her narrow shoulders, eager to stop another confrontation.

"We were just thinking, son, that maybe I could be of more help to you," Tobias said, a shy smile appearing on his broad face. "It just seems to Sister Priscilla and I that you are.... well, struggling. Leading the congregation is a heavy task for any man, much less one so young, and-"

"And you just think you'll take on my job? Maybe push me out in defiance of my father's wishes?"

Tobias looked startled, and then embarrassed.

"Of course not, son, I-"

"I'm not your son, Brother Tobias. I'm your leader. And I'd appreciate it if you wouldn't forget that fact again. Now you and Brother Zac need to set up the guard schedule. I want a guard on that gate starting tonight."

Stamping out onto the porch, Jacob noticed Marie disappearing down the path toward the garden. He looked around, making sure no one was watching, then hurried after her.

All work and no play will make Jacob a very dull boy.

He smiled as he spied Marie drop to her knees next to a patch of ripening strawberries. Her long, dark hair hung in heavy strands down her back, falling just short of her narrow waist.

"Fancy seeing you here," Jacob said, using the teasing, seductive tone that worked wonders on most women. "Just waiting to be plucked like one of those berries."

Marie blinked up at him without smiling.

"Actually, I'm not waiting for anything, Brother Jacob. Other than to be left in peace."

Unfazed by her cool dismissal, he grinned and squatted next to her, reaching out and taking a stray lock of hair in his hand.

Before Marie could respond, a loud shot rang out from somewhere behind them. Jacob felt a bullet whiz past his cheek. A puff of dirt exploded just past them, sending Jacob onto his belly in the dirt.

Marie whirled around, staring at the hedge that separated the garden from the courtyard. Jacob pulled her down on top of him just as another shot sounded. The bullet sliced the air over Marie's head, burying itself in an orange tree fifty yards away.

Using Marie as a shield, Jacob positioned her between him and the hedge, peering past her only when he heard feet scuffling and the gate banging open, then closed.

Jacob sat up and pushed Marie off him, all thoughts of seduction gone, his mind spinning frantically.

The shooter could have easily killed us. So why not finish the job? Was it just a warning? But from who? And for what?

He looked down at Marie, noting the shock in her deep blue eyes.

"Don't mention this to anyone. You hear?"

Marie nodded numbly, her hands trembling as she pushed back her hair and dusted the dirt off her dress.

"It was probably an accident," he said, wishing he could believe his own lie. "They must not have realized anyone was out here."

Quickly making his way to the storeroom, Jacob pulled a gun out of the heavy barrel Buck Henry's boys had loaded into the back of the CSL Produce truck two days earlier. The compact Walther felt light in his hand and easily fit in the wide pocket of his jacket.

Looks like I've been warned. Next time, I'll be ready.

CHAPTER TWENTY-FIVE

The metal gurneys had been positioned side-by-side in the modest autopsy suite at Willow Bay's medical examiner's office. Iris Nguyen pulled back both stiff white sheets and then paused, allowing herself to feel the full brunt of the anger that swelled inside her at the senseless death of the two young, heathy women.

Iris had performed post-mortems on over a dozen violent homicides in the last few years, but the tragedy of each of death still shocked and outraged her.

You never get numb to the horror. At least not deep down.

Pulling on her face mask, Iris forced her personal feelings aside and adopted the crisp, unemotional attitude she'd need to get through the task ahead. She was a professional, and the best way to honor the girls in front of her would be to help find their killer.

The door opened behind Iris and she turned to see Maddie Simpson's plump face peeking into the room.

"I've got the detectives out here asking for you," the receptionist said, her nose flaring in disgust at the smell of decay that permeated the room. "You ready for them?"

Iris nodded, her mind already absorbed in the process to come. When Maddie continued staring into the room, Iris looked over with raised eyebrows.

"Is there something else, Maddie?"

"Are you going to be okay doing this without Wesley? I mean, isn't it against protocol or something for you to do this on your own?"

Irritation prickled at Iris, but she forced her voice to stay neutral. Maddie's thirty years as a government employee had left its mark on the officious woman. Too late to change that now.

"Yes, I'll be quite all right, and no, it isn't against protocol for me to perform the postmortem without an assistant. Besides, Detectives Ainsley and Jankowski will be observing, so I won't really be on my own after all."

A doubtful frown appeared on Maddie's face, but she withdrew from the room, and a few seconds later the door opened again.

Although Nessa and Jankowski were already suited up in full protective gear, Iris had no trouble discerning Nessa's shorter frame from Jankowski's tall, brawny figure. Iris ignored the flutter of interest that arose in her stomach at the sight of the big detective.

"Hey, Iris." Nessa's voice wavered. "Thanks for waiting for us."

"No problem. Come on over," Iris said, foregoing formalities and moving to the table beside Candace Newbury's small white body.

Nodding toward the recorder, Nessa looked up at Jankowski.

"Can you work the recorder for me...since Wesley's not here?"

She saw Jankowski's eyes narrow at the forensic technician's name and was suddenly curious.

They can't possibly consider Wesley a suspect, can they?

Iris hadn't been able to reach her assistant since she'd seen him at the Candace Newbury crime scene two days earlier. She wondered if the questioning had upset the sensitive young man. Or maybe he was still in shock over finding his friend's body.

"You okay, Iris?"

Jankowski was holding the recorder, his eyes trained on hers, waiting for instructions.

"Yes, sorry. Go ahead and begin recording, please."

Melinda Woodhall

After stating her name, the date, time, and the names of the attending witnesses, Iris began her external examination of Candace's body.

"Body is that of a fully-developed, well-nourished white female measuring sixty-three inches and weighing one hundred ten pounds. Appearance consistent with the victim's age of twenty years. Lividity is fixed in the distal portions of the limbs. The eyes are closed. No evidence of petechial hemorrhages."

Iris examined the wounds on the pale forehead, the clumsily carved letters a garish red in the bright overhead light.

"A series of cut marks can be seen on the forehead, each mark approximately one-inch in length. The marks appear to be letters of the English alphabet. I count seven letters: J-E-Z-E-B-E-L."

Having been raised a Roman Catholic by deeply religious parents, Iris was well acquainted with the biblical story of Jezebel and her wicked deeds, but she kept her thoughts on the possible implications to herself for the time being. It would up to Nessa and Jankowski to determine why the killer had decide to mutilate the victim, if indeed there had been a reason.

Moving down to the chest, Iris steadied her voice.

"An irregular pattern of stab wounds are visible on the chest."

She paused to count the wounds and measure them. Finally, she lifted her head and spoke toward Jankowski, still holding the recorder.

"There are forty-seven observable stab wounds, each measuring an average of-"

Jankowski clicked off the recorder, his eyes blazing behind his protective glasses.

"Forget the dry medical jargon for just a minute, Iris," he demanded, his voice hoarse. "I can see what they did to her. That's obvious. What I want to know is *who* did this, and...*how*."

164

Iris recoiled from his obvious fury, her own raw emotions rising up to meet his.

"Actually, it's *your* job, detective, to find out who, why and how. I can only tell you what they did to the victim's body based on the physical evidence. I can't tell you why...and I certainly don't know how anyone can do this to another human being."

Tears sprang to her eyes, and Iris turned away, ashamed of her outburst.

"Stop being such a jerk, Jankowski," Nessa hissed, coming around the table to put a gloved hand on Iris' shoulder. "You're only human. Iris. No need to pretend this doesn't get to you, too."

Iris nodded, sniffling inside the face mask, glad she was hidden from Jankowski's searching gaze.

"Sorry," he muttered, shoulders slumping. "That came out all wrong. I wasn't blaming you, Iris, I was just trying to...to understand what happened."

"From the look of it, I'd say whoever killed Candace Newbury acted out in a blind rage, stabbing again and again without hesitation or mercy."

Nessa gasped at the image conjured by Iris' blunt words.

"The cause of death was undoubtedly multiple stab wounds to the chest. The knife penetrated the heart and lungs, causing massive hemorrhaging."

Iris paused, looking over at Jankowski, her chin lifting defiantly.

"As for who did this, that's obvious. A monster did this. A heartless monster without the slightest regard for human life."

Jankowski blinked, then nodded slowly, a shine of admiration entering his eyes as her words sank in.

"That's more like it," Jankowski said, "Now tell us about Ruth."

* * *

It was more than an hour before Iris led Nessa and Jankowski into her office. She placed a file full of autopsy notes on the desk and motioned for the detectives to sit across from her.

The postmortem on Ruth Culvert had been brutal on them all, revealing in horrifying detail the injuries the young woman had suffered leading up to her violent death.

"I'll be listing the official cause of death as homicide by hanging," Iris said, her voice subdued. "The cut marks to her forehead were superficial, but the blunt force trauma to the back of her head likely immobilized her long enough for the perpetrator to affix the noose and push her over the side of the bridge. The fall resulted in a cervical fracture, causing traumatic spinal cord injury."

Jankowski looked up.

"What about the gashes on her arms?" Jankowski asked.

"Defensive wounds. A knife similar in size to the knife that was used to kill Candace Newbury. But those wounds are superficial. It looks like Ruth fought back."

She gave the detectives a grimly satisfied smile.

"Lucky for us she did. The skin under her fingernails can be processed for DNA."

Nessa banged a small fist on the desk, causing both Iris and Jankowski to jump.

"Getting DNA results back will take ages. We can't wait that long to find out who did this."

Iris put up a placating hand.

"I take it you haven't heard the big news from the crime lab yet?"

Nessa raised an eyebrow at Iris.

"What big news?"

"A private foundation donated one of those new rapid DNA machines to the police department. It was a huge surprise, because the cost for one of these machines is outrageous. Willow Bay could never afford to buy one with the city's little budget."

Jankowski stood and leaned forward, both hands on the desk, visibly excited by the news. Iris had to force herself to look away as the thin material of his shirt strained over his broad shoulders.

You'd think I'd never seen a man before in my life.

She tried to concentrate on what Jankowski was saying.

"What foundation made the donation?"

"It was supposed to be anonymous," Iris said, dropping her eyes.

"What do you mean, supposed to be?" Nessa asked. "You know who it is?"

Iris knew she shouldn't tell anyone what she'd inadvertently discovered. If the anonymous donor knew they'd been outed, they might decide not to make further donations. But if you couldn't tell the police a secret, who could you tell?

"A friend of mine works for the company that manufactures the machines. When she saw one had been shipped to Willow Bay she called me up to congratulate me. Not many small towns are so lucky. During the conversation she sort of let it slip out that a company called Giant Leap Data had paid for the machine."

Nessa looked confused.

"Is that name supposed to mean something to me?"

Jankowski pulled himself to his full height, crossing his arms over his chest. He shook his head and smiled.

"I should have known it would be her."

Nessa looked even more confused.

"Her who?"

Jankowski grinned at his partner.

"I thought you were a detective. So why don't you know anything about the people living in this town?"

Nessa rolled her eyes and turned back to Iris.

"So, who's behind this Giant Leap Data? Someone I know?"

Iris found herself grinning as broadly as Jankowski.

"I'd say so, and someone who knows just how badly we could have used the machine in the past few years."

Iris waited another minute, then decided Nessa wasn't in the mood for guessing games.

"Eden Winthrop co-founded the company. She still owns a considerable number of shares."

Maddie Simpson popped her head into the room before Nessa could react.

"Wesley Knox was looking for you. He says he needs some unscheduled time off." Maddie sniffed with disapproval. "I told him that was against policy, but he didn't listen."

"Thank you, Maddie. I'll take care of it."

Once Maddie had withdrawn from the room, Iris turned back to Nessa and Jankowski, her smile gone, her thoughts shifting to Wesley. She couldn't let them go without pleading his case.

"You can't really think Wesley had anything to do with what happened to the women in that room, can you?"

A guarded look passed over Jankowski's face.

"Wesley knew Candace Newbury. He was also one of the few people who knew that Ruth had witnessed her homicide, and that Ruth was staying at Mercy Harbor. I'd say we have no choice but to consider him a person of interest."

Iris stared at Jankowski in dismay, worried for the young forensic technician, but unable to think of anything else to say that would convince the detectives that Wesley could never hurt anyone. She'd have to have faith that the truth would come out in due time.

It's not my place to say more. The evidence will have to speak for itself.

Nessa stood, motioning for Jankowski to follow her.

"We'll talk to Wesley again as soon as we can. With any luck we can quickly eliminate him and move on to real suspects."

But Iris didn't like the way Jankowski wouldn't meet her eyes, and her thoughts remained on the brooding detective long after he'd left her office.

.

CHAPTER TWENTY-SIX

The interrogation room seemed too small to contain the two big men that sat across from each other at the battered, wooden table. Nessa stood, back against the wall, observing them with mounting frustration. She knew how badly Jankowski wanted to find whoever had killed Ruth Culvert and Candace Newbury, but he was clearly wasting his time with Wesley Knox.

"Tell me again how you knew Candace Newbury?"

Wesley ran a shaky hand through his thatch of brown hair.

"She was a few years behind me at Willow Bay High. We went out a few times, but it was nothing serious."

Not bothering to hide his skeptical smirk, Jankowski made a note on the pad in front of him, then looked back at Wesley.

"And you say you haven't seen her for years?"

Wesley nodded.

"Her parents split, and she went to live with her grandfather. At least that's what she told me. Said he owned some kind of restaurant out in the country."

Watching him rub a fist over one eye, the way Cole and Cooper did when they were upset and trying not to cry, Nessa decided it was time to move the interview along. They needed to talk to Alma and find out if she had been able to find any valuable evidence at the crime scene. Harassing this traumatized young man was getting them nowhere.

"Wesley, did you tell anyone that Ruth Culvert had gone to Eden Winthrop for help?" Nessa asked softly.

Wesley shook his head, his eyes confused.

"Who would I tell? I was too upset about Candy to talk to anyone, anyway. I've been at home the whole time, I swear."

"We're just trying to figure what happened," Nessa said. "We've got two dead girls that knew each other, and one of them knew you."

Wesley dropped his head into his hands, his shoulders shaking. Jankowski opened his mouth to say something, but Nessa threw him a warning look.

"Candy knew lots of people," Wesley said, his words muffled by his hands. "She was real friendly...maybe a little too friendly...but she had a good heart."

Nessa remained quiet, waiting to see what else he would say, knowing more information could often be obtained by silence than through aggressive questioning.

Wesley raised bloodshot eyes to Nessa, his face twisting with the effort to keep his composure.

"Who could have done this to her, Detective Ainsley? It just doesn't make sense. Why would anyone want to kill Candy?"

Nessa met Jankowski's eyes over Wesley's head. She didn't know why someone had decided to kill the innocent young woman, but what she did know was that the killer hadn't been Wesley Knox.

* * *

Nessa waited for Jankowski to walk Wesley out and return to their shared office. She's felt a spark of pity for him when she saw the defeated look on his face.

"At least we can cross him off the list and move on," Nessa said, standing up and gathering her files and notepad. "Let's go into the briefing room and map out what we've got so far."

"Well, that shouldn't take long," Jankowski muttered.

Nessa decided to ignore his pessimism.

"And I've asked Alma to join us as soon as she's done with her initial analysis-"

She stopped short at the door to the briefing room when she saw Detectives Ingram and Ortiz. Ingram was standing by the whiteboard pontificating to his partner.

"...the case that's gonna make my career. Probably will be a record for closing a felony case."

Clearing her throat loudly, Nessa stepped into the room, smiling at Ortiz before turning to Ingram with a puzzled frown.

"Did you forget to check the schedule again, Ingram? Cause I've reserved this room for the rest of the day."

A scowl passed over Ingram's pinched face, but he nodded and gestured to Ortiz.

"I think we're done here anyway, aren't we, Ortiz?"

Ingram's handsome partner nodded agreeably and stood up.

"Yeah, we need to grab some lunch before the hearing anyway."

His comment intrigued Nessa, who turned to look at the words they'd left scrawled on the whiteboard.

"You guys are in court today? On what case?"

Straightening his tie with an exaggerated flourish, Ingram nodded and grinned, revealing an uneven row of small, yellowish teeth.

"We're planning to sit in on Oscar Hernandez's bail hearing. I want to see the bastard's face when he finds out he's not going anywhere until the trial."

The malicious gleam in his small, pale eyes unnerved Nessa, and she turned away in distaste.

So much for an impartial investigation of the case.

She slid her gaze to Jankowski, wondering if Ingram's behavior toward Oscar Hernandez had reminded him of his own misguided pursuit of Wesley. Was he bothered by Ingram's overly zealous pursuit of a man that had yet to be proven guilty of anything other than knowing the victim?

But Jankowski wasn't paying attention. He seemed distracted, ignoring the other two detectives as they exited the briefing room.

Moving to the whiteboard, Nessa erased the notes Ingram had written on Oscar Hernandez. She taped a photo of Candace Newbury to the top of the board, then added a photo of Ruth Culvert next to it. The pictures had been taken during the autopsies. Nessa would have preferred to use something less morbid, but they were the only pictures she had at the moment.

"So, what do we know about the victims?" Nessa asked, raising her voice to get Jankowski's attention.

"We can't let that little weasel become the new chief," Jankowski said, suddenly snapping back to life.

"What little weasel?" Alma Garcia asked from the door.

Willow Bay's senior crime scene technician stepped into the room carrying a slim, black briefcase. She crossed to the long table that dissected the room and began unloading files.

"Who's trying to become the next chief?"

Alma's smooth, round cheeks lifted in a smile when she saw Nessa hesitate and look to Jankowski for help.

"Okay, I'll pretend I never heard anything."

"Thanks, Alma," Nessa said, her face pink. "I mean, for meeting us here. We were just about to get started laying out the information collected so far. We're eager to include your findings on the evidence."

Picking up a marker, Jankowski joined Nessa in front of the white board and added the victim's names under their photos.

"Okay, so what do we know about Candace Newbury?"

Nessa and Alma started to speak at the same time.

"You go ahead, Alma."

Alma nodded and opened a file, taking out photographs of the clothes Candace had been wearing.

"The victim was wearing homemade clothes from the look of it. No tags or labels. Her dress appears to have been stitched by hand."

She laid a photo of the shredded, bloody garment on the table.

"Her shoes were also made by hand, and I'd say whoever made them has considerable skill. The name Putnam has been etched on the insole of the shoe."

Alma produced another photo, this one a close-up of the inside of a leather shoe. The leather was stained, but the word *Putnam* was clearly visible.

Nessa nodded, her mind churning.

"If this shoemaker sells his handmade shoes somewhere locally, or online, maybe we can find out where Candace got them."

Jankowski nodded. His sullen expression turned to interest as he added the information about the shoes and clothes onto the board, then watched Alma reach for another photo.

"I've also cast several sets of footprints at the Candace Newbury scene. My initial analysis is that there were at least four people at the gas station that night. But get this. They were all wearing the same type of shoes."

Alma stared at them with shining eyes.

"And the ground outside Ruth's window had three sets of footprints."

"Let me guess," Jankowski muttered. "They were wearing the same shoes, too?"

Alma nodded, her excitement obvious.

"One of the prints can be matched back to Ruth, but the other two sets of prints must belong to whoever took Ruth."

Nessa shook her head, wanting to make sure she understood what Alma was saying.

"Are you telling us there are two perpetrators?"

Alma lifted a finger, motioning for Nessa to hold her question. She laid a photo of a long black hair on the table.

"We also found a hair on the dress Candace was wearing. It was caught in one of the punctures made by the knife, and it doesn't belong to the victim."

Before the wide-eyed detectives could ask any questions, Alma pulled out a printed report, and laid it on the table next to the photo.

"Thanks to the early Christmas present Santa delivered, I was able to run the DNA on the hair right away. I have some of the results here."

She inhaled deeply.

"The only thing I can really tell you at this point is that the hair belongs to a woman. To find out who this woman is, we'd have to have a suspect to compare them with or get a lucky hit in CODIS."

Jankowski looked stunned.

"A woman? You think a woman killed Candace Newbury?"

"I think the hair tells us a woman was likely at the scene," Alma clarified. "And the footprints indicate there was more than one perpetrator at both scenes."

A horrible certainty settled in Nessa's mind.

"There are two killers," she said, her voice firm. "A man and a woman."

"We don't know that for sure," Jankowski snapped.

Nessa regarded his tense face. He seemed overwhelmed by the flood of information that Alma had presented.

Or is he just refusing to believe a woman could be involved?

She turned back to Alma.

"How long before you can get results back on the DNA from CODIS?" Nessa asked. "How long until we know who this woman is?"

Alma shrugged, but she sounded optimistic.

"Could be within twenty-four hours if we get a full match."

"Good," Nessa said, turning back to the board and writing a string of notes under Candace's name. "Is there anything else?"

Alma raised her eyebrows and held up a fingerprint card.

"I'm still working on the bloody fingerprints we lifted from the door at the gas station. I hope to run those through the database as well by end of the day."

Nessa's felt her phone buzz in her pocket, and she looked down to see a text message from Iris.

Call me now. It's urgent.

Stepping to the back of the room, Nessa tapped in a number and lifted the phone to her ear. Iris answered on the first ring.

"What is it, Iris? What's happened?"

The medical examiner sounded rattled.

"I found something when I went back to finish the autopsy on Candace Newbury."

Nessa hesitated, her heart beginning to thump faster.

"She was pregnant," Iris said, her voice wavering on the words. "The poor girl was about two months along."

CHAPTER TWENTY-SEVEN

The water whipped past Barker's face with icy fury as the flat-bottomed airboat sped across the choppy water of the lake at fifty miles an hour. A bright orange flag waved erratically from the flagpole over Barker's head, ending any hope he'd had of sneaking up on the commune without being seen.

"Do we really need the flag?" he yelled toward the man operating the stick at the back of the boat.

"What?" the heavy-set man named Dooley yelled back, his voice muffled by the massive propeller behind him.

Barker shook his head and gave up. Yelling would attract even more attention than the orange flag.

Steering the big boat toward a canal hidden within a thick cluster of mangroves and swamp maples, Dooley called out again.

"Big gator up ahead...there, to your right."

Frankie clutched at Barker's arm, as if the alligator might jump over the edge of the boat and climb into the elevated chair next to him.

"Calm down, Frankie," Barker yelled, hauling his arm out of Frankie's grasp. "We're up here and the gators are down there."

The boat slowed down as the waterway narrowed and the mangroves grew thicker along the edge of the canal. Barker tried to see past the cordgrass and the towering cypress trees without success.

177

If this boat breaks down, I'm waiting for a tow. No way am I walking through that.

Ten minutes later the canal opened into a wide lake, the banks thickly wooded with pine trees and water oak. Slowing the boat, Dooley pointed to the right, where the tree line faded into a gentle slope.

"That's the backend of the CSL compound," Dooley said, scratching his considerable paunch. "They own those gardens and that grove of citrus trees. Oranges and tangerines I think."

Barker stared over at the neat vegetable patches and symmetrical rows of trees. From what he could see, it didn't appear to be a dangerous place.

Looks more the Garden of Eden than the lair of the beast.

A man walked into view, pushing a wheelbarrow, followed by several women carrying baskets. They looked over at the sound of the airboat's propeller. The man set down the wheelbarrow handles and began walking toward the water's edge.

Dooley raised a lazy hand in a half-hearted wave, then accelerated past the commune's dock, steering the airboat toward a slow-moving tributary. When they were out of sight of the compound, Dooley cut the engine.

"So, that's it." Dooley stifled a yawn. "What else you wanna see?"

"What about the guy who runs the place...Jacob Albright?"

Dooley rolled his eyes in Frankie's direction.

"I thought we already went through that last night, Frankie. Jake's a local boy. Sure, he served some time, but now he's back. That's all I know."

Barker studied the man's chubby face, not liking the defensive tilt to his weak chin. The little man was hiding something.

"You ever see Jake outside of the compound with any girls? Does your good buddy like to party? He frequent any of the bars around here?"

Dooley shook his head, his eyes not meeting Barker's.

"You know, Dooley, you sure are a shitty liar," Frankie said, keeping his eyes on the water around the boat. "Why are you protecting a scumbag that served five years for being a damn pervert? I thought you were a God-fearing Christian boy."

Keeping his eyes on the bottom of the boat, Dooley say back in his chair and crossed his arms over his chest.

"I am a Christian," he muttered, "but around here folks fear Buck Henry more than God. And he and his boys don't like anyone talking to outsiders."

"Who the fuck's Buck Henry?" Frankie asked, watching a water snake slither through the murky water with wide eyes. "And what does he have to do with Jacob Albright?"

Impatient for anything that might lead him to Taylor, Barker was tempted to grab the pudgy man and shake him. Maybe then some valuable information would fall out. Instead he forced himself to remain quiet and listen.

"Buck Henry's the man Jake works for." Dooley looked around as if the alligators might be listening. "He makes...deliveries for Buck, only no one knows what's in 'em."

Barker wondered what kind of deliveries Jacob was so determined to hide. He pictured the CSL produce truck he'd encountered on Highway 42, and the aggressive young man who'd chased Barker away.

Maybe he wasn't hiding information about Taylor after all. Maybe he was just hiding a delivery for the local tough guy.

Barker glared over at Dooley.

"The blond boy that drives the CSL truck. What's his story?"

"He's not from around here," Dooley said. "But I can tell he's a strange one."

Frankie grinned, then leaned over to whisper in Barker's ear.

"My mama always said it takes one to know one."

179

Barker shoved him away and scowled, then turned back to Dooley.

"What do you mean by strange? What's he done?"

Lowering his voice, Dooley leaned toward Barker.

"I seen him coming out of the swamp a few nights back. He was covered in blood. Looked like he'd been huntin' gators and snakes with his bare hands."

Frankie's smile faded, and his eyes returned to the water.

"And he's always carrying a shotgun around. Besides, he just looks like a crazy little fucker."

Dooley looked up at the sun peeking out from behind a gray cloud.

"Look, I gotta get back for my next ride."

"Just one more thing," Barker said, reaching into his pocket and pulling out Taylor's picture.

"You ever seen this girl around here?"

Dooley stared at the picture, then blinked.

"Yeah, I've seen her before. She used to work over at Little Gator's Diner. The only good-looking gal Chester ever had workin' for him other than that granddaughter of his."

Barker's heart hammered in his chest.

"You remember the granddaughter's name?"

Dooley closed his eyes and strained hard as he tried to think, earning a dirty look from Frankie.

"I can't remember," Dooley finally said. "I think Chester called her Honey or Sugar or something like that. All I know is she was a real looker."

"What happened to her?" Barker asked.

Dooley seemed stumped. He shrugged his meaty shoulders.

"I dunno. She just wasn't there one day...just like the girl in that photo. Maybe they done run off together. Can't say I blame 'em. There's nothing but trouble around here for girls like that."

CHAPTER TWENTY-EIGHT

Frankie's stomach lurched along with the airboat as Dooley navigated a wide turn and headed back the way they'd come. Seeing open water ahead, Dooley stomped on the accelerator and jammed the rudder stick forward, causing the boat to hydroplane, and for a heart-stopping second Frankie felt the boat tilt sideways, before it settled onto the water's surface again with a messy splash.

As they sped toward the commune Frankie fumbled for his phone, opening the camera app just as they approached the wooden dock. He held up the phone with numb fingers, willing himself not to drop it over the side of the boat.

Cause there's no fucking way I'm going in after it.

Aiming the camera toward the sloping lawn and citrus grove that was now visible to his left, Frankie saw the figure of a short man standing at the foot of the dock, a rifle held in the crook of one arm.

"He's armed," Barker hollered to Frankie. "Get ready to jump."

Frankie twisted to stare back at Barker, wondering if the older man had lost his mind.

"I ain't jumping nowhere," Frankie yelled back. "He can shoot my ass before I go in that water."

But the man made no move to lift the gun or point it toward the boat. He just watched as they jetted past, his face blank, his white-blond hair reflecting the few rays of sun that had managed to make their way through the overcast sky above.

Using his free arm to wave, Frankie used his other hand to take a random series of shots, training the phone's camera on the man with the rifle and the people working in the garden and the grove.

Once they'd passed out of view, Frankie lowered his stiff hand and dropped his phone back in his pocket.

"You see anything interesting?" he called over to Barker, who was staring back toward the commune.

Barker didn't respond, he just stared into the distance, wearing a dazed look that worried Frankie. The rest of return trip was spent in silence, with Frankie keeping watch for rogue alligators and Barker seemingly lost in his thoughts.

The tiny Viper Airboat office was crowded when they docked the airboat and went inside. A family on a road trip from New Jersey to Naples had booked a swamp tour, and Hank was giving them the obligatory safety talk. Frankie motioned for Barker to follow him back to the Prius.

Pulling out his phone, he began thumbing through the pictures he'd taken, most of which were hopelessly blurry, showing only distorted streaks of water, land and sky. He stopped when he saw the final few photos.

A clear picture of the rifle-toting man on the dock was followed by a shot of several women standing in the garden. One of the women was tall and slim, with long dark hair falling down her back.

"Look at this one, Barker," Frankie demanded, the excitement in his voice causing Barker to grab the phone from him.

Barker stared at the photo, zooming in on the same woman that had caught Frankie's attention.

"Is it her, man? Is that Taylor?"

Frankie watched Barker's face, holding his breath as the ex-detective studied the picture. After a few seconds Barker sighed and shook his head.

"I don't know, Frankie. I've been looking for Taylor for the last two years. I see her on every street and in every car. Anywhere there's a tall girl with dark hair. But none of them ended up being my Taylor."

Frankie placed his long, skinny hands on Barker's shoulders and gave him a shake.

"Stop the pity party, man. That girl back there might be your daughter. She could be alive and safe and only a few miles away."

Barker nodded, his eyes raising to meet Frankie's with both hope and fear.

"And if the murders of those two girls are connected to the commune, Taylor could be in real danger."

CHAPTER TWENTY-NINE

Eli stood by the dock watching the airboat speed across the lake and out of sight. His head hurt, and his eyes burned from fatigue, but he'd still managed to recognize the older man from the other day.

It was the same man who'd been nosing around the truck when he and Zac had broken down. The same one who'd snuck into the compound and confronted Jacob. The one that looked like a cop.

Eli wondered who the other man was, and why he'd been taking pictures of the commune.

They sure don't look like tourists to me. Must be the ones Angel warned me about. The ones that want to destroy the congregation.

Hearing voices approaching behind him, Eli rubbed his sore eyes, took one last look at the water, then began walking up the slope toward the garden. His pulse quickened when he saw Marie among the group of women that had come to gather oranges.

Anxiety flashed through him when he saw the other women in the group. Naomi, Judith and Priscilla crowded around Marie, each trying to harvest as many oranges as possible before the temperatures fell below freezing.

As Eli drew closer to the grove, he slowed down, trying to catch Marie's eye, hoping for a smile.

"You planning to shoot us, Brother Eli?" Priscilla asked as she dropped several plump oranges into a crate at her feet. "Or is that a toy gun?"

"It's a real gun all right, Sister Priscilla." Eli adjusted the rifle in his arms, trying to ignore the headache that was growing stronger. "I'm on guard duty. Brother Jacob says we gotta protect the congregation."

Naomi looked up at the mention of her husband's name, her bright green eyes silently assessing Eli.

"Well, make sure you're careful with that thing, now," Judith said, picking up an empty crate from the stack. "I'm sure Brother Jacob doesn't want anyone to get hurt."

"Listen to your mother now, Brother Eli," Naomi said, as she pulled down a ripe orange. "She always knows just what my husband wants. Why, she hangs on his every word."

Priscilla scowled at her daughter's spiteful remark, but before Eli could react, Judith lightened the tension with a soft laugh.

"I do have a weakness for Brother Jacob," Judith admitted. "He helped Eli when few other men would, and he allowed me to come and be near my boy as well. He's a good man."

Eli instinctively bristled at the words of praise for a man that had proven to be so selfish, before feeling a sense of shame and dread wash over him. Jacob had welcomed him into his flock and called him brother, and yet Eli was sitting in judgment of him, branding him a sinner.

Will I be struck down like Ruth and Candace for my betrayal?

Eli shook the thought from his head, noticing that Marie had kept herself out of the conversation. She worked quickly and silently, focused only on harvesting the oranges, her deft hands reaching, twisting, pulling and dropping the fruit with effortless grace. Eli wondered why Marie was ignoring him.

Maybe she's still shook up after what happened this morning.

He felt bad about shooting at Marie and Jacob in the garden earlier. He hadn't wanted to do it, but Angel had given him an order. He could still hear her ominous voice in his head.

"It is God's will, not mine...you must stay strong."

Recalling the pitiless gleam in her eyes, Eli felt an involuntary shiver ripple down his back. He knew from experience that defying Angel's orders could prove deadly, and he'd given up trying to resist her plans.

Besides, she hadn't wanted him to really shoot them, had she? His head ached, making it hard for him to remember exactly what she'd said, but he was sure she'd just wanted to scare Jacob away from Marie. Deep-down Eli knew he had wanted the same thing.

Brother Jacob's already hurt enough women around here. I don't want him hurting Sister Marie, too.

Circling around the women and their growing stacks of crates, Eli headed up toward the main house. He looked back over his shoulder, hoping for another glimpse of Marie, only to find her staring after him with wide, frightened eyes.

"Brother Eli, can we get some help over here?"

Forcing himself to pull his eyes away, Eli turned to see Ma Verity shuffling through the garden toward the smooth expanse of lawn by the water. Zac was struggling to carry her big rocker while keeping a steadying hand on the older woman's arm.

"What are you doing, Brother Zac? Why are you bringing Ma down here?" Eli glanced nervously at the water, half-expecting to see the men on the airboat returning. "It's not safe."

Zac shrugged, his face sagging with worry.

"I wanted to get some sun, Brother Eli," Ma Verity called out, her voice slurring on the words. "It's too cold for my old bones up in that old house."

Positioning the chair on an even patch of grass, Zac turned to walk back toward the house without a word.

"That boy's not very happy, is he?" Ma Verity muttered at Zac's retreating figure. "Must be worried about poor Sister Ruth."

Eli looked away, avoiding the woman's pale blue eyes, unsure what he should say about Ruth.

Sister Ruth was a traitor...she got what she deserved...

Somehow he knew that wasn't true, no matter what Angel said, and no matter how many times he'd tried to convince himself. Ruth had been innocent. He clutched at the throbbing pain in his head and stumbled toward the women in the grove, driven by a need to talk to Marie. To explain what he'd done and why.

But Marie was gone. Confused, Eli stopped, looking up toward the house, then down to the water; there was no sign of her. The other women ignored him as they hurried to fill their crates. He stood, his head spinning, then moved toward the potting shed. Maybe Marie had gone to collect herbs for teatime.

A cluster of moss-covered oak trees hid the entrance to the wooden shed, and for a minute Eli thought he'd missed it. When he spied the little wooden door, he had to put a shaky hand on the doorframe to stop himself from falling.

Wrenching the door open, he peered inside. The dim interior was cold and silent. He blinked, his eyes trying to adjust to the light, trying to focus on the long white sheet draped over a long table.

Is that a body under there? Could Angel have already gotten to Marie?

He knew it was impossible, but his throat constricted, making it hard for him to draw in a breath as he crept toward the sheet, waves of dizziness washing over him with each step.

"Marie?" His voice sounded hollow in the quiet room.

Lifting a numb hand, he picked up the edge of the sheet and pulled, revealing a tray of purple flowers. Weak with relief, Eli stared down at the blossoms, wondering vaguely if he should bring some leaves back to the house, but not sure what part of the plants were needed to make Angel's special tea.

"She's not here," a voice hissed behind him, the words sending bolts of ice through his veins.

Eli jumped, but he didn't turn around. Temples throbbing, he closed his eyes, resisting the urge to raise his rifle and turn to confront the woman behind him.

"Sister Marie is the one that helped Sister Ruth run away. She's part of the plot against us. The little whore could ruin everything."

Eli shook his head, his hands clenching around the cold metal of the rifle, his mind reeling as she told him what lay ahead.

The killing wasn't over, and Marie would be the next to die.

CHAPTER THIRTY

Marie stepped back from the big window in the kitchen, careful not to be seen by Eli as he scanned the lawn and main gardens then headed toward the west end of the property. She knew without a doubt that he was looking for her. What he wanted with her wasn't as clear.

When Marie had first arrived at CSL, Father Jed had welcomed her with paternal affection, and Eli, also a newcomer to the congregation, had seemed to be the little brother she'd never had.

All the heartbreak and guilt she'd been running from had faded behind the comforting walls of the compound, and she believed she'd found a new family. A family that was based on simple truths, honest work and shelter from the evils of the world outside. But then Father Jed's sudden death had changed everything.

Why did you die, Father Jed? Why does everyone good have to die?

Her mother's face, still beautiful even at the end, flashed into her mind. Her bravely cheerful eyes had hidden any fear, and her soft, accepting smile had denied feeling any pain. But Marie had known the truth; she'd felt it in the delicate, tell-tale trembling of her mother's hand. That trembling had stayed with Marie long after her mother's death, growing stronger, creating fissures in her heart that had been slow to heal.

Wiping away the tears that often followed thoughts of her mother and Father Jed, Marie filled a kettle with fresh water and took down a teacup. She opened the cupboard by the walk-in freezer and reached up to the top shelf for her private supply of green tea.

None of that nasty angel tea for me. It's bitter enough to kill.

Scooping out a small mound of tea leaves, Marie waited for the kettle to boil, keeping a watch out the window for Eli's return. Something had gone terribly wrong with him; the earnest young man she'd first met had become increasingly anxious and aggressive, carrying that dreadful shotgun around, his eyes bloodshot and angry.

And he hadn't seemed at all worried about Candace and Ruth disappearing. In fact, neither Eli nor Jacob had seemed concerned that something may have happened to the young women. They'd just seemed annoyed and angry. But Marie's worry was growing with each passing hour.

Ruth should be back by now. She was just supposed to make sure Candy was safe before coming home. So where is she?

Marie was beginning to suspect that something terrible had happened, and that her shy young friend wasn't coming back.

Pouring the boiling water over the tea leaves, Marie looked through the window, seeing Judith disappear into the barn, a full crate of oranges under each arm. Naomi and Priscilla walked behind her, each balancing a heaping crate in front of them.

The mother and daughter seemed to be having a heated discussion. Marie shook her head as she saw Naomi drop the crate of oranges on the ground and stomp back toward the grove. Priscila stared after her with wounded eyes.

If only Naomi knew how lucky she is to still have her mother.

But it wasn't Marie's place to lecture the young woman, who had her own grief to deal with after she'd suffered a miscarriage earlier in the year. It wasn't surprising that Naomi needed time to mourn, but she'd become withdrawn and bitter, seeming to blame Jacob and everyone else around her.

Lost in her thoughts and worries, Marie didn't hear the footsteps coming up behind her.

"Having a tea break, Sister Marie? Mind if I join you?"

Marie jumped at Jacob's deep voice only inches from her ear. She felt his hot breath on her neck and twisted around, her elbow knocking into her teacup, sending a splash of hot liquid across the counter. Several scalding drops of tea dripped onto the floor.

"You should be more careful, Sister Marie," Jacob snapped, jumping back and inspecting his shoes. "Brother Tobias just finished this pair."

"And you shouldn't sneak up on people, Brother Jacob. You might end up getting hurt."

Seeing that his shoes had been spared, Jacob relaxed again, picking up a kitchen towel. Instead of using it to clean up the spill, Jacob looped the towel around Marie's waist and tugged her toward him before she had a chance to protest.

"You can hurt me all you want, Sweet Marie," he growled in her ear. "In fact, I just might like that."

A rattling cough from the doorway caused Jacob to spin around, panic lighting his pale blue eyes.

"God, Ma, you scared the life out of me."

He crossed the room to take his mother's arm, throwing Marie a warning glare as he passed her.

"I thought you'd gone out to get some sun. Is everything okay?"

Ma Verity squinted at Marie as if she didn't recognize her. Marie responded with a reassuring smile, her outrage at Jacob's actions overshadowed by concern for Father Jed's widow.

"It's okay, Ma," Marie said, not liking the confused look in the older woman's eyes. "Why don't you sit down and have a little tea?"

"There's evil in this house," Ma Verity croaked. "It comes to me at night. It speaks to me."

Alarmed by his mother's garbled words, Jacob stood frozen by her side. Marie almost felt sorry for him. The once sharp, strong woman had lost herself after his father's death, and it was clear that he didn't know what to do to help her find her way back.

Marie decided to ignore Jacob for the time being. She'd have to deal with his unwelcome advances later. Guiding his mother to a chair at the kitchen table, Marie set a teacup in front of her. She pushed past Jacob to get to the special tea and herb concoction Ma Verity preferred, but the cannister was empty.

"No angel tea left, I'm afraid." Marie reach for a scoop of her green tea leaves. "How about I make you some special Marie tea instead?"

Ma Verity didn't respond. She just peered into the teacup as if it held the key to her future. Marie poured the hot water into the cup and watched as the tea leaves began to brew. When she looked around, Jacob was gone. Her shoulders slumped with relief, and she hurried to the window. The gardens were empty. Eli was nowhere in sight. Now all she had to do was watch out for Ma Verity until help arrived.

* * *

"Fresh oranges if anybody wants one."

Judith sounded cheerful as she and Priscilla entered the kitchen. She set a wicker basket of freshly picked fruit on the counter, stopping short when she saw Ma Verity staring into the untouched green tea.

"What happened?" Judith slid into a chair, looking up at Marie. "She having another one of her bad days?"

Marie shrugged, holding back sudden tears. It was all just too much. Ruth and Candace missing, Eli's strange behavior, Jacob's aggression, and Ma Verity's worsening condition. Everything seemed to be falling apart.

"I think she's...confused," Marie finally managed to say. "She was talking about evil...about it coming to talk to her at night."

Priscilla placed a gentle hand on Ma Verity's shoulder, but her eyes rested on Marie's anxious face.

"You don't believe in evil, Sister Marie?"

Suspecting Priscilla was teasing her, Marie shook her head.

"I believe that some people do evil things, but I don't think there's an evil force in the world that can whisper in your ear at night."

"Well, I was raised to believe in the devil." Judith picked up the teacup in front of Ma Verity and deposited it in the sink. "If he's not an evil force at work in the world, I don't know what is."

Talk of the devil seemed to rouse Ma Verity. She looked up, her face twisting in fear, then stood on unsteady legs.

"I...I want to pray," she demanded. "I want to pray that...that the devil stays away. Our congregation needs...prayer...protection..."

Marie watched, feeling helpless, as Ma Verity shuffled out of the room, Judith scurrying behind her. Priscilla waited until the door had closed behind them, then turned to Marie.

"It's sad to see Ma like this. First she loses her husband, and now she's losing her mind."

Marie frowned, offended by Priscilla's callous tone.

"I know how she feels." Marie lowered her eyes to the table. "To miss someone so much...to be crazy with grief."

Priscilla raised an eyebrow and crossed her arms over her chest, waiting for Marie to continue.

"I mean, after my mother died, I kind of...lost touch with reality. I couldn't think straight for so long."

"And now?"

Priscilla's cool green eyes studied her as Marie struggled to answer the question she'd been asking herself more and more lately.

What should I do now? Can I really just go back home after all this time?
Cheeks burning under Priscilla's piercing gaze, Marie shrugged.

"I guess CSL has given me the space and time I needed to find peace...to accept my mother's death...to see how unfair I was to blame my father."

"Your father? Why would you blame him?"

Marie's chest ached at the thought of her father's haggard face. She had tried so hard to forget him, had even tried to replace him with Father Jed. But it was no good; he was her father, and he was all she had left.

"I thought his smoking had caused my mother to get...cancer." The last viscous word stuck in her throat. "I had begged him to quit for so long, but...he always said he couldn't."

Marie didn't trust herself to look at Priscilla. The words she'd said to her father before she'd left still haunted her. Shame washed over her as she recalled the pain in his eyes.

"After my mother had gone, I was so angry. I said terrible things. I told him that he should've died instead of Mom. I said I wished it had been him."

"And do you still feel the same?"

Priscilla's question knifed through Marie.

"I don't blame my father anymore," Marie admitted, "and I've come to accept that nothing can change the past. There's no use wishing things were different."

She met Priscilla's gaze, suddenly ashamed for being so self-centered. The woman was having her own problems. She didn't need to bear Marie's burdens as well.

"Anyway, maybe I'll have to go see my father soon," Marie said, straightening her back and adjusting her face into a smile. "Perhaps it's not too late to make amends."

"Does your father live nearby?"

Marie hesitated. The casual question was an easy one, but it would undoubtedly lead to questions that were more difficult to answer.

"Not too far, really," she said, dropping her eyes. "I'm sure I could manage the trip."

"Well, just make sure you clear it with Brother Jacob, first. Remember the new rules. No one leaves the compound without his approval."

Blood rushed to Marie's cheeks at the thought of having to ask Jacob for anything. How could the insufferable man think he could get away with such a rule?

"Has the rest of the congregation been told about this new rule?" Marie's voice quivered with anger. "Are they all willing to be treated like children, or like...prisoners?"

"I was against it at first, too," Priscilla said, bristling, "but then I realized that it's for the safety of the congregation. Two girls are already missing. Who knows what might happen next."

The words brought Marie's fears for Ruth and Candy rushing back, and a defiant plan began to form.

If no one else cares enough to go look for them, maybe I'll go. And I won't bother asking permission when I do.

CHAPTER THIRTY-ONE

L eo checked his phone repeatedly as the hours passed, waiting for a call or text from Eden to let him know she was all right, hoping she wouldn't put herself in danger in her rush to find Ruth's killer. He'd just pulled the slim, black iPhone out of his pocket again when a text alert sounded. Frankie Dawson had sent through a message with a photo attached.

Leo stared at the close-up shot of a chubby man with small eyes and a stained cap pulled low over his forehead. Leo shook his head at Frankie's accompanying text.

Lil Ray's cousin Dooley. He's an idiot.

Leo was already typing out a reply telling Frankie to stop messing around when another photo came through. The text with this photo was more interesting.

Back of commune. Check out the chick.

Zooming in on the photo, Leo could make out several women and a man. All he could see of one woman was her back. She was tall with long dark hair. The other woman was facing the camera. He studied the women without recognizing either one.

Leo thumbed in a message.

Which one? And why?

As he waited for a reply, Leo sat on Eden's big sofa next to Duke and scratched the soft fur between his ears. Frankie was quick to respond.

The one with her back turned. Could be Taylor.

Leo's heart jumped at the message. He raised the phone and once again studied the back of the slim, dark-haired girl standing in the bucolic garden. Could the girl really be Barker's long-missing daughter?

The security panel on the wall by the door chimed, and an automated voice announced that motion had been detected on the driveway. Leo stood just as the garage door rumbled open, his relief at Eden's return edged with unease. He looked down at Duke.

"Let's hope she's feeling better now, boy."

The golden retriever padded over to Eden as soon as she'd stepped through the door, and she knelt next to him and hugged his warm body against her, dropping her head to hide the shine of tears in her sad green eyes.

"I'm sorry, Duke," she whispered against the golden fur. "I'm so sorry for everything."

Finally, she raised her head to look at Leo, her cheeks pink.

"I guess I owe you an apology, too."

Leo shrugged and grinned.

"I thought love meant never having to say–"

Eden held up a hand in protest.

"Don't tell me you're quoting *Love Story*. Isn't that movie a bit sappy for a tough-as-nails defense lawyer like you?"

Her gentle teasing stung more than he was willing to show.

"You must have gotten me confused with someone else." He pulled her up into his arms. "I happen to have a very soft heart, and I like sappy old movies."

Nestling against his broad chest, Eden let out a deep sigh.

"Well, I am sorry...*again*. I'm just torn up about Ruth. I feel like I failed her so badly. But I don't want to take it out on you."

Leo ran his hand over her hair, liking the feel of the silky, blonde strands though his fingers. He hated to leave her now, but Oscar

197

Hernandez was counting on him, and he needed to get to the courthouse in time for the bail hearing.

"I should have known she was in danger," Eden whispered, her cheek warm against the soft cotton of his shirt. "I should have demanded the WBPD provide protection."

"It's not your fault," he objected, pulling her closer. "You couldn't have known. The man who killed Ruth is the only one to blame."

Eden pushed against Leo's chest and stared up with wide eyes.

"That's just it, Leo. It wasn't just one man that killed poor Ruth. There were two people outside Ruth's window last night. At least two people worked together to abduct and kill her."

Eden's voice faltered as Leo stared down.

"Another pair of killers in Willow Bay?" he asked weakly, not wanting to believe it was happening again.

The last series of murders in the city had been committed by the unholy partnership of Douglas Kramer and Adrian Bellows. They'd been respected residents of Willow Bay, and they'd kidnapped eight girls over a dozen years, killing seven of them before they'd gotten caught. Eden's persistence had made their capture possible, and she and Duke had risked their lives to save the last girl. Leo couldn't believe the city was facing another homicidal duo so soon.

"I know, it's horrible. I still can't get my head around it."

"What you need is some food, and some rest." Leo checked his watch and winced. "How about I make you a sandwich before I head over to the courthouse? Then you can relax here with Duke, and I'll be back before you know it."

Eden shook her head and smiled.

"No, you go on. I'm not very hungry right now. The kids will be home soon, and Barb will be here, as well. I'll eat with them."

Glancing again at the clock, Leo took both of Eden's hands in his and squeezed.

"I hate leaving you at a time like this. You know that, right?"

"I know," Eden said, squeezing back. "But you need to go, and Duke and I will be fine."

Leo wondered if she really would be fine. How could she remain physically and emotionally intact if she kept getting pulled into such dangerous situations? Maybe it was time for Eden to distance herself from the day-to-day operations of the Mercy Harbor Foundation. He opened his mouth to share his concerns, then closed it again.

Asking Eden to give up her work at the foundation would be like asking me to give up practicing law.

They had both dedicated their lives to helping people in desperate need. It was their way of seeking redemption for the past, and it was the bond that had brought them together. Quitting at this stage wasn't an option for either of them.

"If I don't get Oscar out on bond, he'll have to stay in jail until the trial. That could take months, and he has a wife and child that depend on him, and...."

Leo paused, not sure who he was trying to convince, himself or Eden, and sensing it wasn't the right time to plead his case. Eden had too much on her mind now to think about anything else.

"I'll be back as soon as I can." He kissed the top of her head. "And then I promise I'll do whatever I can to help find the bastards that killed Ruth and her friend."

Stopping to ruffle Duke's fur, Leo's eyes fell on a stack of wrapped presents on the side table. Christmas was only weeks away, even if none of them were feeling very festive.

"It might be a strange time to say this, but I'm really looking forward to spending the holidays with you."

Eden smiled then for the first time since she'd heard about Ruth, and she kept the smile on as she walked to the door to wave goodbye.

But as Leo pulled away from the house on Briar Rose Lane, a feeling of dread crept over him, as if someone had walked across his grave. Shivering, he flipped on the heater to warm the frigid air inside the car, promising himself he'd return as soon as Oscar Hernandez had been released on bail.

* * *

The downtown traffic was surprisingly light for a weekday, allowing Leo to arrive at the courthouse thirty minutes before the hearing was scheduled to begin. His luck held out as he pulled into the parking garage. A minivan was just vacating a prime space on the second floor.

Checking his watch, Leo decided to stop by the cafeteria in the courthouse lobby. He had just enough time to grab a cup of coffee and review his notes before heading to the holding room where Oscar would be brought prior to the hearing.

"Leo Steele! I was hoping to see you here."

Leo spun around at the sardonic greeting. Detective Marc Ingram sat slouched at one of the little tables along the wall. His partner, Detective Ruben Ortiz, decked out in a well-tailored suit, waved to Leo from the line in front of the counter.

"What are you boys doing here?" Leo asked, although he was confident he already knew the answer. "Shouldn't you be out looking for the real perp that broke into the Delancey's house?"

Ingram smirked and sat up straight in his chair.

"Oh, I'm right where I'm supposed to be. Here, making sure the real perp isn't released back into society to hurt anyone else."

Stepping into line behind Ortiz, Leo forced himself to take in a full breath, then slowly exhale. He'd need his wits about him if he had a hope in hell of getting Hernandez out on bail with Ingram and Ortiz giving evidence.

"Don't let him get to you," Ortiz muttered, looking back at Leo with a sympathetic grimace. "He can be a jerk, but he means well."

"I'll buy the part about him being a jerk," Leo replied, "but I think we both know the bit about him *meaning well* is bullshit."

Ortiz chuckled as he grabbed his drink off the counter.

"See you in court, buddy."

Leo didn't bother responding. He ordered a black coffee and a bottle of water, then checked his phone for messages while he waited for the cashier to run his credit card. When he turned back around, Ingram and Ortiz were gone.

Juggling his coffee, phone and briefcase, Leo shouldered open the door and held it with his foot for a woman pushing a toddler in an enormous stroller. As she maneuvered the huge contraption through the door, Leo's eyes fell on a collection of Florida's most-wanted posters.

A motley assortment of faces stared back at him, but one caught his attention. He let the door swing closed behind the stroller, studying a black and white image on one of the posters. The grainy picture looked like it had been taken from CCTV, but the woman in the picture was facing the camera, and her face and shoulders were clearly visible.

"What the hell?"

Leo dropped his eyes to the text beneath the photo.

Person of Interest in 2016 Homicide in Pensacola.

The woman had been caught on a hidden security camera leaving the scene of a homicide. Her identity was still unknown. Anyone with information on the woman in the photo should contact local authorities. Based on the violent nature of the crime, the poster warned that the woman should be considered armed and dangerous

Holding his camera next to the poster, Leo navigated to the photos Frankie had sent him just an hour before. The woman in Frankie's photo, the one by the lake facing the camera, was a dead ringer for the woman in the most-wanted poster.

Leo used his phone to take a picture of the poster, then zoomed in on the woman's face, sure that he must be mistaken. But a close-up look at the woman only confirmed his fears.

The woman in Frankie's picture closely resembled a possible murder suspect. Someone considered armed and dangerous. And that woman was standing next to a girl that Barker thought may be his missing daughter.

Head spinning, Leo made his way to a marble bench outside the clerk of the court's office. Who should he tell? He looked at his watch. How much time did he have?

Raising the phone Leo searched for the name and number of the only detective in the WBPD that he trusted to take his concerns seriously. Nessa's voicemail picked up after the sixth ring.

"Nessa, this is Leo Steele. I need to talk to you urgently. Please call me as soon as you get this."

He was about to hang up when an image of Barker's sad, puppy-dog eyes flashed through his mind.

"On second thought, I'm heading over to see you now," he belatedly added through gritted teeth. "This can't wait."

Not letting himself think about how disappointed Oscar Hernandez was going to be when he found out the hearing had been delayed, Leo strode into the clerk of the court's office and hurried to the counter. The cheerful young man behind the counter greeted him by name.

"Hi, Mr. Steele, how can I help you today?"

Ignoring the dull ache in his stomach, Leo forced the words out.

"I need to file an emergency request for my client. We need to request a delay of his bail hearing."

CHAPTER THIRTY-TWO

The front door burst open, letting in a gust of cold air along with Hope and Devon. Moments later Barb Sweeny hurried in behind them, bundled in a thick parka, the kind more commonly seen on a ski slope than in the Willow Bay suburbs.

Duke greeted the new arrivals with a wagging tail, while Eden stood back smiling, pulling her own cotton sweater around her as the frigid air swirled through the living room.

"Why don't I start up a fire?" Eden offered, desperate to keep busy. "I'll get some wood from the garage."

But before she could turn to go, the automated voice of the security system announced that motion had been detected in the driveway. Seconds later Hope was flinging open the door to let in more cold air, and her boyfriend, Luke Adams.

Liking the happy flush that appeared on Hope's face whenever Luke was in the room, Eden turned to the boy and smiled.

"I was just going to put some wood on the fire, Luke. Would you like to help me get some from the garage?"

Giving an agreeable nod, Luke followed Eden to the garage and allowed her to pile several logs onto his outstretched arms.

"You ready for the holidays?" she asked, walking back toward the living room. "Is your family going away on vacation?"

"No, ma'am, we're staying in Willow Bay." Luke's mouth curled into a shy smile. "Don't tell Hope, but I've already got her a Christmas present. Can't wait to see her open it."

Eden trailed behind Luke, touched by his obvious affection for her niece, but also concerned that the teenagers may be getting a little too close for comfort. She'd promised to protect her sister's children, and that meant it was up to her to stop Hope and Devon from making poor decisions or getting into dangerous situations they couldn't handle.

After Hope's abduction the summer before, Eden's anxiety for her niece and nephew had grown along with a lingering fear that something, or someone, might destroy the happy little family they'd worked so hard to build.

Shaking off the cloud of anxiety that was threatening, Eden lit the fire, then went to find Barb. There was no way she could sit at home all afternoon pretending everything was okay, when she felt as if nothing would ever be okay again. She needed to do something, anything, to try to understand what was happening, and to figure out a way she could help.

Barb was in the kitchen, arranging oranges in a bowl.

"The citrus was all on sale today," Barb said, not looking up. "I guess everyone's bringing in the harvest ahead of the freeze. I bought two big bags. One for you and one for me."

"Thanks, Barb. They look delicious."

Something in Eden's voice prompted Barb to look up in concern.

"What's wrong, honey? What's happened to put that sad look on your pretty face?"

The older woman put a soft hand on Eden's arm, and Eden struggled to keep her face composed. She couldn't break down again. Especially not in front of the kids. They'd already been through too much.

"I'm fine," Eden insisted, patting Barb's hand. "I just have loads of work to do. Would you mind if I leave you here to watch the kids and fix dinner while I go into the office?"

Barb cocked her head, her eyes thoughtful.

"Well, when you're ready to tell me what's wrong, I'll be ready to listen. In the meantime, you go on and do what you need to do. I'll take care of the kids and make sure they're fed."

Eden collected her purse and her laptop bag, then stood at the door to the living room, watching the kids as they laughed and talked together in front of the crackling fire. The world outside the warm room suddenly seemed very far away.

Leaving the cozy scene behind, she walked to the garage, Duke following closely behind. She turned to the golden retriever and smiled down at him.

"You've been trapped inside all day, haven't you, boy?"

Grabbing his leash and a blanket for the car, she let the dog climb into the backseat of her Expedition, feeling a little better now that she wouldn't be heading out alone. But as she drove out into the wintry afternoon, she had an uneasy feeling that it would be a long while before they returned.

* * *

The Mercy Harbor administration office was in an uproar when Eden arrived. Rumors about Ruth Culvert's murder had spread from reception, to accounting, to health services. Edgar spotted Eden in the lobby and filled her in on the ensuing drama as she hurried toward the elevators, keeping Duke close beside her.

"Everyone's asking *me* if they should be worried," the security guard said. "But I don't know any more than they do."

"Just tell everyone to be careful," she said, doors sliding open in front of her. "Until we know more, we should all be extra diligent."

The doors closed between them, and Eden let her shoulders slump. How could she reassure the people working at Mercy Harbor that they weren't in danger when even she didn't feel safe?

Once the news broke that Ruth Culvert had been inside a Mercy Harbor shelter when she'd been lured outside and abducted, the staff and residents would have plenty of questions. And right now, Eden didn't have any answers.

Settling Duke on the sofa under the window, Eden sat at her desk, turned on her laptop, and double-clicked on the foundation's client database. She typed in Ruth's name and hit the search button. She wasn't surprised when the *No Matches Found* message appeared.

I would have remembered Ruth if she'd been a resident before.

Eden had met most of the women and children that had taken refuge within the foundation's network of shelters. The names, faces, and heartbreaking stories she'd encountered throughout the last five years had stayed with her.

But why did Ruth have my name with her? And why was Mercy Harbor's address written on that piece of paper outside Ruth's window?

The bloody paper had been turned over to the police once they'd arrived to investigate the scene, but when she closed her eyes, Eden could still see the grisly streaks through her name. Dropping her head into her hands, Eden tried to block the disturbing image.

It took her a minute to realize that her desk phone was ringing. She glanced at the display, but the caller was listed as *Blocked Number*. Clearing her throat, she picked up the receiver and held it to her ear.

"Hello, this is Eden Winthrop."

A woman's high-pitched voice quivered over the line.

"I want to talk to Ruth. I want to know if she made it there okay."

Eden hesitated, trying to make sense of the words.

"Who is this?"

There was only silence at the other end. Eden thought the call had been disconnected, but then she heard soft breathing.

"Please," Eden begged, "tell me who you are and why you're calling for Ruth."

"I'm her friend. I gave her your name. From the newspaper. There was an article saying you help people."

Pieces started falling into place in Eden's mind. The local papers had been full of news about the murders Douglas Kramer and Adrian Bellows had committed. Several articles had referenced Mercy Harbor and Hope House. A few had even included pictures of Eden and extolled her role in catching the killers.

Eden realized the woman on the phone must have seen the articles and sent Ruth and Candace to Mercy Harbor for help. It must have been her handwriting on the note.

"Someone's coming. I've got to go."

The girl sounded scared. Was she also in trouble?

"Please, you have to tell me who you are. You may be in danger."

Gripping the phone tightly to her ear, Eden strained to keep her voice calm, terrified that the girl would hang up before she could warn her.

"Danger? What do you mean?"

The girl lowered her voice, as if she was trying not to be overheard. Eden knew she may not have much time. She couldn't afford to wait.

"Listen to me. Ruth is dead. Candace is dead. Someone killed them. Please, tell me where you are. I'll send the police out to help you."

"Someone's coming," the girl repeated, her voice a hoarse whisper. "I have to go."

Eden stared at the receiver, refusing to believe the call had been disconnected just like that. She pressed the button on the phone to access the number of the last caller. *Blocked Number* appeared on the display.

Frantic to reach the police, Eden dug into her purse for her cell phone. Nessa's number was stored in her contacts. If she could reach Nessa, maybe the detective would have a way of tracking the blocked call. Maybe they could find the caller and make sure she was safe. And if they could track her down, maybe she would be able to tell them who had killed her friends.

Nessa answered on the second ring.

"Hi Eden, I'm in the middle of another call, can I call you back?"

"No, Nessa. I need your help. A woman called asking about Ruth. Said she gave Ruth the note with my name and address."

The words got Nessa's full attention.

"Holy cow, that's great. What's her name? Where is she? We need to talk to her right away and see what–"

Interrupting Nessa before she got too carried away, Eden broke the bad news.

"She didn't leave her name, and her number was blocked."

Nessa gasped, then puffed out a frustrated sigh.

"Sounds like it might have been a prank, Eden."

"It wasn't a prank, Nessa."

Eden was sure the caller had been telling the truth.

"The girl was real, and she was scared, and she knew about Ruth."

A buzz sounded on the line.

"Look, Eden, I've got an incoming call. I'll contact the phone company. See if I can get the number that called you. But that takes time, and there's no guarantee we'll be able to link the phone to a specific location or a person."

"Okay, I understand," Eden murmured. "Just let me know what you find out."

Eden had just set down the phone, her hand cramped and sore from clutching the receiver, when Duke jumped down from the sofa and growled low in his throat. She turned toward the door to see a man standing in the doorway.

"Nathan?"

"You haven't forgotten me already, have you, Eden?"

Striding across the room, Nathan hesitated when he saw Duke.

"It's okay, Duke," Eden soothed. "You remember, Nathan. He's a an old friend of mine."

Nathan held out a hand for Duke to consider. Once the golden retriever had given his tacit approval, Nathan leaned across the desk and gave Eden a loud kiss on each cheek.

"You look great," Nathan said, grabbing her hands in his. "I've missed those green eyes."

"What are you doing here, Nathan?" Eden couldn't believe her ex-partner had followed through on his threat to come to her if she refused to go to San Francisco.

"I told you. I need to talk to you."

A wayward lock of blonde hair fell over his forehead, and Eden automatically lifted a hand to push it back, before pulling away, feeling awkward.

"Really, Nathan, what *are* you doing here?" Eden snapped. "I'm in the middle of another crisis, and I don't have time for games."

"I'm here so we can talk. And I'm not leaving until we do."

Plopping into a chair across from her, Nathan crossed his arms and smiled defiantly at Eden. His blue eyes softened as he saw the stress on her face.

"How about I help you solve your crisis first, and then we talk?"

"No one but the phone company can help me now."

Nathan's eyes widened.

"The phone company? Are you experiencing poor cell reception?"

Eden opened her mouth to protest when she saw the twinkle in his eyes. She shook her head and sat back in her chair, dejected.

"A woman called asking about Ruth, the girl that was...killed," Eden said, her voice weary. "The caller didn't leave her name, and her number was blocked, so now there's no way of finding her."

Nathan frowned, his face sobering at her words.

"And you think this caller may know who killed Ruth?"

"Right, and I'm worried she could be in danger. If I don't find her, she might wind up dead, too."

Nathan cocked his head and scrunched up his forehead like he always did when he was trying to think though a problem.

"You've asked the police to get the number from the phone company?"

Eden nodded, her eyes downcast.

"Yes, but they said it takes time, and there are no guarantees."

"Sounds familiar." Nathan took out his phone and thumbed through his contacts. "When I hear that from one of my contractors I know just who to call. For the right price he can get me any information I need, guaranteed."

It was Eden's turn to frown.

"You mean, you pay someone to steal information for you?"

Shaking his head, Nathan began tapping out a message.

"It isn't stealing, it's borrowing. Now, give me your office number and the time of the call."

Within minutes Nathan had sent though a request for his mysterious contact to find the number behind the call. Eden assumed he'd have to hack into the phone company's database, but she wasn't sure Nathan was being serious.

Would he really pay someone to hack into a private system for me?

She knew the answer without thinking. Nathan was a true friend, and she knew he'd do just about anything to make her happy. The thought made her feel slightly guilty, and she pushed away Leo's brooding face.

"Let me buy you a warm latte while we wait to hear back," Nathan suggested, standing and motioning toward the door. "I can't believe how cold it is here. I only packed bathing suits and flipflops."

Smiling despite herself, Eden stood and let Nathan escort her and Duke down to the garage. He'd come straight from the airport to her office in an Uber, so they climbed in Eden's SUV. Before she could back out of the parking space, Nathan's phone buzzed

His eyes scanned the message, then turned to Eden.

"The number's listed for a business off Highway 42 called Little Gator Diner. Diner's owned by a man named Chester Gosbey."

"Well, call the number. See who answers."

Nathan tapped in the number and waited, but no one answered. After a dozen rings, he ended the call.

"What now, Watson?"

Eden scowled at Nathan, frustration making her voice sharp.

"Please don't tell me you think you're Sherlock Holmes just because you found one phone number."

"Talk about lack of gratitude," Nathan teased, staring into the shadows of the parking garage. "I thought you were friends with that police detective. The one that got shot. Can't you call her?"

Eden rolled her eyes, then pulled out her phone and called Nessa's number. She wasn't surprised when it went to voicemail. She considered calling Leo, then remembered he'd be in court. Oscar Hernandez had a bail hearing. A spark of resentment stirred inside her, but when she glanced over at Nathan, the feeling flickered and faded.

Something about being with Nathan again was helping her see everything more clearly. Nathan was kind and funny and helpful, but he wasn't Leo. And while she was grateful for Nathan's friendship, she knew that Leo was the one she wanted by her side, especially at a time like this.

But Leo isn't here, and there's a girl out there in danger.

Turning the key in the ignition, she looked at Nathan.

"You up for a ride in the country, Sherlock?"

Eyebrows raised, Nathan grinned and buckled his seatbelt.

"I sure am, Watson. And once our mission's complete, you and I are going to have that talk."

CHAPTER THIRTY-THREE

The winter sun set early in December, casting gloomy shadows over the overgrown marshland where Angel searched for the devil's weed. The supply she had in the potting shed was almost gone, and she needed to be sure there would be enough of the poisonous plant to finish what she'd started.

Her mother had warned her about the plant from the time she could walk, teaching her the proper name, Datura Stramonium, and warning that even a modest amount could cause violent illness, terrifying hallucinations and, ultimately, death. Angel had been fascinated by the purple blossoms, intrigued by the idea that something so lovely could be deadly.

After her mother had died, a new family adopted Angel, changing her name, pretending that her previous life, and her real mother, had never existed. But Angel remembered. And eventually she'd been old enough to go out and find the devil's weed on her own. Her new family had proven her mother right. The weed did cause violent illness and death.

The next family that adopted her was less bothersome and more useful. She'd been spoiled and pampered and had decided they were more valuable alive than dead. At least, they had been up until a point. It seemed everyone reached the end of their usefulness to Angel at some point.

Spying the tell-tale flash of deep purple she'd been looking for, Angel crouched in the long grass to harvest the toxic plants. Wearing protective gloves, she withdrew a four-inch, fixed-blade knife, using it to deftly cut down each plant before shoving it into the big burlap sack she'd brought with her.

She liked the feel of the heavy knife in her hand, liked remembering how she'd used both the knife and the plant at different times to take revenge on those that had crossed her. She couldn't decide which she liked best really.

There's a sentimental value to using devil's weed, but the knife is more efficient if time's a factor. Nothing quicker than a sharp, well-placed blade.

The face of the old biddy that she'd killed in Pensacola floated through her mind, bringing a malicious smile to her face.

Angel had wanted to be close to the prison but lacked a place to stay, so when Ursula Mueller had offered room and board in exchange for light chores and help with her medications, Angel had been more than happy to oblige the elderly widow.

But once she no longer had a reason to stay in Pensacola, a few satisfying slashes with the knife had ended the old woman's chronic complaints and incessant whining forever.

Thinking it would have been a shameful waste to leave perfectly good jewelry and cash behind, Angel had helped herself to whatever old lady Mueller had laying around.

A girl needs nice things sometimes, and poor old Ursula certainly didn't have use for them anymore.

Angel hadn't counted on the old woman's interfering neighbor making an unexpected appearance. Initially she'd ignored the pounding on the door, but then had been forced to slip out the back when the neighbor dragged up the apartment manager, screeching that something must be wrong.

With no time to clean up the mess, Angel suspected she'd left incriminating evidence behind, and in her rush she'd forgotten about the security cameras in the parking lot.

Luckily the walls of the congregation have provided refuge, and surely the police have given up looking for me by now, if they'd even bothered.

She shook her head at the memory. It was a shame she hadn't had Eli to act as her little helper that day. Maybe if she'd had his help then she wouldn't have ended up on the state's most wanted list.

But now she had to decide what to do about Eli. She could never tell him who she really was and what she'd done. That would be pushing him too far. The bits of devil's weed she'd been adding to his tobacco pouch had kept him confused and hallucinating, but he was still lucid enough to ask questions, and to have doubts.

If he learned the truth, if he found out everything, even the devil's weed wouldn't be enough to keep him quiet and cooperative.

Angel knew she'd have to accept that Eli was a liability. He knew too much and had seen too much. He would have to be disposed of soon. It was sad but necessary. She'd never meant to keep him around so long, but he'd proven to be an unexpectedly valuable and obedient partner in crime. Without him she'd never have been able to take care of Candace and Ruth.

But poor Eli will have to take the fall. It's his destiny after all.

Eli would be the sacrificial lamb taking the responsibility for her sins. His diminished mental state would make it easy to blame him. She'd made sure of that. Everyone knew that Eli was losing his grip on reality. It wouldn't surprise anyone to find out he'd finally lost control and ended up killing two innocent girls.

Although, after we take care of Marie, I guess that'll make three girls.

She knew she should feel guilty, or at least a little sad, but then, she never had been the sensitive type. If she was to get what she wanted, there was no other way.

* * *

Angel kept herself hidden behind the dense trees and soggy underbrush as she passed behind the Little Gator Diner.

No sense in making old Chester curious about what I'm up to.

A faint, high-pitched sound in the still air made Angel stop and cock her head. She could hear a woman's low, urgent voice. The voice sounded familiar.

Creeping to the edge of the clearing, Angel pushed aside a tree limb and peered toward the old diner. Chester Gosbey leaned on his cane beside his blue El Camino. Marie stood in front of him, her face anxious and her hands clenched into fists at her sides.

"I'm just telling you what the woman on the phone told me, Mr. Gosbey." Marie glanced around the yard as if she sensed that she was being watched. "She said Ruth and Candy are *dead.*"

Shaking his head as if he couldn't believe what he was hearing, the old man leaned more heavily on his cane.

"Who is this woman, anyway?" Chester asked, his gravelly voice skeptical. "And why were you callin' her?"

"She helps people." Marie sounded reluctant to tell Chester more. "I gave Ruth her address because Candy was in...in trouble. They wanted to run away. I thought I was helping."

Chester reached into his front pocket and pulled out an old handkerchief. He wiped his forehead with it nervously and stuck it back in his pocket.

"Why didn't Candy come to me? I'm her grandfather for goodness sake. Why'd she run to strangers?"

Marie dropped her eyes.

"She was embarrassed. I guess she thought you'd be mad since you'd told her not to get involved with Jacob Albright."

Chester sighed, his big shoulders dropping.

"So, what are you plannin' to do now? You wanna' call the cops?"

Marie shook her head and backed away.

"No...I mean, I don't know. I saw that article in the paper a while back about the Willow Bay police chief killing girls, and Jacob keeps telling us that the police are trying to close the commune, so I don't know if I can trust them. But I think I know where I want to go."

Angel leaned closer, straining to hear Marie's words. A branch cracked underneath her shoe, and both Chester and Marie looked around. Angel froze, her heart hammering in her chest, but then Chester broke the silence.

"You go on back to the commune, young lady. Give me time to check out this story and see if it's true. If something's happened to my granddaughter, I need to know about it."

Marie wrapped her arms tightly around herself as she listened.

"Collect your things, then meet me back here after dark. We can decide what to do once I know more. Go on now, hurry!"

Watching with angry eyes as Marie slipped into the trees, heading toward the compound, Angel let the tree limb drop back into place. Frozen in mute fury, she contemplated her options. She had to find a way to stop Chester and Marie before they ruined everything.

The sound of tires crunching over rocks and gravel made her push back the limb and peek out again.

A big black Dodge pickup rumbled toward the back of the diner. Chester propped his cane against the El Camino and folded his arms over his skinny chest.

"We got us a problem," Chester called out as Buck Henry climbed down from the truck. "Jake's fucked up again."

Swiping an orange Gator's cap off his head, Buck raked a big hand through his close-cropped curls.

"What'd that little fucker do now?"

He stomped to the truck bed and began pulling on a plastic tarp he had tucked around something in the back.

"This time it's serious, Buck," Chester said, limping over to the truck and peering in. "He's messed around with some young girls again. May even have killed 'em. Police are bound to come poking around that compound."

Angel strained to see what was in the back of the truck, but the men blocked her view.

"It's a big'un," Buck said, letting the tarp fall back into place. "Twelve-footer at least."

"And the guns?"

Buck nodded to a wooden crate in the corner of the truck bed.

"Yeah, a hundred of those little Walthers we got in last time. That's all I could fit in with the gator."

"You better take those somewhere to offload. And get rid of anything that links you to Jake Albright. He's goin' down, and he'll take us with him if we let him."

Snorting with disgust, Buck stuck his cap back on his head and jerked open the truck door.

"Let me get rid of this load and alert my boys to clean the shop. I'll circle back later. We need to decide what we're going to tell the cops if Jake starts talking. Make sure we've got our stories straight."

"That boy's going to have bigger problems than our little operation to deal with if what that girl told me is true."

Chester picked up his cane and limped toward the diner.

"If I find out Candy really is dead, I'll put that boy down myself. Shoot him with a crossbow just like that gator you got in your truck."

Angel waited for the Dodge to speed away and for Chester to disappear into the diner before she stepped out into the clearing. She'd have to take care of the old man now and see to it that Eli dispatched Marie later tonight. Neither the old man nor the tattle-telling girl would live long enough to tell the cops anything.

CHAPTER THIRTY-FOUR

Iris Nguyen kept her head down as she entered the Willow Bay police station. She passed the front desk with a quick wave to Officer Andy Ford, not meeting his eyes or stopping to chat. The rumors about the homicides had begun to circulate already, and she wanted to avoid uncomfortable questions that she couldn't answer.

Any evidence or information about the cases had to be kept strictly confidential as she worked with the WBPD to identify next of kin and evaluate the autopsy findings.

Not really my place to give out gory details in any case.

It was inevitable that news of the vicious murders would be sensationalized in the media for weeks and months to come, but Iris suspected specific details of the crime scene and the mutilation of the bodies would be held back by the police as part of their investigative strategy.

Approaching the door to Nessa's office, she could hear Jankowski on the phone, the frustration in his voice palpable.

"When we're ready to make a statement, Gabby, you'll be the first person I call. Right now, we're knee-deep in a shitstorm. No way I can take time to pull together *talking points* for the fucking mayor."

Iris froze, unsure if she should risk sticking her head into the office. Maybe it would be best if she came back another time. Perhaps when Jankowski wasn't cursing at his ex-wife, who just happened to be Willow Bay's media relations officer.

"Iris? Why are you standing out in the hall?"

Jankowski stood in the doorway wearing a puzzled frown.

"Um, I just came to give you and Nessa an update and I heard...well, I realized you were on the phone."

Wincing at her words, Jankowski waved her inside.

"Sorry you had to hear that. It's just...these homicides have really gotten under my skin."

Iris smiled, but she didn't reply, reminding herself that whatever was bothering the brawny detective wasn't any of her business.

Although it sounds like his ex-wife is the one getting under his skin.

Averting her eyes from Jankowski's empty wedding ring finger, she forced her thoughts back to the reason she'd stopped by, crossing to stand by Nessa's empty desk.

"I take it your partner is out at one of the scenes?"

Jankowski rubbed the stubble on his chin.

"She's running the bridge scene. I'm handling the scene at the gas station. So, I'd say she's probably gone back out to the river."

"Okay, well, I wanted to let her know that Alma has what she needs from me to run the DNA test on Candace Newbury's fetus."

Dropping her eyes to hide sudden tears, Iris pretended to study the pile of files Nessa had on her desk, mortified by the show of weakness.

"Must be pretty rough on you when a little one is involved."

Jankowski's deep voice was uncharacteristically gentle, and Iris felt a soft flutter in her stomach. A warm rush of blood tinged her cheeks pink.

I need to get a social life before I end up embarrassing myself.

Raising her eyes to meet his, Iris nodded.

"Yes, it is," she said simply, her voice small.

She knew she should add something about *just doing her job*, but it wasn't true, and she didn't think Jankowski would buy it anyway. She felt better as they stood in companionable silence for a few minutes, both seemingly lost in their thoughts. Finally, she sighed and stepped toward the door.

"Well, if you see Nessa, let her know I stopped by. If the father of Candace's baby has been arrested for a felony recently, his DNA should be in the database."

Jankowski's face hardened.

"Yeah, and maybe if we find the father, we'll find the killer."

Recoiling at the icy resolve in his voice, Iris felt a shiver of fear for anyone unlucky enough to be deemed a suspect by the intimidating detective. Wesley's face sprang to mind.

"You've spoken to Wesley, haven't you? He's in the clear, right?"

Jankowski shook his head, but his voice softened as he saw the distress on Iris' face.

"We haven't cleared anyone yet, but maybe the DNA results will help us eliminate Wesley from the suspect pool. He's provided a DNA sample, so it'll just be a matter of time."

Jankowski's phone buzzed as Iris considered his words. She watched as he picked up his phone, holding it against his ear with one big hand while he flexed the other hand into a fist. After a terse conversation, he dropped the phone back on his desk.

"That was one of the crime scene techs. They've widened the perimeter around the bridge. Even brought in dogs who've followed a scent into the woods."

Iris waited with wide eyes, hoping for more information. Maybe even some good news.

"But they've lost the trail in the wetlands. Said we need to bring in a search team familiar with swampy terrain."

"So, what are you going to do?

Jankowski shook his head in defeat, banging his fist on the table. Iris jumped, instinctively taking a step back, unsettled by the sheer physical force of his frustration.

"Can you call in a favor from the state or the feds?" Iris asked in a reasonable voice. "Surely they'd want to help."

"I guess, but I doubt they'll be able to get a search team here and ready to go today, and who knows how far the perp will have run by tomorrow. In the meantime, the tracks will be a lot harder to follow."

"What about local search and rescue options?" Iris suggested, not used to giving up on a problem before she'd found a solution. "There's gotta be someone the WBPD can call on if a child goes missing in the woods or there's some kind of natural disaster around here."

Jankowski's eyes lit up, and he reached for his phone.

"You're a genius, Iris! I know just the man who can help."

CHAPTER THIRTY-FIVE

Nessa arrived back at the station with a pounding headache, the last hour spent shivering by the river, fielding phone calls, and interviewing potential witnesses who had all asked more questions about the scene than they could answer. She'd finally decided she needed a break to grab a cup of coffee and call Jerry. Best to tell him now that she wouldn't be home for dinner. She also wanted to check in with Alma.

Hopefully the DNA results are in, because I have a bad feeling we're running out of time.

Alma was in the WBPD crime lab, standing in front of a shiny machine that looked to Nessa like a bulky desktop printer.

"That your new toy, Alma?"

Alma turned and motioned for Nessa to join her.

"Yep, this is it. This little beauty can produce a DNA profile in about ninety minutes. Then once we have the profile, we can run it through the state and national databases."

She walked over to her computer and tapped on the keyboard.

"Unfortunately getting results back from them can take a little more time." She grinned back at Nessa. "Unless you have friends in high places."

Looking over Alma's shoulder, Nessa couldn't make sense of the numbers and letters she was seeing, but the words, *Partial Match Found*, caught her attention.

"So, you got a match on the DNA from the hair at the Candace Newbury scene?"

"Well, no," Alma said, her voice impatient, "the DNA from the hair on Candace's dress hasn't come back yet, but I did find-"

Before she could explain what she'd found, Andy Ford stuck his head in the door, a red flush suffusing the freckles on his face

"Sorry to interrupt you guys, but Leo Steele is here to see you, Nessa. I told him you were busy on a case, but he's not taking no for an answer."

Andy looked over his shoulder as if he expected Leo to be looming behind him.

"Don't worry, Andy. You just stick him in an interrogation room and tell him I'll be right out."

"Yes, ma'am."

As Andy disappeared down the hall, Nessa turned back to the screen, anxious to hear what Alma had uncovered.

"I submitted the results for the DNA found under Ruth Culvert's fingernails. I haven't gotten results back from the national database yet, but state database results just came back." Alma produced a self-satisfied smile and winked at Nessa. "I have *connections* at the state lab you know."

Nessa didn't bother asking about Alma's connections. She vaguely recalled that Alma had dated one of the state techs she'd met at a forensics conference, but right now she was more interested in the DNA results than Alma's love life.

"The results are a little confusing though. You see, there is a partial match in the database, but it's strange."

"What do you mean by strange?" Nessa asked.

"Well, the DNA profile for the blood underneath Ruth's fingernails is a partial match for a decades-old cold case double homicide up in Tallahassee."

CATCH THE GIRL

Nessa suddenly wished she'd stopped to get that cup of coffee first. Her brain didn't seem to know how to process Alma's words.

"Slow down a minute, Alma," Nessa said. "Just what are you telling me?

"From what I see in the file, a couple named Sally and Kyle Young were killed in their home, and their young child vanished. The DNA profile is a partial match to Sally Young."

Nessa was even more confused.

"So, the perp that killed Ruth may have killed this woman, too?"

Alma shook her head, her thick curls wobbling emphatically.

"No, the perp who killed Ruth is *related* to Sally Young. The profile indicates the perp is her biological child."

Giving Nessa time for her words to sink in, Alma clicked on the *Home* menu and selected *Print*.

"I'm printing out all the information I have so far for you to take with you. And I've already requested a copy of the full file from the Tallahassee archives. It's on its way now I imagine."

The shock of Alma's words, added to her already pounding headache, clouded Nessa's brain. She tried to piece together the information in some kind of logical order.

"The child who went missing almost twenty years ago is the person who killed Candace?"

Alma shrugged, but her big brown eyes were almost as wide as Nessa's baby blues.

"Well, the DNA profile found under Candace's fingernails matches the child. That doesn't necessarily prove murder."

Staring down at the printout, deep in thought, Nessa wondered if the case could get any more complicated.

Two young women have been violently killed and their homicides linked to a decades-old double murder and kidnapping. What'll happened next?

A knock on the doorframe brought her attention back into the room. Andy Ford looked in.

225

"Mr. Steele's getting impatient," Andy said, gulping down a nervous breath, "he says–"

Leo's frustrated face appeared behind Andy, his voice drowning out the young officer's words.

"Nessa, this can't wait. I need to talk to you now."

He stared at Nessa and Alma for a long beat, registering their dazed expressions, then plowed ahead.

"I think I know where you can find a fugitive from Florida's most wanted list. She's a person of interest in an open homicide from 2016 in Pensacola."

Nessa regained her composure enough to hold up a hand.

"Sorry, Leo, but we've got enough homicides right here in Willow Bay to worry about. If you know something about a homicide in Pensacola then we'll need to turn it over to the state. Let them and the local force up there handle it."

Leo ran an impatient hand through his hair as he waited for her to finish. When she had, he spoke in a calmer tone.

"You may change your tune when you find out where the woman is living. You see, she's staying at a commune not too far from where a girl's body was found two days ago. The same commune where your old pal Pete Barker thinks his missing daughter may be staying."

Nessa felt Leo's words like a punch in the gut.

"Taylor's at a commune outside Willow Bay? Is she okay?"

Dropping his eyes, Leo shrugged wearily.

"We don't know for sure that Taylor's there, but there's good reason to think she might be."

"And the woman at the commune? Why would you think she's on the state's most wanted list?"

Leo pulled out his camera and showed Nessa the picture Frankie had taken.

"You recognize anyone in that picture?"

Nessa gasped when she saw the back of the woman with long, dark hair. Lifting her finger to the camera, she touched the image gently.

Taylor, can that really be you after all this time?

Her eyes moved to the woman facing the camera. She tapped the image and looked up at Leo, frowning.

"This is the woman you think is wanted for murder?"

When Leo nodded, she looked back at the photo.

Am I looking at the face of a killer?

The woman didn't look evil or insane. Other than her old-fashioned, homemade dress, she looked like an average woman.

Leo swiped to the next photo, displaying the black and white image in the wanted poster. There was no denying the resemblance.

Alma cleared her throat, reminding Nessa that she had an audience. Andy Ford was still standing in the hall, gaping in at the unfolding scene.

"We're good here, Andy, thanks." Nessa tried to arrange her mouth into a smile. "You can go on back up front."

Once Andy was gone, Nessa turned to Alma and showed her the pictures on Leo's phone. After studying the pictures closely, Alma leaned against her stool and folded her arms over her chest.

"Either it's the same woman or they're twins."

Taking the phone back from Nessa, Leo tapped on the screen.

"I've emailed you both the photos. Now, what are we going to do about them?"

"We've got to go out to that commune right away," Nessa said, already mapping out a plan of action in her head. "But I should at least try to get a warrant first, and that won't be easy at this time of day."

Leo looked at his watch.

"You're probably right. Most of the judges in this town are probably home in front of a fire by now. None of them work past four o'clock anymore."

"Then I'll just have to call them at home. This can't wait. Not if Taylor's in danger."

The image of Pete Barker's sad face brought Nessa's plans to a sudden standstill. She had to let him know she was hoping to get a warrant to search the commune, and that she'd look for Taylor once inside. But she wasn't sure how he'd take the news that a suspected killer may be living at the compound, too.

"We can't tell Barker about this woman until we know more," she said, picking up her phone. "He's worried enough as it is."

First she'd make the call to Barker, then she'd need to update Jankowski.

And I can't forget to call Jerry back and tell him not to bother waiting up.

With the plan she had in mind, it was going to be a very long night.

CHAPTER THIRTY-SIX

Barker kept his eyes on the big gate as he reached for his cell phone. He'd been parked outside the compound for the last thirty minutes hoping to catch someone coming in or out. If luck was on his side he might even see Taylor.

Or the girl that just looks a hell of a lot like Taylor.

Blocking the negative thoughts from his mind, he swiped to answer the incoming call.

"Barker, where are you?"

It was Nessa, and she sounded stressed.

"I'm staking out a commune off Highway 42. I think Taylor may be inside." Barker kept his eyes glued to the gate. "It's called the Congregation of Love, but for some reason they have a guy with a gun guarding the perimeter."

"Please tell me you aren't planning to do anything stupid, like trying to sneak in."

Barker snorted and switched the phone to his other hand so that he could roll down the window. Even with the drop in temperature the car was getting stuffy.

"When have I ever done something stupid? I mean, other than allowing Taylor to run away and not looking for her for over a year." Barker winced at the bitterness he heard in his voice.

Nessa has enough to deal with without me throwing myself a pity party.

"Look, Barker, Leo told me you think Taylor's in that compound, and I just wanted to let you know that I'm going to check it out."

Surprised at her words, Barker held out the phone to stare at it, as if Nessa might be using it to somehow play a trick on him.

"I appreciate that, Nessa, but I know you're busy with those two homicides and I really need to see if Taylor's in there *today*. I can't wait anymore."

"I'm not asking you to wait, Barker. At least not very long. Just give me time to track down a judge and get a warrant and–"

Barker's eyebrows shot up.

"A warrant? How are you going to manage that? Taylor's an adult. Staying at a commune isn't a crime, so what grounds could you have for a warrant?"

There was a pause, and for a minute Barker thought the connection had dropped. Then Nessa responded in the artificially cheerful tone she always used when she was trying to hide something.

"Let me figure that one out, Barker. You just stay away from the compound, and the man with the gun, while I do. I don't want you getting shot."

"What am I supposed to do then, Nessa? Sit here and twiddle my thumbs?" Barker slumped back against the seat. "It seems like dead girls have been turning up every five minutes. I keep thinking Taylor may turn up next."

A black Dodge pickup drove past the compound gate. Barker's pulse quickened, but the driver didn't look over or slow down. He followed the truck's progress in the rearview mirror, then shifted his eyes back to the gate.

"Maybe you can offer Jankowski a hand while I work on the warrant," Nessa suggested. "He's in the woods not too far from where you are, at the gas station where Candace Newbury's body was found. They've found tracks leading into the swamp and are trying to pull together a search party."

"I feel like my whole life has been one big search," Barker muttered, but the idea of stretching out his stiff back and stomping through the woods didn't sound too bad.

"Okay, I'll give you a few hours to see what you can do. But warrant or no warrant, I'm going in that commune tonight."

* * *

Jankowski stood in front of Viper Airboat Rides with both hands on his hips, his lips set in a grim line, disapproval clear on his face. As Barker steered the Prius toward the little wooden building, he looked over at Frankie with a sarcastic smile.

"Guess Detective Jankowski's not too impressed with Hank and Dooley."

"Nobody's impressed with Hank and Dooley," Frankie said, rolling his eyes. "But who else would be dumb enough to let us take their airboat out on the swamp at night?"

Jankowski spotted the blue Prius and waved to Barker. He called over his shoulder to a man leaning against the wooden wall. The man stood, showing off a tall, lanky frame and a red crewcut.

"You gotta be kidding me," Frankie said. "Why'd he bring GI Joe with him?"

"He probably needs all the hands he can get," Barker replied, parking the Prius next to a spindly pine tree. "Why do you think he agreed to bring you along? Besides, Vanzinger's got search and rescue training, unlike your sorry ass."

Tucker Vanzinger lifted a cheerful hand in Barker's direction, then grabbed up a heavy rucksack. The ex-cop owned a truck-stop now, but he still served in the National Guard, and the last time Jankowski had called on him for help, Vanzinger had requisitioned a helicopter to save Nessa and Eden Winthrop from a serial killer's farm in the middle of a hurricane. Finding tracks in a swamp would likely be a piece of cake for the big man.

"Thought you boys weren't coming," Jankowski called out as Barker approached. He lowered his voice. "And when I saw this place I thought maybe you were playing some kind of joke."

Frankie strutted over to the dock, gesturing toward the airboat bobbing up and down in the water.

"What are you talkin' about? This here's the best airboat tour in the preserve...maybe even in the whole county."

Vanzinger raised an eyebrow as he inspected the battered boat.

"It's probably the only one in the county." He didn't look impressed. "Since we're just executing a slow search of the local area she should do the job."

Hank popped up from behind the driver's seat like a backwoods jack-in-the box. He held up the missing life jacket he'd been searching for.

"There ain't nothin' wrong with this boat."

A limp strand of dirty blonde hair fell over his face, hiding one of his eyes. The other eye stared over at Jankowski resentfully.

"She'll get up to sixty or higher if she's in the right mood."

Vanzinger stared at Hank for a long beat, then produced a dazzling smile. He was a Florida native, born in the backwoods, well versed in the unique communication style favored by most country folks. It was one of the reasons why Tucker's Truck Stop was a favorite with the locals as well as the long-distance truckers looking for a friendly chat during their fill-up.

"Well, we sure do appreciate you letting us take this beauty out," Vanzinger drawled. "We'll be sure to bring her back safely."

A frown appeared on Hank's skinny, sunburned face, as if he suspected Vanzinger was making fun of him, but then he shrugged and handed Jankowski the lifejacket he was holding.

"You all have to wear these." It was Hank's turn to put on a wide cheesy smile. "But then you should know that since it's the *law*."

Once Jankowski, Barker and Frankie had climbed into the airboat, lifejackets awkwardly in place, Vanzinger hauled himself up into the elevated driver's seat. He dumped his rucksack on the seat next to him and unzipped it, rummaging around inside.

"Let's search out by the CSL commune first," Barker said, trying to act casual. "It's nearby, it's secluded...it'd be an ideal hiding place for a man on the run."

"Fine by me," Jankowski said. "But we're actually looking for two people. A man and a woman."

The news knocked the wind out of Barker. He hadn't known the police suspected two perps were involved.

Two killers, and one of them is a woman? What the hell...

Pulling out a pile of headsets, Vanzinger distributed one to each man. He slipped a headset over his ears and pointed to the built-in microphone.

"These'll protect your ears and let us hear each other while the propeller's spinning."

He looked down at a slim device on his wrist, then held it up so the men could get a better view.

"GPS navigator, top of the range. It'll track our current position and the exact path we take. We can keep track of where we've been and backtrack as needed."

Jankowski gave him a thumbs up, and Barker looked properly impressed. Frankie rolled his eyes and tried unsuccessfully to cross his arms over his bulky life jacket.

"La-de-da, man, I'm really impressed. Now, can we just get going?" He looked into the surrounding water nervously. "If we sit in one place too long a fucking snake will try to crawl in the boat."

Vanzinger laughed out loud and shook his head.

"Snakes don't crawl, my friend. They slither!"

Before Frankie could respond, Vanzinger flipped a switch, sending the huge propeller spinning, and thrust the stick forward. The boat vibrated beneath them, then slid smoothly out into the water.

Barker adjusted his headphones over his ears and flipped on the microphone. He turned to Jankowski.

"Is this thing working? Can you hear me?"

Jankowski nodded, his eyes scanning the terrain as they moved slowly through the dusky air. The sun was setting somewhere to the west, but the sprawling cypress trees blocked the light. Barker heard a high-pitched whistle, and he looked up to see a massive Osprey nest on top of a withered tree. A bird perched in the nest, spreading its long narrow wings, before soaring into the sky.

"You know, I've been thinking, Barker."

Jankowski's voice crackled through the headset.

"Now that Chief Kramer is gone, we need somebody we can count on to turn the department around. Someone who's been in the trenches. Someone who knows the ropes."

Barker turned to frown at Jankowski, who kept his eyes on the shadowy shoreline.

"What the hell are you talking about, Jankowski? I'm *retired*."

"Come on, Barker. You're too young for retirement. Besides, Willow Bay needs a new chief of police, and the only one I know of going for the job is Marc Ingram." Jankowski wrinkled his nose in distaste. "You'd make a hell of a better chief than Ingram. And who else have we got?"

Anger heated Barker's face as he took in Jankowski's words. He stared over at the detective with narrowed eyes.

"You really are a dumb son of a bitch, you know that?"

Jankowski snapped his head toward Barker, his eyes wide.

"You're mad that I think you'd be the best man for the job?"

"I'm mad because you're too blind to see that, in this case, the best man for the job is *a woman.* The same woman who used to be my partner, and now has the misfortune to be your partner."

Jankowski sat back in his chair, baffled. Then he grinned.

"You know, that kinda makes sense. I'm too hot headed, Ingram's too much of an asshole, and Ortiz is too busy looking at himself in the mirror. Besides, now that I think about it, maybe you are too old."

Vanzinger's voice interrupted their conversation. He was shining a search light into the trees and swamp vegetation.

"See that cluster of mangroves to our left? I see a snake curled up in the lower branches. Everybody keep your hands inside the boat."

A soft groan echoed through the headset, and Barker felt a frantic hand grab onto his arm. He turned to see Frankie's eyes wide with panic. He was pointing a shaky hand toward the dark, thick body of a snake swinging down from the gnarled tree ahead.

"Cottonmouth," Vanzinger said with a laugh. "Venomous, but rarely deadly."

"Calm down, Frankie," Barker snapped. "There's something hiding in this swamp that's much more dangerous than that snake, and we need to find it. Now keep your eyes opened and your mouth shut."

Frankie slumped back in his seat wearing an offended expression, but his eyes remained fixed on the murky water as the boat drew ever closer to their target destination.

CHAPTER THIRTY-SEVEN

Jankowski unhooked his life jacket and pushed it off and onto the floor. He needed to have access to his weapon if something, or someone, sprang out at them from the cover of the woods. The light was rapidly fading, and every shadow seemed to move as he pulled out his Glock, inspected it, then stuck it back into the holster.

"Hey, Tucker, you carrying?"

Vanzinger nodded but didn't look around.

"Yeah, I got a couple crossbows and some AK-47s in my bag."

Frankie stiffened, and even Barker sat up straighter.

"I'm just messin' with you, Jank." Vanzinger chuckled, shifting the stick to navigate around a log in the water. "I just have my personal sidearm. This isn't an official operation, so the Guard wouldn't have let me bring along anything heavier."

Releasing his breath, Jankowski turned to Barker.

"What about you, old man? You got a gun, or maybe a cane, in case we gotta defend ourselves?"

Barker patted the bottom of his life jacket and gave a thumbs up. Looking over at Frankie, who was bundled up in two jackets and a fuzzy hat, Jankowski decided not to ask. They were all safer if Frankie didn't possess a weapon of any kind.

Not that he would use it against any of us intentionally, but Frankie definitely seems the type to be accident prone.

Jankowski's pocket buzzed, and he reached inside to pull his phone out. Alma's text message caused him to bolt upright in his chair. The force of the wind caught his arm unexpectedly, sending it, and his phone, flying up into the air. Grabbing for the little device, Jankowski lurched toward the edge of the boat, then sank to his knees and clutched onto the low side rail.

Slowing the boat, Vanzinger gaped back at Jankowski, who held up his phone with a shaking hand.

"Caught it," he mumbled, climbing back up into his seat. "Just a little accident. No need to worry."

Holding tightly to the phone, he again read Alma's message.

DNA results in. Partial match found in CODIS. Felon Jacob Albright paternal match to Candace's baby. Last address listed off Highway 42.

"Jacob Albright?" Jankowski muttered, not recognizing the name.

"What about Jacob Albright?" Barker's voice was urgent. "Have you found out something about that scumbag?"

The fury in Barker's words surprised Jankowski. For a minute he wondered if he should share the news.

It is confidential information that hasn't been shared with anyone yet. No telling how it could impact the investigation.

Then again, Barker seemed to know Jacob Albright, and may be able to help find him.

"Candace Newbury was pregnant when she was killed," Jankowski said, reluctantly. "And the DNA profile of a felon named Jacob Albright was matched to the unborn baby."

"Holy shit, Barker, you were right!" Frankie yelled. "That guy that owns the compound is a creep."

Barker's face looked frozen in the gloomy air, but his hands clenched into tight fists beside him.

"That bastard's more than just a creep; he's a murder suspect. And he might have my baby girl in his fucking commune."

* * *

They passed by the CSL dock without incident, seeing no one in the deserted garden or groves. Vanzinger navigated the airboat past the far side of the fence and around a bend in the shoreline, then turned off the propeller.

The eerie stillness of the scene was disturbed only by the gentle lapping of the water against the tufts of cordgrass along the shoreline as the men stared at Vanzinger, waiting for orders. He removed his headset and life jacket, then pulled a Glock out of the belt holster he wore under his jacket.

"I kinda got used to my Glock while I was on the force," Vanzinger said when he saw Jankowski checking out his weapon. "Never really looked for anything else."

Jankowski nodded his approval, then gestured at the woods next to them.

"You think it's safe to get out here and scout around? Maybe come up on the commune from the rear and see what we can find?"

Shining the boat's spotlight into the woods past the shore, Vanzinger studied the area, then jumped down from the driver's seat.

"Yeah, it looks like solid ground up that way."

He heaved his rucksack over his shoulder, tapped a finger on his GPS navigator, then pointed to an opening in the trees.

"Okay, let's head that way. Everyone stay together for now."

Frankie followed the men off the boat, then clutched at Barker's arm, his face pale in the rising moonlight.

"What does he mean *for now*? We aren't splitting up, are we? You won't leave me out here on my own, Barker, will you?"

"No one's going to be on their own," Vanzinger said quietly, slipping into the trees. "No one goes anywhere without a buddy."

Nodding emphatically, Frankie scurried after the men.

"You're my buddy, aren't you, Barker? We're buddies, right?"

But Barker didn't reply as they walked single file through the woods. He just stared intently at Jankowski's back, following him deeper into the shadows.

Vanzinger pulled out a slim, aluminum flashlight, keeping the light pointed down at the ground ahead of them.

"You got one of them lights for me?" Frankie called up in a loud whisper. "I could use one of them back here."

Jankowski glared back at Frankie, but the lanky man was too busy swatting at trees and imagined snakes to notice the dirty look.

Pushing aside a swath of palmetto branches, Vanzinger found himself standing in front of a six-foot-high concrete wall. He held up his hand, motioning for the men behind him to stop.

"This is the fence perimeter," he said, shining the light along the length of the wall. "We'll follow it to the edge of the water. See if we can access the compound that way."

Jankowski put a restraining hand on Vanzinger's shoulder.

"We don't have a warrant, Tucker. If we go charging in there I could get in big trouble. And anything we find wouldn't be admissible in court."

Barker pushed his way through a clump of Spanish moss to stand in front of Jankowski.

"So, you don't go in then. You wait out here and keep watch. But the three of us aren't cops, and Tucker's not here in an official military capacity. The most they can do is call the cops on us and accuse us of trespassing."

Jankowski considered Barker's words, then shrugged.

"Okay, let's check it out and see if you can even get in."

Within minutes they were standing at the end of the wall. The tide was low, and the wall ended six feet from the lapping water, revealing a soggy expanse of mud and vegetation.

Placing a tentative foot on the damp ground, Jankowski felt his boot start to sink. He stepped back, struggling to pull his boot out of the sticky mud.

"You guys can try it," Jankowski said, "But I don't know how far you'll get."

"I wouldn't advise it if I were you," a loud voice called out. "Cause you won't be getting too far if this gun has anything to say about it."

A young man with bright red hair and a freckled face stood at the edge of the compound perimeter, a rifle clutched nervously in both hands. The boy had a finger wrapped around the trigger, and Jankowski saw that the barrel of the rifle was shaking.

"Whoa, there now," Jankowski soothed. "We don't want any trouble. I'm with the Willow Bay Police Department, and we're searching the area in relation to a recent homicide."

Keeping the gun trained on Jankowski, the boy shook his head.

"That don't give you the right to come onto private property. You need a warrant to search this place. You got one?"

Barker spoke up before Jankowski could answer.

"I thought this is the Congregation of Supreme Love. So, what's with the weapon? What are you all hiding in here?"

The boy swung the gun toward Barker; everyone except Barker took a big step back.

"We aren't hiding nothin'. We're protecting ourselves. It's our constitutional right to do so, as far as I can remember."

A rustling sound in the bushes behind them caused the boy's finger to tighten on the trigger. Jankowski raised both hands.

"Listen, friend, we aren't here to cause any trouble, but a girl has been murdered. We need to find her killer."

Jankowski saw a flash of worry in the boy's eyes. He inched closer and tried again.

"Has anyone gone missing from your compound lately?"

The boy frowned, but he didn't deny it.

Barker stepped forward, his face earnest.

"I'm looking for my daughter. She's missing, too. I think she might be here. Her name's Taylor Barker. She's about your age-"

A voice called out from the compound.

"Zac? Everything all right out there?"

The boy shuddered, and he stuck the rifle out toward Barker, his hands gripping the metal even tighter.

"You're the man that keeps coming around here bothering us. The one we saw on the highway. I've been warned about you. We knew you'd be back causing more trouble."

Barker didn't seem to notice the boy's agitation, or the gun that was only a few yards away.

"Is my daughter here? I'm not leaving until I find out."

His voice was flat and emotionless, as if he didn't care whether his persistence earned him an answer, or a bullet between the eyes.

"No, your daughter's not here, Mister. No one named Taylor ever stayed here, and we don't know nothin' about her. Now all you get out of here before I have to use this."

"We're going," Jankowski said, pulling on Barker's arm. "We'll continue our search elsewhere. No harm done."

He turned and waited for the other three men to walk into the woods. He felt the barrel of the gun on his back, half expecting the jumpy man to pull the trigger at any minute.

It would sure make Gabby's day to hear that my body's been found dead in a swamp. No doubt she'd love to write up that press release.

The thought of his ex-wife's joy at seeing his dead body was suddenly replaced by the unsettling image of his naked body on a metal gurney in front of Iris Nguyen.

Jankowski let out a sigh of relief as the trees closed behind him, but he knew they'd have to find another way in. Jacob Albright was in that compound, and they had to find out what he was hiding.

CHAPTER THIRTY-EIGHT

The rolling paper rustled in Eli's hand as he took a clump of tobacco from his pouch, sprinkled it onto the thin paper, and began rolling. Fingers shaking, he finally managed to produce a skinny, slightly crooked cigarette. He dug in his pocket for the book of matches he'd gotten from the Little Gator Diner last time he'd made a delivery, ignoring the bloody thumbprint smudged over the grinning alligator on the cover.

Heavy footsteps crunched past the barn, and Eli ducked down just in time. Tobias Putnam was on guard duty at the front gate, and Eli couldn't let the older man know he'd been hiding just inside the door, waiting for a chance to sneak out unseen.

If Jacob finds out I've left the compound, the whole plan will be ruined.

Although Eli wasn't so sure he could go through with the plan anyway. Especially now that Angel had given him his orders. He shook his head, trying to rid his brain of all thoughts about what he'd been ordered to do. He needed a smoke first. But he had to make sure Tobias was far enough away not to detect the acrid smell of the cigarette.

Peering around the doorframe, Eli let his eyes wander over the silent courtyard and up to the main house. Ma Verity's rocker was empty, and the porch had been swept clean. The whole congregation had gone inside for dinner. They'd be gathered in the main dining hall, saying prayers and preparing to eat. His stomach lurched at the thought of food.

Striking a match, Eli held the tiny flame to the tip of his cigarette and inhaled deeply. The smoke filled his throat and lungs, forcing out a raspy cough that he struggled to hold in. A sudden sense of vertigo made him reach for the wall, desperate for something solid to hold on to.

I'll just tell Angel that I can't do it...that I'm too sick.

But deep down he knew he didn't have the guts to face her rage or suffer whatever punishment she would surely send down on him. The slow throb of another headache started in his temple.

I have to do it. It's the only way. It's His will, too.

A sudden scream echoed inside his brain, making him jump and clutch at his head with both hands. The scream grew louder and louder, as if someone was turning up the volume on a stereo.

"No, please, no...."

The sound of his own pleading voice brought Eli crashing back to reality. The screaming had stopped as suddenly as it had started, but the crushing headache remained. Taking a last drag on his cigarette, Eli threw the butt down and ground it under his heel in the dirt.

He needed to leave now, before it was too late, but Angel's words played again in his head, tormenting him.

"Sister Marie is a liar, Eli. I heard her plotting against us with my own ears and He has made his will known to me."

The terrible pleasure in her voice had sent a shiver down his spine.

"Your obedience will earn you a place in heaven at His table, while Sister Marie will disappear into the lake of fire and brimstone reserved for liars."

Eli wasn't sure about heaven or hell, but he was very sure that Angel would have her way in the end. She always did. And Marie would be leaving the commune soon. Once she got past the gate she would head over to the diner, where she would continue to plot against him and the rest of the congregation. At least, that's what Angel had foreseen in her vision. And her visions were never wrong.

The scurrying whisper of feet on the gravel outside his hiding place, and the scent of soap and rosewater drifting in on the cold breeze, alerted Eli that Marie was nearby.

No need to follow too closely. I can easily get there before she does.

Creeping out into the night, Eli stayed close to the barn, holding his rifle down by his side, trying to blend in with the dusky air. His heart beat a painful rhythm in his chest, and his lungs felt scorched and heavy, making it hard for him to take a full breath.

Is this what it feels like to suffer and burn?

Anger mixed with fear as he strained his eyes, trying to make his way through the darkness ahead. It was too risky to use a flashlight or lantern yet. He needed to get past the gate, get out in the woods first, so that no one in the commune, and no one on the highway, would see the light.

Ignoring the mounting pain in his head and chest, Eli scurried toward the concrete fence. The sight of the produce crates stacked up against the wall made his heart drop. He had hoped that for once Angel would be wrong, and that Marie wouldn't have to die. But the crates told the true story.

Marie used these to get out. She's a liar. An enemy of the congregation.

Stepping on the first crate, his foot wobbled, and he had to stop and lean against the fence. A woman's voice spoke behind him. He jerked his head around, holding in the scream that threatened, but no one was there. The night was still empty.

"Hello?" The whispered word trembled in the air. "Who's there?"

Was Angel out there, waiting to see if he followed through on her orders? Had his questions caused her to doubt him?

"Why do we have to kill Marie? She's innocent, and...I like her."

His words had enflamed Angel's wrath, igniting a feverish response.

Innocent? She's no more innocent than Sister Candace or Sister Ruth. They're all whores, betrayers, and liars, yet you still try to defend them. Have you forgotten they're trying to destroy what Father Jed built?

Just the mention of Father Jed made him long for the past, back when he'd first arrived at the CSL compound. From that very first day, the old preacher had shown Eli the true meaning of family, quoting his favorite bible verse in a deep, gentle voice.

"Whoever does the will of My Father who is in heaven, he is My brother and sister and mother."

The simply spoken words had been the foundation on which the congregation had been built. But then Father Jed had been taken from them all. His sudden death had left everyone in the congregation reeling. Ma Verity and Jacob had been hit the hardest, of course, but the congregation was a family, and that meant everyone behind the compound walls had suffered the loss of their spiritual father.

Why did Father Jed have to die?

The question he'd asked himself a million times still had no answer as Eli made his way through the icy black night toward the flickering lights of the diner.

CHAPTER THIRTY-NINE

Marie dropped lightly to the ground, moving away from the wall and into the frigid shadows of the woods. She felt strange dressed in the casual pants, t-shirt and tennis shoes she'd been wearing when she'd arrived at the commune almost two years before. They'd been tucked away in her bottom drawer since then, having been replaced by the simple homemade shift dresses the women at the commune preferred to wear.

But as she'd prepared to leave for the diner, she had pulled on her old clothes instinctively, sensing she would never see her little room, or anything in it, again.

Buttoning up the soft red sweater she'd knitted last winter, she took a last look at the compound that had come to feel like home.

But a true home is wherever your family is, and the congregation doesn't feel like my family anymore. It's time to find my way back to where I belong.

Marie froze at the sound of footsteps nearby, waiting for Tobias Putnam to pass. She wondered what would happen if he noticed the crates she'd stacked against the wall. Would he investigate and try to follow her trail? Would he sound the alarm?

Somehow she couldn't image the kindly old man hunting anyone down. He was one of the few people remaining in the compound that she would truly miss. But even so, she couldn't take any chances he might alert Jacob or Eli. Her intuition told her that they wouldn't hesitate to stop her from leaving using any means necessary.

The moon sat high in the winter sky, but the dense trees allowed only a few drops of moonlight to reach the ground. The worn path to the Little Gator Diner was transformed by the darkness, the winding, scenic trail morphing into a shadowy maze of misshapen trees and grasping, gnarled branches that caught on Marie's long hair as she hurried by.

A fist-sized spider scurried up a branch only inches from her face, but she held back her scream. Swallowing hard, she continued forward, knowing there was no going back now. If she walked back through the front gate, the entire congregation would know that she'd left the compound. And there was no way she'd get back over the wall without the crates to help.

Or is there?

She pictured the sprawling branches of the maple tree that hung over the fence near the potting shed.

I might be able to climb the tree and drop back inside the compound without anyone even knowing I was gone.

But before she could lose her nerve and turn back, she found herself standing in a patch of moonlight behind the old diner. A big black Dodge pickup truck was parked near the back door next to Chester's baby blue El Camino.

Who's there with Mr. Gosbey? Has he already called for help?

The Dodge looked vaguely familiar, but then again, lots of people in the area drove similar vehicles. Anyone that didn't want to stick out as a stranger in the community could drive the truck and blend right in.

Approaching the back of the diner, she saw a sliver of light through the door; it had been left slightly ajar.

Maybe Mr. Gosbey left it open for me, so I wouldn't have to wait out here in the dark.

But the hair on the back of Marie's neck stood on end, and she tiptoed closer to the door, trying to listen to any sound from inside the kitchen. At first there was only silence, then she heard a man's voice coming from somewhere further inside the building, perhaps in the front dining room. She couldn't make out the words, only the deep, guttural tones.

Pushing the door open with one trembling hand, Marie slipped into the brightly lit kitchen. She eased the door shut behind her, and tread quietly across the room.

It had been a long time since she'd been in Chester's kitchen, but it still had the same greasy smell she remembered. Trying not to make a sound, she inched her way to the doorway between the kitchen and the back of the counter.

A tall man with an orange cap stood facing the diner's front windows. He had a phone held to his ear with one hand. The other hand was balled into a fist at his side. She could hear him clearly now, and she strained to make sense of his words.

"You gotta clear the whole fucking lot tonight. Take it to the warehouse in Tampa and dump it. This whole damn operation has gone belly up. We need to erase the evidence and lay low."

The man disconnected the call and looked down, shaking his head. Marie's eyes followed his to the floor. Chester Gosbey lay on his back in a thick pool of blood, his arms splayed out beside him, the front of his shirt torn and streaked with lurid red gashes.

Screaming in horror, Marie gaped at the dead man's face, which had twisted and stiffened around bulging, lifeless eyes. The man in the orange cap spun around, eyes wide with fright. Or was that guilt?

Heading spinning, Marie realized she recognized the man. It was Buck Henry, a regular customer at the diner.

He was always a bit of a creep, but still, he was a good tipper.

The surreal gore of the scene made her stomach heave. She held a hand up to her mouth, trying not to retch.

"Come over here, girl, and give me some help."

When she didn't move, he looked up, frowning.

"Wait, this isn't what it looks like."

"It looks like Mr. Gosbey's dead," Marie cried out, backing away. "It looks like you killed him."

Raising both hands in a show of surrender, Buck moved closer, his left boot slipping slightly on the bloody floor. He steadied himself against the counter.

"I came here to talk to Chester, *that's all*."

Buck took another tentative step forward, his hand moving to his belt. Marie's eyes widened when she saw the gun holster.

"Listen, little girl. The old man was dead when I got here."

"Are you the one that killed Candy and Ruth?" Marie demanded, her fear turning to anger. "Did Mr. Gosbey find out? Is that why you killed him?"

Cocking his head, Buck studied Marie with narrowed eyes.

"You're the girl that Chester told me about. You're the one from Jake's little cult that stuck your nose into our business. You caused this whole mess."

"It's not a cult....and I don't know anything about-"

But Buck wasn't listening. He charged toward the counter that separated them, jumping toward her with animal quickness.

Marie braced herself for the impact, closing her eyes and lowering her head. A loud shot reverberated behind her, and for one terrifying moment she thought Buck's gun must have gone off, and that she'd been shot. But she was still on her feet, and she felt no pain.

Opening her eyes, she saw Buck slumped over the counter facedown; blood seeped from a hole in his forehead, then dripped to the floor. The room was quiet except for the *splat, splat, splat* of the blood hitting the floor.

"I couldn't let him hurt you."

Eli's voice sounded far away to her aching ears.

Can a gunshot burst your eardrums?

Looking slowly over her shoulder, Marie saw Eli standing in the kitchen doorway, his rifle clutched in his hands, his eyes bloodshot and cloudy.

"Eli? What are you doing here?"

The words seemed so trite, given the situation, that Marie was tempted to laugh. But then she saw the crazed look in Eli's eyes. Somehow that look told her he hadn't come to save her, and he hadn't shot Buck in self-defense.

"I'm here to save the congregation...to do her bidding."

"*Her* bidding? *Who's* bidding? Eli, who sent you here?"

Ignoring her questions, Eli raised the gun with stiff, clumsy arms, pointed the barrel toward Marie, and wrapped his finger around the trigger. Closing his eyes, he tightened his finger.

"Wait, Eli, please don't do this.'

Something, perhaps the desperation in her voice, made him open his eyes and look at her. She could see that his pupils were constricted, and his skin was red and feverish, despite the chill of the unheated building.

"Something's wrong with you, Eli. You're sick. You need help."

Shaking his head, Eli struggled to catch a breath. He coughed violently, his face turning red.

"Nothing's wrong with me, Sister Marie."

His voice faltered, and he coughed again before continuing in a raspy croak.

"You're the liar. You're the one that plotted against the congregation. If you hadn't given them the paper, they wouldn't have left, and they wouldn't be dead."

"Who's dead, Eli?"

But Marie already knew who Eli must be talking about. Ruth and Candy were dead, and Eli had killed them.

"The whore and the betrayer,' Eli mumbled, rubbing at his red-rimmed eyes. "Jezebel and Judas."

The rifle slumped in Eli's hand, and his head sagged to the side.

Waiting to see if Eli had fallen asleep, or perhaps passed out, Marie stayed still, quieting her breath, not daring to breathe too loudly for fear of waking him.

After several minutes of silence, Marie slowly took a step to the side, knowing she'd have to circle around Eli to get to the kitchen and out the back door. Two more steps and she was in the kitchen doorway. Before she could step through, a pair of bright lights flooded in through the front window, lighting up the diner.

Eli jerked awake with a start, staring at the headlights in bewildered awe, as if an alien spaceship had just landed in the parking lot.

The headlights belonged to a white Expedition that Marie had never seen before. Not knowing if the SUV belonged to friend or foe, she raced through the kitchen to the back door. Tripping over the doorstep, she fell to the ground next to Buck's black pickup, before jumping back to her feet.

As she looked over her shoulder, Eli burst through the door, rifle in hand.

"Come back here, Sister Marie. I want to...to help you."

Eli's plea faded into a raspy sob behind her. He coughed again, then called out into the night, his voice thick with regret.

"I can't let you go back to Jacob. That would ruin everything."

As Eli began to stumble toward her, Marie turned and ran for the cover of the trees.

CHAPTER FORTY

Leo leaned forward in the passenger seat of Nessa's Charger, finding it impossible to sit back and relax as they sped along Highway 42 toward the CSL compound. They'd spent the last excruciating hour trying to track down a judge and get a search warrant. Only after Leo had called Judge Eldredge personally and made an impassioned argument, along with several ominous statements about the pending judicial elections, had Nessa been able to obtain the needed document.

She was still fuming as they neared the address on the warrant.

"After everything Kramer and Reinhardt did, this town *still* runs on the good old boy network. It's outrageous."

Keeping his eyes on the road ahead, Leo didn't bother to deny it. The same group of old men had been running Willow Bay as long as he could remember, and Judge Eldredge was definitely a card-carrying member of the club.

"Judge Eldredge is bound to retire soon," Leo offered in a distracted voice, his mind already moving to the confrontation that lay ahead. "So, maybe we'll finally get a woman on the bench in Willow Bay."

Nessa raised a doubtful eyebrow but let the matter drop.

"Let's just be glad we got the search warrant so we can find out if Taylor's at the compound," Leo said. "Barker deserves to know."

"Yeah, I can't imagine what he's been doing through," Nessa murmured, slowing down as she looked for the turnoff. "I don't know what I'd do if one of my boys ran off and never came back. I mean, how do you live with something like that?"

Shrugging his broad shoulders, Leo looked over at Nessa. Her face was grim in the glow of the dashboard lights.

"It's amazing what people can endure if they have to. I didn't think I'd make it after my mother's murder, and my father's conviction. Then when my father died, I thought I'd never be happy again. But somehow, in spite of everything, you just...go on."

"I guess there's usually not much choice," Nessa admitted. "But for Barker's sake I hope Taylor's here, and I hope she's okay."

The Charger pulled up to the big gate and Nessa turned to Leo.

"I should really wait for Jankowski to back me up when I serve this." She studied the walls of the compound. "Or maybe call on one of the uniforms to come out here?"

Leo raised both of his eyebrows and crossed his arms over his broad chest.

"Don't tell me you're going to back out on me now, not after everything I've done to get here."

He watched the indecision play across Nessa's face.

"Come on, Jankowski's off in the woods hunting down a killer, and the boys you've got in uniform are greener than I am."

When she still didn't speak, he sighed.

"Okay, how about you swear me in as a deputy?"

This statement got Nessa's attention. She drew in a deep breath, then let out a reluctant laugh.

"You are entertaining if nothing else, *Deputy Steele*."

Leo grinned at her and put his hand on the door handle.

"Okay, forget the ceremony. But let's do this before I lose my nerve, and before they realize why we're here."

253

Zipping up her windbreaker, Nessa opened the door and stepped out into the frigid night, exhaling delicate puffs of silvery air. She put one hand on her holster, as if assuring herself that the big Glock was still there, then pulled out a thin flashlight and switched it on. Raising her other hand, she gave a thumbs up and signaled for Leo to follow her up to the gate.

Leo reached the driveway just as Nessa pushed the little buzzer on the security panel.

"I don't hear anything," Nessa said, pushing the buzzer again. "You think it works?"

Footsteps sounded from inside the gate before Leo could respond. He instinctively stepped in front of Nessa as the gate swung open, ready to confront whoever might appear, prepared to defend himself and Nessa if needed.

I talked Nessa into coming here. It's only fair I go in first.

But Nessa slipped around him, one hand shining the flashlight straight ahead as the other reached into her pocket and pulled out the warrant.

Holding the warrant out in front of her like a sword, she greeted the big man that answered with a curt nod.

"I'm Detective Ainsley with the Willow Bay Police Department. I have a search warrant for this property."

Nessa tried to shine the flashlight past the man's massive frame, but he blocked the view, his face a wide mask of confusion. Leo saw that he cradled an old rifle in his left arm.

"Are you the property owner, Jacob Albright?"

"No, ma'am, I'm not." The man's voice was warm, almost friendly. "I'm an elder of the congregation, Tobias Putnam."

Nessa looked down at the man's leather shoes.

"Putnam?"

Nodding, the man stepped back and waved them into the courtyard, lowering the gun to his side.

"I need you to put your weapon down, Mr. Putnam."

When the man hesitated, Nessa took a stepped forward, but she didn't reach to pull her own gun.

"Now, Mr. Putnam. Lay it over by the wall there out of the way."

Tobias nodded and bent to lean the rifle against the wall.

"It's not loaded," he said, a flush creeping over his plump cheeks. "Jacob insisted we all carry them when we're on guard duty, but I didn't want anyone accidentally getting shot."

Leo eyed the man's work pants, lumberjack shirt, and well-worn coat. They were the clothes of a simple man who was used to a long day's work; they reminded Leo of his father.

"Where is Jacob Albright?" Nessa asked, her voice tense now.

"He's in the main house," Tobias answered, pointing back toward the two-story building behind him. "But he's not gonna be very happy to see you. Maybe I should let him know you're here first."

Leo thought he saw movement in the shadows of the big barn that sat across from the main house. Had someone slipped inside?

A commotion on the front porch drew his attention. An old woman shuffled out, her dress hanging loosely on her thin frame, her hair a disheveled tangle around her shoulders.

"Mrs. Albright?" Nessa called. "Are you Verity Albright?"

The woman frowned and squinted toward Nessa. She seemed to think about the question, then nodded.

"Yes, ma'am, I'm Verity Albright. Who are you?"

"I'm a detective with the Willow Bay Police Department, and I have a warrant to search your property."

The woman lowered herself into a rocking chair without responding. Tobias Putnam hurried up the stairs.

"Ma, these folks are asking to see Jacob. They want to look around the compound."

"I wondered when ya'll would show up." Ma Verity began to rock slowly back and forth. "It's about time."

Nessa followed Tobias up the steps to the porch. Leo trailed after them, his eyes scanning the barn and the fields beyond.

"Is there something we should know then, Ms. Albright?"

Leo thought he heard a touch of sympathy behind Nessa's words. The old woman closed her eyes and lifted her face toward the sky, her mouth curling into a wide smile as she rocked.

"You should know there's evil here."

Ma Verity opened her eyes and stared at Leo.

"But my Jed protects me. He watches over me and Jacob."

Tobias cleared his throat and looked over at Leo with an embarrassed smile.

"Jed...Father Jed...he was her husband, but he passed away over a year ago. It's been hard on her." Tobias gave Ma Verity a fond look. "She gets a little confused sometimes."

Nessa nodded her understanding, but continued to stand in front of the rocker, eyes on Ma Verity's face.

"Why do you think there's evil around here, Ms. Albright? Has something scared you?" Nessa stepped closer, keeping her voice quiet. "Have you seen someone doing something? Something evil?"

"Why, the angel told me, of course." Ma Verity's eyes took on a defiant gleam. "Nobody believes me, but I've heard her. She speaks to me. She told me that my Jed is coming back to me. That he'll protect me from the evil that's invaded the congregation."

Leo put a hand on Nessa's shoulder, then pointed to the window behind the porch. A group of women stared out, their faces pale and scared behind the frosty panes.

"We'd better get on with the search, Nessa. If Jacob isn't here, we'll have to carry on without him."

"Oh, my boy's here all right," Ma Verity said, still rocking. "You all can go on in. He'll be up in his room with his wife."

Nessa glanced back at Tobias; he only shrugged. The big man obviously wasn't going to offer any objections to them going inside.

But Leo still felt vulnerable as Nessa stepped to the door and turned the knob. Jacob Albright was a convicted felon, and something told Leo he wouldn't take their arrival as placidly as Tobias Putnam had.

A petite woman with dark hair and nervous green eyes stood just inside the hall. When Nessa moved into the room, she called out in a sharp voice.

"Tobias, what's going on? Who are these people?"

"They're from the police, honey," Tobias called back from the porch. "They say they've got a warrant to search the whole place."

The woman's stunned expression hardened into outrage. She rounded on Leo.

"What could you possibly be looking for in this commune? We're law-abiding citizens who just want to be left alone. Has that become a crime?"

"Priscilla!" Tobias raised his voice as he stepped into the hall behind Leo. "These folks are just here to do their job. Let's let them do it and go."

Huffing indignantly, Priscilla crossed her arms over her chest and stared at Nessa suspiciously.

"What exactly are you expecting to find?"

"We're investigating the homicides of two women who we have reason to believe lived here: Candace Newbury and Ruth Culvert. We're also looking for a missing woman named Taylor Barker."

Priscilla gaped at Nessa, then shook her head in disbelief. Leo heard a deep voice beside him cry out.

"God Lord, no!"

Tobias grabbed Leo's arm, his big hand twisting Leo to face him.

"Sister Ruth and Sister Candace? They're dead?"

His face was stricken, his mouth trembling with emotion.

"It was bad enough when we thought they'd run away." He swiped at his eyes with the back of a big, weathered hand. "But dead? Why would anyone want to hurt those young girls?"

"That's what we need to find out, Mr. Putnam."

At the use of his name, Leo saw Nessa's eyes drop to the older man's shoes again. Then she cleared her throat and looked over her shoulder at the crowd of people that had started gathering in the hall.

"I need everyone to stay together, and I'd like you to all wait in one room and wait to be questioned." She turned to Tobias. "Is there a room where you all can go?"

Tobias nodded numbly, waving the congregation down the hall.

"Yes, ma'am. There's a meeting room where we hold services. We can all fit in there for now."

Priscilla Putnam didn't budge. She still appeared to be in shock over the news about Ruth and Candace.

"My daughter," she said suddenly. "Naomi's upstairs. She hasn't been feeling well. I brought her some tea..."

The little woman suddenly bolted for the stairs, her feet pounding toward the second floor. Nessa hesitated, then hurried up after her, calling over her shoulder to Leo.

"I've got this. You just make sure everyone's secured in the meeting room."

He watched Nessa disappear into the shadows above, then followed the crowd as they moved down the hall. As he reached the meeting room, a high-pitched scream echoed down the stairs.

"Don't let anyone leave this room," he yelled to Tobias, before racing away and mounting the stairs two at a time.

A light shown from a door at the end of the hall. Muffled cries were coming from the room. Leo suddenly wished he'd brought his own gun along. But it was still securely locked in the glovebox of his BMW back in the parking garage. Slipping down the hall, he peered into the room, heart hammering against his chest.

Priscilla Putnam knelt next to a clawfoot bathtub; her upper body was halfway submerged in the water as she clung to the limp body of the girl floating in the water.

"My baby," she cried, her voice raw. "My little Naomi."

Nessa bent to pull Priscilla away, but the distraught woman resisted, too upset to listen to Nessa's pleas.

"Help me, Leo," Nessa urged, her feet slipping on the water that covered the slippery floor. "We've got...to try...to resuscitate her."

Rushing to Nessa's side, Leo wrapped his arms around Priscilla and dragged her back from the edge of the tub. He held her writhing body firmly against him as Nessa grabbed the lifeless woman in the tub under both arms and heaved her up and over the side.

Ignoring the protests from Priscilla, Nessa maneuvered Naomi onto her back and listened for breathing while checking for a pulse.

"She's still got a weak pulse, but I can't feel her breathing," Nessa cried out, turning panicked eyes to Leo. "I'm gonna try mouth-to-mouth."

Priscilla grew still in Leo's arms as the words sunk in.

"She's still...alive?"

Nessa nodded, tilting Naomi's head back, pushing her long, wet tangle of hair out of the way. She swirled a finger around the girl's slack mouth, then bent her head and puffed in a deep breath.

Raising her head, Nessa counted slowly, then puffed again.

By this time Leo had released his grip on Priscilla and they were both watching Nessa with hopeful eyes.

Pausing to listen again, Nessa closed her eyes and sighed in relief.

"I think...she's breathing."

Face flushed and sweaty, Nessa placed a gentle hand on the slippery skin above Naomi's heart and listened again beside her mouth. After a long, tense beat, she gave a weary thumbs up.

"Yep, she's breathing."

Priscilla released a low groan and slid across the floor to her daughter. She cradled the girl's head on her lap and looked up at Leo.

"We don't have a phone here." Her voice wavered. "Can you...can you call an ambulance?"

Taking his cell phone out of his pocket, Leo dialed 911. Priscilla's eyes stayed on him as he explained the situation to the operator and gave them directions to the compound.

When he hung up, he saw Nessa inspecting the room, her eyes searching for something. Leo raised an eyebrow at her and cocked his head, not sure what she was hoping to find.

Maybe she suspects it was an overdose? Or maybe it wasn't an accident?

The possibility of suicide crossed his mind as he watched Nessa pick up a cup of tea on a table near the tub. She raised the cup to her nose and sniffed, recoiling quickly.

"I thought I tasted something bitter on her lips," Nessa said, looking down at Priscilla. "What is this?"

"It's the angel's tea we use to calm our nerves." Priscilla stared up with a dazed expression. "It's a special blend. We grow the herbs in the–"

Naomi whimpered, then called out.

"Ma? Is that you, Ma?"

"I'm here, baby. Mama is here."

But Naomi just shook her head, her voice a scared croak.

"Ma...no, please...Ma..."

Leo turned around to see Tobias Putnam standing in the doorway, his face pale and sagging with worry.

"Is she...is she gonna be okay?"

Nessa, her clothes wet and clinging to her, crossed the room and put a damp hand on Tobias' arm.

"She's breathing on her own for now, and we've called an ambulance. You wait with them here while we try to find Jacob."

A look of guilt flashed into the older man's eyes.

"He was in his office. I didn't know, I swear." He swallowed hard, then pointed to the window. "He ran out when I was coming up the stairs. I think he's...leaving."

Leo slid to the window and stared out into the dark. A figure was wrenching on the door of the delivery truck parked in the courtyard. Leo turned questioning eyes to Tobias, who held up a ring of keys.

"But Brother Jacob won't be going anywhere in the CSL truck. I made sure to lock that up tight and secure the keys as part of my guard duty."

Spinning back to the window, Leo pushed it open and leaned out into the cold night.

"Jacob Albright! Stop right where you are and put your hands up."

Nessa appeared beside him, her gun in her hand, pointing toward the open window. But the shadowy figure had already hefted a large carryall over his shoulder and was running toward the open gate.

Knowing it would be useless to call out again, Leo and Nessa ran toward the stairs, pounding down at top speed. As they flew out of the front door, Leo noticed that the congregation had gathered on the porch, their faces shocked and scared.

He hesitated, eyes scanning over each face, hoping to see Taylor, fearing that he'd see the face of the woman in the wanted poster; none of the faces looked familiar.

"Come on, Leo, he's getting away," Nessa called, halfway across the courtyard.

Pushing Ma Verity's empty rocker to the side, Leo jumped off the porch and followed Nessa out into the dark night beyond the gate.

CHAPTER FORTY-ONE

E den gripped the steering wheel in frustration, not ready to give up and admit she was lost. Her cell reception had grown progressively weaker as she'd driven further and further away from Willow Bay, and eventually her map app had frozen completely, leaving her to find her way to the Little Gator Diner on her own.

After another ten minutes of tense driving, she saw the glow of a neon sign and pulled off the highway and into a small parking lot. The sign flickered off, plunging the building into momentary darkness, before flaring on again, revealing the alligator's wide grin.

"Well, here we are," she said, turning to prod Nathan, who had fallen asleep during the long drive. "Should I park in the front?"

She drove closer to the front of the building, looking up just as the Expedition's headlights flashed through the darkened windows of the diner, illuminating the interior like a well-lit stage.

The slumped figure of a man was visible behind a long counter. As Eden watched, he jerked his head up and stared out at her. She could see at once that he held a long rifle in his hands.

"Nathan, do you see that? That man has a gun, and..."

But Eden's words trailed off as she watched the man spin around. She caught a glimpse of a small, pale face behind the man, before he disappeared through the doorway into what Eden assumed was the kitchen. She kept her eyes on the now empty diner.

"There's a girl in there...she looked scared."

Duke lifted his head and blinked up at Eden as she impulsively stepped on the gas and steered the big SUV around the diner toward the back lot.

"What are you doing, Eden?" Nathan yelled, holding on to the grab bar for dear life.

"I'm trying to see where that man is going."

Reaching the edge of the asphalt, Eden hesitated for a split second, then accelerated forward, bouncing onto the expanse of dirt and gravel that led to the rear of the diner. Two vehicles were parked beside the back door. The door was wide open, swaying back and forth in the icy breeze.

"Over there!"

Nathan pointed toward a dense cluster of trees lit up by the Expedition's headlights. A woman in dark pants and a red sweater ran toward the woods, her long, dark hair fluttering behind her. The man from the diner ran after her, rifle in hand, his white-blonde hair shining in the dark like a halo around his head.

"Come back. I don't want to hurt you!"

Eden heard the man's desperate yell just as the woman vanish behind a massive cypress tree. She watched him stumble forward, almost fall, then regain his balance and charge into the dark woods after the fleeing woman.

Wrenching open the car door, Eden stepped down onto the gravel. The cold air surrounded her, quickly seeping through the blouse and pants she wore.

I knew I should have brought my coat, but at least it's stopped raining.

She looked back at Nathan, who had unfastened his seatbelt and was already reaching for the door handle.

"I've got to try to help her." Eden ignored the crush of fear in her chest. "I'm going to go inside and see if there's anything I can use as a weapon. You stay here and protect Duke."

"Wait, Eden, don't–"

But Eden had already hurried through the open door. The kitchen lights were on, and she saw right away that the room was empty. She looked around for something to use to defend herself. Something that could help her protect the young woman in the woods.

A rack of knives sat on the kitchen counter, but she hesitated, not wanting to use a weapon that might end up inflicting a fatal wound. If she could find a heavy stick, or something she could use as a club, perhaps she could sneak up on the man and knock his gun away. He had seemed to be on the small side, and she thought he looked confused and disoriented.

Maybe a well-timed blow will be enough to disarm him.

As she stood looking around the room, she became aware of a sickly-sweet, coppery smell. It seemed to be coming from the dining room. She crept toward the doorway, peering into the dim room beyond. The smell was growing stronger and Eden held her hand to her mouth, resisting the urge to gag, as she realized what it was.

It's the smell of blood. The stench of death.

She looked out into the diner, her eyes falling on the two bodies just as Nathan spoke behind her.

"What's that smell?"

Jumping at his sudden words, Eden pointed wordlessly toward the dining room, struggling to catch her breath. Her throat had constricted, making it impossible to breath, and her chest felt heavy.

"Holy shit!"

Nathan turned away from the gory sight, his face pale. He looked over at Eden, suspecting at once that she was in the early stages of a panic attack. Eden stared back at him, desperate to stop the spinning in her head. She sank to the tile floor and lowered her head between her knees, forcing herself to inhale a long, slow breath, then exhale even more slowly. After a minute of deep breathing, Eden raised her head and looked at Nathan.

"I'm all right. I just got a little dizzy. But I need to go after the...the girl. We need to at least try to help her."

Shaking his head in disbelief, Nathan knelt beside Eden and grabbed her cold hands in his.

"You can't do this to yourself anymore, Eden."

His voice sounded infinitely weary.

"It's too dangerous. It's too much. Think of the kids. Think of Duke. Hell, maybe even think of me once in a while."

Nathan ran a shaky hand through his hair.

"What would any of us do if you get yourself killed?"

Pushing his hands away, Eden got to her feet. She looked down at Nathan, who was still kneeling on the greasy tiled floor.

"I let my sister *die*, Nathan. And I promised myself I'd do whatever it takes to stop another woman from suffering her fate."

Eden wiped at her nose, resisting the urge to sniffle.

"If you can't understand that...if you won't accept that, then you can't accept *me*."

Walking to the back door, Eden spoke without turning around.

"Please, Nathan, if you want to help, watch out for Duke. Don't let anything happen to him while I'm gone."

* * *

The moon provided enough light for Eden to make her way toward the edge of the woods where she'd seen the girl and the man enter, but after she'd stepped under the blanket of sprawling trees, their branches heavy with Spanish moss, she found herself in total darkness.

Reaching into her pocket, she pulled out her cell phone. The small words *No Reception* at the top of the screen sent a shiver along her already freezing spine. Forcing herself to remain calm, she put a finger on the phone's display and swiped up, then tapped on the flashlight icon.

A bright beam shone onto the ground in front of her, revealing a muddy path. Several sets of footprints were clearly visible.

All I have to do is follow the footprints. Once I find the girl, I can figure out how to save her.

Moving swiftly though the trees, she kept her eyes open for a fallen branch that she could use as a club when needed. She'd been waking no more than five minutes when she heard the sound of someone approaching. Stepping off the path, she huddled under a sable palm, fumbling with her phone to turn off the flashlight.

As she waited in the dark, she listened to the footsteps coming closer. Her ears strained to hear, and she realized that there was another sound coming from behind her: the soft, dangerous rattle of a snake.

Reacting instinctively, Eden leapt back onto the path, determined to get away from the terrible rattling. She flew down the path in the dark, colliding roughly with the solid figure of a tall man, who cursed and stumbled backwards, weighted down by an enormous carryall.

The collision had knocked both Eden and the man's flashlight to the ground, and as Eden jumped back to her feet, she saw the man's face as he scrambled for the flashlight.

"Who the hell are you?" he demanded, grabbing Eden's arm. "And what the fuck are you doing out here in the dark?"

Gasping at the viciousness of the man's words, and the iron grip he had on her arm, Eden fought to get away. Her eyes dropped to the big carryall. The massive bag had landed on the sharp edge of splintered branch, and one of the seams had ripped open, revealing a pile of handguns packed in between thick bags of white powder.

"What's...that?" Eden asked numbly, her mind whirring as she realized what she was seeing.

The man gripped her arm even tighter, drawing her closer to him, his clenched teeth only inches from her face. He pulled a little handgun from his waistband, waving in front of her eyes.

"Now, I asked you a question. Who the hell are you?"

Holding back the scream that hovered in her throat, she tried to think of Duke and Nathan waiting for her in the car. If she screamed they may come and try to help her. And if either of them ended up getting hurt, it would be all her fault.

No, this is my fight. It's up to me to figure out what to do.

As Eden opened her mouth to speak, a scream shattered the nearby sky. The big man whirled around, startled, and Eden took the opportunity to slip out of his grasp. She'd gotten only a few yards away when she heard the gun explode behind her and felt the bullet zip past her shoulder.

Skidding to a sudden stop, Eden legs threatened to buckle underneath her. She braced for the next shot, shivering in the cold, overcome with fear. Suddenly the man's arm was around her throat, tightening, pulling her back against his rock-hard chest.

"You're not going anywhere, lady," the man growled. "You see, I may need a hostage to get me out of this, and you'll do just fine."

CHAPTER FORTY-TWO

Jankowski looked over his shoulder; Barker had once again fallen behind. The ex-detective had been dragging ever since their little search party had retreated from the compound wall with a rifle trained on their backs. They'd walked over a mile since then, searching for tracks leading to or from the gas station where Candace Newbury's body had been found, finally stumbling onto a dirt path that showed signs of recent use.

"You okay, old man?" Jankowski called back, moving aside so that Vanzinger could examine the trail.

"Yeah, I'm doing...really...great." Barker bent over and put his hands on his knees. "Just need to take a little breather."

Vanzinger pointed his flashlight down toward the dirt path and motioned to Jankowski.

"You see these footprints?"

He crouched down, pointing a long finger at several imprints in the crusted mud.

"These are from two different people. Maybe a man and a woman. And look here..."

Vanzinger moved the beam of the flashlight closer to the path, focusing on a spattering of rusty drops in the dirt.

"Looks like blood to me."

Jankowski squatted beside Vanzinger and studied the footprints. He immediately recognized the imprint pattern from the gas station crime scene, as well as the scene outside the Mercy Harbor shelter where Ruth Culvert had been abducted.

"The techs found prints like these at both scenes," Jankowski told Vanzinger. "They think they're from some kind of custom-made shoes."

Looking back to make sure Barker was still on his feet, Jankowski noticed Frankie hovering beside the older man, one spindly hand gripping Barker's upper arm in support.

Maybe Frankie isn't a total waste of space after all.

As Jankowski turned back to Vanzinger, a high-pitched scream echoed through the trees, causing every hair on his head to stand up straight.

"That's Taylor!" Barker yelled. "That's my daughter screaming."

Barker's face was deathly pale in the moonlight, his eyes bright and glassy. Turning in the direction of the scream, he charged into the underbrush without another word.

Starring after Barker in stunned silence, Frankie turned to Jankowski with wide eyes.

"Where the fuck does he think he's going?"

Jankowski moved toward Frankie, calling out as he ran.

"Barker, wait!"

But his words were drowned out by a deafening gunshot. Spinning toward Vanzinger, Jankowski expected to see his ex-partner sprawled on the ground, but Vanzinger was still crouching by the path, his hand already taking the gun from his holster.

"This way," Vanzinger hissed at Jankowski, keeping hunched over as he began moving further down the path. "Follow me."

Jankowski looked back at Frankie, who was still standing frozen in fear on the path, then back at Vanzinger's retreating form, knowing he only had seconds to decide what to do.

"Go find, Barker," he called to Frankie, gesturing toward the trees. "Find him and meet us back here."

Not waiting to see if Frankie would follow orders, Jankowski turned and raced after Vanzinger, fumbling for his flashlight and his Glock as he went.

* * *

Vanzinger lifted a finger to his lips, signaling for Jankowski to stay quiet, before holding two fingers in front of his eyes, gesturing for Jankowski to survey the clearing ahead.

Crawling over a clump of cordgrass, Jankowski felt his right knee sink into a puddle of muddy water. He continued along the uneven ground, staying hidden behind tree trunks and overgrown bushes, until he was able to see what Vanzinger was pointing to.

A man stood upright in the middle of a small clearing. His left arm was looped tightly around the neck of a tall, blonde woman; he held a gun to the woman's temple with his right hand.

Jankowski held back a gasp as he recognized Eden Winthrop.

"If I loosen my grip, you better not try to run again." The man waved the gun in front of Eden's face for emphasis. "Next time I promise you, I won't miss."

Lowering his arm, the man pushed Eden forward, training his gun on her as he moved toward a big carryall that had split open on the ground. He used his free hand to pick up a small, black handgun that had fallen into the dirt and shoved it back into the bag.

Jankowski glanced at Vanzinger, wondering if he had seen the pile of guns and bags of white powder in the carryall. From the gleam in Vanzinger's eyes, Jankowski assumed he had.

"Okay, we're gonna head over that way toward the old diner," the man said, pointing down the path with his gun. "I can get a car there. We'll be over the county line before anyone knows we're gone."

Eden shook her head, her face twisting in panic.

"I don't think we should go that way. There's-"

"Shut up!" the man shouted, pointing the gun closer to her face. "Don't you tell me what to do!"

Rage ignited in Jankowski's chest as Eden recoiled from the gun.

Only a total piece of crap treats a woman like that.

He waited for the man to turn back to the carryall, holding up his hand so Vanzinger could see his fingers as he counted down.

Three, two, one...

As the man reached for his bag, Jankowski and Vanzinger burst out of the undergrowth, guns pointing at his startled face.

"Police!" shouted Jankowski. "Drop your weapon, now!"

The lightweight Walther fell to the ground as the man tripped backward over his carryall, landing in an icy puddle of murky water. A tiny green tree frog jumped across his chest, then splashed out into marshland beyond the trees.

"Keep your hands where we can see them."

Jankowski kept his gun trained on the man while Vanzinger turned to Eden with worried eyes.

"Are you okay, Ms. Winthrop?"

Jankowski wasn't surprised that Vanzinger remembered Eden, but he was impressed at how calmly the guardsman had reacted to seeing her again. It had been only a few months since he'd been called out to rescue her the first time.

"How...how did you find me?" Eden stammered, confusion and relief competing in her green eyes.

"Let's just say we got lucky," Jankowski offered, glad that Eden appeared to be unharmed.

Stooping to pick up the Walther, Vanzinger flipped the safety lever, removed the magazine, and inspected the chamber. He dropped the unloaded gun into the carryall before turning to the man on the ground.

"Stand up and keep your hands high."

The man stood and raised his hands, his Adam's apple bobbing in his throat as he kept his eyes on the barrel of Jankowski's Glock. Vanzinger patted him down, stopping at his pants pocket, pulling out a thin wallet.

Opening the wallet, Vanzinger pulled out a driver's license.

"Jacob Albright. That you?"

The man didn't speak, but his jaw tightened, and his eyes dropped to the ground. Vanzinger held up the license for Jankowski to see.

"Sure looks like him in this picture," Vanzinger said.

Jankowski stared at the license, then at the man. Could this really be the scumbag whose DNA profile had been a match to Candace Newbury's unborn baby?

Feeling the rage ignite again in the pit of his stomach, Jankowski stepped closer to Jacob, pointing the Glock straight ahead, keeping it leveled at his chest.

"You like hurting women, Jacob? Is that it?"

Jacob frowned, then shook his head.

"You got the wrong man, *officer*. I never hurt anybody. I'm just tryin' to run a business here."

"Is that why you spent five years in the state pen?" Jankowski snarled. "Because you never hurt anybody?"

Jacob narrowed his eyes, looking closer at Jankowski.

"How'd you know about my record? What is this, some kind of setup? You trying to pin something on me that I didn't do?"

Shaking his head in disgust, Jankowski looked Jacob straight in the eyes.

"Your DNA tells the whole story. It tells me you got Candace Newbury pregnant, then decided that was inconvenient. So, you killed her. That sound about right?"

Eden gasped from behind Jankowski.

"Are you saying *he's* the one that killed Ruth's friend? Did he kill Ruth Culvert, too?"

Jankowski didn't respond. He watched Jacob's eyes widen in shock as Eden's words sunk in.

"Candy and Ruth are *dead*?"

The blood drained from Jacob's face as the realization that he was a murder suspect rolled through him.

"I didn't kill anyone," he sputtered, looking to Vanzinger, then to Jankowski, before turning his eyes toward Eden.

Charging past Jankowski, Eden pointed an accusing finger at Jacob, her face flushed red with emotion.

"Why did you kill Ruth? Why'd you hang her from the bridge? What did she ever do to you?"

Jankowski reached out to pull Eden back, but it was too late. Jacob grabbed her and twisted her around so that she faced Jankowski's Glock. He wrapped a thick arm around her neck and dragged her back toward the woods, using her as a shield.

"If either of you move I'll snap her-"

But Jacob didn't get a chance to finish his sentence. A heavy cane appeared out of the dark, whooshing through the air, connecting with Jacob's head. Jankowski watched in surprise as Jacob crumbled to the ground unconscious. Seconds later a blonde man in a well-tailored coat stepped out from behind a thick, moss-covered tree trunk. He threw the cane down on the ground at Jankowski's feet.

"Well, I guess that stopped him."

Holding a shaking hand to her throat, Eden looked at the man.

"I thought I told you to stay in the car, Nathan."

"Well then I'm glad I don't take my orders from you anymore," Nathan replied with a weak smile. "Besides, Duke was worried. He wanted to check on you."

At the sound of his name, Duke bounded out through the trees, his golden coat splattered with mud, but his tail wagging.

Observing the happy reunion with worried eyes, Jankowski watched as Nathan pulled off his coat and wrapped it around Eden's quivering shoulders. He turned to Vanzinger, who was kneeling beside Jacob, inspecting his head injury and checking his vital signs.

"He's out cold," Vanzinger said, "but he'll make it."

Jankowski looked back into the woods, wondering if Barker was okay, and if he and Frankie had found the source of the scream. A prickle of unease stirred inside him.

This isn't over yet. Not by a long shot.

Holding Jacob's driver's license in his hand, Jankowski faced Eden and Nathan, his voice somber.

"This man, Jacob Albright, is a suspect in two homicides, and he's also the man Pete Barker thinks may be involved with his daughter's disappearance."

Eden looked up and frowned, pulling Duke closer to her in the chilly night air, her body tense as Jankowski continued.

"Barker and his friend, Frankie Dawson, are back there in the woods. They heard a scream and went to investigate."

Vanzinger snapped handcuffs onto Jacob's prostrate body, then hesitated, holding up a hand.

"Listen..."

They stood still, straining to hear the sound that was coming closer in the night.

"It's an ambulance," Eden murmured, cocking her head. "And it's coming from that direction."

Jankowski meet Vanzinger's eyes, nodding in silent agreement.

"We're gonna go see what's going on over there," Jankowski said, holstering his Glock. "See if we can find Barker and Frankie. Try to find out what the ambulance is doing here."

"You mean you're going to leave us out here, with *him?*"

Nathan looked aghast as he surveyed Jacob, still unconscious on the ground. He pulled Eden against him as if to shield her, but she shrugged out from under his arm and put both hands on her hips.

"We're not staying out here on our own, and I'm not going back to that diner. There're two dead bodies back there."

Jankowski's jaw dropped open at the news. The situation was much worse than he'd feared. His mind began to spin with possibilities, and he remembered Barker's pale face, suddenly terrified that something bad had happened to his old friend out in the woods.

"We can't leave them unguarded until we know what's going on," Vanzinger chimed in, looking a bit dazed. "They'll have to stay with us until we find a secured location."

Nodding in resignation, Jankowski checked Jacob's hands one last time. They were tightly locked in the cuffs. He and Vanzinger then dragged the big bag of guns and drugs off the path, concealing it behind a wilting palmetto bush and a few clumps of Spanish moss.

"Okay, let's go find out what the hell's going on."

Vanzinger led the little group in single file formation down the path toward the siren's wail. Jankowski brought up the rear, his unease growing as they advanced deeper and deeper into the woods.

CHAPTER FORTY-THREE

Barker squinted into the darkness ahead, cursing himself for not bringing a flashlight. The trickle of light through the trees revealed an army of deep shadows around him, along with a few delicate patches of moonlight. The only thing that was keeping his feet moving forward was the single scream that had pierced his heart.

He knew without a doubt it was the same high-pitched scream he'd heard whenever he'd sat next to Taylor on a roller coaster; the same scream he'd heard that last time they'd all gone to the beach as a family, when Taylor had sworn she'd seen a shark

I know my Taylor's voice. I know my girl's nearby.

Trying to catch his breath, he felt Frankie shivering heavily beside him. He wasn't sure if Frankie was shaking from the cold night air, or from outright fear, but either way, Barker was glad to know he wasn't alone.

"Look," Frankie whispered, pointing a long finger toward an opening between two enormous maple trees. "Someone's there."

Barker watched as the slim shadow of a girl slipped into the patch of light. She stopped, as if sensing that she was being watched, and looked around, pausing long enough for Barker to see her silhouette.

"Taylor," he tried to call out, but his mouth was dry, and the word came out as a hoarse whisper.

Licking his lips and stepping forward, he opened his mouth to yell, then felt a hand smash across his face, smothering his cry. Struggling against the tight grip, Barker could feel Frankie's heart thudding against his back.

"There's a man with a gun right behind her. Right there..."

The frightened whisper sent a bolt of panic through Barker's body. He ignored the wave of dizziness that threatened to engulf him, and instead shook off Frankie's hand and began inching ahead, straining his eyes to get a better look at the dark figure creeping toward his daughter. A shimmer of light reflected off the metal of the rifle, pinpointing the man's position.

Moving silently forward, Barker tried not to think about anything but reaching the man's hiding spot before he fired the weapon. Keeping his eyes on his target, he didn't see the girl dart into the shadows; all he saw was the man raising the gun and taking aim.

Barker hurdled blindly toward the dark figure, colliding with the man just as he was lowering the rifle. He hadn't taken the shot. Barker rolled off the man, grabbed the gun and wrenched it away. He turned desperate eyes toward the patch of light where Taylor had stood. She was gone.

"Taylor!" Barker shouted, his breath coming in gasps. "Taylor...it's me. It's Daddy."

Pushing himself to his knees, he grabbed onto a tree branch for support, then pulled himself up into a standing position. Frankie ran up beside him, pointing after the blonde man, who had already disappeared into the trees.

"You wanna go after that little shithead?"

Barker tried to speak, but his head was spinning, and his legs had gone all wobbly. He grabbed onto Frankie's arm, wanting to beg him to go after Taylor, but unable to speak. Suddenly, even the tiniest specks of moonlight had disappeared; everything went dark.

* * *

"How long has he been unconscious?"

Nessa's voice sounded close by. Barker smiled, liking the dream.

If only the dream were true.

In the dream he was safe; Nessa had come to save him, and everything would be all right.

"Not long." Frankie sounded worried. "Some jackass with that rifle over there was chasing a girl. Barker thought it was Taylor."

Feeling the glare of a bright light on his face, Barker forced his eyes open, squinting up at the faces peering down at him. For one surreal moment he felt as if he were in his coffin, and the three people above him were paying their respects.

Did I die? Is this what it feels like to be dead?

Nessa smiled at him, moving the flashlight away from his eyes.

"You awake, partner?"

Barker nodded, his mouth dry, but his head was no longer spinning. The image of Taylor's silhouette in the moonlight flashed into his mind. Panic filled his eyes as he struggled to sit up.

"Taylor," he croaked out. "She was here...I saw her."

"Hold on, Barker." Leo reached out to put a restraining hand on his shoulder. "You're in no shape to be running around this swamp chasing anyone."

"Not if you've had another heart attack," Nessa agreed, her eyes bright with tears. "When I saw you laying here, I thought...well, I thought we'd lost you."

Shaking his head, Barker tried to speak, but his throat was too dry, and he began to cough.

"Don't try to talk, Barker," Nessa insisted. "We've got the ambulance crew on their way over. Just rest for now."

Frustrated, Barker cleared his throat, determined to force out the words he needed to say. He grabbed Nessa hand and squeezed.

"Stop wasting time here with me, Nessa. Go find Taylor."

He looked at his ex-partner with pleading, puppy dog eyes.

"Please, just save my girl."

Nessa nodded, then looked up at Leo and Frankie.

"I'm gonna go look for Taylor. You guys stay here with Barker until the paramedics get here."

Raising a hand in protest, Leo shook his head.

"No way I'm letting you go on your own. We use the buddy system out here." Leo smiled down at Barker, then looked up at Nessa. "Frankie can be Barker's buddy, and I'll be yours."

"Just get going," Barker said, moving his eyes toward the clearing where Taylor had been. "Who's that?"

An old woman with long white hair stood on the path. She wore a stained dress and carried a wicker basket over her arm. Frankie gave a low whistle under his breath as Nessa and Leo turned to the woman in surprise.

"Ms. Albright? Did you want to tell us something? Did you see the girl that ran that way?"

The woman nodded, offering a small smile, as if she had a secret.

"Will you show us where she is?" Nessa asked, stepping closer.

Barker didn't like the glassy look in the old woman's eyes, and he didn't like the idea of getting help from anyone related to Jacob Albright.

"How do you know she's telling the truth, Nessa?" Barker called.

Leo looked between Barker and Nessa, then studied the woman.

"And didn't you say one of the killers might be a woman, Nessa?" Leo asked, keeping his voice quiet.

"Oh, I always tell the truth." The woman's smile grew sad. "Just like my dear Jed always told me: the truth will set you free."

Holding back further words of caution, Barker watched Nessa and Leo follow the woman down the path. He stared after them with sunken, worried eyes until they'd disappeared into the shadows.

CHAPTER FORTY-FOUR

Angel waited in the potting shed for Eli's return. He'd been away too long. Something must have gone wrong at the diner. Maybe Marie had escaped, or perhaps the girl had used her wiles on the smitten boy and persuaded him to have mercy. Anger brewed in Angel's chest at the possibility.

After everything I've done for that boy, would Eli really betray me?

She hadn't thought the simple young man would have the nerve to turn against her, but as the minutes ticked past, and he still hadn't returned, she began to have doubts.

Drawing the cover back from the tray of devil's weed, she surveyed the delicate flowers, transfixed as always by the power the pretty plants bestowed on those who knew their secret.

Who wouldn't want to wield the power of life or death? Only sanctimonious old fools, like Father Jed.

Irritated by the thought of the old man, she paced to the window. If Eli didn't come soon, she'd have to go find Marie on her own. Shaking her head, she wondered why she'd let herself count on Eli for something so important in the first place, when she'd known all along he couldn't stay around forever.

He's been helpful all these years, but he does have his limits.

A noise outside the shed made Angel stand still and listen. She made out the scrabbling of hands and feet on the old maple tree beside the wall. Someone was coming over, and they were coming fast. The door to the shed rattled, then opened.

Marie's tall, slim figure filled the open doorway, before slipping inside. The door swung closed behind her, and Angel heard her moving to the far wall. A match flickered in the dark, and the lantern on the wall flamed to life, lighting up the little room.

"So, he betrayed me after all."

Angel's cold words startled Marie. She jumped and spun around in fright, knocking against a watering can, sending it clattering against the wall.

"Sister Judith, you scared the life out of me."

Marie's bright blue eyes shone like sapphires in the lantern light. She glanced down self-consciously at her clothes.

"I guess you're wondering what I'm doing in here and...and why I'm wearing these clothes."

"I know exactly what you're doing, and why," Angel sneered, no longer bothering to hide her contempt. "You're a liar, and a whore."

She raised her hand slowly, displaying the knife, gratified to see the terror that filled the young woman's eyes.

"Are you scared?" Angel taunted, waving the knife slowly back and forth. "Your friends were scared, too. Before I killed them."

"You? You killed Candace and Ruth? But...why?"

Shrugging her wide shoulders dismissively, Angel stepped closer.

"Because they got in my way. They tried to take what I wanted. So, they had to die."

Marie took a step back, her eyes moving around the room, searching for an escape from the ruthless woman in front of her.

"They never did anything to you, Sister Judith," Marie said, her voice quavering. "They...they trusted you."

"They never even knew me," Angel spit out. "They had no idea who they were messing with."

She took another threatening step forward, brandishing the knife.

"I did the congregation a favor by getting rid of them both."

Angel was enjoying the rare chance to brag about everything she'd accomplished. It felt good to finally get the recognition she deserved.

"Candace was nothing but a whore. She seduced Jacob. She tried to destroy him. And then Ruth betrayed us all by helping her run away. Imagine the damage they could have done to Jacob's reputation if I'd let them."

Marie grabbed the lantern off the wall and thrust it toward Angel in a defensive gesture. The firelight danced over her stricken face.

"Is this about Jacob? Did you kill Candy and Ruth for *him*?"

"I did it for me, actually,' Angel admitted, "But Jacob is part of my plan, so I couldn't let your friends ruin everything, now could I?"

Marie's obvious confusion amused Angel, and she laughed as she leaned toward the lantern, blowing out the flame with one big puff of air. Darkness settled over the room, the only light coming from the moon shining through the little window.

"You really don't get it, do you, *little girl*?"

Shaking her head in panic, Marie moved back as far as she could, stopping only when she reached the wooden wall. Angel watched her fade into the shadows with disdain.

This is going to be too easy. Just like all the others.

She held the knife up in the moon's soft glow, admiring its shine.

"This knife is the perfect weapon when there isn't much time. I have to say it dispatched of your little friends quite nicely."

Angel looked back at the tray of devil's weed and waved one arm in an exaggerated flourish over the deadly plants, enjoying the pungent scent that hung in the air.

"But my sweet devil's weed, well, it offers a more subtle end when there's enough time to linger."

She stalked closer to Marie, trembling with the need to feel the power of the knife again, but first wanting the girl to understand how brilliantly her plan had succeeded.

"You see, I've taken care of the last bitch standing in my way. By now Naomi is floating dead in the tub, her tea sweetened with a fatal dose of my lovely devil's weed. Young Jacob is free to marry again."

Even in the dim light Angel could see Marie's eyes widen in shock. Something about the look irritated her.

"You thought you were going to have him, didn't you?" Angel waved the sharp blade next to Marie's throat. "But he needs someone to help him. Someone strong and merciless. Someone like me."

Shadows seemed to move beyond the window, and Angel paced over, looking out into the night, before turning back.

"With all the *distractions* out of the way, Jacob and I can run CSL together, and under my control the free labor...I mean, *the congregation*...will make us a lot of money. It'll be nothing like the pathetic refuge for losers that old Jed built."

"But Father Jed saved you and Eli," Marie cried out. "He let you come live here when you had nowhere else to go. How could you betray him?"

Thrusting her face within inches of Marie, Angel grinned.

"It was easy. The old man was too trusting. All it took was an extra strong cup of my angel tea, and...well...as simple as a heart attack."

As Angel let her head fall back in a full-throated laugh, Marie raised the gardening shears she'd detached from the hook on the wall and swung them in a wild arc.

Ducking just in time, Angel felt the shears swoosh over her head and crash into a support post behind her. Before she could regain her balance, the door to the potting shed burst open, revealing a tall man with thick black hair and angry eyes. A small woman with red curls and a big black gun pushed past him.

"Police! Get your hands up, now!"

The woman flicked on a high beam flashlight, illuminating the little room and the young woman standing against the wall.

"Taylor? Oh, my goodness, honey, is that really you?"

Angel swung her head toward the girl, her eyes narrowed.

"I knew you were a liar, *Sister Marie*. Unlike everyone else, I never bought your innocent *poor little me routine* for a minute."

"I'd shut up right now if I were you," the tall man barked at her, his face hard. "I've recorded enough of what you've said to put you away for a very long time."

Holding up his cell phone, he tapped the screen. Angel heard her own voice coming from the little speaker.

"This knife is the perfect weapon when there isn't much time. I have to say it dispatched of your little friends..."

"Shut it off, Leo," the policewoman snapped, glaring at Angel. "It makes me sick to my stomach to hear that."

Leo tapped the screen again as a shadow stepped into the doorway. Ma Verity stood just outside, staring at Angel with red, watery eyes. She stopped and picked up the gardening shears laying by the door and held them up with trembling hands.

"That's the angel I told you about. The one that talks to me."

Angel stared toward the door, holding back a satisfied smile.

Looks like my savior has arrived.

CHAPTER FORTY-FIVE

E li stood behind Ma Verity, his eyes moving past her, meeting his mother's gaze. He gripped the rifle he'd found by the front gate with trembling hands. He'd known since he was a little boy that it was his duty to obey his mother in all things. She was an angel, as she had often told him. An angel that had given him a new life when his real parents had abandoned him; an angel that gave only death to those she saw in her visions.

A bright light shone in his eyes, intensifying the throbbing in his head as he squinted into the little shed, trying to see who was inside. A man and woman stood by his mother. The woman had a big gun in her hand, but she held it pointing down. Their unfamiliar faces turned to him with angry expressions.

"Nobody move or I'll shoot."

He raised the rifle toward the strangers, but they seemed far away and blurry. Lights flashed before his eyes, and he heard the voice shouting in his head, over and over.

His will be done, Elijah. His will must be done.

Keeping the rifle in front of him, Eli moved past Ma Verity, ignoring the old woman. She wasn't a part of the task set before him.

"You've arrived right on time, Elijah, just as I saw in my vision."

The victorious smile on Angel's lips made Eli's stomach hurt. It meant blood would soon follow.

"Now, you can finish the work that He has given to you."

Eli moved forward into the room. Marie stood by the wall, her blue eyes wet with tears, her whole body shaking with cold and fear.

This is His will, not mine. His will must be done.

The words in his head were growing unbearably loud. He swung the rifle toward Marie. Movement out of the corner of his eye told him the stranger's gun was now trained on him, but he didn't let himself think about that. He just needed to finish the job. Then it would all be over.

Marie's words penetrated the fog that had descended over him.

"Your mother killed Father Jed, Eli. Did you know that?"

He squinted at her, trying to make sense of her words.

"Don't listen to her, son," Angel hissed. "She's a liar. She's lying about this just as she lied about everything else, even her name."

Shaking her head, Marie held Eli's gaze.

"I'm not a liar, Eli. I haven't been honest about my name, but that's because I needed to get away from my old life for a while. I wasn't trying to trick anyone or hurt anyone."

Ma Verity's voice sounded behind him.

"The girl's speaking the truth, Brother Eli. She came seeking refuge, and Jed took her in. Just like he took you in, boy."

Angel scowled at Ma Verity, narrowing her eyes in a way that frightened Eli. He didn't want to have to hurt the old woman, too.

"Ignore the old fool, Eli. She's been touched by evil."

The pain in Eli's head was getting stronger. He felt like it was going to explode. He tried to focus on Marie, but her face was fading in and out. A voice echoed through the little shed. At first Eli thought it was only in his head, but then he realized it was coming from the big man's phone. It was his mother's voice.

"...the old man was too trusting. All it took was an extra strong cup of my angel tea, and...well...as simple as a heart attack..."

The image of Father Jed's worn face hovered in Eli's mind. Could his mother really have killed the old preacher? Had he been named in one of her visions? But if he had, why had Angel lied about it?

If she lied to me about Father Jed's death, what else has she lied about?

The rifle trembled in his hands as the confusion and pain in his head swelled. Something was definitely wrong with him.

Has she done something to me, too? Am I next on Angel's list?

The big man stepped closer to Eli, hands raised beside his head.

"You don't have to do this, Eli. It's obvious you're sick. You haven't been thinking straight. Put the gun down. Let us help you."

Eli turned to Angel, his red-rimmed eyes searching for a sign that she understood why he couldn't do it. That she wouldn't be mad at him if he let the man help him.

Without warning Angel lunged at him, grabbing the rifle with strong hands, seizing it from his grasp.

"If you don't have the guts to do it, then I will."

She swung the rifle toward Marie, her face contorted with hate. The man's arm flew out, knocking the barrel of the rifle toward the ceiling just as Angel pulled the trigger, producing a harmless click.

"The gun...wasn't loaded," the man said in disbelief, as the woman next to him tackled Angel, knocking her to the ground.

"Stop them, Elijah! Don't let them do this to your mother."

But Eli's head was spinning with sickening speed, all sights and sounds around him obliterated by the excruciating pain, as he fell onto the tray of devil's weed with a heavy crash.

* * *

The flashing lights of an ambulance lit up the sky as Eli opened his eyes. He felt as if he'd been hit over the head with a hammer, but the spinning had receded, and he could see more clearly. Trying to sit up, he realized an I.V. had been inserted in his arm. He raised a weak hand to pull it out and found that both arms had been cuffed to the sides of the stretcher.

"Just lay back and relax. You're not going anywhere right now."

The woman standing beside him was petite with red curls. She wore a jacket with the letters WBPD on the back.

"I'm Detective Nessa Ainsley, and I'm placing you under arrest."

Nessa called out to a man standing by the ambulance, which was parked in front of the main house.

"Leo! I'm gonna read him his Miranda right. I'd like a witness."

Eli recognized the dark eyes of the man that had spoken to him in the shed. Had he meant what he'd said about helping him?

Jogging over to stand by Nessa, the man looked down at the I.V. and frowned, before crossing his arms over his chest.

"I hate to be the one to say it, but he doesn't seem to be in any condition to understand his rights, Nessa."

Nessa raised her eyebrows and put her hands on her hips.

"Leo, I thought you'd given up law to become my deputy."

Her words earned a grudging smile from the man as Nessa stared down at Eli and spoke in a clear voice.

"Elijah Dunkel, you have the right to remain silent. If you do say anything, what you say can be used against you in a court of law. You have the right to consult with a lawyer and have that lawyer present during any questioning. If you cannot afford a lawyer, one will be appointed for you if you so desire."

Not waiting for Eli to respond, Nessa walked past him to stand in front of the porch steps. Angel sat stiffly on a straight-backed chair, her hands handcuffed behind her back.

Tobias Putnam, his expression grim, stood guard between Angel and Ma Verity, who was seated in her rocking chair undergoing an examination by a paramedic

"Judith Dunkel, I'm placing you under-"

"My name's not Judith, and I've got nothing to say."

"Well, whoever you are, I'm placing you under arrest on suspicion of first-degree murder, as well as attempted murder."

Ignoring the woman's stoic expression, Nessa proceeded to read Angel her rights, then looked over at Tobias.

"We're real lucky you unloaded the guns so no one would get shot. You might just have saved a life."

A pink flush spread over Tobias' plump face.

"You're the one that saved a life today," Tobias sad, his eyes bright with unshed tears. "My Naomi would be gone if it weren't for you and Mr. Steele."

He glared over at Angel, his mouth trembling with emotion.

"She's pure evil. I never believed in the devil...until now."

Shaking his head, Leo stepped forward, standing in front of the people on the porch as if he were standing in front of a judge and jury.

"From what I've seen this woman isn't an angel or a devil. She's just a cold-hearted killer who preys on good, decent people. And based on Florida's most wanted list, this isn't the first time she's hurt someone."

Eli watched Angel flinch at the words, but she kept her eyes fixed straight ahead.

"No, this is far from the first time, isn't it, Judith?" Nessa asked, joining Leo by the porch. "You've been doing this for many years, haven't you? Were Sally and Kyle Young the first people you killed? Or does it go back even further?"

Jerking her eyes to Nessa, Angel stared at her in stunned silence, before glancing nervously over at Eli.

"You see, Judith, we have DNA from the Young family crime scene. And guess what that DNA tells us?" Nessa walked back toward Eli, her voice softening. "It tells us that your son, Eli, is really *their* son."

Shaking her head, Judith dropped her eyes, refusing to look up.

Memories came flooding back to Eli at the mention of his real parents, Kyle and Sally Young. He'd been only five years old when his nanny, Angel Dunkel, had told him that his parents had left him. That they didn't want him anymore. That she would be his new mother.

"Brandon," Eli said, his voice cracking on the word. "My name isn't Elijah Dunkel. It's Brandon. Brandon Young."

The courtyard grew silent. Then a soft voice spoke up behind him. "Hello, Brandon."

He twisted his head around. Marie stood next to the stretcher, looking down at him with solemn eyes.

"I'm Taylor. Taylor Marie Barker."

He stared at her with haunted eyes, his rage at Angel's betrayal overshadowed by his shame at having taken part in her crimes. Then he dropped his eyes without speaking, knowing there was nothing he could say to make up for everything he'd done.

Can I ask Marie to forgive me when I'll never be able to forgive myself?

But as she turned way, a small part of him was relieved. No matter what happened to him in the future, at least her nightmare was over.

He'd just closed his eyes and allowed himself to relax back against the stretcher, when the front gate burst open. A man with a red crew cut ran into the courtyard, followed by a muscular man in a WBPD jacket that matched Nessa's.

"Where the heck have you been, Jankowski?" Nessa called out.

Jankowski stopped to catch his breath, his eyes taking in the scene around him.

"We caught Jacob Albright out in the woods. He was making a run for it with a bag of drugs and guns."

"So where is he?" Nessa asked, looking over his shoulder.

"Don't worry, he's not going anywhere. We left him tied up out there. Vanzinger can help us find our way back with his GPS navigator once we're good and ready."

"Why in the world would you leave him out there?" Nessa griped, rolling her eyes. "You boys too weak to carry him back?"

Shooting Nessa a dirty look, Jankowski jogged back to the gate and opened it wide, motioning to someone on the other side.

"Hurry up there, you two. We haven't got all night."

A tall blonde woman in an over-sized man's coat staggered through the gate, followed by a blonde man without a coat. A golden retriever trotted in after them, tail wagging at the sight of all the people standing around.

"Eden? What...what happened to you?"

Leo rushed forward, pulling the woman to him in a tight hug. He looked to the blonde man, shivering beside her.

"Nathan? When did you get into town?"

The man laughed wearily and shook his head.

"It's a long story. Once I thaw out, I'll tell you all about it."

"I'd love to sit here chatting, ya'll, but we need to get Barker some help,' Nessa said, raising her voice. "He fainted in the woods and needs someone to bring him back. He's out there with just Frankie Dawson for company."

Taylor gasped, hurrying to Nessa's side.

"My dad's out there? And he's hurt?"

Nessa nodded, biting her lip.

"Sorry, Taylor, I guess I shouldn't have said anything until we'd gotten your father back here safely. I wasn't thinking."

"No, I'm glad you told me," Taylor insisted, grabbing Nessa's arm. "I want my father. I want to go find him before it's too late."

CHAPTER FORTY-SIX

Barker rolled onto his side, drawing his legs up into a fetal position, trying to pull his jacket down far enough to cover his knees. The damp air was bitterly cold, and thin patches of ice had started to spread on the soggy ground around him.

Trying to make Barker more comfortable, Frankie had taken off one of his jackets and stuffed it full of maple leaves and Spanish moss to make a pillow. But the ground was still painfully hard, and Barker's back had started to complain.

"I don't think they're coming back," Frankie muttered, pacing back and forth with the flashlight Vanzinger had left behind, trying to keep warm. "We'll be found here in a few days, frozen stiff, or maybe eaten by snakes.

"Snakes don't eat people, Frankie."

But Barker was beginning to think Frankie might be right. Jankowski and Vanzinger had been gone for over an hour, and they couldn't stay out in the swamp all night without shelter.

"You ever seen that movie, *Anaconda*, Barker?" Frankie shuddered. "I tell you, I'll never look at snakes the same way again."

Smiling in spite of himself, Barker sat up, still lightheaded, but determined to get to his feet.

I just need to rest a few more minutes. Take time to build up my strength.

He closed his eyes, breathing deeply, feeling the cold, crisp air fill his lungs. He tried to ignore Frankie's incessant pacing, tried to meditate the way the doctors had taught him after his heart attack.

Breath in...two, three, four. Breath out...two, three four...

Sudden rustling in the trees, followed by a gasp from Frankie, prompted Barker to open his eyes. He stared at the familiar face in front of him, then blinked, scared he was only dreaming.

"Taylor Marie Barker," he said, his voice weak, "where have you been, young lady? I've been looking everywhere for you."

Taylor dropped to her knees in front of him, taking his hands in hers. He stared at her, drinking in the bright blue eyes.

"You look just like your mother did at your age," he whispered, lifting a finger to wipe a tear from her cheek. "She was beautiful, too."

"I miss her so much, Dad," Taylor said, swallowing hard. "And I've missed *you*. I'm sorry for leaving, and for...everything I said."

Barker tried to smile, struggling to hide any evidence of the scars her long-ago words had left behind.

"I'm sorry, too, honey. For not coming for you sooner, and for not seeing how much you were hurting after your mother..."

The sound of Nessa clearing her throat made Barker look around. He'd been so absorbed in Taylor that he hadn't noticed his ex-partner standing at the edge of the clearing next to Jankowski.

A member of the Willow Bay Fire and Rescue team stood behind them, adjusting a lightweight stretcher that had been mounted on one, sturdy all-terrain wheel. The man pushed the contraption toward Barker, his navy-blue uniform fading into the shadows.

"You aren't really gonna try to put me on that thing, are you?"

The fireman grinned, sizing up Barker's girth.

"I'm gonna try. But first let me get you warmed up and take your vitals. Make sure you're fit for transport."

Digging through a sizable backpack, the fireman pulled out a thermal emergency blanket and wrapped it around Barker's shoulders.

"I've never had to use this before." He sounded impressed. "Usually I'm treating people around here for heat stroke."

After taking Barker's temperature, blood pressure, and pulse, the fireman frowned, studying Barker's sunken eyes.

"Everything seems normal. No arrythmia, your BP's good, even your temperature's on target." He almost sounded disappointed. "When's the last time you had something to eat or drink?"

Barker opened his mouth, then closed it again. He couldn't remember the last time he'd eaten anything. And he hadn't had anything to drink all day.

"I've been busy," he said, a flush of shame spreading across his face as everyone stared down at him. "It's been a few...days."

"Dad!" Taylor's eyes were wide. "Why haven't you been eating?

A rush of anger surfaced at her words.

"I was worried about you, young lady!"

Their eyes met, and for an instant it seemed like they were back where they had started. Like they'd never been apart. Taylor broke into a smile first, and then Barker followed.

Damn, it feels good to see that smile again.

He held out his hand, and she clutched at it, holding on tight.

"We better get you to the hospital," the fireman said after a tactful pause. "Dehydration can be very dangerous."

The fireman looked around and waved over to the detectives.

"Can I get some help?"

Jankowski jogged over and took one of Barker's arms. The fireman grabbed the other arm, and they hoisted Barker to his feet, then lowered him onto the stretcher.

"I feel like such an idiot," Barker moaned as they began to wheel him up the narrow path and into the woods.

He turned to see if Taylor was following after him, fearful of letting her out of his sight. She was right behind him.

"Just be glad it wasn't another heart attack," she said.

Barker raised his eyebrows and peered back at his daughter.

"How do you know about that?"

Nessa popped up beside Taylor.

"Sorry, Barker. You know I have a big mouth."

Barker laughed, happy to be surrounded by his two favorite women in the world. He suddenly felt like a very lucky man.

"Yeah, you do have a big mouth, Nessa. But I think you'd make a great chief of police anyway."

He looked around for Jankowski, who was walking in the rear, trying to keep the stretcher balanced as it jutted over rocks and potholes in the path.

"You think so, too, right, Jankowski?"

The burly detective looked up like a deer in head lights.

"What was that, Barker?"

"I was just saying that you think Nessa should be the next Willow Bay chief of police. Isn't that right?"

Jankowski's mouth curled up into his usual wiseass grin.

"Sure, you've got my vote, Nessa. If that counts for anything. I've always wanted a hotheaded redhead for a boss."

Falling into a comfortable silence, the little group continued down the dark path. Barker sensed the night was growing steadily colder as they neared the compound.

"I don't want to go back in there, Dad," Taylor said, her voice suddenly small, and scared. "Not now."

Nessa gestured toward the waiting ambulance.

"You go on to the hospital with your father, Taylor. Although we will need to get a full statement from you tomorrow."

Looking past the gate, Barker could see Vanzinger standing by a police cruiser. Jacob Albright was sitting in the backseat, a large white bandage wrapped around his head.

"Yes, you come with me, honey," Barker agreed as they loaded the stretcher into the ambulance. "After all this time, there's no way I'm ever going to let you go again."

Taylor smiled, squeezing her father's hand, and as the ambulance drove away from the compound, she didn't look back.

CHAPTER FORTY-SEVEN

The Sacred Hearts Cemetery slumbered under a bright winter sun, offering the illusion of warmth to the chilly day. Taylor stood by the gravestone in a faux fur jacket, her long, dark hair falling loose down her back. Oversized sunglasses hid her red, puffy eyes and the tears that streaked her cheeks. She sniffled as she read the words etched into the marble: Caroline Ferguson Barker, Beloved Wife and Mother.

"I can't believe it's been three years."

She sniffled again as her father bent to place the bouquet of calla lilies in the headstone's bronze vase. He paused, brushing a few dead leaves away, then stood up and put an arm around her shoulders.

"Time doesn't stand still for any of us, honey," Barker said, squeezing her tighter. "That's why we have to make the most of the time we have."

Pulling a tissue out of his pocket, Barker tucked it into her hand.

"Stop sniffling, and blow."

Taylor smiled, her father's unsolicited advice no longer a source of irritation. She was glad to have someone looking out for her again.

"I just feel so guilty," Taylor admitted, her voice thick. "Like I failed her somehow. I know it doesn't make sense, but..."

"Remember what Reggie told you during your session?"

Barker paused, then sighed when Taylor didn't answer.

"She said whatever you feel is okay. Your feelings don't have to make sense or meet anyone's standard of normal. Remember?"

Removing her sunglasses, Taylor wiped at her eyes.

"I know. I guess I'm just beginning to understand *how* I'm feeling. I still don't know *why*, but at least it's a start."

Taylor had been home for the past two weeks, settling back into the house on Bullrun Road where she'd grown up. She'd been surprised at how easy it was to fall into the same old routines, and how much it hurt for her to think of her father living there alone for the past two years.

I've got a long way to go, and a lot of making up to do.

Looking down at the calla lilies, she knew coming to see her mother's grave was a first step. The counselor she'd been seeing, Reggie Horn, had suggested she wait until she felt ready, and Taylor had put it off for the last two weeks, scared of what she would feel.

But Christmas Eve had seemed like the perfect day for a visit. Her mother had loved Christmas, and she'd always gone out of her way to make it special for Taylor. So now Taylor knew it was her turn to make an effort. Stooping next to the marble headstone, Taylor laid a little knitted stocking next to the vase.

"I put a note to Santa in there."

Taylor suddenly felt silly for making the childish gesture.

"That's real nice, honey. Your mother would have liked that. She always loved the little cards and notes you made for her."

Barker kept his eyes on the stocking, a sad smile appearing.

"You know, she kept them all. They're still in her memory box in our closet. I thought you'd want them once you came home."

The simple words triggered the recurring sense of shame and remorse she'd been struggling with ever since she'd gotten home.

"I'm sorry, Dad. I never meant to hurt you."

The words were a lie; they both knew it. She had meant to hurt him when she'd left. She'd wanted him, and everyone else, to hurt just as badly as she had been hurting. But she knew now that she'd been terribly wrong, and that she'd run away from the one person who could help lessen the pain.

"You lost your mother. You were grieving. Grief makes us all do things we normally would never do."

Barker ran a hand through his hair, and Taylor noticed with a pang how gray he'd gotten, sure that his worry for her had played a role.

"I can't say I haven't suffered, but I do understand, and I'm so glad you've come home."

"Me, too,' Taylor admitted. "I was happy at CSL for a while, but it never truly felt like home. Especially after Father Jed was gone."

Thinking of Father Jed was still hard, but she'd gone to visit Ma Verity and the others at the commune the day before, and she felt as if she'd somehow made peace with her time there.

"It was great to see Ma Verity looking so much better. She seemed like her old self again."

Taylor glanced at Barker, feeling awkward, but knowing she couldn't treat her time away as a secret that she couldn't talk about, or as something to be ashamed of. Reggie had told her that openly communicating with her father would help them rebuild their trust in each other.

"She's taking on the leadership role, and has asked Tobias Putnam to help her, now that Jacob's back in jail." Taylor sighed, then lifted her chin. "I think they're going to be okay."

"I'm glad to hear that, honey. It sounds like they were good to you before...well, before things started going wrong."

Sliding her sunglasses back on so that Barker wouldn't see the fresh batch of tears, Taylor took his hand in hers and squeezed.

As if sensing her mood, Barker squeezed back, then let go.

"I'm gonna leave you to have a few minutes alone," he said, clearing his throat. "I saw Dr. Horn's car when we pulled in, and I'm thinking maybe I'll go say hello."

Taylor blinked, then raised her eyebrows.

"Since when have you started calling Reggie, *Dr. Horn*?"

Barker blushed, looking around awkwardly, as if he wanted to avoid the conversation.

"Well, she is your doctor, isn't she? So, what's the problem?"

Shrugging, Taylor shook her head.

"It isn't a problem, Dad. You go say hi. Tell her hi from me, too."

As Barker turned to go, Taylor called after him.

"But remember, Reggie's my doctor, not yours, so don't start telling her all your problems."

Barker didn't respond to her playful comment. He just started walking toward the front gate where a small figure sat on a bench under a weeping willow.

Taylor watched him walk away, glad that his stride was strong and his back straight. The doctors at the hospital had determined his collapse in the woods had been caused by dehydration and exhaustion. His heart was doing fine. They'd administered intravenous fluids, keeping him in overnight for observation, and he'd seemed okay since then.

But Taylor's pleasure at her father's good health dimmed as she remembered that not everyone who had survived that terrible night was doing okay. During her recent visit to the commune, she'd noticed that Naomi had become withdrawn and depressed. When she'd asked Priscilla about it, the normally reserved woman had dissolved into tears, confiding that the doctor told Naomi that the toxic tea had likely caused her miscarriage.

"Naomi was already devastated to have lost the baby, but to know that Judith made it happen, and that it could have been prevented..."

Priscilla's voice had trailed off. She was all too aware of the futility of all the thoughts of *"what if"* and *"if only"* her daughter kept playing over and over in her mind. Nothing any of them did now could change the heartache caused by the devil's weed.

The devil's weed, or datura stramonium, as they'd come to know as its official name, had devastated them all. Only after suffering through weeks of withdrawal had Naomi and the rest of the congregation been able to return to some semblance of normal again.

Taylor suddenly wondered if Eli had known about the devil's weed, and if he'd recovered from the effects of the poisonous plant.

No, his name's not Eli, it's Brandon. And he's a victim, too.

She knew her father still blamed Brandon Young for his role in the killings, but Taylor wasn't so sure that was fair. The young man had been kidnapped as a small child, brainwashed by a psychopath his whole life, and then given a hallucinogenic poison that made him hear voices. What chance did he have to resist or refuse to go along with her murderous plans?

Just the thought of a young boy growing up without a loving mother made Taylor's eyes fill with tears again. She looked down at her mother's name etched in marble and realized how lucky she'd been to have had such a wonderful mother.

Who did Brandon Young have for a mother? A heartless serial killer.

The image of Judith Dunkel's evil face hovered in her mind, and Taylor closed her eyes and shook her head.

No, I won't let her hurt me anymore. I hope they lock her up someplace where she can never hurt anyone again. I hope they throw away the key.

Opening her eyes, Taylor's gaze fell on the little red stocking. She didn't need to take out the note to remember what she'd written. As she stood in the cold air above her mother's grave, her voice was quiet, but strong.

"You might be wondering what's in that note, which, by the way, is in a stocking that *I knitted*. Yep, I actually learned how to make something, Mom."

Taylor swallowed hard on the word, then cleared her throat.

"Well, maybe it's silly, but I asked Santa to make me and dad happy again. I mean, that's what you always wanted for us, so I figured it's the only thing I have left to give you."

She stood still, breathing in the cold air, surprised that she didn't feel sad or lonely anymore. She wasn't sure what she was feeling, but that was okay. She was okay.

"Merry Christmas, Mom. I think I'm gonna go find dad now."

She looked up to a sky that was as blue as her mother's eyes and smiled. It was time to go find her father. It was time to go home.

CHAPTER FORTY-EIGHT

The lights from the Christmas tree cast a festive glow over the boys' heads as they crawled beneath the prickly branches to count their presents. Nessa laughed as Cole dragged out a book-sized box and groaned, before stuffing it back under the tree to look for something more exciting.

"I've got more presents than Cole," Cooper shouted, his smile revealing a gap where his front teeth used to be. "I've got six presents and he's only got five."

"You both have the same number of present," Nessa interjected, before an argument could erupt. "Although I'm not sure either of you deserve anything other than a bag of coal."

Balancing a tray of hot chocolate, Jerry shouldered his way through the kitchen door, laughing as he made his way to sofa.

"You say that every year, Nessa, and yet every year you end up buying them more presents than the year before."

Nessa rolled her eyes and crossed her arms over her chest.

"Yeah, well one of these years those two are gonna wake up to a bag of coal and nothin' else." She winked at Jerry. "And I'm gonna tell Santa that's all they deserve, too."

Ignoring her threats, the boys returned to their respective piles, shaking each box vigorously, listening for any noise that might reveal the gift inside. Anything that sounded like clothes or books earned a hearty groan of despair.

Jerry snuggled next to her on the sofa, handing her a cup of the hot cocoa and an iced sugar cookie in the shape of a snowman.

"I thought we were saving these for Santa," she said, biting off the snowman's head. "What if he gets mad and skips the presents?"

Cole rolled his eyes, but Cooper looked concerned. He tilted his head and frowned over at Nessa.

"Do you really think Santa will skip our house, Mama?"

"No, I don't think so, little man," Nessa replied. "He's always come before."

Cooper contemplated her answer, then frowned again.

"But this year I haven't been that good. I threw that baseball through the window, and my room's been a mess."

Holding back a smile, Nessa considered his words.

"Well, everyone makes bad choices sometimes, but they usually get a second chance to set things right."

Cooper nodded and went back to his presents, seemingly happy with her answer. But Jerry was staring at her, one eyebrow raised.

"You've changed your tune," he said in mock confusion. "Lately you've been calling for all heads to roll, and now you're saying everyone deserves a second chance?"

"Not everyone," Nessa clarified, sounding testy. "Not Judith Dunkel, or Angel Dunkel, or whatever her damn name is. She's had all the chances she deserves. That woman's definitely on my naughty list, and if I have anything to say about it, she'll be getting a life sentence for Christmas."

Both Cole and Cooper looked over with wide eyes.

"Ya'll go on into the kitchen and eat your cookies in there."

She waited for the boys to disappear through the door, then turned back to Jerry, her Christmas cheer deflated.

"So, what's your point, Jerry? Why are you trying to annoy me?"

He laughed again, but this time Nessa didn't join in.

"I'm not trying to annoy you, Nessa, but I think you're kidding yourself if you think you're going to magically turn into some kind of hard-nosed cop so that they'll make you the chief."

Incensed by his words, Nessa opened her mouth, then snapped it shut again. She stood up, walked to the front window, and looked out at the street, trying to calm her nerves before she said something she'd regret. She didn't want to ruin anyone's Christmas, especially her own.

"I'm sorry if I'm misunderstanding what's going on, but it just seems like you're conflicted, and you won't talk about it."

Sighing, Nessa walked back to the sofa and sat down. She took another bite of the snowman, followed the bite with a sip of hot chocolate, then slumped against the back of the sofa.

"I am conflicted, Jerry. I can't seem to figure out right from wrong anymore. Or who's good and who's bad."

Her mind spun with the events of the last year, and she tried to block out all the bad memories, all the bad guys, all their dirty deeds.

Only it isn't just the bad guys anymore is it, Nessa? Now there are even bad women going around raising hell.

She looked at Jerry and shrugged.

"A lot has happened lately. I guess it's kinda getting to me. I just keep thinking and thinking."

Jerry reached out and took her hand.

"Thinking about what?"

"Thinking about our boys and how lucky we are that they're home and safe. But then I think about someone like Brandon Young. Someone who was abducted when he was just five years old. That's only a year younger than Cooper for goodness sake."

She tried to swallow but her throat was too dry. She tried sipping her hot chocolate, but that just started her coughing.

"So, what then?" Jerry asked, his eyes curious. "You're feeling sorry for Brandon Young? You think he shouldn't be prosecuted for his role in the murders?"

"I don't know. I just feel like everything's mixed up."

She ran a hand through her red curls, not sure how to say what she wanted to say.

"It's just, one day I'm answering to my chief of police, and the next day I'm arresting the guy. Then two weeks ago I track down a man who's been involved in the brutal murders of two young girls, and today I'm feeling sorry for him."

She stared over at Jerry, shoulders slumping.

"I don't know what's wrong with me. Maybe I'm not made of the right stuff to be in charge. Maybe I'm too soft, maybe-"

"All right, I get it. But I definitely don't agree. You are made of exactly the right stuff to be in charge. The examples you just gave prove that."

"What do you mean?"

Jerry stared at Nessa, all laughter gone, his eyes serious.

"What I mean, is that Willow Bay needs a chief who can see beyond just the black and white of a situation. You're that kind of person. You can see when a person is abusing power, and act to stop it. You can see when someone has been victimized and have mercy. Those are good traits for a leader, Nessa. It isn't weakness that you're describing. It's called decency and fairness. Things that Kramer never had."

Dropping her eyes, Nessa felt a smile threaten.

"You really think I'm chief material?"

"I think you're solid gold, Nessa. The best thing out there."

Pulling Jerry in for a hug, she let the smile spread into a wide grin.

* * *

Cole and Cooper had just finished icing a new batch of Christmas cookies when the doorbell rang. Nessa looked over at Jerry expectantly, but he just shrugged.

"Maybe it's Santa," Cooper bellowed, running into the hall and swinging the front door open. "Oh, it's just *you*."

He shuffled back into the room.

"Mom! It's for you."

Hurrying to the door, Nessa was surprised to see Jankowski leaning against the door frame.

"Sorry to bother you at home, but you weren't answering your phone, and there's something on Channel Ten that I think you're gonna want to see."

"Merry Christmas to you, too, partner." Nessa said, sniffing at the air by the door. "Are you wearing a different cologne?"

A blush started to creep up Jankowski's neck, and he turned away, not answering her question.

"Just turn on your television."

"Wait," Nessa called, holding up the cup of milk she'd just poured. "Come in and have a drink."

Eyeing the milk with amusement, Jankowski shook his head.

"I can't stay. There's...someone waiting for me in the car, and–"

"Are you on a date? Is that why you're wearing all that cologne?" Nessa looked over his shoulder, trying to see into the tinted windows of his Dodge.

Jankowski blocked her view, the blush deepening as she studied his face. He was definitely hiding something. Or someone.

Grabbing her jacket off the hook by the door, Nessa charged past Jankowski, making a beeline for his Charger. As she stepped in front of the car, she met the eyes of the woman sitting in the passenger seat.

Iris Nguyen smiled out at her. She gave Nessa a stiff little wave, then opened the door and climbed out.

"Hi Nessa, how are you tonight?" Iris asked, a nervous smile pasted on her flushed face. "Are your little ones excited about Santa? Have they hung up their stockings yet?"

Putting both hands on her hips, Nessa refused to be distracted.

"Some detective I am. How come I didn't know you were dating my partner, Iris?"

A disgruntled voice sounded behind her.

"Because this is the first date we've had," Jankowski muttered between clenched teeth. "And from the looks of it, you're going to make sure it's the last date we ever have."

Grinning at Iris, Nessa motioned for her to come into the house.

"It's the holidays, you two. Come in. Have a drink and a cookie."

Nessa waited for Jankowski and Iris to troop inside before calling out to Jerry that they had visitors. When Jerry saw Jankowski and Iris, he immediately turned back to get the tray of cookies.

"So, what's the big story you couldn't wait for me to see?"

She switched on the television, clicking through the stations until she found Channel Ten. Her mouth fell open as she saw the headline.

All Charges Dropped Against Accused Assailant, Oscar Hernandez, Amid Allegations of Police Misconduct.

"What the heck happened?" Nessa asked. "When did it happen?"

"Today, during the Hernandez pretrial hearing. His legal counsel discovered that Marc Ingram had never checked the defendant's alibi," Jankowski said. "It seems Ingram also ignored other evidence that would have eliminated Hernandez as a suspect."

Nessa frowned, confused as to why the story was breaking news.

"If they just found this out today, how come Channel Ten jumped on it? I mean, police incompetence always makes for a good story, but a primetime, *we-now-interrupt-your-program*, news report?"

The grim look on Iris' face told Nessa that the medical examiner knew why the story was getting so much attention.

"Another woman was attacked last night," Iris confided. "It was pretty brutal. The crime scene techs found evidence at the scene that linked this new attack to the first one. Same gated community as the last. Same MO and signature."

Nessa gasped as she realized what they were saying.

"And Oscar Hernandez was still in jail last night, right?"

Jankowski nodded, his face hard.

"Yeah, Ingram pushed the judge not to give the guy bail. Said he was a danger to society and a flight risk. Ends up the guy had an airtight alibi for the night of the first attack, but Ingram didn't follow up. Instead of going out and looking for the real perp, he locked up an innocent man."

Nessa grimaced, unable to hide her distress.

"And the real perp attacked someone else."

"That's what it looks like."

Jankowski's eyes widened as he looked over at the television. A slim woman with a shiny bob and a bright-pink bomber jacket was trying to fend off reporters outside the Mayor's office. A stocky reporter with thick glasses stuck a microphone in the woman's face.

"Hey, Gabby, it is true the police planted evidence? Is it-"

Jerry flipped off the television, pointing to Cole and Cooper who stood in the doorway trying to see the screen.

"We've got little eyes and ears here," Jerry said. "And it's Christmas Eve to boot."

Ushering Jankowski and Iris through the door and back to the Charger, Nessa wondered if there was anything she could have done to prevent Ingram from making such a tragic error of judgement.

"I'm going to ask for the chief's job," she told Jankowski without preamble. "I'd made my decision already, and now that Ingram has publicly disgraced the city with this new screw-up, I think the mayor and the city council will be looking for a different candidate."

"That's a great idea." Iris's eyes shone with enthusiasm. "Willow Bay needs someone like you to clean things up."

"I agree, and I'll back you, for sure," Jankowski said. "But I hope you know what you're getting yourself into. Now that the press has gotten a hold of the Hernandez mix-up, you can bet they're going to keep hyping it up to increase ratings."

Nessa nodded, trying not to think of the difficulties ahead.

"I'm not expecting it to be easy, you know." Nessa gestured back toward the house. "But my boys live in this town, and I wanna make it safe for them and all the folks around here. If I don't, who will?"

"I guess you're right," Jankowski said. "At least I hope you are."

After the Charger had pulled away, Nessa saw that Jerry was standing on the porch. She wrapped her arms around his waist and rested her head against his chest, wanting to enjoy a rare moment of quiet before the next storm rolled in.

CHAPTER FORTY-NINE

The courthouse was all but deserted as Leo exited the building and made his way to an empty bench outside. He'd waited as long as he could after the hearing was over for the reporters to give up and go away, but the security guards had finally kicked him out, eager to go home and begin enjoying the holidays.

"You still here, Mr. Steele?"

Oscar Hernandez stood on the sidewalk. After all the excitement of the day, his shirt still appeared to be freshly ironed, and not a hair on his head was out of place. The only sign that he'd been through a traumatic ordeal was the slightly shell-shocked look on his face.

"I had to file the official motion for dismissal," Leo explained, moving over so that Oscar could join him on the bench. "Really just a formality but I wanted to wait for the press to clear out anyway. It's usually easier to stay out of sight until the fervor dies down."

Nodding agreeably, Oscar sat down and took out his phone.

"I told my old lady to wait for me to call." He tapped on the phone and put it to his ear. "I didn't want her and my little boy to be here if things didn't go my way, you know?"

Leo nodded, feeling guilty about the two weeks Oscar had spent in jail while he'd prepared the pretrial motion for dismissal and investigated the little evidence submitted by the district attorney.

"Hi, honey, it's me," Oscar boomed into the phone. "I'm officially a free man again. They even gave my cell phone, wallet, and lucky rabbit foot back."

Oscar thrust a ball of white fur on a key chain toward Leo, laughing when the lawyer recoiled.

"I'm waiting outside the courthouse with Mr. Steele right now if you wanna come pick me up."

Growing quiet, Oscar held the phone to his ear, listening. He nodded a few times, as if the person on the other end of the call could see him, then let out a deep sigh.

"It doesn't matter, baby. I'll find something else." Oscar lowered his voice, turning away. "I was getting tired of that job anyway, you know? We'll be okay."

Leo kept his eyes on a file in his lap until Oscar had ended the call.

"You got plans for Christmas, Mr. Steele?"

Leaning back against the bench, Oscar stretched out his long legs and crossed his arms over his lean chest.

"Not really," Leo admitted. "I've been so wrapped up with...well, with your case, that I didn't make any plans."

"You got kids?"

Leo thought of Hope and Devon, then shook his head.

"No, none of my own. Not yet, anyway."

Tapping on his phone, Oscar thumbed through a few screens, then held the phone toward Leo.

"That's my boy. He just turned two in October."

A little boy in a tiny suit and tie stared back at Leo from the screen. He was a miniature version of his father, right down to the neat hair and lopsided grin.

"He's a handsome boy," Leo said, hesitating, then adding, "and I'm glad you're going to be home to play Santa for him tonight."

"Thanks to you, man."

Oscar looked away, clenching his hands into tight fists on his lap.

"I owe you, Mr. Steele. If there's ever anything you need..."

Leo winced, feeling like a fraud. Knowing that he'd somehow failed the young man beside him.

"I just wish I could have gotten you out on bail, Oscar. I'm sorry I wasn't able to do that. I know what it's cost you."

Anger stirred in Leo's belly at the memory of Marc Ingram's testimony in front of Judge Eldredge, who had presided over the bail hearing. The elderly justice, annoyed that the hearing had been delayed by two days, had clearly bought into Ingram's performance.

Eldredge probably thought Ingram was going to be the next chief of police, which would explain why he'd listened to the whiny little detective.

Shaking his head, Oscar turned to Leo, his voice earnest.

"Don't apologize, Mr. Steele. I'm glad you didn't get me out sooner. If I'd been out of jail last night, I'm sure that Detective Ingram would have tried to pin both those attacks on me." Oscar drew in a shaky breath. "I might have gone down for life!"

"I wouldn't have let it come to that, Oscar," Leo said, but the possibility that Oscar could have been blamed for the second attack wasn't farfetched.

I wouldn't put anything past that weasel Ingram.

The streetlight in front of them flashed on, and Leo realized the sun was setting. He'd have to decide what he was going to do soon.

"There's my ride, man!" Oscar yelled, standing up and waving to a Toyota Camry that was heading in their direction.

Rolling to a stop at the curb, the Camry's driver stuck her head out of the window and squealed. Leo could see a boy's small, excited face in the backseat.

"Merry Christmas, Mr. Steele. I hope Santa's good to you!"

Leo waited until Oscar and his family had disappeared around the corner in the Camry, then stood and began walking toward the parking garage.

He'd done what he could for Oscar Hernandez. Now it was time for him to go home and figure out what to do about his own life

* * *

By the time he steered the BMW into his neighborhood, Leo's stomach was starting to grumble. He'd skipped lunch in his rush to finalize the motion for dismissal, and his breakfast had consisted of a slightly mushy banana and a Venti black coffee from Starbucks.

Distracted by the question of which restaurants might deliver on Christmas Eve, and how quickly they could get to his house, it took Leo a few seconds to register that a familiar blue minivan was parked on his driveway.

What in the world is Pat Monahan doing here on Christmas Eve?

Driving past the van into his garage, Leo could see that the vehicle was empty. He turned off the BMW and hurried into the house, wondering if Pat had decided to go out of town over the holidays and left her van on his driveway for safekeeping.

He detected the delicious aroma of Italian spices as he opened the door and stepped into the kitchen. Pat stood by the oven, an apron over her work clothes and a potholder in one hand.

"You're just in time for dinner." Pat opened the oven door to reveal a bubbling pan of eggplant parmesan. "I hope you're hungry."

"You have no idea, Pat," Leo said, his mouth watering. "Although I'm not sure you and I will be able to finish all that on our own."

Before Pat could respond, Leo heard a flush coming from the bathroom off the hall. He turned to the door just as Frankie Dawson shuffled in and sat down at the kitchen table.

"Hey, Leo. What's up?"

Looking back and forth the between Pat and Frankie, Leo wondered if he'd forgotten making plans with them. Could he really have been that absorbed in the hearing?

"Frankie? Pat? What's going on? What are you doing here?"

Spreading butter onto a tray of crispy garlic rolls, Pat looked over at Leo and rolled her eyes.

"What does it look like we're doing? We're making you a meal to celebrate your big win today."

"My big win?" Leo repeated, still dazed. "You mean, getting Oscar Hernandez's case dismissed?"

Frankie stood up and walked toward the oven, looking at the garlic rolls with hungry eyes.

"Duh! Of course, we mean getting Oscar Hernandez out of jail. It was a bogus charge, and you proved it. That's a pretty big deal. I should know."

Shooing Frankie away from the oven, Pat nodded her agreement.

"Yes, if it wasn't for you, Leo, both Oscar Hernandez and Frankie would still be behind bars for crimes they didn't commit. I'd say that's reason enough to celebrate."

Leo couldn't argue with the logic, but there was something about Pat's behavior that didn't feel celebratory. The expression on her face looked more like pity than admiration.

"Okay, Pat. What's really going on?"

Dropping her eyes, Pat bent over and pulled the heavy tray of pasta out of the oven, sliding it onto the stovetop with a defiant clatter.

"Well, if you must know, I didn't want you to be alone. Not on Christmas Eve." She busied herself with taking out plates and silverware. "It just doesn't seem right."

Leo frowned and took the potholder from her hand.

"Why did you think I was going to be alone?"

Pat sighed and looked over at Frankie, who shrugged.

"Well, Barb told me that she was making dinner for Eden and the kids tonight." She hesitated, biting her lip. "And she said that Eden's ex had come over to eat with them last night, and..."

"Yes?" Leo asked, his voice deadly calm.

"And that he was showing around a ring."

The silence that followed was deafening. Leo stood still, trying to let her implication sink in. Pat winced at the stricken look on his face. She put a soft hand on his arm.

"I just...didn't want you to be alone."

Regaining his composure, Leo turned to Frankie.

"And how did you get involved in this charity event?"

For once Frankie didn't make a joke.

"I stopped by your office to tell you some good news and found Pat all worked up. When she told me why, I thought maybe you'd need a friend tonight. You know, like, to keep you company."

Feeling as if he'd swallowed a stone, and that it had lodged in his chest just above his heart, Leo tried to smile.

"Well, tell me your good news, then."

A pink flush colored Frankie's cheeks, and he dug his hands in his pocket, searching until he found a loose stick of gum. He pulled off the wrapper and shoved it in his mouth, chewing nervously.

"Helps me with the whole no smoking crap," Frankie explained. "And, I should really wait until Barker is with me so that we could tell you together, but he's spending the holidays with Taylor, so..."

Crossing his arms over his chest, Leo leaned against the counter. There was no rushing Frankie, and in any case, he was no longer in a hurry to eat.

"What's Barker got to do with this?" Leo finally asked.

"He's gonna be my new partner."

Frankie beamed at Leo's stunned expression.

"Barker and Dawson Investigations. That's what we're gonna call our business. We figure this town needs a couple of experienced PIs."

Pat laughed as she arranged the eggplant and rolls onto plates and set them on the table.

"Well, it certainly sounds...interesting."

A reluctant smile emerged on Leo's face at the idea of Barker and Frankie riding around like Starsky and Hutch.

"I think it's a great idea, Frankie. I'll be the first one to call on you guys for investigative services once you're up and running."

Frankie stuck half a garlic roll in his mouth, trying to talk and chew at the same time.

"Mates rates for you, Leo."

Sitting down next to Leo, Pat looked over with miserable eyes.

"I shouldn't have told you about Eden...or the ring," she said, pushing her pasta around on the plate. "I should have minded my own business."

Leo shook his head, not wanting to admit he'd lost his appetite.

"You should do what you feel is right. And you wanted to help a friend. Don't feel bad for that. Besides, I knew Nathan was still in town. So, it's not surprising he's going over there for dinner."

"So, why don't you go over there, too?" Frankie asked, his plate almost empty. "Or invite Eden over here?"

The question had been eating at Leo all day: why hadn't he tried to make plans for Christmas with Eden?

Leo shoveled a forkful of pasta into his mouth so that he wouldn't have to respond. It was hard to explain, but something about the last few weeks had planted a seed of doubt that he would be able to make Eden happy. With Nathan in town, doting on her and the kids, and with Leo tied up with the Hernandez case, an uneasy feeling had taken hold, and a terrible idea simmered in his mind like a fever.

Maybe she's better off with Nathan. Maybe he can make her happy.

Leo finished his meal, walked Pat and Frankie to the minivan, then went back into the empty house. He wasn't prepared to see Eden, even if it was Christmas Eve. He wasn't ready to face the truth.

CHAPTER FIFTY

Eden heard footsteps on the stairs and quickly switched the channel, not wanting Hope or Devon to see the news about the Hernandez case, or to learn that an unidentified assailant had attacked another woman in Willow Bay only the night before. She didn't want anything to ruin the warm holiday spirit that seemed to fill the house.

"Can we open a present tonight?" Devon asked, charging into the room, his wide blue eyes hopeful. "Just a little one? Please?"

Before Eden could respond, Hope joined her brother by the tree.

"Mom used to always let us open one present on Christmas Eve."

Recalling Mercy's love of Christmas brought a mist of tears to Eden's eyes. Her sister had adored Santa as a child, and once she'd had children of her own, she had gone all out to make the holiday special for Hope and Devon. Now it was up to Eden to carry on the family tradition.

"Okay, but just one," she agreed, smiling at Devon's shout of joy.

Hope picked up a small box wrapped in silvery paper, then paused.

"Should we wait for Leo to get here before we open these?" she asked, watching Eden's face carefully. "He is coming over, isn't he?"

Nodding cheerfully, Eden tried not to show her underlying worry. *The hearing is over, and Leo won his case. So why hasn't he called yet?*

She'd seen the news like everyone else and had been thrilled that she would finally get to spend some time with Leo now that he'd gotten the charges against Oscar Hernandez dismissed.

"Of course, he'll be here, honey. He's just been busy."

Ripping off the paper around a box of Legos, Devon cheered.

"Cool! Then Leo can help me put this together when he gets here!"

A voice from the kitchen called out, accompanied by the warm scent of something baking in the oven.

"I need a taste tester in here." Barb stuck her head into the room. "Who can make sure these cookies are yummy enough for Santa?"

Devon jumped up and raised his hand, running toward the kitchen at full speed, his Lego set already forgotten on the floor.

"Is everything okay between you and Leo, Aunt Eden?'

Hope's voice was quiet, and Eden got the impression her niece had been waiting for the opportunity to ask the question. She decided the girl was old enough for an honest answer.

"I don't know, honey," she admitted. "I thought Leo would be here by now. Or would have at least called."

She patted the cushion beside her, motioning for Hope to join her on the sofa in front of the fireplace.

"He's been working on an important case these last few weeks, but that's over now. I guess I was kind of expecting him to show up tonight so we can celebrate."

Hope tilted her head and frowned.

"Why don't you just call him and tell him to come over?"

"I guess I thought he might still be busy wrapping things up. I didn't want to bother him."

Eden still felt responsible for getting Leo involved in the hunt for Ruth's killer, which had prompted him to ask for a delay in Oscar Hernandez's bail hearing. When Hernandez had been denied bail a few days later, Leo had been devastated. Since then Eden had tried to give Leo all the space he needed to focus on the case.

But maybe I've given him too much space.

Putting an arm around Hope's shoulder, she pulled her niece closer, wanting to reassure her that everything would be okay. That she and Leo were good. But suddenly, Eden wasn't so sure.

A familiar holiday song drifted over from the television, and Eden looked over to see the opening credits for her favorite Christmas movie, *It's a Wonderful Life.*

She remembered watching the movie with her father and Mercy when she was a little girl. How long ago that had been. But the movie was still a classic.

"I love this movie," she said, reaching for the remote to turn up the sound. "Although your mother always complained about it being in black and white."

Impulsively jumping up, Eden hurried to the kitchen just as Devon was testing another cookie. Duke blinked up from his cozy spot by the door, hoping for an after-dinner walk.

"You two come in here and watch *It's a Wonderful Life* with Hope," she told Barb and Devon. "Duke and I have an errand to run."

* * *

Leo's house on Knightsbridge Drive was dark when Eden's Expedition pulled into his driveway. The other houses in the family neighborhood all seemed to be lit up with strings of Christmas lights, inflatable reindeers, and nativity scenes. A jolly plastic Santa stared at Eden from its position in the yard next door.

"Come on, Duke, let's see if he's home."

Opening the back door to allow the golden retriever to jump down beside her, Eden glanced up at the dark windows with a frown.

Could he still be at the courthouse, or at his office?

She crunched up the gravel walkway, shivering as a gust of frigid wind blew through her hair. As she knocked softly on the front door, she noticed a stack of unopened newspapers on the porch. A few seconds passed, then she heard the soft metallic click of the deadbolt.

"Looks like it's my night for unexpected guests," Leo said, swinging the door open and motioning for her and Duke to come inside. "Pat and Frankie just left a little while ago."

Concerned by the depressed tone of Leo's voice, Eden closed the door behind her, and looked around the empty room. The only light in the room came from the fireplace.

Taking Leo's hands in hers, she looked at him with worried eyes.

"What's wrong, Leo? What's happened?"

She could only assume something had gone terribly wrong for him to look so miserable when he'd just won a dismissal for his client.

Leo pulled his hands away and stalked over to the fireplace, gazing down into the flames. Eden decided to try again.

"I thought you said you were looking forward to spending Christmas with me."

She crossed to where he stood and put a finger under his chin, turning his face to hers, but he dropped his eyes.

"So why are you sitting here in the dark, all alone?"

"I thought it would be easier if I left you and Nathan to enjoy the holidays without me butting in."

Confused by his words, Eden blinked, then shook her head.

"I don't understand. Nathan left Willow Bay this afternoon. He wanted to get home for Christmas morning."

When Leo didn't look up, it began to dawn on her that Leo thought something had been going on between her and Nathan. She wasn't sure if she should feel guilty or offended.

"You don't think there's something going on between me and Nathan, do you?" She stepped closer, wanting to feel his warmth. "Do you, Leo?"

Slowly, Leo shook his head, raising his dark eyes.

"No, I guess I don't," he admitted. "It's just that Nathan's spent so much time with you lately, and I've been so busy, and...well, it doesn't seem fair for you to have to always come second to my practice and my clients."

"So, what are you saying?' Eden asked, her green eyes searching his face. "Are you saying you don't want to be with me anymore?"

"I'm saying that you'll be better off without me."

His soft words broke Eden's heart, and she pulled him to her with a cry of protest, wanting to erase the pain in his eyes.

"I'd be miserable without you," she said, pulling back to look up at him. "And I don't want Nathan or anyone else, but you."

"What about the ring?"

Leo's question hung in the air as Eden stared at him blankly.

"The ring? What ring?"

Sighing, Leo stepped back and ran a hand through his hair.

"The ring that Barb saw Nathan showing off yesterday at your house. She told Pat all about it."

"If she told Pat all about it, she should have mentioned that the ring was for Nathan's new partner. A woman he plans to ask to marry him tomorrow morning when he gets back to San Francisco."

Her words seemed to hit Leo like a slap. He stared at her, stunned.

"You mean he hasn't been trying to get back together with you?"

Eden shook her head, raising her eyebrows.

"And you don't want to get back with him?"

She shook her head again, this time crossing her arms over her chest with a stern look.

"No, Leo. Nathan and I are just friends, and if anything, my time with him has proven to me just how much I want to be with you."

"Even though I'm always at work? Even though I defend people you might not like me defending?"

Eden nodded, a smile spreading over her face at the hopeful look on Leo's handsome face.

"Yep, even then," she said. "I'm proud of you for what you do, Leo. I'm not angry that you spend your time helping other people. And I'm sorry for the way I acted when Ruth was killed. I was upset, and I reacted badly, but that doesn't mean I want you to change."

Relief spread over Leo's face as her words sank in. Eden dug in her purse and pulled out a package wrapped in bright red paper with a big green bow.

"Duke and I got you this present."

Taking the package, Leo pretended to shake it and listen for clues, then slowly unwrapped it to reveal a framed picture of Eden and Duke wearing matching Christmas sweaters.

"To put on your desk, so you won't forget about us when you're working on your next big case."

"It's perfect. Thank you...both of you."

Leo bent to scratch between Duke's ears, then lowered himself onto the rug in front of the fire. Pulling Eden down next to him, he took her hand in his and studied it.

"I'm sure Oscar Hernandez was happy to be released in time for Christmas," Eden said, liking the way the firelight played off his dark eyes. "And you must be relieved, too."

"I am glad for Oscar, and angry about what happened. He seems like a good man, and this whole thing has been hard on him."

Leo's jaw hardened as he spoke.

"And, of course, there's still someone out there that has attacked two women. Based on the reports I've seen, this guy's a real psycho."

The anger in Leo's eyes softened as he looked at Eden.

"I worry about you and Hope, you know. And all the women out there that this sick bastard might target."

Lifting her hand to push back a lock of dark hair from Leo's forehead, Eden tried not to think of the man that even now might be lurking in the dark, searching for his next victim.

"For now...just for tonight...let's not think about any of that, Leo. Let's just be glad that we're together, and that it's Christmas, and-"

"Hold that thought," Leo said, pushing himself up and hurrying out of the room.

Minutes later he was back, kneeling next to her, holding a small, unwrapped box.

"Sorry I didn't have time to wrap this," he said, his eyes suddenly shy. "I wasn't sure this would be the right time. But I hope it is."

A nervous flutter in her chest made her feel slightly breathless as she opened the box. She gasped when she saw the ring inside.

"It was my mother's engagement ring. I know it's not very big, but it means the world to me. Just like you do."

Blinking back tears, Eden took the ring out of the box and slid it onto her ring finger.

"Does this mean...are you asking me to...?"

Leo laughed, his eyes bright.

"I'm kneeling in front of you, giving you my mother's ring. So, yes, this means...will you marry me, Eden? Will you make me the luckiest man in the world?"

Eden paused, thinking back to everything that happened to lead her to this moment, and to the man in front of her, then nodded.

"Yes, Duke and I will marry you."

Pulling Leo down next to her, Eden snuggled against him, wanting to tell the kids her exciting news, but knowing that it could wait. Their movie wouldn't be over yet, and she didn't feel like moving anyway. It felt too good to be protected from the bitter wind outside, safe and warm in the glow of the fire. She smiled as she felt Duke settle his warm body next to hers.

Sometimes it really is a wonderful life.

ACKNOWLEDGEMENTS

I WROTE THIS BOOK DURING A SCORCHING FLORIDA summer, taking refuge in my cool, quiet writing nook while the long, hot summer days ticked by. I deeply appreciate my wonderful family giving me the time and the solitude needed to finish this book before fall rolled around.

I often remind myself how lucky I am to have my amazing husband, Giles, and five lovable children, Michael, Joey, Linda, Owen and Juliet. They never fail to give me encouragement when I need it the most. Their unwavering love and support keeps me writing.

My life would be much more difficult without the help I receive from my extended family, including Melissa Romero, Leopoldo Romero, Melanie Arvin Kutz, David Woodhall and Tessa Woodhall. I don't know what I'd do without them.

I can't finish a book without giving thanks for having a mother who loved to read. I grew up surrounded by bookcases packed full of wonderful books; the joy my mother got from those books inspires me to write.

The feedback I've received on the first two books in the Mercy Harbor series provided useful insight and inspired me while writing this third book. I'm so thankful for the readers and reviewers who took the time to share their thoughts with me.

ABOUT THE AUTHOR

Melinda Woodhall is the author of the page-turning *Mercy Harbor Thriller* series. After leaving a career in corporate software sales to focus on writing, Melinda now spends her time writing romantic thrillers and police procedurals. She also writes women's contemporary fiction as M.M. Arvin.

When she's not writing, Melinda can be found reading, gardening, chauffeuring her children around town and updating her vegetarian lifestyle website.

Melinda is a native Floridian, and the proud mother of five children. She lives with her family in Orlando.

Visit Melinda's website at www.melindawoodhall.com

If you'd like to leave a review for *Catch the Girl*, please visit: http://www.Amazon.com/gp/customer-reviews/write-a-review.html?asin=B07V5WQMT2

Made in the USA
Columbia, SC
03 September 2020